A SAM PR

INNOCENT CONSPIRACY

DAVID ARCHER

USA TODAY BESTSELLING AUTHOR

PROLOGUE

T he house lights dimmed and people began to cheer as the spotlight speared through the darkness to illuminate the man and woman who stepped out from behind the curtain onto the stage at Canterbury Arena in Denver, one of the greatest performance venues in the city. The audience, all eighteen thousand of them, erupted into raucous screams, cheers, and applause as the exciting music died down.

"Ladies and gentlemen," called the announcer over the incredible noise, "the seventh annual Web Wide Awards Presentation Program is both delighted and excited to welcome this year's host and hostess, Aaron Zachary and Jennifer Larkindale!"

The music continued to swell as the young celebrity couple made its way up to the podium, and then the big kettledrums rolled briefly just before silence settled to engulf the entire building. The incredibly loud cheers and applause died down quickly as the two young celebrities smiled and waited patiently.

When the volume had gotten just barely low enough, the young man standing at the podium looked at the lovely young lady beside him. "Jennifer," he said, "I know this is actually your very first time hosting an awards program in front of a live audience. I'm curious, but is it shaping up to be everything you expected?"

Jennifer's smile was wide and absolutely radiant, offering strong competition to the brightly colored satin designer gown she wore. "Oh, it's absolutely amazing, Aaron," she said. "Just a year ago, when I was a guest on this very program, I never would have dreamed that I would be standing here tonight, getting ready to announce the names of this year's incredible breakout superstars in web-based television."

"But you were on this stage a year ago," Aaron said, his own smile almost overshadowing hers. "I remember that very well, because I was the one who was given the honor of presenting you with last year's Top Web Video Discovery award."

The audience went ecstatically crazy again, cheering and applauding even more loudly than they had before. Jennifer's self-produced, independent web-based TV series, entitled Life After Jeff, had become a global favorite since the day she first started writing, producing, and starring in the fifteen-minute episodes. The show chronicled the day to day life of a sixteen-year-old girl whose boyfriend was one of several kids who were brutally slaughtered one day by a school shooter. It had drawn international attention and acclaim for its incredible realism in capturing the depth of the emotional impact of such a loss, even though the story was entirely fictional.

"And I still think that could only have been a dream," Jennifer said. "I'm just a small town girl from Arkansas, not some kind of TV celebrity, but this has been an incredible experience. I never would have believed that my little video hobby would come to affect so many people so deeply. The fans have been, oh my gosh, they have been just absolutely wonderful, and I hope I can continue to honor and entertain all of them for a long time to come."

Aaron led the the crowd in the cheering applause this time. It went on and on for another half minute, and then finally died down again.

"I'm sure you're always going to do well," Aaron said. "But tonight, we're here to pay well deserved tribute and honor a number of different web-based shows and the casts and crews that make them happen. I don't know about you, but I am personally very deeply honored to be able to host this year's show, because this actually makes it my second in a row. I'm also terribly, terribly excited to be working with Jennifer, because I just happen to be one of her biggest fans."

"Well, then, let me tell you that the feeling is absolutely mutual," Jennifer said. "Aaron, your music is so incredibly awesome, so beautiful and inspiring that I'm actually the president of the Fayetteville chapter of your fan club."

"Are you telling me that I actually have a fan club?" Aaron asked, feigning surprise. The audience erupted into laughter, and after a moment, he composed his face to be more serious. "Tonight, Jennifer and I are privileged to be presenting awards to those web-based series, movies, and music videos that have had the most impact on the lives of their own fans. All of the nominees, and all of the votes, came directly from you, the fans who watch all of the shows and love all of the characters and the music, and tonight the winners will be revealed."

"That's right, Aaron," Jennifer picked up as he paused. "We'll be letting the whole world know about all of the brightest and most talented new stars in the web video universe, from the actors and actresses, themselves, to the shows and music!"

"And while we're at it," Aaron resumed on his cue, "we'll also be giving you some exciting examples of the finest entertainment to be found on the World Wide Web! Get ready for an absolutely incredible night of surprises and delights as we stream this award presentation program live to the entire world!"

Over the next three hours, Aaron and Jennifer were cheered and applauded as they presented more than three dozen awards in as many categories, ranging from short, topical videos to independently produced feature-length movies, music videos from several different music genres, and even recognized several popular actors and actresses. It was very much like many other award shows that had been on television over the years, with various musicians, most of them discovered on YouTube, performing their music, and with special appearances by some of the stars of the new shows from the preceding year.

The final award of the evening, of course, was the one that everyone was waiting anxiously to see presented, though. It was the very one Jennifer had been honored to earn just the year before, the Top Web Video Discovery Award, and everyone was waiting on the edge of their seats to find out whether one of their favorites had garnered the most votes for this coveted spot.

Winning the Top Discovery Award was almost as big a deal as if you had gotten a major movie or recording contract. While you might already be well known to many thousands of fans, this award would thrust you to the top of the web video heap for a long time. It wasn't at all unusual for the winners of this award to move on to star in major movie or TV productions, or be signed by a major record label, and everyone in the audience was hoping it would be their own favorite who took home the prize.

At last, it was time. Aaron and Jennifer took the podium once more.

"Each year," Aaron began, "Web Wide Awards allows you, the fans of the shows and the music, to contribute names to a database of your favorite artists who have appeared on the many web videos seen during that year. Two months ago, all of those hundreds of names were listed on the Web Wide Awards website for a week as potential nominees, and every single one of you was allowed to choose up to three of them, the people you wanted to see nominated for this award. In order to actually be a nominee, each of these artists had to be chosen by at least twenty percent of the fans."

"In some of the previous years," Jennifer continued, "this nomination method has resulted in up to a dozen nominees for the Top Web Video Breakout Award, but this year you have selected only five, and they are undoubtedly the best of the best. All five of their names were posted on the Web Wide Awards website for a full thirty days, and you were then each allowed to vote for only one to be the winner. A number of vote tallying techniques and methods were used to make absolutely sure that each fan could vote only one time, so that the results we are going to present tonight can be revealed with confidence."

"And the nominees are," Aaron said, and the audience erupted again as he held a card up in front of his face. He had to wait for the noise to die down before he continued. "Penelope Winston, from the independent YouTube video series, The Girl In The Room Upstairs, which is a delightful show about a family who moves in to a new home and finds that one of the bedrooms is haunted by the lonely, friendly ghost of a teenage girl. What began as a short indie film project received so much attention and acclaim that Penelope was encouraged to continue it, so she wrote and produced several more episodes, and it evolved into a series with a new episode posted each week. Penelope lives in Edmonton, Alberta, in Canada, and is fifteen years old."

A screen behind him showed a live video of Penelope Winston sitting on a tall chair, waiting backstage, and the fans applauded.

"Next," Jennifer said, holding up her own nominee card. "Lamar Morrison, an incredibly talented indie music artist. Lamar started recording some very simple music videos of himself when he was only twelve years old, but this past year has seen him doing something new and gaining quite a following. His exciting new music videos are even more interesting because they show what appears to be a ten piece band made up of several copies of himself, as he plays all the instruments and provides all the vocals. Lamar's music is outselling many of the top label artists from all around the world, and some of his songs have already been used in three feature Hollywood films. Lamar lives in the tiny little town of Walterboro, South Carolina, and is only eighteen years old."

Lamar, sitting on a tall chair of his own, waved at the audience from the screen.

"Number three," Aaron announced when the cheers and applause died down enough, "is Paula Murkowski, also an indie music artist. Paula began recording herself playing piano so that she could listen for errors, and it was her friends who convinced her to start posting them as music videos for everyone to see about a year ago. Her clear, sweet voice has resonated with millions of people all around the world, and she has been invited to perform at a number of different exciting events, including a special performance for none other than the Queen of England. She lives in Bristol, England, with her family, and she is twenty-two years old."

Paula could be seen on the overhead screen, tears of excitement and happiness streaming down her face as she blew kisses to the audience.

"Number four," Jennifer resumed, "is Max Petrelli, star of the web video series, Freaktown High, which is a science fiction comedy about a high school whose science teacher accidentally creates a wormhole to other dimensions. Max plays Max Peters, the brainy student who has to figure out how to fight and defeat the strange, sometimes diabolical creatures that come through while keeping most of the school from ever finding out just what's really happening. Max says he actually created the show just for fun, but it has grown to become a worldwide phenomenon because of the ingenious, old school style special effects he comes up with. Max lives not that far away in the town of Montrose, Colorado, and is fifteen years old."

Max, a skinny kid with an obvious and serious case of acne, was laughing and waving wildly on the overhead screen.

"And number five," Aaron said with a flourish, this time raising his voice to be heard over the cheers that didn't seem to want to stop, "is Alexei Romanov, yet another indie music artist. Alexei has burst on the scene because of his incredibly beautiful and sensual singing voice, which some people say is the most unique voice they've ever heard. Alexei lives with his sister in the city of Moscow, Russia, and is twenty years old."

On the screen over and behind them, a pale, thin-faced young man was seen smiling and waving.

The kettledrums rolled as Aaron picked up the sealed envelope that would name the winner.

"Jennifer, I think it would be more appropriate if I let you read off the winner, are you ready?"

Jennifer smiled broadly. "Oh, yes, Aaron, absolutely," she said, as Aaron ripped the envelope open and passed the card inside it to her. "And the winner is," she said, pausing dramatically and causing the entire audience to hold their breath.

On the overhead screen, all five of the current nominees were shown sitting on stools side by side, holding hands and smiling triumphantly.

"The winner is," Jennifer said again, "Max Petrelli, the creator and star of Freaktown High!"

The nominees all cheered for Max, who seemed genuinely surprised and even stunned. He sat there for a moment until Alexei and Paula pushed him off his stool, and the music swelled as the curtains opened and Max stumbled for a second as he came from behind them. He caught himself and looked up at Aaron and Jennifer, then took only one more step before his legs suddenly collapsed underneath him. He fell to his knees and stayed there, just staring at the two of them for a couple of seconds, then pitched forward onto his face.

A few people began to laugh, obviously thinking he had only fainted, but then Aaron and Jennifer rushed over to him just as a stage hand got there, and it was Jennifer who screamed when the stage hand rolled the boy over and they saw the blood spurting out of his chest.

The house security guards went into sudden action, sealing off all the exits from the building as police were called and began flooding in. Because of the size of the crowd that had been expected, the company that owned the arena maintained two ambulances on site, and paramedics got to Max within less than two minutes. They quickly determined that he had been shot in the chest and had a collapsed lung and internal bleeding, and they worked to stabilize him as quickly as possible, then loaded him into an ambulance and raced for the hospital.

As a number of hours passed and the Denver police tried to determine exactly what had happened, only one thing became apparent: someone had shot Max with a rifle from high overhead, up in the lighting of the building, and the shooter was apparently long gone before anyone even realized what had happened.

The audience was required to remain where they were, sitting in their seats for well over 3 hours, while the police continued to conduct their initial investigation. It was shortly before they were finally released, at shortly before midnight, when Aaron Zachary and Jennifer Larkindale walked solemnly out onto the stage again.

"Ladies and gentlemen," Aaron said, "We've just been given the first official update regarding Max Petrelli's condition. He was rushed directly in to surgery within minutes after they got him to the hospital, and the doctors were able to remove the bullet, which they say was lodged right next to his heart. He's currently listed as being in critical condition, but the doctors say there is definitely still hope for him to make a complete recovery."

Jennifer leaned down to the microphone. "I'd like to ask everyone to just stop whatever it is that you're doing for the moment, and please, just say a prayer or just spend a moment of silence for this young man. This is a terrible thing that's happened here tonight, and I am sure we all hope and pray that whoever did it is caught quickly and spends the rest of his life paying for what he's done."

The hall was completely silent for more than a minute as Aaron and Jennifer stood in their spots with their heads bowed. When they looked up at the crowd once more, a young woman who was sitting in the front row began to applaud. A few others joined in with her a couple of seconds later, and then the entire hall erupted into cheers and applause. There were numerous shouts of, "Max! Max!"

The audience was released about fifteen minutes thereafter, and everyone made their way out of the building and headed for home. The news over the next few days would continue to cover the story, and, no matter who they might have voted for, the whole world watched and cheered as Max Petrelli slowly recovered.

The day after the shooting, however, there was no sound applause at the downtown Denver headquarters of Web Wide Awards, Inc. The company, despite the fact that it was not a big corporation, had quickly rallied to do what damage control they could, pledging that they would never again let such a thing happen at one of their events, and promising to make an announcement over the next few days on how they planned to prevent it.

In their business, it was always necessary to begin planning the next major award event as soon as each one was finished. With such a shock rocking their world, the Board of Directors, which consisted of two people, decided to immediately arrange for better, more professional security for the next event, and to arrange personal protection for all of the nominees for the major award the following year.

"Who was that local security company," asked John Morton, the CEO, "the one we heard about on the news last week? I can't remember the name, but I'm pretty sure that they're based here in Denver, aren't they?"

Annie Porter, who was not only his executive assistant and fellow board member but also his girlfriend, looked up from going over the video of the event on her computer. "Windlass Security Services," she said. "Do you think we ought to give them a call?"

"Damn right," Morton said. "We need to get them on board, get them established now, before we even start the winner's tour that's coming up. They do offer personal protection services as well as security guards, right?"

"I'm looking at their website right now," Annie replied. "Yes, they do. And get this, every single one of their security people is ex-military, like Green Berets or Navy SEALs. These people are a lot like Blackwater, and they actually have their own investigations section and everything."

"Investigations? Really? What can you find out about them, are they any good?"

Annie spun her laptop around so John could see the photograph on the monitor screen. "I'm sure you've heard of Sam Prichard, right?" she asked, letting him look at the picture. "He's the guy who stopped the terrorists from tossing in a nuclear bomb at Lake Mead, and tracked down that stolen super chip a few weeks back."

"He's done all of that, and then some," John said. "This says he's actually in charge of their entire investigations team, and runs the whole show." He looked up from the computer to her eyes and nodded his head. "Get us an appointment to talk to them, and the sooner we can meet with them, the better."

1

"Daddy, look, come and look at Bo!" Kenzie called out. "He's crawling all by himself, he's crawling!"

"I see that," Sam said. He looked over at his wife. "Isn't that just a little bit early? Isn't he a bit too young for that?"

Indie shook her head at him, and chuckled. "Sam, he's actually coming up on seven months old, babe. It might be just a little early, but not really all that much. Wow, but would you look at him go?"

Beauregard Prichard was named, to the surprise of many, after the ghost of an old Civil War soldier. Beauregard, almost everyone who knew anything about him was convinced, was actually nothing more than a figment of his grandmother's imagination. Kimberly Perkins, Indie's mother, seemed to have some strange, somewhat eerie ability to pick up bits and pieces of the future, but something in her childhood upbringing caused her to find that ability frightening. As a result, she had developed the habit of blaming all of her precognitive episodes on Beauregard, a ghost she was sure she had picked up years earlier while she and her daughter were living in Kentucky.

Bo didn't particularly give a rip who he was named after. At that moment, all he seemed to be concerned about was the musical toy on wheels that his big sister, Mackenzie, kept dragging away from him. He had followed it a good ten feet, with his proud parents beaming down at him as they stood by the front door, watching him and getting a kick out of his progress.

"Mackenzie, I told you over and over, don't tease him," Indie said. "Let him catch it. If you don't let him catch it sometimes, he'll give up trying to get it."

"Okay, Mommy," Kenzie said, "I'm sorry. Come on, Bo, you can catch it, I'll pull it slower."

Bo suddenly found the toy stopping just within his grasp, so he snatched it up with a happy sound and then sat down. Picking it up caused it to make even more music, which in turn caused Bo to laugh even louder.

"Okay," Sam said, "C'mon, Kenzie, we gotta get a move on. If I stand here watching him much longer, I'm liable to forget that I have a job."

Indie turned to face him and stretched her face up for a kiss, which he was more than happy to provide. "Okay, babe," she said with a smile and a hug. "You have yourself a good day, and I'll see you tonight for dinner. I love you, Sam."

"Love you more," Sam said quickly, and then he and his daughter were out the door like a shot. He leaned on the rail just a bit as he went down the front steps, then put his cane lightly to work as he walked to his car. He held the seat forward so Kenzie could climb in and get buckled up, and then the Mustang's big, powerful engine fired up as soon as he turned the key. Sam backed out of the driveway and headed toward Kenzie's school, dropped her off, and then turned the car toward his office.

As the chief investigator for Windlass Security, Sam felt like he had just about made it to Easy Street. Most of the time, all he really had to do was sit in his office and send various members of his team out to handle whatever minor investigations were going on at the time. Usually, it would turn out to be something as simple as figuring out who was taking boxes of screws home from a factory, or determining how someone had gotten a compromising photograph of a local executive. The latter cases weren't really all that hard to figure out, because compromising photographs don't usually exist unless you put yourself into a compromising situation.

Sometimes, though, something a lot bigger actually came along. Sam's very first case after taking the job with Windlass had been to track down a stolen prototype of a chip that could allow a computer to communicate directly with the human brain, and find the thief who stole it. That case had started out seeming like nothing more than a simple theft, but rapidly evolved into a matter of national security that threatened the entire world. Sam and his team, after being infiltrated by the actual mastermind behind it all and led on a wild goose chase, had finally determined who the culprit was and taken steps to stop him from literally trying to take over the entire world.

Since then, things had settled down and mostly been pretty easy. Sam admitted to himself and his wife that he truly enjoyed going to work at his office every day, and he felt certain that he had the best possible team working with him. No matter what case came along, Sam Prichard had absolute confidence that they could handle it.

He pulled into his reserved parking space in front of the old automotive shop that was the Windlass Security Company's headquarters building, and made his way leisurely inside. His hip wasn't hurting too awfully badly that day, and that always helped, but he was feeling pretty good in other ways, as well. The toughest case the team had on their plate at the moment was almost comical, and involved tracking down the stripper who seemed to have left a party thrown by the CEO of a local bank with the memory stick that contained some of his bank access codes. It was encrypted and was probably secure, but if it were to find its way into the wrong hands, the bank could potentially be ruined.

Sam grinned as he thought about it. He had decided to put Summer Raines on that case. A raving beauty, there wasn't a man in the world she couldn't crack, or a woman she couldn't intimidate, if she really put her mind to it.

He walked into the foyer of his office and broke out into yet another smile. Jenna Smalley, his secretary, was holding out a cup of coffee for him, something she tried to do every morning.

"How do you always manage to know exactly when I'm coming this way?" Sam asked her, but she only grinned and put one of her pudgy fingers to her lips.

"It's a trade secret," she said in a stage whisper. "You wouldn't want me to give them all away, now, would you, Mr. Prichard?"

"Oh, of course not," Sam said with a chuckle. "Besides, I know good and well you can get into the building security videos from that computer of yours, so it's not really all that hard to figure out."

"Spoilsport," Jenna said. "Ruin all my fun! See how you are?"

Sam chuckled again as he went into his office and closed the door behind himself. He sat down at his desk and turned on the monitor for his computer, then began looking through the reports that his team members had completed overnight.

Summer had found the sticky-fingered stripper at a sleazy bar in LoDo and explained just how badly she intended to ruin the girl's life if the missing memory stick wasn't returned, which resulted in some frantic bra digging, which closed that case neatly. Sam added yet another memo praising her for a job well done, then approved her expense account request for the very small bar tab she had run up in the course of the night's work.

Walter Rawlings, Windlass' somewhat legendary and almost supernaturally gifted crime scene analyst, had been sent on a trip to Salt Lake City a couple of days earlier to help determine how a thief had managed to walk off with a 600-pound statue of an angel. He always traveled and worked with a partner, Steve Beck, a retired police detective from Golden who was actually an old friend of Sam's. Steve had reported that Walter had, as usual, figured out exactly how the crime was committed within 10 minutes of being on the scene.

The statue was housed in a small room which was located just off the foyer of the building. A large, sealed glass window allowed all of the people passing by to see and admire the statute, but no one was allowed to ever get close or touch it. The room containing it could be entered only from the back, through a highly secure maintenance passageway, and the door to the statue itself was secured with 3 different locks that required three separate people to open them. It had always, until this theft had proven the thought wrong, been considered one of the most secure and theft-proof display systems in the world, but the statue had suddenly and inexplicably been missing one morning. A close examination of the room found nothing had been disturbed, other than the glaring fact that the statue itself was gone.

The building had been built more than a century earlier, in the late eighteen hundreds, and was constructed of stone on solid ground. There was absolutely no conceivable way that anyone could explain how the statue had been removed from its accustomed place until Walter had walked into the room and looked around.

"They took it out through the floor," he said, and all of the police officers standing in and around the room scoffed at him.

"Man, that's impossible, because we're standing on solid rock," said the detective in charge. "There's no basement, no way to take it down."

"They took their time, and they cut a tunnel in from the building across the street," Walter said. "That building across from this one is the only one anywhere nearby that has a basement, so it had to start from over there. Then they used some heavy hydraulic jacks to hold up the floor under the statue while they cut all the way around it under the walls, and then they just lowered the whole thing down. They used some sort of lift to move the statue onto a flat cart and wheeled it away, then they just jacked the floor back up. You can't see the cuts because they're under the walls around the room, but they're there, because the dirt that should be in the space where the floor meets the walls is gone. The jack is still down there and holding the floor up, so if you go across the street and find the entrance to the tunnel, you can follow it to find the jack."

A warrant to search the basement of the building across the street was quickly secured, and the basement entered. What looked like a small storage room had been built against one wall, and when it was opened, they found the rock and dirt that had been carefully dug out of the tunnel packed all around inside it. The tunnel was there, exactly as Walter had said it would be, and the police officers followed it all the way to the jack that was holding up the section of floor under the room where the statue had been kept.

Security footage from a camera on the first floor of the building with the basement had captured images of four men going into the basement each day for two weeks, and then it caught them coming up a couple of nights earlier with something large on a hand truck. Still pictures were captured from the video and had been run through facial recognition, and the thieves had been identified. Now, the police only hoped to catch up to them before the solid copper statue could be sold or melted down for scrap.

Sam couldn't help laughing as he read the report not just once, but twice. He'd seen several times already what Walter was actually capable of, and it was just about as uncanny as Kim/Beauregard and her predictions of the future. Walter had assured him more than once that there was nothing supernatural about it at all, though; he just had a natural knack for seeing how things work and noticing small details that almost everyone else would miss, and determining what had to be truth out of the many possibilities that presented themselves.

Each of his team members was able to report success in their individual cases, but this was something Sam had grown accustomed to. They were a good team, and each of them was already a highly trained and experienced investigator in his or her own right, and the respect they showed him as their team leader was awesome.

The phone on his desk rang, and the light told him it was the intercom line. He picked it up and said, "Yes?"

"Ron and Jeff are here to see you, Mr, Prichard," Jenna said.

Sam smiled. Ron Thomas and Jeff Donaldson were the two men who had founded Windlass Security, after they had left their jobs as electronic and computer technicians for the Department of Homeland Security. They had chosen to enter the private sector when their former boss, Sam's old friend Harry Winslow, had been promoted and sent to work in the DHS headquarters in Washington, D.C. They had been after Sam to come work for them for quite some time, and he had finally decided to accept the offer a couple of months earlier.

"Send them on in," he said with a grin. He replaced the handset in its cradle and looked up at the door as the two men entered.

Ron and Jeff stepped inside and closed the door behind them. Sam stood and shook hands with each of them, and then they sat in the chairs in front of his desk.

"I just want to know," Jeff said, "why it is that she always calls you 'Mr. Prichard,' but Ron and I are just Ron and Jeff. Can anybody explain that to me?"

"It might have something to do with the fact that you used to date her," Ron said. "I told you that was going to come back to haunt you someday, remember?" He turned and smiled at Sam.

"Both of you at once," Sam said. "Must be because there's something big getting ready to happen."

"We think there certainly is," Jeff said. "Sam, did you hear about the shooting at the Web Wide Awards show a couple nights ago? That kid that was shot, right on live video?"

"Oh, yeah, Saturday night," Sam said. "Indie and I were actually sitting in our living room and watching it when it happened. That kid was very lucky to live through that shot. Have you heard anything about who did it?"

"I agree the kid was lucky," Ron said, "but as for who did it, that's still a mystery, and now the company has come to us to ask for our help in solving it for them. They'd like us to assign you and your team to find out who the shooter was and bring him to justice, and we're going to be providing security for all of the winners as they go on their big victory tour next month."

Sam nodded that he understood. "Do the police have any leads at all? Or am I working in the dark, here?"

"None that we've heard anything about. The shooter or shooters seem to have gotten in and out without being seen, and they must have known exactly where every security camera was, because there is no sign of anyone carrying anything into or out of the building that could be a rifle. They did find a few people, they said, who seemed to be carefully keeping their faces away from the cameras, but they've managed to identify most of them and cleared them."

"Has anyone tried to claim responsibility for it?" Sam asked. "Or has there been any indication of any kind of motive behind the shooting?"

"The answer to both questions is a great big fat negative," Ron said with a frown. "At this point, the sad fact is that you probably know just as much as the police do. How would you feel about taking on this kind of a case?"

"I feel pretty good about it," Sam said. "If anyone is going to be able to find the shooter, or shooters, it's my team. Of course, we've got to consider the possibility that it was an inside job of some sort. I'd like to get Walter to look the scene over as soon as possible, because that will probably tell us more than anything else, I think."

Jeff nodded. "He and Steve are due to fly back into the airport from Salt Lake City at noon," he said. "I'm sending somebody out to the airport to pick them up, so they should be back in the city by one at the latest. Meanwhile, the two people who actually own Web Wide Awards are coming here in about twenty minutes, and we'd like you to sit in on the meeting with us. In fact," he said, glancing around at Sam's big conference table, "I think we should probably just have it in here."

"I'm more than happy to oblige," Sam said. "Should I ask Jenna to get any kind of presentation ready? You know how she loves to do presentations."

"I don't actually think were going to need one, in this case," Ron said. "In fact, I don't think you should even bring in any of the team. In this particular case, I think the only face they need to know is yours for the moment. We can introduce the others to them when and if the time comes, but it may turn out to be better for them to be unknown quantities, at least for now."

"I can agree with that, mostly," Sam said. "However, I'm sure I'm going to want to put somebody inside their organization, and I think Jade would be the right one. They are primarily a web company, so just about everything they do is going to involve computers, and that was her specialty. How many people are going to be coming to this meeting?"

"Just two, the owners," Ron said. "John Morton and Annie Porter constitute the entire Board of Directors. John is the CEO, Annie is the COO and John's assistant, but she's also his girlfriend. The two of them own ninety percent of the stock in the company, so they are the ones who get to run the show. I really do mean that literally, with no pun intended."

"Okay, then," Sam said, "no problem." He reached over and picked up his phone and punched button one for Jenna.

"Yes, Mr. Prichard?" Jenna asked as she answered.

"Find Jade Miller and ask her to come to my office, please," Sam said. "Tell her I said to look as computer geeky as possible."

"Yes, sir."

"She'll be here shortly," Sam said, putting the handset back in its cradle. "Is there anything you can think of that I need to know before we get into this meeting?"

Ron and Jeff looked at each other and grinned, then turned back to look at Sam. "Just that solving this case will get a huge bonus for you and your team," Ron said. "And I do mean huge, like, really huge."

Sam grinned. "Then I can assure you that we are going to solve it," he said.

There was a tap on the door a moment later, and Sam called out for Jade to come in. A very pretty Asian woman, she was a highly skilled investigator who was very capable with just about any kind of computers. In a former life as a Dallas police detective, she had specialized in cybercrime, and she was extremely knowledgeable about it. She stepped inside and saw the three of them, and her eyebrows rose slightly behind the fake horn-rimmed glasses she was wearing.

"Either there's something special about to happen," she said, "or I'm in some really big kind of trouble."

"Or possibly both," Sam said with a grin. "Is that what you call geeky?"

Jade almost crossed her eyes trying to look at her glasses. "What? Computer nerds wear glasses, right?"

"I guess it'll pass," Sam said. "Come on in and have a seat." They moved to the conference table and sat around it, and Sam began to fill her in about the new case with help from Ron and Jeff.

"It sounds incredibly intriguing," she said. "I take it you're going to want me undercover inside their company?"

"That's the idea I had in mind," Sam replied. "I want you to get into their computer system and see if you can find anything out of the ordinary. I can't say that anyone inside is involved, but something like this could easily destroy a company like this. If someone wanted them out of the way, maybe a competitor, they'd almost certainly want to have someone on the inside."

"You don't think Max Petrelli was the actual target?" Jade asked.

"I suppose it's possible, but he's a kid. Unless his little web TV show was actually interfering with someone else's, I have to think that the motive was more about Web Wide Awards. Having their brand new superstar shot and killed on stage, just as he is about to receive his big award, could make it look like the company didn't take reasonable precautions for his safety."

Jade nodded, then turned to Ron and Jeff. "Did they have any security there at the program?"

Ron nodded. "They did, but they just hired the usual security guards that work for the venue. Most of them are minimum wage high school dropouts. I'm not saying they didn't do what they could, but they were far from professionals. There is already a small amount of backlash against them on social media for not providing better security."

"That's why," Jeff added, "they just arranged to hire us to safeguard their winners on the tour that begins next month. Eight of their award recipients are going out on a bus tour around the country for three months. Five of them are musicians who will be performing, and the others are comedians. We're putting three full security teams on them, so they'll be covered at all times, and each one will have their own personal bodyguard, twenty-four-seven."

"That's good," Sam said. "Who are you putting in charge?"

Ron grinned. "Who else? Rob Feinstein. He's a highly respected former Navy SEAL, and the men don't bat an eye at taking orders from him. He's also got the brains necessary to run an operation like that, and he can think for himself when he has to."

Sam was nodding his head. "I agree completely. I watched him when we were in San Francisco, and the guy knows his stuff."

Ron's cell phone vibrated and he touched the Bluetooth earpiece on his ear. "Go ahead," he said. "Okay, send them back to Sam's office." He tapped it again and looked at Sam. "They're here."

A moment later, Jenna ushered John Morton and Annie Porter into the office. Jenna asked if anyone would like something to drink, but everyone declined and she disappeared into the foyer.

"John, it's good to meet you face to face," Ron said. "I'm Ron Thomas, we spoke on the phone yesterday afternoon. This fellow to my right is Jeff Donaldson, my partner; that's Sam Prichard at the head of the table, and Jade Miller is one of our investigators. Sam, Jade, this is John Morton and Annie Porter. They own Web Wide Awards, and they've built it from the ground up."

They shook hands all around and then were seated.

"John, Annie, we've been talking a bit about your case," Ron said, "sort of getting Sam in the loop. He'll be taking lead in the whole investigation, and using our assets as he sees fit. We'll let him take over from here, if that's all right."

John and Annie both nodded and smiled, looking to Sam. "We heard a lot about you, Mr. Prichard," John said. "We're really hoping you can find out who did this and why."

"So am I," Sam said with a grin. "As it happens, my wife and I were both watching your program when the shooting took place. We're both very glad the young man seems to be improving."

"Aren't we all," Annie said. "I was right there in the front row, I thought I was going to have a heart attack."

"I can imagine," Sam said. "Let's talk about this for moment. The first thing I'd like to ask you is whether you have any idea who might want to harm your company. I understand there's a lot of talk about how you could have done better at providing for the safety of your contestants. Something like this could easily damage your reputation, even cause your company to start losing revenue."

"That's absolutely true," John said. "Obviously, that's precisely why we're here right now. As for who might want to see us suffer? Just about any of the major video streaming companies, they would come to mind first. Some of them offer their own awards, so it's possible they can see us as some sort of competition that they needed to eliminate. There are also other award companies, some of them even older than we are. They just didn't have the marketing skills that propelled us to the top. They might feel that bringing us down would leave a vacuum they could move into. I know that a few of them have already posted articles about our failure in the security area, pointing out that they would naturally have done better."

"Even though it never would've occurred to them," Annie said, "before this happened."

"That's probably right," Sam said. "Hindsight can make wise men of us all." He paused for a couple of seconds. "What about Max Petrelli? Do you know of anyone, or any organization, that might have wanted to harm him?"

John looked mildly shocked at the quest. "Max? If you look on social media, absolutely everybody loves that kid. Freaktown High is one of the most popular shows online, and the production quality is absolutely amazing for a teenage amateur. Even before we recognized him, he had offers from three major studios to buy the show, but he didn't want to sell. He wants to stay independent and do his own thing without worrying about what corporate sponsors might think. He's making a small fortune on every episode, but he controls just what he decides to advertise."

"But what about rival shows?" Jade asked. "Because of the nature of your business, you've got your finger on the pulse of internet video. What other shows might become more successful if Freaktown High were to suddenly go off the air?"

John and Annie looked at one another. "Probably the closest rival he's got," John said, "would be Tim Wilson's Lucidar. That's a show about a demon who possesses the body of a teenage boy who was in a coma, brain dead. He takes over that kid's life, but then he starts to like being human, so he ends up fighting against evil to protect his new human teenager friends. It's a pretty good show, to be honest, but it just doesn't have the pizzazz of Freaktown High. It can't even compare on special effects, and Max deals with lots of different otherworldly creatures while Tim has to fight the same devil and demons every week. If Max was gone, Tim still wouldn't be able to get much bigger."

"All right, that makes sense," Sam said. "What about your sponsors? Would any of your sponsors be in danger over what happened? Is there any backlash against them?"

"Well, not that we've heard," Annie said. "I deal with the sponsors, and I haven't seen anything online or heard anything from them to indicate that they have any concerns about themselves. We got a couple that may pull their support for our program, but just about any kind of bad publicity can cause that to happen."

"Who are they?" Jade asked. "The ones that are talking about dropping you?"

"Canterbury Soft Drinks," Annie said. "They're actually our biggest sponsor, so that could definitely hurt us. There is also Mama O'Malley's Snack Cakes. They're both afraid that sticking with us might cause a problem for them down the road, but we're hoping they'll stay on board. To be honest, we told them we were meeting with you today about taking over all our security in the future, and that seemed to calm them down quite a bit."

"I'm glad," Sam said. "When we're finished here, Ron and Jeff will talk to you about the security arrangements. My area is strictly investigating the current situation. Now, I understand that the two of you own the majority of the stock in your company. How many employees do you have?"

"Well, quite a few," John said. "We have to keep track of literally hundreds of thousands of videos each year, including movies, series, and music and comedy standalone videos. We've got twenty people that do nothing but scan social media looking for what's likely to go viral next, and another twenty who just handle the databases that record each video's popularity. As the popularity numbers go up, we focus more attention on them. If they go down, they may fall completely off our radar. We've got interviewers and video crews that go all over the world to talk to potential breakout stars, and a lot of people who do nothing but work on our annual presentation show. Altogether, we probably have around two hundred employees."

"Jade is highly skilled with computers," Sam said, "and I'm planning to have her go undercover inside your organization to look for anything that might help us solve this.

Is anyone going to think it strange if someone new comes in today or tomorrow?"

"I don't think so," Annie said. "We have a couple of openings right now, anyway. Where do you want to put her?"

"She's going to need access to your entire computer network, and she should be able to interact with as many people as possible. What she's looking for is the possibility that whoever did this had someone inside your organization helping them to plan it. See, there are two distinct possibilities. First, the target was Max Petrelli. I understand that seems farfetched, but it's not unthinkable. The other is the possibility that the target was whoever won that final big award, and that's the more likely scenario. It wouldn't have mattered which of the nominees you chose, the winner would have been the one who got shot. Now, in either case, the shooter had to have had some kind of advance knowledge about those last few minutes of the program. He almost certainly had somebody, either inside your organization or at the venue end, who could provide that kind of information."

John and Annie looked at each other again, and Annie shook her head. "I don't want to believe that," she said. "I don't want to believe that anyone in our company would willingly participate in something like this."

"We understand that," Sam said, "but unfortunately, human nature is such that there can be many reasons why someone will betray another human being. Money, power, jealousy—if we can figure out why this happened, it will probably lead us directly to who actually pulled the trigger and who helped them to do it."

"We'll do whatever you need us to do," John said. "How about this? What if we say Ms. Miller is Annie's new executive assistant? She'd have access to everything, and full run of the headquarters building. Nobody would even think to question what she was doing in any department, because they'd see her as representing Annie."

Sam looked at Jade, who nodded and smiled. "That sounds perfect," she said. "When do I start?"

"First thing tomorrow morning," Sam said. "The rest of the team will be working from the outside. Some of them will work with the police, and others will be working in the dark. Even you won't know about them unless it becomes necessary, but trust me when I tell you that they are the best I've ever seen at what they do."

Annie looked at Sam with a sad smile. "Thank you, Mr. Prichard," she said.

HARVEY REILLY WAS GOING to be late for his first day at work, and there was absolutely nothing he could do about it. His car, the old faithful friend that had carried him all through high school and college, had just shot off its last backfire, and he knew it. Unfortunately, it chose to do so more than three miles from the TV station where he was starting work that day as a mobile cameraman, and he'd been warned that Mr. Lenox, the station manager, had no tolerance for tardiness. According to the stories he'd been told, more than one new employee had been fired on their very first day for showing up late.

He had managed to make the old Durango coast to the side of the road, but there was no way he was going to get it to go any further. That loud "bang" had sounded like more than a normal backfire, and when he got out and looked behind the car, the trail of oil confirmed his worst suspicions. The engine had blown, and there was no fixing it with something as simple as an oil change this time!

He stood there beside the car and wished he'd left his apartment an hour earlier, but wishing wouldn't get him to the station, so he just started walking, holding his thumb out to every car that passed. He was still walking fifteen minutes later, with only five minutes left to make the final two miles, when a nice new Toyota sports car pulled up beside him and stopped.

For a split second, he thought he must be imagining it, but then the passenger window rolled down and a pretty girl smiled at him. "Aren't you the new cameraman? You need a ride? Hop in."

Harvey climbed in as quickly as he could, and the girl smiled again. "Buckle up, I don't need any seat belt tickets. I'm Wendy Dawson. I'm the reporter you'll be assigned to. I saw you when you came for your interview the other day." She put the car in gear and they were on the way.

"I'm Harvey," he said, "and I can't thank you enough! My car just blew its engine, and I thought I was gonna be late and get fired! I've heard stories about Mr. Lenox."

She laughed. "Yeah, he can be a bear. You just gotta know how to handle him, but yeah, being late the first day wouldn't be it. Good thing I saw you, huh?"

Harvey smiled and leaned back in the seat in a sigh of relief. "Best thing ever! I can't thank you enough!"

"No problem," she said. "Besides, Lester in personnel said you were gonna be my cameraman, so I need you! If you didn't make it, I'd have to keep working with Stewart, and he's an ass!"

"You're sure I'm being assigned to you? I mean, you're pretty big at the station."

She giggled again. "Yep, starting today. I've been waiting months to get my own cameraman, but they said I had to wait till they hired somebody new, because everyone else was already assigned; or I could keep using Stewart, and nobody wants to work with him. Mr. Lenox likes to put teams together, and then not mess with 'em, and Stewart is just the backup guy. If we do okay together, we'll be working together for years. As I get promoted to bigger and better stories, you'll go with me, and if I ever make anchor, you'll be in the studio with me, then, too."

Harvey grinned. "Then I guess my job is to make you look good, right?"

Wendy looked at him coquettishly. "Hey, he's not only cute, he's got a brain! Yeah, the better you make me look, the better we do as a team."

Harvey caught it; she'd actually said he was cute. He'd already come to the conclusion that he would be working with the prettiest reporter he'd ever seen, so her comment gave him a bit of a thrill. He dug down deep for courage—girls always sort of scared him, ever since he misunderstood June Dungy in the third grade and thought her offer to trade lunches with him was a ploy to make him her boyfriend—and said, "Well, making you look good is gonna be pretty easy. You look awfully good already."

As soon as the words were out of his mouth, he regretted them. *You look awfully good already?* What kind of line was that?

Wendy smiled, though. "Aw, thanks," she said. "I think we're gonna get along great!"

2

Everyone but Walter and Steve were present in the building, so Sam sent Jenna to round them all up and bring them to his office. They arrived one at a time, taking the seats they had been accustomed to around the conference table.

John and Annie had already left the office, going to Ron's office to finalize the financial arrangements involved in hiring Windlass. They would be meeting Rob Feinstein and the security detail shortly, but Sam wanted to get busy on the investigation.

Jade was already present, so Summer took her usual seat beside her friend. Summer was a petite blonde who could only be described as "stunningly beautiful." She referred to herself as a specialist in information acquisition, which was her way of saying she was a skilled interrogator. She was ex-military and proficient with many weapons and martial arts. Her looks, she often said, were nothing but a tool that she could use to accomplish her mission. With only a very few exceptions, she could wrap just about any man around her finger.

The next to arrive was Denny Cortlandt, the former SAS commando. Sam often referred to Denny as "the chameleon," because he could transform instantly from one persona to another. The Liverpool native could become, in a split second, somebody from the Bronx, from Texas, a Brazilian, an Australian, German, French, Italian, or any of a dozen other different personalities. He kept multiple fake identities and was a master at infiltration, whether overt or covert.

Darren Beecher followed him. Darren was a former FBI agent who had worked with the famous Behavioral Analysis Unit as a profiler. His skills at being able to read the facts of the situation and produce a description of the type of person they were looking for had become invaluable, and he was often able to predict a suspect's, or a potential victim's, next move.

Jenna brought in a tray with numerous cups, sugar and creamers, and a carafe of coffee, then opened the video display screen built into the wall. "I took the liberty of putting together a bit of a presentation for you," she said. Sam only grinned, because it seemed like Jenna could always put together a presentation within minutes. There was no doubt in his mind that she had turned on the omnidirectional microphone on the table during his meeting with Ron, Jeff and the clients, using what she learned as the basis for research. They were about to see the results.

"Go for it," Sam said. The others around the table chuckled, for they had also grown accustomed to Jenna's multimedia talents.

She pressed a button on the remote she held and the logo for Web Wide Awards appeared on the screen, with the faces of its owners superimposed over it. "Web Wide Awards was formed about ten years ago, when John Morton and his girlfriend, Annie Porter, disagreed with some awards given by another website to some YouTube videos. Those awards were chosen by a panel that seemed to ignore what the fans had to say, and both John and Annie felt this was a mistake. By creating an award system that allowed the fans to generate all of the nominations and vote for the winners, and then honoring their choices, Web Wide Awards quickly rose to prominence as the most coveted award any video work could hope to earn. For internet videos, this is the equivalent of winning an Oscar. Web Wide Awards has become so respected and trusted that even some of their quarterly winners have gone on to receive recording and film contracts from established producers."

Summer waved her hand in the air. "Wait a minute," she said, "explain that. Quarterly winners?"

"Oh, yes," Jenna said. "Every quarter, Web Wide Awards allows the public to nominate videos and artists for the quarterly award. The quarterly awards are done with less fanfare, without a live webcast. The winners are presented with their awards privately by a representative of Web Wide Awards and a two-man film crew, who may literally fly around the world in less than a week. Video of each of these award presentations is displayed on the Web Wide Awards website. The quarterly award includes the quarterly award trophy, Honorable Mention on the website, and a cash prize of 5,000 dollars that can be used for any purpose. They give awards to music videos, series, and movies, usually a total of about eight awards per quarter. And winning the quarterly award does not guarantee you a chance at the annual."

"Okay, just curious," Sam said, "but did Max Petrelli win any of the quarterlies this past year?"

"Two of them, in fact," Jenna said. "First and third. His award for the first quarter honored a single episode of his show, which took a powerful stance on bullying, while the third quarter award was for outstanding production values. He's the only person to win two quarterly awards and the annual award in the same year."

"Interesting," Sam said. "Okay, go ahead."

The image on the screen changed to a shot of the stage from the night of the shooting. Aaron Zachary and Jennifer Larkindale could be seen rushing toward a fallen Max Petrelli. A stagehand was already on his knees beside the boy.

"Two nights ago, as the award program was coming to its end, the winner of the Top Web Video Breakout Award was announced. It went to Max Petrelli, for his homemade series Freaktown High. As he was walking out from backstage to receive the award, he seemed to stumble for a second, recovered, and then fell flat. When he didn't move for a couple of seconds, stage crew and the hosts went to check on him and found that he was bleeding profusely from a gunshot wound to his chest. The police and paramedics were called, and Max is now recovering from emergency surgery at the hospital."

The screen changed again, and Sam grinned. The image that appeared was of his friend Karen Parks, a Denver homicide detective.

"This is Detective Karen Parks of the Denver Police Department. She's heading up the police investigation, and she's already aware that we're being brought in. I took the liberty of calling her a few minutes ago and asking her to come to this meeting, and she should be arriving shortly. She will be sharing all the information she has, but she says it isn't much at this point." Jenna grinned. "She said this is one time she'll be glad to have Sam Prichard on a case, and intends to let you take lead on it."

"She's a good cop," Sam said. "She'll be an asset, trust me."

"Currently," Jenna went on, "the theory is that the shooter came in through a delivery entrance that was not secured, then climbed up into the lighting racks over the main auditorium. There are catwalks up there, and it is believed the shot came from about the middle of the third catwalk, which would put the shooter roughly dead center over the audience. The bullet that was removed from Max was a 5.56 mm round, and was probably fired from an AR-15 that was fitted with a sound suppressor. An initial examination of the video footage did not reveal the sound of a gunshot, but when the footage audio was enhanced, they found a spike of sound that matches the characteristics of such a gun."

An example of the rifle she was describing appeared on the screen.

"The police do not have any leads, and Detective Parks admits that she is stumped. They examined security footage from cameras along the route they believe the shooter took, and found several people who seemed to keep their faces averted from the camera, but most of them have already been located and cleared. There were only two who have not been identified, and efforts are underway to correct that, now."

There was a tap on the door and Nadia Jenkins, one of the office girls, opened it and poked her face inside. "Mr. Prichard? There's a Detective Parks here to see you."

Sam smiled and made a "come on" motion. "Send her on in, please," he said.

Nadia stepped back and Karen Parks entered the room. It was the first time she had been in Sam's new office, and she nodded appreciatively as Nadia closed the door behind her.

"Fancy digs, Sam," she said. "Thanks for the invitation."

"No problem," Sam said. He indicated his secretary, standing in front of the video screen. "Jenna thought of it on her own, before I got the chance. I was just briefing the team about the case. Have you got anything new?"

Karen took an empty seat beside Sam, set her briefcase on the table, and reached for the coffee. "Nothing new," she said. "This thing has us stumped, at the moment. I'm working on the theory that the shooting was designed to hurt the company behind the awards, rather than the boy who was shot. He was just the target of opportunity."

"From everything we've learned so far," Sam said, "I agree with you. It looks to me like someone is out to put Web Wide Awards out of the awards business." He turned to Jenna. "Do we have any information on what the blow back has been for them?"

"Well, a couple of their bigger sponsors have made noises about pulling out on them, but the general public support for the company is only growing. People from all over the world are posting on social media that the shooting was something no one could have predicted, so Web Wide Awards should not be held responsible. Of course, everyone agrees security should be greater in the future, but it's likely that the company's revenues will actually go up for this quarter, because of the shooting."

"That's pretty heavy," Summer said. "I'm just wondering out loud, but could anyone have predicted that that might happen? That could be a motive for the shooting, right there."

"I'd think it would be very difficult to predict," Darren said. "Often, when any sort of terroristic action takes place in any kind of corporate event, the company behind it suffers tremendous loss of reputation. Of course, there are precedents for this sort of thing; there have been companies who were victimized in similar ways and came out a bit stronger than ever, but that would not be the rule, by any stretch of imagination."

"I spoke to three different stockbrokers," Karen said, "and they said the same thing. They don't think it's likely anyone really could've guessed that something like this would boost any kind of public support for the company. The opposite would be a lot more likely to happen, with the public blaming them for their favorite new star being almost killed."

"Then we'll put Morton and Porter toward the bottom of the list of potential suspects," Sam said. "I'm more inclined right now to focus on finding out who would benefit if Web Wide Awards were to go out of business."

"That could be a pretty big list," Karen said. "It isn't just other award companies that might gain, but think about production companies. For the past several years, this company has been pretty well ruling the online video world. Most people wouldn't realize it, but until you made it onto their website, you weren't likely to make any money off your video work at all. If they lost that edge, then very expensive marketing would become the only way to make a show hit, which would just about wipe out most of the indie artists who've been winning these awards and making a name for themselves. Most of them, especially when they're just getting started, don't have the kind of money it would take to draw the kind of viewers they need. One of the things Web Wide Awards does is review almost every new indie video that comes along. Anything they give a decent rating to suddenly seems to gain traffic, and traffic translates into dollars."

"So, you think the production companies might be out to shut them down?" Jade asked.

"I don't know," Karen said, "this is just speculation. All I know is that the internet analysts I've spoken to tell me that the free promotion Web Wide Awards gives to new web videos they like is equivalent to spending a quarter million on advertising. That's a hell of a lot of promotion that a new indie video artist gets for free, but it will cost a production company at least that much money to draw the same amount of traffic. There's probably a lot of them who would be glad to see this outfit go out of business."

"All right," Sam said, "we'll look closely at that. Jade, we need any information we can get on any conflicts the company has had, whether with other award outfits, with production companies, with anybody. If anyone has displayed significant animosity or made any effort to create problems, we need to know it."

"She's the one who's going undercover?" Karen asked.

Sam nodded. "Yes. She knows computers and networks, so she can look through their system for any indication that there might've been someone working on this from the inside. My gut says the shooter had someone feeding him information, and if we can find out who that person is, it'll probably lead to the shooter."

"Can I throw something out, mate?" Denny asked. Sam nodded, so he went on. "Right, so there are certain questions we definitely need the answers to. First, we need to know who fired the shot. Second, we need to know why the shot was fired. Third, we need to know about any assistance the shooter had from inside this company. Fourth, we need to know how the shooter got in. Fifth, how the shooter got out. Sixth, we need to know why nothing long enough to be a rifle appears on any of the security video. And seventh, just because I'm a bloody bugger who wants to know, we need to find out who put up the money for this hit, because a shot like that took a pro."

"I'd say," Sam said with a grin, "that just about sums it up." He turned to Karen. "I got a couple of guys on the way back from Salt Lake City," he said. "As soon as they make it back here, I want to take them directly to the Canterbury so they can get a look at the actual crime scene. Walter Rawlings has a knack for figuring out exactly how a crime took place, and I need his input on this."

"I've already gone to the mayor this morning," Karen said, "and gotten his blessings to let you take the point position. To be honest, he seems a little bit pissed that you're working for Windlass instead of the city, but he gave me permission to let you run the show. I've got three detectives and a half dozen uniforms on this case with me, and we are available as you need us. The only thing I'm going to ask is that I get to stay close, so I can answer the mayor when he calls."

"No problem," Sam said. "You can stick with me as much as you can spare the time for, and I'll make sure you get copies of every report."

Karen grinned at him. "Reminds me of when we worked Juvie together."

"Yeah, it does," Sam said. "I just hope you're not as pigheaded as you were back then. And speaking of pigheaded, we need to break for lunch. Walter and Steve will be back at one, so we need to meet back here by then."

The group broke up and went their separate ways, and Sam invited Karen to join him for lunch in the break room. "I smuggled in some frozen pizza," he said. "Sometimes, when I'm too busy to think about going out for lunch, I just pop one in the microwave and chow down."

Karen burst out laughing. "Yep," she said. "Just like when we were working juvie division. I think we lived on pizza back then."

"Which is why I stopped eating it at all for a couple of years. I didn't start up again until I got partnered with Betty Beauchamp. She couldn't get enough of the stuff, and it finally started to smell good again."

"Oh, gosh, I just barely remember Betty. Whatever happened to her, anyway?"

"Oh, I thought everyone knew," Sam said. "We were digging into a robbery at one of the convenience stores in LoDo, and we figured out who had done it and went to pick them up. When we got close, one of the idiots started firing at us. Of course, we both drew our guns and fired and took the shooter down, but a few minutes later Betty started feeling weird and fell over. That's when we found out she had been hit. It was a twenty-two, and it hit her in the lower abdomen. Made a tiny little hole that closed up afterward and hardly bled at all, and the doctor at the ER said it wouldn't be that big a deal to take out. Unfortunately, it had nicked her intestines in a couple of spots, and she developed some nasty infections. Almost died from it, actually, but she suffered enough damage that they had to take some of her intestines out. That was the end of her police career, and I understand she writes detective novels now."

"Hmph," Karen said. "Bet she makes more money than we do."

Sam winked at her. "Speak for yourself," he said. "I'm doing pretty good, here."

"Yeah? You better call me the next time you have an opening, then."

They made it to the break room and Sam pulled a couple of small pizzas out of the little upright freezer he had bought and put there, and then grabbed them each a root beer. They sat down at one of the little tables as the pizza turned around and around in the microwave.

"So what's it really like?" Karen asked. "Working for these guys, I mean."

"It's pretty great," Sam said. "I don't have to worry about whether I have a case, the pay is fantastic, and most of the time all I do is sit in my office and read reports. Every once in a while, like with this case, I have to spend some time out in the field. I don't mind, because it's all part of the business. Very rarely do I miss a night of sleeping at home, though."

"I heard something about these guys still working for the government sometimes?"

"Yes," Sam said, nodding. "In fact, just to work here, you have to have a security clearance. All of the investigators and most everyone else has top secret, special restrictions clearance. There isn't much we can't see or know about."

"Yeah, well, you already had that. How hard is it to get a security clearance? Just in case you ever did have an opening, I'm just wondering."

"Unless you've got something questionable on your record," Sam said, "it shouldn't be that big a problem. And if an opening does come up, you can bet I'll be in a hurry to give you a call about it. You'd be a terrific asset to this team, Karen."

"Yeah, and I bet you say that to all the girls. It's really just a thought, Sam, I'm not sure I'd ever leave the PD. How are the benefits? That's one area where being a cop doesn't seem to be all that advantageous."

Sam grinned. "The benefits are awesome," he said. "Pays for everything, and I mean everything. Not even a copay or a deductible."

"Dammit, I'm jealous, now. That's better than the coverage we got, I got a thirty percent deductible I have to pay on everything."

"Oh, I remember," Sam said. "This is definitely a pretty sweet job."

"It sounds like it. Now all you have to do is solve one of the most difficult crimes I've ever seen."

Sam grinned. "Yeah," he said. "But I got one hell of a team working with me."

"It certainly seems like it," Karen said. "Sam? Thanks for working with me on this. You and I both know that the only reason the mayor is letting you take lead is so that he can say it's your fault if we don't come up with the shooter. He's putting me with you to try to make sure we know everything you do, and I don't really like being used as a spy. I just want to get that out in the open, so there aren't any surprises down the road."

Sam laughed. "Of course I know that," he said. "Just be sure to spell my name right when you file your reports."

"GOOD MORNING, MR. REILLY," said the news producer, Jillian Ross. "I've talked with personnel, and we've assigned you to our most up and coming reporter. Her name is Wendy Dawson, and she'll be—oh, here she is now. Wendy, come meet your new cameraman; Harvey, this is Wendy! Wendy, this is Harvey Reilly."

"We've met," Wendy said, and then she winked at Harvey. "Good to see you again."

"Um, yeah," he said, following her lead. "You, too."

"Okay, good, then we can get down to business. Wendy, I've scheduled you to cover the Levinson funeral this morning, it's at the First Baptist Church on 12th Street at ten, and you've got the Terrell wedding today at three, but then I got a call this morning about a new park opening up. That's at one, and it's over at Buckingham Street and Fifth Avenue, so I need you to cover that, too. Harvey, working with a reporter sometimes means surprises that can hit at any minute, so I got you a van assigned, but let me tell you, I had to twist arms to do it. It's our oldest van, I'm afraid, but it'll have to do. You're to keep it with you all the time, even drive it home. That's so if a story comes up in the middle of the night, which has definitely been known to happen, you can just meet Wendy there and have all your gear ready."

Harvey grinned. That would solve his problem on getting to work, at least. "No problem, sounds great!"

Jillian looked at them. "Okay, then, go get your gear and your van, and make sure you're at the church on time! Scat!"

Harvey and Wendy walked out of her office together. "I've got to go sign out my camera and stuff, and I'll meet you at the motor pool, okay?"

She smiled. "Sounds good. I'll grab us some coffee on the way." She turned and was gone before he could tell her how he liked his coffee, but he figured he'd cover that another time. It was nice of her to offer, and he'd drink it with mud in it before he'd complain about someone so pretty being so nice!

The video equipment they gave him was not the most modern or up to date, but he could work with it. He had three cases to carry with sound equipment and wireless microphones, plus the old Sony FDR camera; between them all, they must have weighed close to a hundred pounds, but he was stout enough to handle it. He'd had to carry even more at times in school, when he worked for the college station.

He found his way to the motor pool and looked around for a moment before he saw Wendy waving at him. She was standing next to a van that looked like it belonged in a junkyard, but it had the station's logos painted on both sides, the front and the rear, and had a satellite transceiver antenna on top, so he figured it must be theirs. He walked over to it and opened the side doors, then set his gear down on its floor while he looked at the mess inside.

"Holy crap," he said. "This is a mess!"

"Wow, it is! I can't believe they'd give us a van that's so torn up!"

He looked at the stuff that was strewn around it for a moment. There were spilled coffee cups, candy wrappers, and goodness knows what some of those sticky messes were! "I'll be right back, I'm gonna need some cleaning supplies."

Wendy smiled. "Okay, I'll be here. Oh, here's your coffee!" She passed him a cup.

He took it and smiled. "Thanks," he said, and took a careful sip. To his surprise, it was exactly the way he liked it, just sweet enough, but not too sweet. "Hey, perfect!" he said as he walked back toward the building in search of cleaning supplies.

As soon as he got back, he started cleaning out the trash and sticky residues that seemed to be all over the interior of the van. He worked fast, and it wasn't long before all the trash had been carried out and dropped into a garbage dumpster that was standing nearby.

Harvey looked inside the van and grinned. "Okay," he said, "I guess it could've been worse, but I'm not sure how."

Wendy grinned and bumped him with her shoulder. "Oh, c'mon, it wasn't that bad! We can make it work for a while, don't you think?"

He looked at her and grinned, her beautiful eyes making him agree with her. "Yeah," he said. "It does look lot better already." He climbed inside and started wiping the shelves that were supposed to hold his equipment, and seemed to lose himself in the work. Wendy took some of the paper towels and a spray bottle and began cleaning the seats and dashboard.

"Thanks," Harvey said when he realized what she was doing. "I'll do that, if you want."

"No, I don't mind. I mean, we're just about gonna live in this thing together for a while, we might as well work together to make it as nice as we can, right?"

The thought of spending so much time with Wendy suddenly appealed to Harvey, and he smiled. "I guess so," he said, and went back to cleaning the shelves and racks. When he was done, he started putting all of his gear into its proper places, and by the time he'd finished that, Wendy had the cab looking great. In fact, other than a few rips in the seats, it didn't look bad at all.

"Well," he said with a grin, "I gotta tell you, this thing looks a whole lot better than it did an hour ago! It's a little after nine, and we've got the funeral at ten, so I guess we better get going! Ready to take it on its maiden voyage?"

Wendy smiled. "Let's do it!" she said, and Harvey climbed into the driver's seat. The keys were in the ignition, so as soon as she was settled, he turned them to start it up.

3

The little Cessna jet touched down to the tarmac at Denver International at 11:49, a little more than ten minutes early. Windlass personnel were accustomed to the charter jets they used beating their predicted arrivals, however, so the car was already waiting on the tarmac when the plane came to a stop. The copilot opened the hatch and let it down, and Steve and Walter stepped off into the mile high sunshine.

Roger Bowman, one of the regular security guards Windlass employed, had been designated as the driver for the day, and was standing beside the car with a smile on his face. He opened the back door of the black GMC SUV and took their bags to the back as the two men climbed inside. He slammed the tailgate and then got behind the wheel.

"How was it, guys?" Roger asked. He'd known both Steve and Walter for more than a year, and liked them both.

Steve Beck had been a police detective in Golden, Colorado, twelve years earlier when Sam Prichard had been a brand new recruit in the police academy. The two of them had gotten to know each other because Steve was a regular guest instructor, and had quickly become friends.

Walter Rawlings was only twenty-six years old, and described himself as a highly functioning autistic. He had an innate ability to look at hundreds or thousands of apparently random factors and connect them, seeing clues that anyone else would miss because it didn't seem possible they might be relevant. He was already becoming something of a legend in the law enforcement community nationwide, because of his ability to walk through a crime scene and understand exactly what had taken place, even when other crime scene experts were completely stumped.

"It was pretty wild," Steve said. "Salt Lake City PD thought we were nuts when Walter told them what had happened, but they turned into believers when he proved to be correct."

Roger laughed. "And how much did they offer him to come work for them directly?"

"I don't know," he said, "how much was it, Walter?"

"Sixty-five thousand," Walter said. "Sixty-five thousand a year."

Roger whistled at that. "Wow, that's got to be an awful lot for a CSI. Most of them don't make that much, do they?"

"Nowhere near," Steve said. "And especially not to start. Good thing we pay him a lot more than that, right?"

"Nah," Roger said, "Walter wouldn't leave us, would you, Walter?"

"No. I like my job. I like traveling, and I like Steve. And I like Sam."

"See?" Roger asked. "Not a thing to worry about. Listen, guys, have you had lunch yet?"

"Not really," Steve said. "They gave us a snack cake and a can of pop on the plane."

"Well, in that case, I'm supposed to swing through a drive-up window and get you something to eat, because they want you back at the office ASAP. There's a hot new case and Mr.

Prichard wants to talk with you about it before you go look at the crime scene."

"Let me guess," Steve said. "We're going to the Canterbury? Where that kid was shot on a webcast the other night?"

"Bingo," Roger said. "The company has hired us for security and to find out who the shooter was. I heard the Denver PD is even taking backseat on this, can you believe that?"

"I believe it," he said. "Sam Prichard is running the investigation, it can't get any better for them." He turned to Walter. "Walter, what do you want for lunch? We have to get it and take it with us back to the office."

"I want Popeye's," Walter said. "The spicy kind."

Steve chuckled and looked at Roger. "You heard the man," he said. "Popeye's it is."

There was a Popeye's on the way, and Roger steered the big SUV through the drive-up lane. They got their order and were back on the road only a couple of minutes later.

When they entered the building, Steve spotted Kate Higgins, another of the office girls, and asked her to let Sam know that he and Walter would be in the break room. She said she would, so the two of them continued on their way. Sam found them sitting at a table a few minutes later, each of them munching on a chicken leg.

"Good to have you back," Sam said. "And good work in Salt Lake City. Did they catch the thieves yet?"

"I got a call as we were headed for the airport this morning," Steve said. "They caught them, and the statue had been recovered. If I recall correctly, that means the company gets a twenty percent bonus."

Sam chuckled, shaking his head. "Ron and Jeff will be delighted with that news," he said. "No, actually I think it's Eileen who will be excited. The guys don't seem to worry a lot about the money, whether it's coming in or going out. I think they leave all that up to her."

"They should," Steve said. "I've seen that lady negotiate the contract for the company, she's like a shark. She squeezes the client for every dime she can get and then gets them to agree to a bonus for full satisfaction. It's the bonuses that really make the money, but that makes it sound like we keep our fees low. I don't know what she did before this, but she's definitely good at what she does now."

"She certainly is. Listen, as soon as you guys finish eating, the three of us are going over to the Canterbury Arena. You heard about the shooting there the other night?"

"Oh, yes," he said. "It was all over the news, you couldn't get away from it."

"Good. I want Walter to take a look at everything there. They think they know where the shot was fired from, and they got an idea how the shooter got in and out, but absolutely nothing is showing up on security video that could be a rifle. I know there are rifles that can be taken apart, even carried in your pockets, but this thing must've happened so fast that the shooter would've had to take it apart on the fly. That doesn't sound to me like it would be easy to do, but maybe I'm behind the times."

"No problem," he said. "Walter can figure it out, right, Walter?"

Walter only nodded.

Sam was smiling again. "Great," he said. "We'll head over there as soon as you guys are ready."

It took a few minutes for them to finish eating, and then Steve, Walter, Sam, and Karen Parks all climbed into another of the company's SUVs. Sam got behind the wheel and drove into Denver proper.

"Okay, here's what we've got," Sam said. "The shooting occurred in what was supposed to be the last few minutes of the program. Mr. Petrelli, the victim, had just stepped out from behind the curtain when he stumbled, but then it looked like he caught himself and was coming on out. He took one step, and then fell flat on his face. When the stagehands and program hosts got to him, they turned him over and saw blood on his chest. The building was locked down immediately and police and paramedics were called. Paramedics got Petrelli stabilized and rushed him off to the hospital, but no one else was allowed to leave. The police interviewed everyone who was present, but no one reported hearing a gunshot or seeing anything out of the ordinary. After enhancing the audio recordings of the program, they did find what seems to be the sound of a suppressed gunshot hidden behind the music."

"What's the current theory on the shooting, Sam?" Steve asked.

"Right now, police believe the shooter was on a catwalk above the audience. They pinpointed the spot they think he had to have chosen, based on the angle of trajectory. The only problem with this theory is that there is no sign of anyone entering or leaving the building with something long enough to be a rifle."

"Probably a take down rifle, then," Steve said. "Carry it in, put it together, make the shot, take it down, and carry it out."

"I thought of that, too," Sam said. "A take down rifle, though, still occupies a lot of space. With the exception of a few women's purses that have already been cleared, we don't have any video footage of a bag large enough to fit that description. Now, it's possible that the shooter had the individual pieces hidden inside his clothing, of course, but even that should be detectable. I mean, you'd almost have to be wearing some fairly heavy clothing with straps or pockets hidden inside to hold the parts. That should be noticeable, and it would probably make you walk differently than normal."

"That's a good point," Steve said. "We'll just let Walter do his thing. Okay, Walter?"

"Yes. I think I know how it happened already, but I want to look at the crime scene."

Sam looked at him in the rear view mirror. "You have a theory already?"

Walter nodded. "I think I figured it out already," he said. "But I want to look at the crime scene before I say anything."

The drive to the Canterbury Arena took forty minutes, and all of them had to show their IDs to get into the building. It was still on police lockdown after the shooting, with one of Karen's detectives holding down the fort for the police department.

"Sam Prichard," Karen said, "this is Detective Russell Dolby. I've had him keeping an eye on things here while I play the politics game down at the mayor's office. The city's CSI team has already done their thing and got nothing, so all we're doing right now is keeping it secure. Russ, this is the famous Sam

Prichard, and these gentlemen are Steve Beck and Walter Rawlings."

Dolby held out a hand and shook with Sam and Steve, but Walter kept his hands in his pockets and Dolby caught the wink Steve gave him. "It's a pleasure to meet all of you," he said. "Mr. Prichard, I've been hearing about you since the day I first met Karen."

"Pleasure is mine," Sam said. "Mr. Rawlings is our crime scene expert. We need to let him look around the area for a while, so he can figure out exactly how this shooting ended up happening."

"Yes, sir," Dolby said. "If you'll follow me, I'll show you where we believe the shooter came into the building." He turned around and started walking away, and the four of them followed.

Walter looked at the employee entrance Dolby showed them for a couple of seconds, then turned around and started walking toward the metal stairs that led up to the catwalk over the audience area. He went up them with everyone else following, stood at the top for a moment and looked around, then started walking across on the central catwalk. This was also known as the third catwalk, and was the one the police had concluded was used by the shooter.

Walter was looking down at the open grating that formed the floor of the catwalk as he followed it along. He stopped almost dead center and looked toward the stage, where a wooden X stood in the exact spot where Max Petrelli had stumbled. He looked at the stage for moment, then turned and looked down at the grating under his feet for another moment before looking upward.

There were dozens of horizontal cables and pulleys overhead, part of the system of specialized lights and cameras that could be moved to just about anywhere under the roof. The actual house lights were below the catwalks, and bright enough to make it almost impossible to see past them. When those lights were off, however, the sheer darkness guaranteed that no one would be able to see what was happening over their heads.

Walter pointed at one of the cameras that was hanging about fifty feet away. "I need that camera over here," he said.

Karen turned to Dolby, who shrugged and then walked slowly across the catwalk and down the stairs. He went to the control booth and spoke to the people inside it for a moment, and the camera Walter had asked for came moving slowly and smoothly toward him.

Walter waited until it was hanging just over his head, then suddenly started climbing on the railing of the catwalk.

"Walter, please be careful," Sam said, but Steve put a hand on his shoulder.

"Don't bother," he said. "When he's after an answer, nothing is going to stop him."

Sam, Karen, and Steve stood transfixed as Walter stood on the two rails, his legs spread wide. He held onto the camera, which was huge. It measured almost four feet long by two feet high and almost a foot wide. From where he was standing, Walter could just see the top of it.

There were a couple of flashes as he took pictures of something with his phone, and then he suddenly dropped back to the floor of the catwalk. The whole thing shook ominously, but it held.

"Well?" Steve said. "What do you think?"

"The reason you never saw the shooter on camera," Walter said, "is because he was already in the building. He didn't have to carry a rifle in or out, because it was already here."

Sam's eyes went wide. "What? Was it hidden on top of the camera?"

Walter held out his phone, showing the photograph he had taken. It showed a stripped down rifle mounted on some sort of electrically controlled tripod. There was a video camera affixed to a scope on top of the rifle, and an electrical solenoid was mounted just in front of the trigger. On one side of the receiver was a small plastic box with an antenna, with wires running to the solenoid. As they'd expected, there was a large sound suppressor on the end of the barrel.

"The rifle was already there, ready to take the shot. All the shooter had to do was sit somewhere out of sight and watch the video through the scope until just the right moment, then send the signal to fire the gun."

"Holy cow," Sam said. "It was done by remote control? We need to find out who has access to those cameras. The arena must have a maintenance crew that takes care of things like that, right?"

"They do," Karen said. "I have a list of all of their employees. It's on my computer, back in your office. Do you honestly think one of them is the shooter?"

"Not particularly, but I can't rule it out. What we need to find out is how long it's been since this camera was actually serviced. Then we can start scanning security videos since that time to see who might have been up here to install the gun."

"What amazes me," Karen said, "is that it might have been there for weeks. Unless somebody got up to that camera the way Walter did, that gun would be invisible. Who would ever think to check up there?"

"The Secret Service, maybe, if the president was going to be here. Other than that, probably nobody, but I can tell you who will always check things like that in the future."

Karen grinned at him. "Windlass Security?"

"You bet your ass. I've dealt with remotely controlled robots before, and we know that we live in an age where remotely controlled weapons are a distinct possibility. Absolutely anything that might have a line of sight toward somebody we're protecting will have to be checked out in the future."

"You know," Karen said, "the shooter might not have been here at all. If it's remotely controlled, he could have been just about anywhere."

"No," Walter said. "The whole roof is a metal grid work. That would block almost any signal that came through, unless it was connected to an antenna outside the roof. The controller had to be here inside the building, under that roof, or it wouldn't have worked. It was probably just something on a smartphone, or on a tablet."

Sam nodded. "He's right," he said. "That roof would almost act like a Faraday cage. The signal to control the aiming mechanism and fire the gun would have almost had to come from inside the building." He looked around at where Dolby was making his way back to them across the catwalk. "We need to get our technicians in here to take that gun down. I want it taken out to our tech labs, so Q can figure it out. It's even possible we can find some kind of digital signature that might lead back to whoever built it."

Dolby looked at him. "Q?"

Sam grinned. "His name is really Fred, but he comes up with such fantastic gizmos and gadgets that everybody calls him Q, like in the James Bond movies. He and his technicians can do just about anything when it comes to gadgetry and electronics."

Dolby shook his head. "I hope you'll forgive me for saying so," he said, "but it sounds like you have way too much fun. I don't suppose you're doing any hiring, are you?"

"Back off, buddy," Karen said. "I've already got first dibs on any job openings Sam has."

"Oh, well," Dolby said. "Can't blame a guy for trying, right?"

"Sure I can," Karen said. "Watch me."

Sam had taken out his phone and called their headquarters. "Jenna, I need you to get Q and a couple of his people out to the Canterbury Arena, with tools. Tell Ron I said they need to hurry."

"Yes, sir," Jenna said. "I'm on it."

The phone went dead and Sam put it back into his pocket, then turned to Karen. "Well, that explains why you never saw anything that could have been a rifle on the security cameras. It was already here, probably long before it was needed. Its placement tells me that the shooter knew well in advance where the winner would come out from behind the curtain. I wonder if that was the camera that was focused on Max when it happened."

"I'd bet on it," Steve said. "I mean, that would make sense. Mount it on the camera that's already going to be pointed in the right direction, and you would only have to make minor adjustments with the aiming mechanism. And it isn't like an actual sniper shot, there's no wind or weather concerns. How far is it from here to where the kid was hit?"

"Approximately one hundred and ninety-six feet," Walter said.

"See?" Steve said. "That's an easy shot, even without fancy electronic gizmos."

Karen sent Dolby down to wait for the technicians while the rest of them stayed on the catwalk. "I don't know about you," she said to Sam, "but I don't want to let this puppy out of my sight. As screwy as this case is, I wouldn't put it past the realm of possibility for that gun to disappear if we take our eyes off it."

"I doubt it," Sam said. "Maybe it's just been the heavy police presence, but no one has tried to get it out yet. I can't imagine they'd try it after we'd found it." He grinned. "At the same time, I want to make sure Q gets it without any problems, and I want a clear chain of custody on it. We'll run ballistics on it just to confirm that it's the weapon that fired the round that hit Max, but I'm a lot more interested in what those electronics might have to say. I learned a lot about smart electronics lately, and different designers do things different ways. It's quite possible our shooter left a signature of some kind."

The four of them stood around and talked about possible scenarios around the shooting, killing time until Q and his team arrived forty minutes later. Q was a short, stocky man, and he turned out to be too short to see over the top of the camera. Luckily, one of his technicians—a man named Cooley—stood almost six foot four. With Q holding onto his legs to brace them, he stood on the railing the way Walter had and removed the screws that held the articulated tripod onto the top of the camera. Wearing rubber gloves so that he wouldn't leave any fingerprints or skin oils, he finally lifted the rifle down and passed it to Vicki Freeman, the other technician who had come with them.

"This is a class 2 Bluetooth setup," Vicki said. "The shooter had to have been within ten meters of it when it was fired." She scowled. "Well, under most circumstances, anyway. It's possible he might've used a Linksys dongle modified with an external antenna. That would let him have a range of up to a hundred meters."

Q shook his head. "That would require a class 1 device, like a laptop. Even a tablet would only have class 2, so I don't think that's a viable scenario." He looked at Sam. "I think she was right the first time. The shooter had to be within ten meters, about thirty three feet." He looked over the rail to the seats below. "I don't know if it's going to help anything," he said, "but it's almost twenty feet down to the seats below us. If you start at the one directly below and draw a radius out about twelve feet, then make a circle at that radius, your shooter was sitting within that circle somewhere." He looked up at Sam. "Of course, that's assuming the camera was right here when the gun was fired. If we can get a copy of the video footage from this camera at the time the victim was shot, we should be able to determine exactly where the camera was at that moment. That would let you know for sure where the shooter had been sitting."

"That gives us something to work with, anyway," Sam said. "What about the electronics on the gun? Any chance you can find any kind of leads back to the shooter from them?"

"Remote controlled guns aren't nearly as uncommon as you might think," Q said. "What's really different in this case is the fact that they used Bluetooth. Radio control or cell signal is most common, but somebody went to the trouble of creating an app and wiring up a Bluetooth transceiver to both the aiming and trigger mechanisms. You can find a dozen articles and videos online about how to use Bluetooth to make remote control cars, things like that. Somebody finally decided to adapt it to something a little more sinister."

"So just about anybody can learn how to do it?" Sam asked.

"I'm afraid so, Sam," Q said. "But that doesn't mean they didn't leave some Easter eggs for us. We can find out where and when this rifle was built, which will lead us to where it was sold. The Bluetooth device should be able to tell us what phone or tablet it was paired with, which will almost certainly be one of the prepaid variety, but that will give us the ability to identify where it was purchased and how the activation was paid. That information might lead to identifying the person who bought it and used it."

Sam grinned. "Q," he said, "that's the best news I've heard all day."

"NEWS SEVEN, THIS IS Production."

Harvey picked up the microphone. "Go ahead, Production."

"News Seven, you're closest to Canterbury Arena. Police scanner says they found the weapon used in the shooting Saturday night, get over there and get the story."

"Roger, on the way," Harvey said. He hung up the microphone and looked at Wendy. "Get ready, we're getting in on the biggest news story of the week."

"Well, get us there," Wendy said. She took a compact out of her purse and looked in the mirror, then pulled out a brush and ran it through her hair.

They pulled up in front of the arena a couple of minutes later, and Harvey got her wired up quickly. He grabbed his camera and followed her into the building, where Wendy spotted Detective Karen Parks and several other people, including the locally famous Sam Prichard.

"Detective Parks," she said, holding out her microphone, "we've been told that you found the weapon that was used in the recent shooting. Can you comment on this for me?"

Karen frowned, but turned to face the camera. "Yes, Wendy," she said. "An investigator from Windlass Security examined the crime scene and found a rifle that had been modified to operate by remote control. The rifle was mounted on one of the overhead trolley cameras, and is being removed for further examination. That's all we know at the moment."

"Detective, why is Windlass Security examining the crime scene?"

"The mayor has authorized Denver PD to work with Windlass investigators on this case," Karen said. "Web Wide Awards has hired Windlass to handle all future security arrangements, and to investigate the shooting itself. Sam Prichard is their lead investigator, and the mayor has the utmost confidence in his abilities and leadership."

Wendy turned and held the microphone out to Sam. "Mr. Prichard, since you seem to be in charge, can you tell us any more about what's going on?"

Sam smiled at the camera. "At this point, we're planning to keep some of the details under our hats, but as Detective Parks has said, we did find a remotely controlled rifle mounted on one of the cameras. Ballistics will have to confirm it, but at this point we believe this is the rifle that fired the shot that struck Mr. Petrelli."

"And do you have any leads on who might have been behind this?" Wendy asked.

"At this point, Wendy, all I can say is that we're exploring different possibilities. Hopefully, finding the weapon will help us to narrow down our search."

"Thank you, Mr. Prichard, and Detective Parks," Wendy said. She turned up to the camera. "This is Wendy Dawson at the Canterbury Arena, for Channel 6 news."

Sam and Karen walked away as Harvey kept the camera pointed at Wendy. "Production, how's that?"

"Very good, News Seven," said the voice in his headset. "Excellent work."

Harvey turned off the camera and nodded at Wendy, who relaxed. "I think that's the first update they've given out on this case," Wendy said. "And we got it! Harvey, this could be a big break for us."

"Yeah," Harvey said. "This is turning out to one helluva first day on the job."

4

As a precaution, and with the agreement of the Denver Police Department, Sam ordered a thorough search of all the equipment in the Canterbury Arena, including all the other cameras, the booms, sound equipment, and everything. No other weapons were found, but the searchers developed a maintenance regimen that would keep better track of every possible location where a remotely controlled weapon could be hidden.

"I want copies of all security video for the last ninety days," Sam told Dolby. "Everything, every bit of video from anywhere inside that building. Our shooter got in there at some point when there was no one else likely to interfere with what he was doing. I'm going to put someone on scanning through that video and see if we can figure out when that happened."

"All their security video is stored on a remote server," Dolby said. "They already provided access to it, so I'll get the login and password and send them to you."

"That's even better. Any idea how far back they go?"

"Yeah, they hold a year's worth of video, just in case they need to go back and look for something."

"Perfect," Sam said. "Give me that information as soon as possible."

Sam thanked him, and then he, Karen, Steve, and Walter got into the SUV and headed back to Sam's office.

"Walter," Sam said as he was driving, "what made you suspect remote control?"

"The catwalks," Walter said. "They only use those for maintenance on the equipment. Nobody would be up there during the show, and when we walked onto it, little bits of dirt and stuff were falling off our shoes onto the seats below. When the police interviewed everybody after the shooting, somebody would most likely have mentioned dirt falling from overhead. When you said nobody noticed anything unusual, that's when I started thinking that it had to be something remote, and the cameras were the most likely place to put the gun."

Karen looked at Sam. "And you send this guy out to consult, right? How much do you charge? I want him looking at every crime scene of mine in the future."

Sam chuckled. "I don't know how much they charge for Walter's services," he said, "but it's enough that he only gets called in on a case when nobody else can figure it out."

"Sometimes we do it for free," Walter said.

"That's true," Steve said. "We've gone out a few times on pro bono, for small departments that need our kind of help. I'm not sure Denver PD would qualify, though."

Karen laughed. "And I'd probably never get them to pay up. Our city is run by a bunch of cheap bastards."

They got back to the office a few minutes later, and Jenna handed Sam a small stack of messages. Jade Miller had met once again with John Morton and Annie Porter, and would be introduced to the company staff the following morning as Annie's new assistant. She had gone home early to start planning her wardrobe and work on a cover story.

Summer Raines had gotten a list of Web Wide Awards employees from Morton and Porter, and asked Darren Beecher to help her go over them. She was looking for employees who might be considered unhappy or disgruntled, and they were poring over the records in search of complaints and reprimands. They had already identified seven potential suspects, all but one of whom were male. Summer would start working on them as early as that evening.

Denny Cortlandt, after hearing that the weapon used was a very professional remotely controlled rifle, was reaching out to contacts in the intelligence community, looking for any leads on professional assassins or hit men who might have been in the area when the shooting occurred. He didn't expect to get any results before the following day, but promised to keep Sam in the loop.

Sam checked his emails when he got into his office and found that Detective Dolby had sent him the login information for the Canterbury's security video server. He grinned, then picked up his phone and called his wife, Indie.

"Hey, good lookin'," he said when she answered. "How's your day going?"

"Pretty good," she said with a smile in her voice. "Kenzie and Bo have been playing all day, and now they're both so worn out that they're sleeping. How's yours?"

"We got called in on the Web Wide Awards shooting," Sam said. "Denver PD wasn't getting anywhere, so the company hired us to investigate, and the mayor agreed to let us take the lead. He assigned Karen to work with us."

"Cool," Indie said. "We haven't seen much of her lately, tell her she needs to come to dinner one evening soon. Any word on the boy who was shot?"

"It looks like he's going to pull through, which is good. Listen, I took Walter out to the arena a while ago, and as usual, it only took him a couple of minutes to figure out what was going on. Turns out the rifle was mounted on top of one of the big cameras that run on cables overhead, and was set up to operate by remote control. I've got the access information for the server that stores all the security video for the arena; we need to search through it to find out when the gun was mounted, and who did it. Is that something Herman might be able to help with?"

"Hmm," she said. "I'd need to know which security cameras to look at, which ones could actually spot that camera. Oh, and I'd need to know what camera it is the gun was mounted on."

"Okay," Sam said. "I'm sending you the access information, and the phone number for Detective Dolby. He's out at the arena heading up the on-site part of the investigation. Tell him who you are, and he'll get you all that information. Don't forget to log your time, so you can bill for it."

"Oh, I won't forget," she said, chuckling. "I like getting a little extra money I can play with. I'll call Dolby now, and get Herman started. Love you."

"Love you more," Sam replied. The call ended and he leaned back in his chair.

Karen had made a stop at the ladies room, and came in just at that moment. "So, what's next?" she asked.

"I just sent the security video information to Indie," Sam said. "She's going to put Herman on it, so we should know something about when the gun was installed by tomorrow at the latest. You said you had a list of employees for Web Wide Awards? Summer and Darren went over it, looking for disgruntled employees who might have a grudge against the company, and they found a few potentials. Summer will be working on them, but another angle we want to look at is whether any of them might be vulnerable to blackmail. Sometimes, people can be forced into acting as accomplices; we need to get some sort of an idea about what skeletons might be rattling around these people's closets."

He hit button one on his phone and Jenna answered immediately. "Yes, sir?"

"I need Darren Beecher, please," Sam said.

"Yes, sir," the secretary said. The line went dead, and Darren tapped on the door less than two minutes later.

"Come on in," Sam said. "Darren, my gut tells me that somebody inside Web Wide Awards was involved in this, somehow. The shooter knew exactly where the winner would be coming out of the curtain, and the placement of the rifle indicates he had that knowledge for some time before the program. I know you and Summer were going over the employees looking for those that might be disgruntled, but did you happen to notice any particular individuals who might be susceptible to blackmail?"

"Actually, I did," Darren said, taking a notepad from his pocket and consulting it. "There are three that I can name off the top of my head, and probably several more. I ran basic background checks on each employee as we were going through them, and some of these people aren't exactly who you would think they are. I'd need a little more information to really compile a list, but we can start with the ones I noticed already."

Sam got up and moved to the conference table, the three of them sitting together at one end. Sam took a notepad and pen off a side table and laid it in front of him.

"Okay, who's first?" Sam asked.

"The first one I noticed was a guy named Charles Barr. He's their senior video producer, and he seems to be very good at his job, but he's got some things in his past that he'd probably like to keep quiet. First off, he's got some experience that he doesn't list on his resume. About eight years ago, he got his start doing video work in the porn industry. Back then, he was known as 'Goodie Barr,' and he produced videos involving just about every kind of not quite illegal fetish you can imagine. Web Wide Awards has a reputation as a wholesome, family-friendly company; somehow I doubt they'd be pleased if that information were to come to light. Just having him in a senior staff position could make them look pretty bad."

Sam was making notes as Darren spoke. "Okay, I'd say that definitely makes him vulnerable. It could do some pretty serious damage to the company's reputation, I'm sure. Did you see any indication that the owners know about his past history?"

"I can't tell for sure," Darren said, "but I'd say they probably don't. I really don't think they'd mention him publicly as often as they do if they were really aware of where his experience came from."

"Okay," Sam said. "Who's next?"

"That would be Patricia LeClair. She's their spokesperson; she appears in their TV commercials, and she presents the awards they give out each quarter. Unfortunately, the background check revealed that she didn't exist until four years ago, just before she got hired. I did a little deeper digging, ran her drivers license photo through facial recognition against the database in the state where it was issued, and found out that she was originally known as Angela Stubblefield. Ms. Stubblefield spent four years in state prison for being an accessory to murder. Apparently her boyfriend at the time tried to rob a drug dealer and ended up killing the guy, and she tried to give him an alibi. She was still on parole when she changed her name, quite unofficially, but I checked with the state parole board there and they don't want to pursue any additional charges against her."

"Then, as long as she stays out of trouble," Sam said, "she should probably be all right. Still, this is something that could hurt the company if it ever came out. That's enough to put her on a suspect list, as far as I'm concerned."

"Yeah, I'll say," Karen said. "She skipped out on parole and they don't want to do anything about it?"

"We're talking about Illinois," Darren said. "Her parole would be over by now, anyway, and she hasn't gotten in any more trouble, so they're willing to just let it go. I guess they have a lot more people on parole than they have parole officers to handle."

Karen shook her head.

"Okay, and who else?" Sam asked.

"This last one may not be that big a deal," Darren said. "Judy Lowery is the woman who gets the award winners all dressed up and presentable for the annual show. She does a complete makeover on them, everything from clothes to hair to makeup or whatever else she thinks they need to make them look their best. The issue is that she has something of a secret life; two or three times a month, she puts on leather and spends an evening with men or women who have a fetish for humiliation. She tells them how disgusting they are, makes them do things that humiliate them, that sort of stuff, and they actually pay her for this. She has a website where she calls herself a humiliatrix, and I didn't even think that was a word until I googled it. There's nothing illegal about what she's doing, but I'm not sure it would sit well with the company's advertisers and fans if it were to get out."

"I'm pretty sure it wouldn't," Sam said. "As you pointed out, they promote themselves as being family-friendly. Something like this could potentially impact their reputation, but I'm not sure how much. The real question is whether she would be willing to cooperate with the shooter in order to keep it secret."

"She might not," Karen said. "After all, she's just in the background. How many people do you think ever even hear about her? And a lot of people in that lifestyle don't consider it any kind of big deal, anyway."

"That's what I'm thinking," Sam said. "The other two are pretty prominent, and the secrets they have hidden away would be potentially damaging. This woman, nobody knows who she is except the people she works with; if it came out that she has this secret life, most people would just consider her some random employee of the company who wasn't even important. It might make some people laugh at them, for not knowing what she was into, but I don't think it would really hurt the company that much."

Darren nodded. "That's why I said it might not be that big a deal. I mean, after Fifty Shades of Gray came out, I don't know that too many people are all that shocked about the weird little fetishes people get into." He shook his head. "What a world, huh?"

"Isn't it, though?" Sam asked. "On the first two, Charlie Barr and Patricia LeClair, let's see what we can find out on their financial situations and personal communications. We need to see if there are any strange phone numbers or emails that have cropped up in the last few months, or if they've either paid out or received unusual amounts of money. Once we get that information, I'll pay them each a visit."

"I can do that," Darren said. He glanced at Karen. "Should we run it through the police and go for warrants?"

"Hey, I know good and well you guys don't bother with that kind of thing," Karen said. "That's probably why you solve cases faster and better than we do. Do your thing, and if you find anything that we need to use in court, then I'll get a warrant so we can uncover it properly."

Darren grinned. "Okay, just checking." He got up and left the room, and Sam and Karen grinned at one another.

"I'm surprised you didn't put Indie on that," Karen said. "She could dig out that information faster than anybody."

"I've already got her working on scanning the security video," Sam said. "Herman can do it a lot faster than any human possibly could."

"Yeah, no kidding. I'm half surprised you don't have her in an office right down the hall."

"We've actually been talking about that," Sam said. "Now that Bo is getting bigger, she's thought a bit about actually coming to work here. Right now, they got her set up as a consultant, though, and that might work better for her. Lets her work from home, so she's there for the kids."

"Yeah, I can see where that would be nice. I missed out on an awful lot of my own kids growing up, with the hours we put in back in the day. I guess those were the dues we had to pay to get to where we are today, right?"

"I don't know," Sam said. "If I hadn't gotten shot when I did, I'd probably still be on the force today."

"Yeah, and you'd probably still be single, too. Getting married did you a world of good, Sam. You were always a good guy, but Indie has definitely made some improvements."

Sam smiled. "You think I don't know it?"

SUMMER RAINES WAS SITTING in her cubicle, going over the list of potential suspects that she and Darren had put together. Each of them, based on items found in their personnel records, seemed to fit the description of disgruntled employee. Disgruntled employees were known to take revenge against their employers, or to perpetrate horrific acts to make the company or particular individuals suffer. Summer was planning to find out if any of these people were likely to have taken things to that extreme.

Walter's discovery of the remote control rifle had already made its way throughout Windlass. Because of the technical skills involved in constructing it, Summer focused first on two of the names on her list. This is because both were employed in the company's electronics maintenance department, where they repaired computers, video cameras, and other complicat-

ed electronic equipment. Constructing a Bluetooth enabled remote control device didn't seem like it would be all that difficult a task for either of them.

First up was Tom Linden. Tom had been with the company
for almost six years, and Summer found that just slightly amazing. The reason she was so surprised was because Tom had
spent at least two months out of every twelve in one drug rehab
program or another. Most companies won't put up with repeated trips to rehab, but Tom was still there. In fact, he had worked
in almost every department in the company at one time or another.

That didn't mean he was some kind of favorite or pet, however. He'd been written up repeatedly by various superiors, including his own department manager, the HR manager, the
bookkeeping department (for trying to bill personal purchases
to the company), and even by both John Morton and Annie
Porter. It was when Summer was examining all the complaints
that she figured out just how Tom managed to stay put.

Tom Linden was Annie Porter's half brother, three years
younger than she was.

Annie's father had died in an auto accident when she was
only two years old, and she had no memory of him whatsoever.
Her mother had raised her alone for a couple of years, then met
and married Thomas James Linden, and a year later had given
birth to a son, whom she named Thomas Raymond Linden. He
grew up being called Little Tom, and was adored by his big sister.

His father was quite an athlete and outdoorsman, while
Little Tom was anything but. He was extremely intelligent, and
had incredible hand to eye coordination, but he couldn't hit a

baseball with a bat to save his life. Fishing and hunting made him cry, he was too short for basketball, too skinny for football and just too darn chicken for hockey. By the time he was ten years old, his father had abandoned the family and run off with a younger woman. Big Tom hadn't been seen in years, and Little Tom blamed himself.

His drug problems had mostly been related to prescription medications that he was given to help with anxiety and depression, but he appeared to have a tendency to abuse them rather severely. The symptoms would become obvious pretty quickly, and big sister Annie would stage yet another intervention. Tom would go into rehab, do his twenty-eight days and come out determined not to ever let it happen again. A few months later, the cycle would repeat.

To Summer, Tom seemed like a likely candidate for the starring role in a workplace shooting. Every time he was written up for being late, or being obviously stoned on the job, he would write a response that basically said everybody else was wrong, the world was out to get him and nobody really understood him at all. It was the typical "poor little me" act that people used to avoid accepting responsibility for their own failures and actions.

Summer took out her cell phone and dialed Tom's personal number. It rang a few times, but finally he answered it cautiously.

"Hello? Who's this?"

"Hi," Summer said brightly. "Is this Tom Linden?"

"Um, who's calling?"

"Oh, I'm sorry, how silly of me. Tom, my name is Candy Simmons, and I got your name and number from a mutual friend of ours who thinks you and I might be quite a good match. I was just calling to see if maybe you might like to get together for dinner tonight."

"I—wait a minute, you're who?"

"Candy Simmons," Summer said. "You remember Dave Newman? He met you back when you were both in, well, you were both in a bad place and working on getting better. Remember him? He told me all about you and said he thought maybe you were just the kind of guy I've been looking for, and since I'm free tonight, I thought maybe you might like to have dinner with me. You know, just to see if maybe we might really like each other. Pretty please?"

"Dave Newman? Was that the guy they called sweaty Dave? Yeah, I think I remember him. So, what, this is like some sort of blind date thing?"

Summer giggled. "Well, not exactly," she said. "I mean, it's not the kind of blind date where you don't get to know who the other person is until it's too late. Hang on, let me send you a picture of myself. It'll just take a second." She held the phone away from her ear and turned on its camera, snapped a quick selfie and sent it to his number. "There. Did you get it?"

"Um, yeah," Tom said. "Just a sec, let me look." She could hear him take the phone away from his ear, and then she heard a couple of beeps as he pressed the buttons that would let him see the incoming image. She also heard the sharp intake of breath when he got a look at her picture.

5

He was off the line for almost 30 seconds, and had a smile in his voice when he came back. "So, yeah, I'm not busy tonight either," he said. "Do I, like, need to send you a picture of me now?"

"No, that's fine," she replied. "Dave showed me a picture of you, and I think you're pretty cute. That isn't too forward, is it? Sometimes people tell me I'm just a little too forward."

"No, no, that's fine," Tom said. "So, do you want to meet up somewhere, or would you like me to pick you up for dinner?"

"Well, since this is the first time we ever met," she said, "I think maybe we should just meet up somewhere. What kind of food do you like?"

"Oh, I can go for just about anything. You just pick a place, and say what time. I'll be there, and I'm buying."

"Oh, you don't have to pay for dinner," Summer said. "I was planning on paying for it, since I'm the one inviting you."

"No, we can't have that, now," Tom said. There was a chuckle in his voice as he went on. "Besides, what would people think if somebody who knows either of us very well saw me letting you pay for dinner? Maybe I'm a little bit old-fashioned, but I still believe the man is supposed to be the one to pay for the date."

Summer giggled. "Well, okay," she said. "I guess this is a date, sort of. Maybe just our first date, right?"

"The first of many," Tom said. "Now, come on, you were going to tell me where and when."

She let out a sigh. "Okay, okay, I've got it. How about if we go to," she paused for dramatic effect, "Shanahan's? Would that be okay?"

Shanahan's was a wonderful place to eat, but it was not for someone on a budget. Summer almost giggled when she heard the split second of hesitation in Tom's voice, but then he recovered himself and agreed enthusiastically.

"Sure, Shanahan's sounds great. What time is good for you?"

"Well, I'm at work right now," she said. "I need to run home and get a bath and do my hair and makeup, all that girly stuff. Why don't we say about six thirty? Is that okay, or is that too early for you?"

"Six thirty is great," Tom said. "I can't wait to meet you face to face."

"Oh, me, too," Summer said. "After everything Dave told me about you, I really am looking forward to this." She giggled again. "Maybe this simple dinner will turn into something even more exciting," she said. "Like, maybe, breakfast? I'll see you at six thirty. Bye bye." She cut off the call before he could say anything else, then let herself collapse into a fit of laughter.

A moment later, after she had composed herself, Summer stopped at Sam's office and smiled at Jenna. "Is he in?"

"Yep," Jenna said with a grin. "Just a second." She picked up the handset and pressed a button on her phone and then said, "Summer is here to see you." She waited another couple of seconds, then said, "Yes, sir," and motioned for Summer to go in.

Summer stepped inside the office and found Sam and Karen sitting at the conference table. They were looking at the employee list on Karen's computer and making notes.

"That's exactly what I came to talk to you about," Summer said. "Tom Linden, who happens to be Annie Porter's half brother, has had more complaints and write ups than anybody else in the company. Every time he gets written up, even if it's by his sister, he writes a nasty response that is so full of suppressed anger that I'm surprised he hasn't gone postal yet. If he was anybody else, he would've been fired a long time ago. If I had to pick a prime suspect for the shooter, that would be him."

Sam looked at her, his eyes slightly narrowed. "Do you have some reason to believe he was actually behind this shooting?"

"No, not really," Summer said. "I just feel like there's enough anger and animosity in him that we can't dismiss it out of hand." She grinned. "That's why I called him up and asked him for a date tonight."

Karen's eyebrows shot upward. "You did what?"

"I called him up and gave him some line about how a mutual friend thought we were ideal for each other, then I sent him a selfie. He's buying me dinner at Shanahan's, tonight. By the time I leave him tonight, I'll know whether he's capable of murder, or even attempted murder. At the very least, I'll be able to scratch him off the potential suspects list."

Sam was grinning. "Just don't get too carried away," he said. "Unless you come up with something that indicates guilt, don't push him too hard. He's still the client's brother, so without any evidence, it would be easy to alienate Ms. Porter."

"Go easy on him? Sam, I will interrogate that boy up one side and down the other, and all he's going to do is thank me for giving him a wonderful evening. He's not going to get what he's hoping to get, but he'll definitely be happier than he is now."

Karen was staring at her, her eyes still wide and her mouth half open. Sam grinned and took pity on her.

"Karen, Summer believes that her looks are a tool to be used in the course of her work. In the short time I've been here, they've proven to be quite effective. Men just naturally seem to want to talk to her, and she can steer the conversation onto whatever she wants to know about. A highly effective interrogation technique."

"Yeah," Summer said. "Especially when I start taking off clothes. I never go as far as they want, but it's like strip poker; the more clothes you take off, the more the guys try to bluff. In this case, the farther they think I'll go, the more they want to tell me to keep me going."

"Oh, really?" Karen asked. "Too bad they didn't have her at Guantánamo Bay. No telling how much sooner we'd have gotten bin Laden."

Summer giggled, then waved at Sam and Karen as she walked out the door. "I'm going home to change for my date," she called over her shoulder.

Karen shook her head. "Dolby is right," she said. "Sam, I think you are having way too much fun in this job."

"Yeah, sometimes," Sam said, "but it has nothing to do with looking at Summer. She's a gorgeous woman, but she can't hold a candle to Indie. You want to know the most fun I have running this team?"

"Heck, yes," Karen said. "Tell me, already."

"It's when they come in from a field assignment and tell me about how it went. I don't care how simple the case is, at

least one of them is going to find some way to set some part
of the world on its ear. A few weeks ago, I had to bail Summer
out of jail because she chose the wrong fictitious name to use.
It just happened to be the name of a woman who was wanted
for being a meth kingpin, but the funny part is that the woman
they were really after looks enough like Summer that the cops
who arrested her couldn't tell the difference. I had to post her
bail, then convince the local magistrate that they had the wrong
woman. It seems they didn't know much about fingerprints,
like the fact that they could have compared them by eye and
seen that they had the wrong person."

"Okay," Karen said, "you might find that funny, but I doubt
that she did."

"No, you're right," Sam said. "Summer was pretty pissed off
about the whole thing at the time, but she can laugh about it
now. Even better than that was when Denny Cortlandt actually
got caught breaking in to the jail in Tucson, Arizona. He actually managed to convince the sheriff there that he was with the
FBI and had been assigned to test their security system. Shook
hands with the sheriff, patted him on the back and told him
what a great job they were doing, and they actually let him walk
out the door."

"They didn't even try to stop him?" Karen asked, incredulously. "I would've at least insisted on calling the local FBI office to verify his story."

"And that's exactly what they did," Sam said. "Denny handed them his card, which had a local number for the FBI office
printed right on it. The sheriff dialed the number and it came
straight to my office phone. Jenna answered, and when the
sheriff asked if he had reached the office of the FBI in Tucson,

she smiled and said that he certainly had, and could she transfer him to Special Agent in Charge Frank Perron. He said he would be willing to hold for a moment, and she buzzed me. She told me Denny was in Tucson trying to retrieve some top secret information from a DEA agent who was undercover inside the jail, and had apparently been busted trying to get in. She told me I was SAC Frank Perron and to get on the phone and confirm whatever Denny had told them, so I did."

Karen was laughing by this point. "Sam! You realize you're sitting here confessing to crimes, right?"

"Nope," Sam said with a grin. "I'm sitting here telling you jokes. Ain't my fault if you believe they're true."

"Whatever," Karen said. "Look, it's almost 4:30. I think I'm going to call it a day, unless you need me for something else."

"No, that's fine," Sam said. "I'm about to quit myself for the day. By the way, Indie wanted me to invite you to dinner one evening soon. I don't think she meant tonight, because she'd want a day or so to prepare, but it's been a while since we had you and the kids over."

"Getting me there isn't the problem," Karen said. "It's those overgrown two-year-olds I call my teenagers. They find some reason to go somewhere before I ever get home each day, and they never come back before I go to bed. I don't know how either of them is ever going to find a job, because all they do is sleep through the day."

"Well, it's worth a try. Maybe I can get David on the phone and twist his arm a bit. He can round up Katie and drag her along, I'm sure."

Karen rolled her eyes. "That sounds like a plan," she said. "Now, if you manage to pull that off, then I really will believe you're a miracle worker."

She waved as she took off out the door, and Sam started thinking about his own quitting time. He was just about to call home to see if he needed to pick anything up on the way when Jenna beeped in.

"Sir, your wife is on line two," she said.

"Thank you," Sam said, and then he punched the button for line two. "Hey, babe," he said. "I was just about to call you..."

"Sam, Herman found what you're looking for, I think," she said. "I'm sending you a link by email, check it out now."

"Okay," Sam said. "You sound awfully agitated. Is there something about this that's going to be a surprise?"

"Well, it surprised me," she said. "I think you might find it just a little bit surprising, yourself. Click the link and watch the video."

"I'm opening my email, now. Give me a moment, and I'll... Okay, got it. Just clicked the link and it's opening, and okay, I just hit play."

On his computer screen, he saw the view from one of the security cameras that was up near the ceiling in the theater. Almost directly opposite from where the camera was mounted, he could see someone approaching the center of the catwalk. As he watched, the big camera swung down on its trolley lines and hung just over the catwalk, exactly where Walter had checked it out earlier that day.

The camera focused on the man and zoomed in tight, but from the side. It showed part of a youthful face on a skinny frame, and Sam thought for a moment that it looked like many people he had seen that day. The man stopped beside the camera and removed a backpack he'd been wearing, slung it over one shoulder, then climbed up and straddled the railing just as Walter had done. At that point, the camera itself made it impossible to see what he was doing.

Whatever it was, it was taking some time. Sam hit the fast forward button, scanning ahead a few seconds at a time until he saw motion again. After about ten minutes, the fellow climbed down, slung the backpack on properly again, and walked back the way he had come, and just before he would've disappeared through the doorway that led to the rear maintenance stairs, he stopped and looked back at the big camera. His face was obscured by a hanging cable at that point, but Sam could see his body clearly, and it suddenly struck him that something was off.

A few months earlier, Sam had dealt with a cold murder case in which the only witness insisted that the "man" he had seen running away from the scene of the crime was a woman. He based that determination on a personal study of the differences between the way men and women walk, something he had undertaken on the advice of his high school drama teacher. Sam had listened to the young man's explanation of those differences, and that suddenly came back to him now.

That wasn't a skinny young man; that was a thin young woman, doing her best to look like a man. The physics of the female anatomy, however, meant that certain motions were going to be different from the way a man would make them, and this one's sudden stop and turn were undoubtedly feminine.

"Indie," Sam said, "that's not a man, it's a woman."

"Yep," Indie said. "Your shooter is a woman, and she looks to me like a teenager."

"She definitely looks young," Sam said. "You really think she's a teenager?"

"Well, very young," Indie said. "Very petite, and blonde. I can't get a good look at the face or hands, so I don't really have anything to go by other than the way she moves, but she's as agile as any athlete I've seen. She could be older, but I just get the feeling she's not more than very early twenties."

"Okay. Let me get this out to everybody now, and I'll be on the way home in just a few minutes..."

"Hold on, Sam," Indie said, cutting him off. "You missed the most important part. You wouldn't want one of your team to catch it before you do, would you?"

Sam froze, looking at the screen again. "Okay, let me play it again. Hang on." He refreshed the screen and hit the play button again. It opened as it had before, with someone coming across the catwalk from the opposite side of the theater. The big camera, hanging back toward the rear, suddenly started moving forward until it paused over the catwalk.

"I got it," Sam said. "Our shooter mounted the gun on the camera, but she had an accomplice in the control room. That's the only way the camera could have been at just the right place at that moment for her to work with it."

"Oh, you got it," Indie said. "Now, one last thing. Did you notice the time stamp on the video?"

Sam looked quickly, then groaned. "Three o'clock in the morning? The place should have been locked up tight."

"Yep. Three o'clock in the morning, five weeks ago today. When you get home, you get your prize. Just remember that your children will be here, so you have to settle for a kiss until later."

Sam chuckled. "A kiss from you is definitely a prize worth winning," he said. "I'll be home soon, babe."

"Okay, love you." The line went dead.

Sam sent the video link out to all of the team, including Karen Parks, along with a note explaining that he and Indie had come to the conclusion that the person they saw in the video was female, and that there had to have been an accomplice in the arena's control room. There was a time stamp on the video, so the first thing he wanted to find out was whether any of the arena employees were clocked in and present in the control room at the time.

He left his office and walked up the hall. Ron and Jeff were still in their own offices, which were side by side and had an adjoining door between them. He stepped into Jeff's office and crooked a finger, and Jeff got up to follow him into Ron's.

"I just sent you a video," Sam said. "It's the one Indie found, showing someone apparently mounting the gun on the camera. We can't get a good look at the face, but she and I are both convinced that what we're seeing is a woman trying to disguise herself as a man. Indie thinks she's pretty young, possibly even a teenager. This makes me wonder about rivals for the award; it's definitely conceivable that a teenage girl who could put together a popular online TV series might be able to make or get her hands on a remotely controlled rifle."

"That's certainly possible," Ron said. "Most of these kids end up doing their own special effects, so they undoubtedly learn some things about electronics and engineering in the process. Jade will be able to get into their computers tomorrow, you should have her start looking at that angle."

"Already sent her the email. She'll know what to do, trust me."

"It would certainly look good if we can bring this to a rapid conclusion, Sam," Jeff said. "We're actually starting to get quite a reputation for our investigative services, and a good part of that is because of you coming on board."

"Yeah, well, I appreciate it," Sam said, "but I don't know that I'm really making that much difference. To be honest, either Darren Beecher or Steve Beck could probably do my job as well as I do."

"Oh, no way," Jeff said. "Sam, you always sell yourself short. Steve and Darren are good investigators, don't get me wrong, but you have some innate ability to spot things that no one else does. You'll chase down all the leads, but in all your cases I've read about, it seems like you always have this sudden burst of epiphany at the last minute that gives you the actual solution. I don't know of anyone else who can do that the way you do, and besides, you got certain assets that no one else has. And speaking of your special assets, I don't suppose Beauregard has had anything to say about this case yet, has he?"

Sam rolled his eyes. "No, and I'm hoping he keeps it that way. And on that note, I'm going home. You know how to reach me if you need me. Otherwise, I'll see you guys tomorrow morning."

"Oh, wait," Ron said. "You won't see us tomorrow. Jeff and I have to fly to New York in the morning, early."

"New York? Working on a new contract up there?"

"You could say that," Jeff said. "Actually, we're going to evaluate the security arrangements for some kind of major internet conference that will be held there next week. NYPD is handling the outside security, but they're bringing us in for the conference itself."

Sam whistled. "Pretty sweet," he said. "You guys are doing fantastic for such a small, new company."

"Yeah," Ron said with a grin. "This is what happens when you're the best at what you do."

That got Sam to laugh. "And look," he said, "you've even managed to stay modest and humble."

6

"Honey, I'm home," Sam called as he entered his house. Kenzie came running from the kitchen, with Indie right behind her. Sam collected hugs and kisses from both, picking Kenzie up and carrying her back to the kitchen.

"Daddy," she said, "the grandmas are coming."

Sam looked at his wife and raised an eyebrow. "The grandmas are coming?"

"Yep," Indie said. "And before you ask, yes, Mom says Beauregard has a message for you. I don't know what it is, yet, but she says it's important."

"That's ironic," Sam said. "Jeff just asked me a bit ago if Beauregard had anything to say about this case. I was hoping to get through one without having to deal with him."

"It's just Mom's way of trying to help," Indie said. "I'll confess I wish she didn't have to rely on Mr. Figment so much, but it's the only way she can cope with being able to see the future. You know that, Sam."

"I know, and Beauregard has been helpful too many times for me to disregard what he has to say."

"Daddy," Kenzie said scoldingly, "Beauregard just wants you to be safe, that's all."

Sam squeezed her tight and kissed her on the cheek. "I know," he said, "and we appreciate it, don't we?"

The little girl giggled as Sam's five o'clock shadow rubbed her cheek. "Daddy, that tickles!"

"It does? Well, let's do it some more," Sam said, and then he rubbed his chin against her face and neck while she squealed in delight.

A sound from down the hall caught their attention, and Indie turned to Sam. "You woke up your son," she said. "That means you get to take care of him for a while. I'm trying to make dinner."

"Yes, ma'am," he said. He set Kenzie down and followed her as she ran down the hall. Bo was still in the nursery they had set up just off the master bedroom, but Indie was in the process of setting up his own new bedroom upstairs. Sam privately looked forward to when the bedroom became occupied.

Bo was standing in his crib and broke into a smile when he saw his daddy entered the room. "Da da," he said, and Sam's smile matched his son's.

"Hey, buddy Bo," he said as he picked the little boy up. "You ready to come out and play?"

The gurgles seemed to translate to the affirmative, so Sam carried him to the changing table and took care of necessities. The diaper went into the container that was set up for it, but the pants Bo was wearing were fine, so Sam put them back on him and they headed for the kitchen.

"Here's Bo, Mommy," said Mackenzie.

Indie turned and gave the baby a quick kiss, then went back to cutting up vegetables.

"We're having roast?" Sam asked.

"Yeah," Indie said. "I had a taste for it, so I figured it would be good for dinner tonight."

"Fine by me," Sam said. "One of my all time favorites."

"I caught the news a little while ago," Indie said. "They say Max is out of intensive care, now. I guess they expect him to make a full recovery."

"That's good," Sam said. "Of course, he's probably looking at a long road of physical therapy and probably psychological. PTSD is nothing to take lightly, and getting shot is one of the worst ways to get it."

"Really? Seems to me you always shrug it off like it's no big deal. How do you know Max isn't just as tough as you are?"

"I don't exactly shrug it off," Sam said with a grin. "Every time, it takes something out of me. I'm just lucky enough to have the best possible therapy waiting for me at home."

"Yeah," Kenzie said. "You got me and Mommy, and now you got Bo, too."

"That's exactly right," Sam said. "Nothing can get a man through something traumatic like the love of his family."

"But it would be a lot better if you'd stop getting shot," Kenzie finished. She shook her head and sighed. "That's pretty rough on us, too, you know."

"I'm doing my best," Sam said. "It's been a couple months, and last time I only got shot in the thigh. That wasn't too bad."

Sam put Bo into his highchair and Kenzie got him a bottle of milk. Bo smiled at his big sister as he took it, then plugged it into his mouth and began working at trying to drain it.

Sam opened the refrigerator and found a bottle of root beer, then sat down at the table beside his son. A sudden stabbing pain in his ankle made him yelp and look down to find Samson, their cat, trying to use Sam as a means of righting himself. Samson had survived a bout of distemper when he was a kitten, but it had left him seriously handicapped in his motor control. He had a tendency to flip over now and then, and he never seemed to understand why his back legs would somehow pass his front legs whenever he was trying to run. Occasionally, he would find himself on his back and unable to turn over, so he would dig his claws into whatever was closest and use it to pull himself back upright.

"Ow, Samson," Sam said. "I am not your scratching post."

Kenzie laughed, and Bo took the bottle out of his mouth to join in.

In self preservation, Sam reached down and picked up the cat. Samson was usually content to sit in his lap, and began purring almost instantly. Sam stroked him as he got himself into a comfortable position, and the cat was asleep within a minute.

Sam and Indie chatted while she made dinner, and he told her all of the details of the case. Because Indie was one of the most accomplished hackers any of them had ever known, and had been instrumental in helping Sam during certain cases when he worked with Harry Winslow and the Department of Homeland Security, Windlass had authorized Sam to use her as a consultant on any case. Harry had seen to it that she had a top secret security clearance, which was still necessary since Windlass had a contract with the government and could work on cases involving national security.

"So, you're thinking someone was out to hurt the company, Web Wide Awards?" Indie asked. "You don't think the kid was the actual target at all?"

"That's the way it looks to me," Sam said. "The problem is that whoever's behind it is going to be frustrated. So far, the company seems to be gaining greater sympathy from all of their supporters. The only detrimental effect so far is the possible loss of some sponsors, but one of them is Canterbury Soft Drinks. They're the biggest sponsor, and the reason Web Wide Awards gets to use the arena for their annual awards show."

"That would definitely hurt them," Indie said. "Imagine what it would cost to actually rent a venue like that."

"I don't know that that would be such an issue," Sam said. "The Canterbury Arena has eighteen thousand seats, and tickets for the event were like thirty dollars apiece and it was a sellout. I suspect the arena made some serious money that night; Web Wide Awards probably didn't have to pay a dime, and most likely got part of the gate."

"Okay. Then Canterbury is probably the company that loses on the deal, if they drop sponsorship. It would seem to me that they ought to wait and see how this all turns out before they make any decision."

"And that seems to be what they're doing," Sam said. "Annie Porter said that they seemed to calm down a bit when they found out we were coming on board to handle security and investigation."

There was a knock on the front door, and then it opened as their mothers walked in.

"Grandma!" Kenzie yelled, and took off running. Grace, Sam's mother, caught her and snatched her up into a hug, then turned and passed her to Kim, Indie's mom. Both women smothered the girl with kisses, then put her down and came into the kitchen.

Kim sat at the table across from Sam, while Grace reached up into the cabinet for a couple of glasses and poured them each some iced tea. Indie, who had the roast in the oven by then, wiped off her hands and joined the rest of them at the table.

Grace leaned close to Indie and whispered in her ear, "Send Kenzie out of here for a few minutes." Indie glanced at her, then told Kenzie to go find something on the TV. She waited until the sounds of the latest Disney show could be heard, then nodded at her mother.

"Okay, go ahead," she said.

"Sam," Kim said slowly, "I know you don't like it when Beauregard has a message for you..."

"It's okay, Kim," Sam said. "He's helped me out too many times for me to keep being a grouch about it. What's he got to say this time?"

She looked down at her glass. "He says," she began, "that this case you're working on now is going to be one of the hardest you've ever had. He said that if you're not careful, you'll end up hanging the wrong person for a crime they didn't commit, and..."

Sam looked at her for a few seconds, waiting for her to go on. "And?"

Kim slowly raised her eyes up to meet his. "Sam, he says Death is stalking someone close to you, and will strike before you finally solve this case."

Sam's eyebrows shot upward. "What? Did he happen to say who? Or how?"

She shook her head. "He says he doesn't know. All he got is that you may be going to arrest the wrong person, so you'll have to figure that out, and that Death is after someone close to you.

It sounds like someone you know is going to die because of this case."

Indie was staring at Sam. "Sam," she said softly. "Oh, Sam, what are you going to do?"

Sam was still staring at his mother-in-law. "This isn't acceptable," he said. "You tell Beauregard to go back to spook land or wherever and get me more information. I need to know who he's talking about, or at least how it's supposed to happen. Maybe I can stop it if I know how."

There were tears leaking down Kim's cheeks. "Sam, you know he's never been wrong, but he hardly ever has all the details. He says he'll keep looking for more information, but for now that's all he's got."

"Well, then this is going to be a first. This time, he's going to be wrong. First off, there's no way I will arrest anyone unless the evidence is conclusive, right? That's a given. If there's any doubt at all, that's not good enough for me. And as far as anyone getting killed, I'm not gonna let that happen. You can tell that old spook he's way off, this time."

"Sam," Grace said, "don't take it out on her. As much as Beauregard irritates me, the fact is he's always been right, as long as we've known Kim. It doesn't matter whether he's real or just in her imagination, he's always been right, and you know it. You need to stop being stubborn and hateful, and be thankful that you're getting any advance warning on this at all."

Sam forced himself to calm down, but his emotions were churning on the inside. He'd only known most of his team for a couple of months, but they had all become his friends. The thought of losing any of them was shocking, horrifying, and not something he was going to take lying down.

"Okay, Mom's right," he said. "Kim, I'm sorry I snapped like that. I really do appreciate the warnings that Beauregard gives, but I can't just accept this and act like there's nothing I can do. If one of my team is in danger, I have to do everything possible to save them. Even Beauregard has to understand that."

"Of course he does," Kim said. "He says he doesn't know if you can change what he sees or not, but that's why I had to tell you about it. You can't possibly do anything to prevent somebody getting killed if you don't know it's coming, so he's been after me all day to make sure I told you."

Sam looked to her. "But he thinks there might be a chance I can change it?"

"He says he doesn't know if you can," Kim said. "The problem is that he can't tell you who it is that's going to die, or what they'll be doing at the time. If you knew either of those things, you might have a chance. Other than that, there really isn't much you can do."

Sam chewed on the inside of his cheek for a moment. "How about when? Does he have any idea how soon it will happen?"

"He says it won't happen tonight or tomorrow, but that's as far as he can see."

"Then the first thing I'm going to do tomorrow is put everybody on the buddy plan," Sam said. "Nobody works alone on this case." He put his hands over his face. "I've got to find someone to work with Jade. She's going undercover inside the company, to try to get into their computer systems and look for any indication that somebody inside was working with the shooter. At the moment, if anyone is at risk, it would probably be her."

Kim shrugged. "You could be right, but Beauregard doesn't know. For what it's worth, he says he's really sorry he can't give you more information."

Sam nodded but said nothing. He took out his phone and walked out the back door onto the deck, then sat down in one of the Adirondack chairs. He dialed a number and put the phone to his ear.

"Hello?" A deep voice answered the phone, and Sam couldn't suppress the grin that it brought to his face. Rob Feinstein was a huge man, and a gentle giant until someone was in danger. At that point, he became one of the deadliest men Sam had ever known. He was one of the supervisors in the security division of the company, and Sam had worked with him on the brain chip case.

"Rob? It's Sam Prichard. I need a favor, and I don't know who else to ask."

"You don't need to ask anyone else," Rob said. "What can I do for you, sir?"

"Well, I know you've heard about Beauregard, right?"

"Yes, sir," Rob said. "Ron told me a bit, and you filled in a couple blanks out in San Francisco."

"Well, Beauregard just informed me that—unless I can do something to change it—somebody close to me is going to die during this case that I'm on. The one most at risk would be Jade Miller, because I'm sending her in undercover. I need somebody who can go in with her, shadow her and watch her back. Got anybody I can borrow for that?"

"Absolutely," Rob said. "I'll give you Stacy. Anastasia Stepanov is one of the few women who made it through Spetsnaz training in Russia. She came to the U.S. after she was discharged, and she's been with us for a year, now. Excellent soldier, and exactly who you need. I would willingly let her watch my back, I can tell you that."

"Perfect. I'll make the arrangements. Can you get hold of her and tell her to contact Jade? I'll call Jade now and let her know what's going on."

"Sure thing. I'll tell her to wait fifteen minutes."

Sam cut off the call and dialed Jade's number.

"Jade, it's Sam," he said when she answered. "Listen, I have reason to believe that you might be in some danger on this case. I called Rob Feinstein, and he's arranged for someone to cover your back. Her name is Stacy, and she'll be contacting you shortly."

"Okay," Jade said. "Can you tell me any more about what kind of danger?"

Sam sighed. "You've heard about Beauregard?"

She giggled. "Yeah, you told us about that," she said. "I take it he's predicted something?"

Sam hesitated. "Yes," he said. "He says there's a risk that someone close to me is going to die on this case."

The giggling vanished. "Okay, so Stacy is going in with me. How do I explain her?"

"I'll handle that right now. You arrange to meet up with her in the morning, and both of you report to work at Web Wide Awards."

"Yes, sir," Jade said. "Talk to you tomorrow."

"Later," Sam said. He cut the call and then dialed the cell number he'd been given for John Morton.

"This is John," Morton said as he answered the call.

"John, it's Sam Prichard. I'm going to be sending a second operative with Jade Miller tomorrow. Her name is Stacy, and she needs to stay with Jade at all times."

"Stacy," John said. "Okay. Any special reason?"

"Let's just say I feel the need to have someone watching Jade's back. If I'm right about someone inside your company being involved in this mess, she could be in danger."

"That's good enough for me, Sam. I'll let Annie know."

Sam thanked him and ended the call, then went back into the kitchen.

"Okay, I've got Jade covered," he said. "She's the one who's on the front lines of this one." He sat down at the table again. "Kim, if Beauregard says anything else, I want to know it immediately. Call me, and I don't care what time it is or what I'm doing."

She nodded sheepishly. "Okay, Sam, I will," she said.

They sat and talked while they waited for dinner to be ready, and Sam tried to keep his mind on the conversation, and off the case.

SUMMER WALKED INTO Shanahan's at six twenty and spotted Tom instantly. She was wearing a silky, short black dress over fishnet hose and shockingly red heels that matched the lipstick she had applied. Tom saw her a second later and almost fell out of his chair, then did a double take when he realized that the beauty walking toward him was actually his date.

He was on his feet in an instant, standing there looking happily dumbfounded. Summer made sure that her walk was as suggestive as possible, and knew that she was capturing not only his attention, but that of almost every man and most of the women in the place. This was okay with her, because it would put Tom slightly on the defensive as he tried to keep her attention focused on himself.

"Tom?" She said with her brightest smile in place. "I'm Candy, it's great to meet you at last. Oh, my, you're even taller than you look in your pictures."

Tom stretched himself up to his full five foot eleven and smiled. "I hope that's not a problem," he said.

"Oh, no, not at all," she said coquettishly. "I love to be able to snuggle in under a man's shoulder, and you look perfect for it. Come here, let's try." She grabbed his arm and pulled him close, then wrapped it around herself as she snuggled up against his side. "See? Perfect."

She let go and sat in the chair across from where he'd been sitting, and instantly reached across and took his hand.

"Wow," she said. "I can't believe we're finally here together. Dave's been trying to get me to call you for I don't how long, but I had kind of a bad breakup a couple months ago, and it took me a little time to get past that. What all did he tell you about me?"

Tom's face froze. "Actually, well, I haven't heard from Dave in quite a while. To be perfectly honest, the first time I ever heard of you is when you called today."

Summer looked shocked. "Seriously? That butt head. He told me that you were all excited about meeting me. Are you sure he never mentioned me? He said you really liked my pictures, did he ever even show them to you?"

Tom grimaced. "I'm afraid not," he said, "but I can tell you that I absolutely loved the picture you sent me today, Candy,

I think you've got to be the most beautiful woman I've ever seen."

Summer blushed, a talent she had developed in high school. She learned that whenever she needed to seem shy or innocent, all she had to do was think about the time her best friend Dena got her drunk and talked her into streaking through the old soldiers' home when she was fourteen. To this day, the memory never failed to embarrass her, but the flush on her face always made her seem sweet and innocent.

"See? There you go. Dave told me you were a real sweetheart." She let go of his hand and stroked the back of it with one fingernail. "So, tell me about Tom."

7

Stacy had called Jade just minutes after she got off the phone with Sam, and they made arrangements to meet at Starbucks the following morning. Jade was there waiting when she walked in, and the two of them got coffee and sat at one of the tables for a moment.

"So," Stacy said, with just a slight Russian accent. "What is it we're doing at this place?"

"Well, I'm going to be posing as Ms. Porter's new assistant," Jade said. "The idea is to make it possible for me to wander throughout the entire building and be able to watch everybody, as well as get into their computer system. I don't know what they've got in mind for you, but Sam says you'll be with me all the time."

"That works for me," Stacy said. "My job is to keep you safe. I can do that best if we are together."

Jade smiled at her. "Then, shall we go? We have to go through the motions of getting hired, so we have appointments at human resources in half an hour."

"I'm following you," Stacy said. She picked up her coffee and followed Jade out the door, then they each got into their own cars for the last short drive to the Web Wide Awards headquarters.

The building was close to downtown, one of several modern structures made of steel and glass. It had its own parking garage underneath, and the two girls managed to find parking spaces side by side. They chatted like old friends as they walked to the elevator and rode it up to the second floor, where the signs told them they would find the human resources department.

It wasn't hard to spot. When the elevator opened, they were looking directly at the main entrance to HR, so they stepped inside together. A lady at the front counter looked up and smiled.

"Hi," she said. "How can I help you today?"

"I'm Jade Miller, and this is Stacy Stepanov. We were told to report for work today."

"Just a moment," the lady said. She turned to a computer and tapped the keyboard, then smiled. "Okay," she said. "You two are the new assistants for Ms. Porter. I'm personally very glad to see you, because that poor girl works herself just about to death. You might think I'm kidding, but I'm not. Hold on just a moment, while I get someone to get you both started on your paperwork."

"No problem," Jade said.

Five minutes later, the two of them were sitting at a table filling out paperwork. There were numerous forms, all of the normal paperwork that must be done when you start a new job, and they went through the motions of filling it out.

It took almost half an hour, and when it was finished they were both escorted to the top floor, to Annie Porter's office. Annie looked up with a smile and thanked the lady who brought them in, then closed the door behind them.

"I'm glad you're here," she said. "John told me about Mr. Prichard calling last night. Stacy, it's good to meet you."

"The pleasure is mine," Stacy said.

"Okay, well, I think what we'll do is introduce you at the morning meeting. Ten o'clock every morning, we have a short meeting, usually lasts about fifteen minutes, and you'll both be introduced as my new assistants. Jade, we're going to say that you are here to learn all about the business so you can fill in when I need to be out of town, and Stacy, your story is that you are an efficiency expert. That way, the two of you should be able to ask any questions you want and get straight answers. Just the fact that you work directly with me should be good enough, but with some people, you just never know. Do either of you have any questions at the moment?"

Jade smiled. "I have one," she said. "Can you tell me what computer operating system you use?"

"Oh, just Windows on all of the office computers. We've got the latest release, with all the bells and whistles. Our servers run on Linux, of course. They're down in the server room on the first floor. Are you familiar with Linux?"

"Yes, very," Jade said. "Cybercrime used to be my specialty, and it almost always involved some sort of fraud on a server. I became proficient with just about every operating system and most programming codes. I was just curious what you are using. What about database? Are you using Oracle, or SQL?"

Annie's eyes widened. "Um, for that you'd need to talk to John, or somebody down in coding. I'm afraid that's a little out of my area of expertise." She squeezed her eyes almost shut in a self deprecating gesture. "I'm pretty much just the advertising salesman around here. John runs everything else, he's the genius. He built the original website all by himself, and figured out how to make money off it. I didn't even really get involved until about a year later."

"Oh, no problem," Jade said. "I was just curious."

"Oh, okay," Annie said. She glanced at her watch. "We've got about twenty minutes before the meeting starts. How about if I give you a quick tour?"

JENNA LOOKED UP AS Sam walked into his office and smiled. "Summer is looking for you," she said. "I don't know what it's about, but she's got a smile on her face."

Sam grinned. "Tell her to come on, then," he said. "I could use something to smile about." He went into his office, but left the door open.

Summer arrived a moment later and closed it, then sat in the chair in front of his desk. "I thought you'd like to hear a report on my interrogation from last night," she said. "Tom Linden?"

"Yes, and judging from the smile on your face, I suspect you must've enjoyed yourself. How did it go?"

"Well, I can tell you he's not our shooter," Summer said. "He couldn't possibly be, since he was actually in Vancouver at the time, but he just doesn't really have the kind of personality that could do something like that. I got him to talk about himself quite a bit, and he really opened up after a few minutes. I asked him what it was like to work for his sister and her boyfriend, and he absolutely idolizes both of them."

"Wait a minute," Sam said. "You told me that he always writes some nasty responses whenever he's written up, even when it's his sister doing it. What happened to all that anger you were talking about?"

"You know, it's funny," she said, "because I didn't even have to find an excuse to ask that question. He was telling me how a lot of the other employees think he's boss's pet, so John and Annie told him they want him to act angry at them a lot. They say it cuts down on some of the complaints they hear about him, but the beauty of it is that he's often the first one to hear when somebody else gets their panties in a bunch. If it sounds like something serious, he goes straight to his sister after work and tells her all about it. According to him, and I found evidence to back it up in the employee files, they've actually managed to stave off some potentially serious problems that way. The disgruntled employee finds his problem suddenly disappearing, with no idea why. Tends to make them think things weren't really all that bad, after all."

"Wow. And his drug problems?"

"Those are not even real, it's all part of his cover inside the company. Apparently he really went to rehab once when he was in his late teens, but he's been clean ever since. They use his history to keep him looking like the black sheep of the family, and he disappears for a month every now and then. Everybody thinks he's in rehab, but he's actually taking care of some special errands for Annie or John. That's actually why he was in Vancouver; he was up there talking to a couple of small TV producers about some new project they've been working on. He flew home the next morning, after he actually saw the shooting on the show."

"I see," Sam said. "So he's off the suspect list?"

"Definitely," Summer said. "On the other hand, he gave me a few names to add to it. One of the guys in the marketing department, Bryce Nicholson, has suddenly come into some money. Tom was telling me that Bryce invited him to go out on his new boat this weekend. That might not be such a big deal, except it's a hundred thousand dollar house boat, and Bryce claims he got a windfall that let him pay cash for it. I was going to ask if I might call Indie and ask her to take a look at his financials."

Sam nodded. "Absolutely," he said. "So, how did Tom take it when the evening came to an end?"

"Oh, that was no problem at all," Summer said, grinning. "I just told him I had herpes and had to wait until it was dormant again before I could do anything, and he seems to have decided I'm not really his type, after all."

Sam was still laughing when she got up and left the office.

A minute after Summer left Sam's office, Jenna buzzed him to tell him that Steve Beck was waiting. Sam told her to send him in, and Steve entered a second later.

"Steve," Sam said. He got to his feet and shook hands with his old friend. "How's it going?"

"That's what I'm here to find out," Steve said. "I like working with Walter, but I'd like to get out of the office once in a while and act like an investigator again. Got anything you can put me on?"

"I do, actually," Sam said. "It's Max Petrelli, the boy who was shot. I understand he's out of intensive care now, and I'd like you to go out and talk to him. I know the police have already spoken with him, and he doesn't seem to have any idea what might have motivated this thing, but I'd like to see what you can get out of him. He probably doesn't know anything about the shooting, but he might have some ideas who could be upset with the award company. I'd like you to see if you get any feelings from the things he might say."

"Sure, Sam," he said. He was grinning. "You mind if I take Walter along? He tends to be pretty good at reading people. Might pick up something I miss."

"That'll be fine," Sam said. "Let me know if you find out anything, or just what you think about it all."

"Will do," Steve said. He made a mock salute as he turned and walked out.

A moment later, Denny Cortlandt tapped on the door and Sam waved for him to come inside. He shut the door behind himself and took the chair in front of the desk.

"Got something that might interest you, mate," he said. "According to Interpol, there's a hit man named Reynard who came to the States about three months back. What makes him worthy of notice is the fact that he's been known to use remote control weapons on several occasions. I checked with some friends at NSA, and the last contact they had on him was in St. Louis ten weeks ago. Facial recog on a security camera got a hit on him, but he was gone before anybody could get there. It's possible he was on his way this direction, but he's off the radar at the moment. I've sent his photo to your email."

Sam turned to his computer and downloaded the email, then opened the photo and looked at it. It showed three people, two men and a woman who were apparently walking through what looked like an airport. One of the men was singled out with a red circle around his face, and Sam knew this had to be Reynard.

"He's got a hard look to him," Sam said. "Almost feral."

"True. Of course, Reynard is probably not his real name. In fact, it's the name of a mythical fox, one who was almost human and was known as a trickster in European folktales. I suspect that's why he uses the name."

Sam leaned back in his chair. "Is he the type to take corporate-style jobs? The only way I can see this shooting involving somebody like him would be if there is some serious money behind it."

"That's for real," Denny said. "His fee starts out at two hundred grand, and goes up from there if there's any difficulty. If he's our boy, then there's some real money behind trying to hurt Web Wide Awards. Problem with that is that just about any of their potential competition would have the kind of money we're talking about. Give you any thoughts?"

Sam shook his head. "Not right off the bat," he said. "I'm like you, I think pretty much any of their competition would have that kind of money. Why don't you dig around a bit, see if you can come up with any potential suspect competitors?"

Denny levered himself out of the chair. "Righto, boss," he said. "I'll get to it, then."

Darren Beecher showed up about ten minutes later. "Where's Detective Parks?"

Sam grinned. "She hasn't made it in yet," he said. "What have you got?"

"Well, I looked at both Barr and LeClair pretty closely. It occurred to me that your wife could probably find more than I did, but so far they look pretty clean. No unusual financial transactions, and nothing that looked odd as far as personal communications. The only thing I found is that Charlie Barr might have a side business going on, taking in editing work for some of the kinds of people he used to work for. I think that sort of thing could potentially blow up in Morton's and Porter's faces, but I don't know if it should be up to us to say anything or not."

"I think I might," Sam said. "If he had put that all behind him, I'd probably leave it alone, but if he's still messing around with it, that could cause problems if it got out. I think what I need to do is go and have a talk with each of them, feel them out for myself. Why don't you come along, give me your take on it as well?"

"No problem," Darren said. "Just tell me when."

"Give me five minutes, and we'll head over there. I'll meet you out front, okay?"

"No sweat," Darren said. He left the room and Sam picked up the phone and called his wife.

"Hey, babe," he said. "Just checking in. Everything okay?"

"Everything's fine here," Indie said. "You doing all right?"

"Yeah. I'm getting ready to head out to Web Wide Awards and talk to a couple of people, and I just wanted to check in before I go. I don't suppose Beauregard has had anything more to say, has he?"

"Not that I've heard," Indie said. "I'm sure Mom would call you first, after what you said last night. I've been working with Summer this morning. Other than that, your kids are in the living room watching TV and I'm just trying to keep track of everything going on here."

"Okay, baby," Sam said. "I guess I really just wanted to hear your voice for a minute."

"Oh, that's so sweet. I love you, Sam."

"Love you, too," Sam said. He hung up the phone and rose from his chair, told Jenna where he was going, and walked out the front door of the building. Darren was waiting for him, just looking at the beautiful Mustang. "Climb in," Sam said. He slid behind the wheel as Darren got in, and then they took off toward Denver.

"When we get there," Sam said, "remember that if we run into Jade, don't let on that we know her. As far as Charlie Barr and Patricia LeClair, feel free to speak up if you think of a question that needs to be asked. I don't necessarily think they're involved, but I'd hate to miss something."

"No problem," Darren said. "I'll sit back and observe unless it's something important. Sometimes, I learn more just by watching expressions and body language than by asking questions."

"That's why I wanted you to come along," Sam said with a grin.

It was almost ten by the time they arrived, and the receptionist told them they would have to wait. Charlie and Patricia were both in the usual morning meeting, but should be free within the next twenty minutes or so. Sam and Darren sat in the waiting area and browsed through some magazines.

In one of them, Sam found an article about Web Wide Awards, and read through it. It gave a bit of history of the company, talking about how it had grown from a nearly invisible little website to a multimillion dollar enterprise that was known throughout the world. It was the premise of letting the people decide who deserved the awards that brought on their success, according to the author. All other award programs had their own panels that made the decisions, and though many of them claimed to pay attention to what the public wanted, the winners they chose were not always the ones the public thought most deserving. John Morton and Annie Porter had changed the playing field by allowing the public to have control over who they gave their awards to.

However, there were those who felt the public simply didn't understand the video industry well enough to make those decisions, and so some of the other awards were still around. They were not quite as recognizable as the Web Wide Awards, but they were still there and still had some impact on the video industry.

The article interviewed some of the officers from the other award companies, and Sam was particularly interested in the response from the president of the Web Video Institute, which claimed to analyze all web video to make its determination on quality of production. Gerald Sharp, the president, was quoted as saying, "The Web Wide Award is a joke. It doesn't take into account any of the thousands of hours of effort that go into the proper production of a video, but pats a bunch of kids on the back for putting together their own childish little programs with the family's camcorder. Sooner or later, the public that they claim as their supporters are going to figure out that those awards don't mean anything, because nobody with a brain is behind the choice of who gets them. When that happens, Web Wide Awards will be gone, but the Institute will be right here to take up the slack."

Sam passed the article to Darren, who quickly read through it. His eyebrows rose when he got to that quote, and he looked up at Sam. "Is it just me," he asked, "or does it really make sense that people are going to put more stock in their own choices and opinions than in the choices and opinions of a self-styled expert?"

"I don't think it's just you," Sam said. "I feel the same way. Apparently, so do an awful lot of the public, because it's the Web Wide Awards they seem to be in favor of."

The receptionist came and got them at that point, telling them that the morning meeting was over and both Charlie and Patricia were available to meet with them. Sam asked if there might be a room they could use so the conversation could be more private, and the receptionist led them to a small interview room off the lobby.

"If you wait just a moment," she said, "I'll bring Mr. Barr right away."

The interview room had a couch and a couple of chairs. Sam and Darren sat down on the couch to wait, but Charlie Barr came in just a couple of minutes later. They stood and shook hands with him, showing him their IDs.

"Mr. Barr," Sam said. "I'm Sam Prichard, and this is Darren Beecher. We are with Windlass Security, and we'd like to talk with you for a minute about the shooting that happened the other night."

Charlie nodded and sat in one of the chairs, as Sam and Darren took the couch again. "Sure, no problem," he said. "Real pity about that kid, but I hear he's going to be okay."

"Yes, that's our understanding as well," Sam said. "Mr. Barr, I was wondering if you can tell me what you know about how the shooting happened."

Charlie's eyes went wide. "How it happened? How would I know? Way I understand it, somebody was waiting up overhead with the gun, and shot the kid when he was coming out from behind the curtain. That's all I know."

"Yes, that's what happened," Sam said. "What I'm looking for is your opinion on how it happened. I mean, you're the senior video producer, right? Were you in charge of putting together the whole production for that show?"

"Well, yeah," Charlie said. "But all that means is that I put together the itinerary of the program, make sure the right people are on cameras and editing and all that stuff. I don't actually physically do any of it, not myself."

"Oh," Sam said. "I thought you were the one who actually decided what camera angles to use, that sort of thing. Isn't that part of your job?"

"Well, yeah, sort of. We do a storyboard, kind of like a comic strip of how we want the show to look. From that, we decide which camera angles we want to use and things like that."

"But you aren't actually the guy in charge while it's being filmed?"

Charlie was squirming just a bit in his seat. "Well, yeah, I was there. I mean, I was in the booth watching the monitors, just to make sure everything went smoothly."

Sam nodded. "Okay, that's what I thought," he said. "Now, how long ago was this storyboard done?"

"The storyboard? Oh, that was probably two, three months ago. We had to get it all worked out way in advance, so that we'd be able to get all the right sound and video equipment in place. I mean, we had six different bands performing that night, and a few other people, as well. If you don't have it all planned out long before time to shoot, you don't even want to think about what all can go wrong."

"Okay," Sam said. "I got that. Now, who would've had access to the storyboard? Or maybe I should ask, who would have known what camera was going to be used for each shot?"

Charlie seemed confused. "Well, probably the whole vid crew. That would be everybody who was in the booth, and the Steadicam operators on the stage. All of us had to know what camera was being operated when, and we had a cue sheet set up for that."

"Does a cue sheet actually say which camera? I mean, like if one of the big overhead cameras is going to be used, would that be on the cue sheet?"

"Yeah, of course. You got to have that so you know when to have each camera in position and ready."

"So the cue sheet would have said that camera 4C was going to be on the curtain for the winner of the big award at the end of the show, right?"

"Yeah, of course. That's so the booth can make sure the camera is positioned where they want it before the shot begins."

"So it all works pretty much the same way it did when you were in the porn business, right?"

"Yeah, pretty..." His eyes went wide, and he stared at Sam. "What? I don't know what you mean."

8

"Oh, come on, Goodie," Sam said. "Did you really think you could keep that a secret? It wasn't even hard for us to find out about it."

"I just—look, that was all a long time ago, and I really..."

"It was a long time ago, until you decided to start taking in some outside work again. I'm sure it's a nice little side income, Charlie, but it's probably not something you'd want your bosses here to know about, am I right?"

Charlie licked his lips, but seemed afraid to say anything more.

"Charlie, I don't care what you're into," Sam said. "What I do care about is finding out how the shooter knew that camera 4C was going to be the one pointed straight at the winner when he came out from behind the curtain. From what you're telling me, he had to have gotten hold of a copy of that cue sheet. Now, from what I've read in the past, most video productions keep everything a secret. So you tell me, Charlie, how did somebody get hold of that cue sheet?"

"Well, how the hell should I know? I didn't give it to anybody. There's thirty-seven people in the production department, why don't you go talk to the rest of them?"

"I probably will before this is over," Sam said. "At the moment, though, I'm talking to you. And you just happen to be the one man in the video department who would probably do just about anything to keep a nasty secret from coming to light. So, tell me, Charlie," Sam went on. "Who was it that wanted the cue sheet, and threatened to out your little secret if you didn't give it to them?"

Charlie's eyes couldn't have gotten any wider, but Sam would have sworn they did anyway. "Nobody! I swear, I don't know what you're talking about. As far as I know, nobody here even knows about any of that."

"I'm not worried about somebody here," Sam said, getting to his feet and leaning over Charlie. "I'm concerned about somebody who wanted to set up a gun with a remote control trigger, and needed to know exactly what camera would be pointed in the exact direction of the winner of that award at what moment. Now, anybody who's willing to shoot a young kid like Max Petrelli isn't going to bat an eye at blackmailing you or anybody else for that information. So, tell me, Charlie, who wanted it? Who came to you and said that if you didn't cooperate, they were going to make sure your bosses find out all about Goodie Barr and his past?"

Charlie's face was flushed, and his mouth was opening and closing, but no words were coming out. Darren leaned close.

"Charlie," he said softly, "look, man, we know you didn't intend to be involved in this thing. You just wanted to keep the past in the past, right? We understand that, we really do. We don't even have a problem with that, but whoever you gave that cue sheet to has shot that poor kid and hurt your company even worse than your secret getting out could do. You don't want to let them get away with that, do you?"

"But I don't know," Charlie said. "I swear to you, I don't have any idea how this happened. I didn't give the cue sheet to anybody, not to anybody. If I did that, I could lose my job."

"Yeah?" Sam asked. "And what do you think would happen if the blackmailer went to John and Annie? Do you think you would have been able to keep your job if they found out what you used to do, what you've been doing again? They pride themselves on being a family-friendly company, so how do you think they'd feel about knowing their main producer was taking on side work making porn movies?"

"Charlie," Darren said, still speaking softly, "look, man, it's written all over your face. I told you, we know this is not your fault, and you're not going to be in any trouble over it, as long as you tell us what happened. If you don't, and it all comes out like it's bound to do, then you could be charged as an accessory to attempted murder. That would be the end of your entire career, wouldn't it?"

Charlie's mouth was working again, but tears had started running down his cheeks. He finally closed his mouth and took a deep breath, then looked directly into Darren's eyes.

"It wasn't like that," he said. "It was about six weeks ago when they came to me. They never mentioned the porn work in the past, they just threatened to tell on me for doing some side jobs lately. I mean, it shook me up so bad I quit, I'm not doing that anymore, I swear. I just needed a little extra money, so I took a couple of jobs for one of the companies I used to work for. I shouldn't have, and I wish I never did, but it's too late to change it now."

"And all you had to do was give them a copy of the cue sheet?" Darren asked.

Charlie nodded. "Yeah, that and the security code for the back door. I swear, I didn't have a clue what they were trying to do, I never would have gone along with it if I had. They said they were reporters, just trying to scoop everyone else on the awards. I never would have gone along if I'd known what they were really doing, I swear that."

"Charlie," Sam said, "who was it? Who did you give the cue sheet to?"

"I don't know," Charlie said. "I never seen them before, or since. It was a man and a woman, both of them fairly young. The only one I talked to was the woman; she's the one who approached me, and I only ever seen him sitting in the car."

"Can you describe them? And what about the car?"

Charlie swallowed. "The girl, she's maybe twenty-five or so, about my height and pretty thin. Might weigh a hundred pounds if she was soaking wet, I guess. Blonde hair and dark eyes, kinda cute but not pretty. The guy, I never got a real good look at him. He was taller than me by a couple inches, probably, and had his head shaved bald. Never saw his eyes, never got that close to him."

"What about the car? Do you know what kind it was, what color?"

"It was a new one," Charlie said. "One of those little ones, the hybrid thing. Prius, that's what it was. Toyota Prius, sort of a dark red." He was looking at the floor, but he raised his eyes up to look into Sam's. "Am I in trouble?"

"That isn't up to me," Sam said. "I can tell you that you should have come forward, even after the shooting happened. If you had come forward then, you probably would not be in any real trouble at all. Now, I don't know. It all depends on the prosecutor."

"Are you going to tell John and Annie?" Charlie looked like he was about to collapse.

"Charlie, I'm afraid I don't have any choice."

Charlie leaned back on his chair and began to cry. Sam sat and watched him for a moment, then took out his phone and called Karen Parks. It took him a moment to explain to her what was happening, and she told him she'd be right there.

Sam left Darren with Charlie and walked out of the room, then returned ten minutes later with John Morton. Charlie started bawling like a baby when John walked in, but he didn't try to deny anything when Sam explained what they had learned.

"Charlie," John said, "you could've come to me. I might not have been happy about you doing that kind of stuff, but I wouldn't have fired you over it. If you had only come to me, we could've caught these people before anyone got hurt. Now, we've got a boy in the hospital who almost died, and that looks bad on all of us. He was our responsibility while he was on the show, and we let him down."

"I'm so sorry," Charlie sobbed. "I'm so sorry."

"I know you must be," Morton said, "but I'm afraid it's too late for that. Charlie, I'm gonna have to let you go. This is going to come out, now, and I can't afford to let it look like we're protecting you. I'm sorry, Charlie, but you're fired."

Charlie sobbed a moment more, then started to get up from his chair.

"Not yet," Sam said. "A police detective is on the way, and you're going to have to go downtown and answer questions again. After that, they'll decide whether there are any charges to be filed against you."

Karen arrived a short time later and Sam repeated what they had learned to her with Charlie sitting there. She kept her face impassive through it all, but then she had a uniformed officer take Charlie back to her own office for further questioning.

Once he was gone, she and Sam both turned to John Morton. "I don't know what's going to happen to him," Sam said, "but the story is going to hit the news. His past, and even the things he's doing lately, are going to be public knowledge by the end of the day. You did the right thing by letting him go, but you might want to start working on a press release."

John nodded. "Yeah, I guess so. Is this going to help you get to the bottom of it?"

"I hope so," Sam said. "At least we've got some general information. We got descriptions of the two people involved, and we know they were driving a Prius, which was most likely a rental car. That may give us a name, but I suspect it won't be genuine."

"All right," John said. "I better go and let Annie know what happened."

He walked away, and Karen looked at Sam. "Don't beat yourself up," she said. "That fellow had plenty of chances to come forward and do the right thing."

Sam looked at her, confused. "Beat myself up? Hey, I'm not the least bit worried about Charlie Barr, he made his own bed and he can darn well lay in it. I'm just feeling a little bad for John and Annie, because this is going to be more mud splashed on them. Coming right on top of the shooting, it could do them some serious damage right now."

Karen shrugged. "But it also shows that they really are doing all they can to find out what happened. If he words his press release properly, there's a good chance they could get another popularity boost out of this."

"Yeah, maybe," Sam said. He turned to Darren. "Good work in there," he said. "You caught me off guard when you started talking to him, because he just about had me convinced he didn't know anything at all. What gave it away?"

"His left pinky," Darren said. "He started digging the nail of his pinky into his palm. It's something I've seen people do, a way to keep themselves from thinking about the fact that they're telling a lie, thereby avoiding the normal telltale signs. There was a survivalist writer, guy named Kurt Saxon, he wrote this series of books called The Poor Man's James Bond, and that was one of the tricks he promoted. It doesn't really work, but an awful lot of people read those books."

Sam blinked. "I'd never heard of that one," he said. "Does it really work?"

"Not very well. Especially if your interrogator knows about it."

"I guess I learn something new every day," he said. He glanced at the clock on the wall. "We've still got some time. Let's go and talk to Patricia LeClair."

The receptionist brought Patricia in, and she took the same chair Charlie had occupied. She seemed nervous, so Sam gave her a smile. "Patricia, thanks for coming," he said. "I'm Sam Prichard and this is Darren Beecher, we are investigators with Windlass Security. We're trying to find out just what happened to Max Petrelli, and that led us to some questions we wanted to ask you."

"Okay," the young woman said. "I'm pretty sure I don't know anything, but whatever I can do to help."

"Well, in particular," Sam began, "we were wondering if anyone has approached you lately to ask for information about the national awards show. Have you had any kind of unusual contacts, maybe somebody asking you about the itinerary for the program?"

Patricia's eyebrows narrowed. "No," he said. "I don't really have much to do with the show, as far as putting it together, I mean. All I do is make some of the announcements, and I do some of the commercials for it."

"Okay, but this is very important. Has anybody asked you any kind of unusual questions about the show, or about the company, in the last few months? Has anybody tried to pressure you into giving them information?"

Her nervousness seemed to increase. "No, I told you," she said. "Nobody's asked me anything like that. Why are you asking that?"

Sam leaned forward and looked her in the eye. "Patricia, somebody got some pretty serious inside information about how the program was going to be run. We already know that one other employee, Mr. Barr, was actually blackmailed, so we're looking at other employees who might be vulnerable to that kind of pressure."

Patricia swallowed. "But what would that have to do with me?"

"As I said," Sam went on, "we're looking at people who might be susceptible to blackmail. I think that could describe you, couldn't it, Ms. Stubblefield?"

Patricia's eyes went wide, and her mouth opened and closed a couple of times with nothing coming out. After a few seconds, she closed her mouth and then the tears began to stream down her cheeks.

"Yes, we know who you are," Sam said. "Unfortunately, people with skeletons like yours rattling around in their closets sometimes feel that they have to do whatever it takes to keep their secret. If we can find out about you, so could someone else, so I'm going to ask you one more time. Has anyone tried to pressure you for information or cooperation that might have helped them to accomplish the shooting that happened the other night?"

Still crying, she began shaking her head. "No, I swear," she said. "Nobody knows. I don't know how you found out, but I was careful, I made sure nobody could ever connect me to my past." She sniffled a couple of times. "What's—what's going to happen now?"

"Well, your home state has decided they're not interested in prosecuting you for skipping out on your parole, so you're not in any direct legal trouble. I'm not sure what's going to happen when Mr. Morton and Ms. Porter find out, but I'm afraid we have no choice but to tell them the truth." He glanced at Darren. "Darren, would you mind to ask them to come down?"

"No problem," Darren said. He got up and walked out of the room.

"That's not who I am, not anymore," Patricia said. "Look, Mr. Prichard, I was young and stupid and I thought I was in love. When Bernie was arrested, he swore up and down he was innocent and I believed him. I tried to help him, I said he was with me, but too many people knew I was lying. I was arrested for perjury and obstruction of justice, and I pled guilty. I did my time, I paid my debt to society, and then I just wanted to start over." She laughed, but there was irony in it. "You know who told me how to do it? It was my parole officer. She said she wanted to give me a break, but I think it was just because she didn't want to have to do a lot of paperwork on me every month. She knew I didn't have any family, so she told me how to change my name and start over. I just happened to pick Denver to come to, and I was looking for a job when I heard about auditions for this one. I came to the audition and nobody was more surprised than me when I got hired."

"Patricia," Sam said, "I'm not going to say I don't feel sympathetic, because I do. The only thing I can tell you is that secrets almost always blow up in your face. If you had taken some opportunity over the last few years to tell your boss the truth, it's possible they would've been willing to help you keep the secret, but keeping it from them is what made you a liability that we had to explore."

Darren came back in, with John Morton and Annie Porter right behind him.

"Mr. Prichard?" John asked. "Mr. Beecher said you needed to speak to us again."

Sam looked up at them, then turned his eyes back to Patricia. "Ms. LeClair actually has something she needs to talk to you about. Like Mr. Barr, she had a secret that could have allowed someone to blackmail her, and could have put your company at risk. She swears that no one has approached her, and I think she's telling the truth. However, I think it's necessary for her to tell you what she's been keeping from you."

Annie sat down on the arm of the chair and put an arm around Patricia. "Pat? What is it?"

The whole story came out, and Patricia explained to them the same way she had tried to explain to Sam. She had made a mistake when she was young, had paid the price for it, and was only trying to start over.

John shook his head. "Pat, it would've been better if you had come to us about this back when you were hired. I realize that might've been scary, but if there's one thing Annie and I have come to understand, it's that everybody makes mistakes. I'm pretty sure we would've been willing to accept you, even then." He looked at Annie and raised his eyebrows.

"Pat," Annie said, "is there anything else you've been keeping from us? Any other secrets we need to know about?"

"No, no, I swear," Patricia said. "This has been the best thing that ever happened to me, working for you. I would rather die than do anything to hurt you or the company. I don't have any other secrets, I swear I don't."

Annie nodded, then looked back at John. He seemed to read something in her eyes, because he turned back to Patricia with a smile.

"Then we'll say no more about this. On the other hand, if anyone ever docs find out about it and try to pressure you, you will come straight to us, right?"

Patricia started bawling, and Annie pulled her close. "I will," Patricia said between her sobs. "I swear I will."

John leaned over and patted her shoulder, then motioned with his head for Annie to take Patricia out of the room. When they were gone, he turned to Sam.

"Like I told her," he said, "everybody makes mistakes. If you look back at when I was a teenager, you'll find an incident where two kids died while riding in the car I was driving. We were hit by a drunk driver, but I almost went to jail over it because one of those kids was only fifteen and was out after curfew. I was sixteen at the time, and the district attorney wanted to charge me as an accessory to manslaughter. I got lucky and the court threw it out, but it left me unwilling to judge other people."

"I think Patricia is a fine young woman," Sam said. "I agree, people make mistakes, and I'm glad to see that she's turned her life around. The problem was that keeping the secret put the rest of you at risk. Now that it's out in the open, she's no longer a danger to you or your company." He paused for a second. "There is, however, one other thing you probably need to know about."

Sam told him about Judy Lowery, the stylist who helped their nominees look good on camera, who also was involved in the fetish lifestyle. He wasn't terribly surprised when John began snickering.

"Judy? Are you serious?" John asked. "Wow, I never would've guessed. Still, that's something she does on her own time. I can't really hold that against her, I don't guess." He had to work for a moment to get his snickering under control. "Oh, I can't wait to tell Annie about this. She'll probably turn red."

He held up a finger to ask Sam to be patient for a moment, then managed to stop laughing. "Okay," he said at last. "Is there anyone else you needed to talk to?"

Sam shook his head. "Not at the moment. For right now, those were the only three that we felt might have been a security risk. With Charlie's admission that he provided the itinerary for the show, I think we've pretty well ascertained how they got their information. Now, I just want to find these people and bury them under the prison system."

9

"Hello," Indie said, answering her phone.

"Indie, it's Summer. Sam said I could give you a call to look into something I stumbled across last night."

"Okay," Indie said. "Give me just a moment, I'm in the middle of changing a diaper."

"Oh, goody," Summer said. "I think about having a baby someday, but then I think about diapers and start to have second thoughts."

Indie laughed. "Ah, it's just something to deal with. Believe me, the rewards of being a mother are worth it. Hang on, I gotta set the phone down for a moment."

Summer waited patiently for about a minute and a half, and Indie came back on the line. "Okay, I'm at the computer now. What have we got?"

"The guy's name is Bryce Nicholson, and he's a graphic designer in the marketing department at Web Wide Awards. Apparently he's been saying he came into a lot of money recently, and even bought himself a big fancy houseboat. He keeps it out on the Aurora Reservoir, if that matters."

"Hang on," Indie said. "Sam sent me a list of all their employees, so I can get his social. That'll let me check his financial standing, credit report, all that stuff."

Summer heard the keys clicking for several seconds, and then Indie said, "Aha! Yeah, he came in to some money, all right, but it's probably legitimate. About three months ago, he got a little over four hundred thousand dollars from the sale of some land. I dug a little bit deeper, and it turns out he inherited the land from his grandparents a couple of years ago. It's been up for sale since he got it, originally listed for almost double what he got. He's lowered the price a couple of times, and I guess somebody made an offer he couldn't refuse. Here's the purchase of the houseboat, he paid cash but got it at a discount. Looks like it was a repo, so he got it for what was owed on it, I guess. About seventy-four thousand."

"Well, it was worth checking. We're looking for somebody inside the company who might have been blackmailed or bribed into helping the shooter, so I figured I should at least ask you to check it out."

"No problem," Indie said. "That's why they keep me on as a consultant. Hey, how about you and Jade and I take a girls' day sometime soon? I could stand a day out without kids or testosterone."

Summer giggled. "Sounds great," she said. "I'll talk to Jade and see when might be good, okay?"

"Sure, just let me know. Maybe we can get some time this weekend. Sam can watch the kids."

STEVE AND WALTER GOT to the hospital about the same time Sam and Darren had arrived at the Web Wide Awards headquarters, and Steve was surprised to find that there were no police guards on Max Petrelli's room. Considering the fact that the boy had been shot on a worldwide webcast, Steve would've expected the city to want to make sure he was safe for as long as he was there.

When he tapped on the door to the room, however, he understood. The man who opened the door was wearing the black uniform of a Windlass Security guard, and he broke into a smile when he saw Steve and Walter standing there.

"Hey, Roscoe," Steve said. "I wasn't aware they already had you on duty here."

"Oh, yes, sir," said the big black man. "Mr. Thomas put us on yesterday. One of us is with Mr. Petrelli and his family every minute."

"That makes me feel a little better," he said. "I was expecting to see the police here, and a little shocked when I didn't. Now I understand." He stepped into the room with Walter following him, and Roscoe turned to the people who were sitting in chairs around Max's bed.

"Steve, Walter, these are Mr. and Mrs. Petrelli, Max's parents, and his sister Gina. Folks, this is Steve Beck and Walter Rawlings. They're two of the investigators working on the case."

Steve shook hands with Marco Petrelli and nodded to his wife and daughter, who looked to be younger than Max. Walter waved, but didn't extend his hand.

"Mr. Beck," Petrelli said, "have there been any developments in the case?"

"All I'm allowed to say, sir," Steve said, "is that we are exploring many different angles. I can tell you that our boss, Sam Prichard, is probably the best investigator I have ever known, to the point that the government has recruited him on several occasions. If anybody can find the people who did this to your son, it's going to be Sam."

Petrelli nodded. "Mr. Thomas and Mr. Donaldson were out here last night," he said. "They were telling us about him, but they also brag about the rest of you. We are awfully grateful to the award people for hiring you folks." He turned and looked at his son, who was watching them from the bed. "It's hard to believe anybody could do something like this. I hope you catch the bastard and put him away."

"That's our goal," Steve said. "Hey, Max. How are you feeling?" He stepped closer to the bed and the boy held out his hand.

"I feel like an elephant sat on me," Max said. "Right on my chest, it hurts."

Steve nodded. "Yeah, I've been shot a couple times," he said. "That's a pretty good way to describe it."

Max chuckled, then winced. "It only hurts when I laugh," he said. "But it's given me some terrific ideas for plot lines and new special effects."

"Yeah? At least you haven't lost your sense of humor. Getting shot always turned me into a grouch, at least for a few days. You feel like talking a little bit today?"

"Sure," Max said. "The doctor says I'm going to be fine, I guess I was lucky the bullet didn't do any major damage. They said the bullet was right next to my heart, but not actually touching it. All the blood was from tearing up the blood vessels in my skin, I guess that was a mess."

"Well, good," Steve said. "I wanted to learn a little more about you, so I went home last night and found your show on the internet. Reminds me of some of the shows I watched when

I was a kid, like Star Trek and The Twilight Zone. I got right into it, watched the first five episodes one after another."

Max grinned. "Thanks," he said. "I'm really glad you liked it. It's kind of a silly premise, but it lets me do all kinds of different things. What did you think of the slithering soul eater?"

"I was wondering how you did that one," Steve said. "It looked like a short, fat snake, so at first I thought it was just somebody's arm wrapped up in a costume, but I could see the whole thing as it slithered across the floor. Can you tell me the secret?"

Max laughed again, then winced once more. "It was a piece of dryer hose with leather wrapped around it, and there was a little remote control car in each end. Me and a buddy of mine were controlling the cars to make it look like it was just wiggling along across the floor."

"Well, it was pretty slick. Max, this is my friend Walter. Walter actually doesn't shake hands, but he's an absolute genius when it comes to figuring out how people do things, and especially figuring out how a crime happened. We took him out to the Canterbury Arena yesterday afternoon, because nobody could figure out how the shooter managed to get out of the building after you were hit. All the security cameras got nothing, so we were all pretty stumped. Walter, he goes out there and we took him up on the catwalk where they think the shot came from, right? He looks around for about a minute, then points at one of those great big cameras they have on the trolley lines overhead. He says I want to see that camera, so they roll it down to where we were at, then he jumps up on the rails of the catwalk to look at the top of it. Turns out there was a rifle mounted up there, set up on a remote control so that somebody could aim it and fire while sitting in the audience. Probably did it with a cell phone."

Max's eyes were wide. "Holy cow," he said. "All the cops couldn't figure it out, but he found it that fast?"

"That's what he does," Steve said. "Now, the reason I told you that is because while we were on the way here, I got him to watch your episode number five. That's the one with the girl who rips out some guy's heart and eats it, right on camera. I gotta tell you, that was the most realistic and goriest thing I've ever seen, and I wanted to know how you did it. I let Walter watch it, and he told me what he thinks you did to make it look that real. I'm gonna let him tell you, because I want to know if he's right. That okay with you?"

The boy was grinning from ear to ear. "Shoot, yeah," he said. "Go for it. I don't think anybody will ever figure that one out."

Steve motioned for Walter to come closer. "Walter, tell him about the girl who ate the heart."

"You showed the girl shove the guy against the wall," Walter said, "then she stuck her hand through his ribs and pulled out his heart. Then she took a bite out of it, and blood ran all down her face."

Max nodded, still grinning. "Right, yeah," he said.

"You cut the camera after she pushed him against the wall," Walter said. "Then you built a false wall and put him behind it, with just his head and shoulders and arms sticking through it. You hung a shirt on him that was just like the one he was wearing before, but you had a dummy body there. The chest of the dummy was rubber, and you had a split in it so her hand could go right through, and that broke a plastic bag full of fake blood.

Then she grabbed the heart inside and yanked it out, and took a bite out of it. You made the heart out of marshmallow, with food coloring to make it look red and blue, and you filled it with fake blood. I think the fake blood was cherry juice, but I couldn't be sure."

Max's eyes were so wide that Steve was afraid they were going to pop out. "Holy cow," he said. "That's almost exactly right. The heart was made of marshmallow, that's true, but it wasn't cherry juice. It was strawberry syrup with some whipped cream mixed in to make it thicker. That is incredible, I can't believe you figured that out."

"I'm pretty good at it," Walter said. "It's what I do."

"Well, I'm just amazed. That was incredible."

"I thought you might get a kick out of that," Steve said. "Listen, Max, I need to ask you a few questions. I was wondering if, anytime before the award show, did anybody contact you and talk about you getting the award? I don't mean the award people, I mean somebody else, somebody you wouldn't expect."

"Well, there were a lot of people who sent me messages about being nominated," Max said. "Most of them were pretty positive, but there were some people who told me I didn't deserve it and shouldn't even be up for it. Of course, most of them thought some other show should get it, so I just kind of ignored those. I didn't really talk to anybody much about it, other than the people from Web Wide Awards and my family and friends."

"Did any of those messages make it sound like Web Wide Awards was a bad thing? Like they were hostile against the company or anything?"

Max screwed up his face as he thought. "Not that I can remember," he said. "Most of them are either from my fans, or from people who don't like my show and think one of the others is better. You always get people like that, so I just ignored them."

"Probably a smart move," Steve said. "If you had to make a guess about who might have been behind this, what would you say?"

Max gave him a goofy grin. "I'd say it had to be Penny Winston," he said. "I don't really believe it was, but she is one of the most competitive people I've ever seen. The whole time we were sitting backstage, she kept telling the rest of us that there was no way any of us would win, because she had it in the bag. When they called my name, she looked completely shocked for the first few seconds. If I was going to believe anybody would want me shot, it would probably be her."

"She does a show of her own, right? Kinda like yours?"

Max nodded. "Yeah, and it's pretty good. It's about a ghost. These people move into a house, and find this lonely ghost girl stuck in one of the bedrooms. Penny plays the ghost."

"She wouldn't do that," said Gina, Max's sister. "She's too nice for that."

Max grinned. "You gotta forgive Gina," he said. "She's a fan of Penny's. I'm pretty sure she even voted for her over my show."

"Hey, I got to know her while we were here," Gina said. "She's really nice."

"I'm sure she is," Steve said. "Besides, I don't think it's too likely that she'd have the kind of money it took to put this together. I'm afraid there was a lot of money involved, and the target actually seems to have been the award company. I think somebody thought that, if you got shot, it would hurt the company pretty badly. We're trying to figure out what other award or production companies might benefit if Web Wide Awards were to be out of business."

Max pursed his lips. "Well, there are some other awards," he said thoughtfully. "I got the Net Video Achievement Award six months ago, at least for the U.S. Hey, Penny won the same award for Canada, now that I think about it. Oh, and there's the Starbright Award, that's another big one. They're out of the U.K. I guess either one of those would probably become the one everybody wants, if Web Wide Awards was gone."

"Okay, we'll check those out. Can you think of any others?"

Max shook his head. "Not off the top of my head," he said. "And they got me on some pain pills, so my brain might not be working all that well, anyway. If I think of any, I can tell Roscoe or one of the guards, they can call you."

Steve took his business card out of his pocket and handed it to Max. "Or you can call me," he said. "My cell number is on the bottom, in case you can't get me at the office. Listen, Max, I don't want you to spend a lot of time worrying about it. I think we're going to get to the bottom of this pretty soon, so don't lose any sleep over it, okay? You just need to concentrate on getting better. I want to see where you take the show from where it's at now."

Max and his family thanked Steve and Walter for coming, and they said goodbye and left the room. When they had gotten down the hall, Steve turned to Walter. "So, what did you think?"

"Max is smart," Walker said. "He doesn't know who did this, but he doesn't really understand that it wasn't about him or his show. I think he thinks it's all his fault, somehow."

"That's not uncommon," Steve said. "PTSD. It sucks."

JADE AND STACY HAD been wandering through the headquarters building since the meeting, and Jade felt that she was getting a pretty fair grasp of how the business worked. It made its profits on the sale of advertising, but there were multiple revenue streams involved.

First, their website got literally millions of visitors per day, as people came to the website to check the rankings on their favorite shows. This had led to them serving as the most popular guide to the many web video programs, which they defined as any series of videos that went from episode to episode. It didn't really matter what the subject was, or whether it was based on fiction or reality. There were shows that focused on particular industries, such as automotive programs, and then there were the many shows that were script based and ranged from comedies to dramas to science fiction and beyond.

Because so many people came to the website to learn more about the shows, or to see where their favorites were standing in the rankings, the areas of the web pages around the actual content were extremely valuable. Advertisers paid as much as a thousand dollars a day to have one of the more popular spots on the homepage, and there were many, many such advertisers.

The company also produced an electronic magazine, or e-zine, called WebVid. This magazine was available free to anyone with an email address, and a new issue was put together every month. It went into great detail on the shows that it featured, and offered lots of biographical information about their creators, stars, and casts. It was essentially another website, and the advertising opportunities it presented were easily as great as those on the main website.

Then, there was the daily video news program they produced. Designed like a regular news program from television, it ran stories that were connected directly to web video, whether they were series or music videos or any other kind that captured the interest and imagination of the public. The show was recorded five days a week, Sunday through Thursday, and was webcast on weekdays. It often saw more than five million viewers in a single day, and featured video commercials that were highly effective for the advertisers who purchased them.

Shortly after lunchtime, Jade and Stacy went to the company's accounting offices, which were on the top floor, along with the executive offices. There, they met with the company's chief accountant, Andrew Wilson.

"Mr. Wilson," Jade said. "I was looking forward to meeting you. I understand it's your job to keep track of all the money this company makes. From what I see, that must keep you pretty busy."

Wilson laughed. "More than you can imagine," he said. "Between them all, my bookkeepers have to keep track of thirty-seven individual revenue streams, which range from advertising to merchandise sales to production services and several other things that I don't even understand. It doesn't matter, though, because all the money that comes in has to be carefully accounted for. Uncle Sam gets really upset if he thinks you're hiding any of it."

"I can imagine. So, just what kind of total dollar amounts are we talking about?"

"This is the part where everybody looks at me like I'm crazy," Wilson said. "That's because it's very difficult for most people to believe the kind of money that can be made on the internet. However, when you've got approximately forty-two million pairs of eyeballs looking at your website each day, an awful lot of businesses want to be placed in front of those eyeballs. Each pair of eyeballs will see an average of twenty-three different advertisements each time they come to the website, and most of them come back several times each day. That can give you as many as 1.6 billion ads served each day. At an average cost of one tenth of a cent each, we're looking at roughly one million, six hundred thousand dollars per day in advertising revenue alone. Merchandising can generate another two hundred thousand per day, as many of those people browse through our gift shop online and decide there's a poster or something they simply can't live without. When you add in every stream of revenue, we end up with a total of close to 2.2 million dollars per day."

Jade's eyes were wide, and Stacy's were about to pop out.

"Are you serious?" Jade asked. "That's over eight hundred million a year."

Wilson nodded. "Yes, and those are just averages. During the week of the quarterly awards, and the two-week period around the annual awards show, those numbers will triple or even quadruple. What it boils down to is a fairly regular annual revenue of slightly over one billion dollars."

"Wow. No wonder you've got such a beautiful building downtown."

"Oh, but we haven't discussed the overhead," Wilson said. "There are over two hundred and twenty employees in the company, and that adds up to a payroll of about twenty million a year. That's not counting the top executives, who can take home another forty million between them. We've got our own advertising bills to pay, which adds up to several million dollars each year, and there's an incredible amount of travel involved. With the cost of our servers and the bandwidth necessary to be able to stream live video the way we do, we spend another six to eight million a year. Altogether, counting building and equipment costs, travel, servers, bandwidth, employees, taxes, and everything, the company net each year gets cut down to about three hundred and fifty million dollars."

"Is that all?" Stacy asked, her face deadpan. "I could live on that."

"A bunch of us could," Jade said. "That's some serious net profits. Maybe I should be in the internet business."

Wilson laughed. "Well, now that you work here, you are," he said. "And while it can be quite an adventure, I should probably warn you to buy stock in your favorite aspirin company. Believe me, you're going to get a lot of headaches from now on."

10

Sam went back to his office and started writing his own report, detailing the conversations he had with Charlie Barr and Patricia LeClair. He was almost finished when Jenna announced that Karen Parks was there. Sam told her to send her in.

"So," he said, "what's going to happen with Mr. Barr?"

"John Pemberton says he may decide to charge him as an accessory to the shooting," she said. "On the other hand, he's doing his best to cooperate. If he does face charges, John's probably gonna go for a plea bargain that will keep him out of prison." She grinned and winked. "I told him you'd appreciate that."

"I'm not sure John wants to do me any favors," Sam said. "He was trying to get me to come to work for him when I took this job, but he wanted me to go after corruption in the police department. I didn't really want to do that, considering just how many dirty cops have already tried to kill me before. The way I see it, that would've shortened my life expectancy and put my family at risk."

"Damn right it would," Karen said. "If you ask me, you were extremely lucky with the last couple cases you dealt with on that. Lemmons in particular wanted you dead, and I'm not sure Carl Rivers wasn't trying to kill you. Hell, Forsyth shot me

in the ass, remember that? If you'd taken that job, I would've
been staying as far away from you as I possibly could."

Sam chuckled. "Can't blame you," he said. "Anyway, at least
we know who was on the inside. Any information on the
Prius?"

"Michaelson Auto Rental has a dark red Prius that seems
to be the one we're looking for. We went through their rental
records already, looking at everyone who rented it during the
time period Charlie's talking about. It was out every day around
that time, but only one name didn't check out, Henry Yenko.
He fits the general description Charlie gave us, tall and bald-
headed, so we're pretty sure it's him. Unfortunately, the name
comes back to a man in Clearwater, Florida, who hasn't been
anywhere near Denver in years."

"Rental company get a copy of the driver's license?" Sam
asked. "They usually do. Any chance it had our guy's actual
photo on it?"

"They got it, and we got it. It does show a bald man, but
there's no way to know if it's the same guy or not. Unfortunately, Michaelson doesn't have security video in their office, so
there's no way to be sure if we've got the right guy or not."

Sam looked at her for a moment, then picked up his phone.
He called Indie and asked her to look for cameras close to
where Michaelson's office was located.

"Yep," she said. "I've got a traffic camera right there on that
corner, and the bank across the street has a security camera on
the drive-thru lanes that's pointed almost exactly at Michaelson's front door. What am I looking for?"

"Karen, what was the date when they rented the car?" Sam
put the phone on speaker so Indie could hear her response.

"You're looking for a tall man with his head shaved. Probably has a thin young woman with him. I don't know how they got there, but they left in a dark red Toyota Prius."

"Okay," Indie said. "The bank uses Laredo Security Video Services, and Herman already has a backdoor into them. Give me a few minutes to find the archives and track down the right date. Any idea on a time?"

"Yeah," Karen said. "It would've been between 10:05 and 10:15 that morning."

"Okay, that narrows it down. Hang on, I'm getting there. Got the right date, but this thing stores video in three-minute increments. I've gotta pop a few open to get the time stamps. Okay, here we go. I see a taxicab dropping off a man who looks like he's got his head shaved, and yes, there is a young woman with him. They went directly inside the building, so I did not get a good look at his face. I'm skipping ahead, looking for when they came out. There they are! Oh, that couldn't be better if they had posed for it. I'm sending you a link to the video, Sam, but I'm also sending you a really nice still shot of both their faces. And before you ask, I'm going to run them through every facial recognition database Herman can find."

The computer chimed in front of him, and Sam opened the email. He downloaded the attached photo and looked at it, then turned the monitor so Karen could see it.

"Thanks, babe," Sam said. "You are definitely the best."

"Sure, sure," Indie said. "I bet you say that to all the hacker girls."

"Nope," Sam said with a grin. "Only the one I married. Love you, babe, talk to you soon."

They hung up and Sam clicked the link to the video. They saw the front of the Michaelson building, and then the couple stepped out. For a brief second, they were looking straight at the camera, but Sam was quite certain they didn't realize it.

"Send me that picture," Karen said. "I want to get an all points out on them right now."

Sam forwarded the email, then printed out the photo and picked it up. He stared at it for a moment, then shook his head.

"What's that about?" Karen asked. "Why are you shaking your head?"

"I don't know," Sam said. "I guess they kind of look familiar. Probably just reminds me of someone I've known in the past, but I would almost swear I've seen both of them before."

He opened the email on his phone and downloaded the picture again, then sent it by SMS to all of the investigators. He included the note that these seemed to be the people who had gotten the cue sheet from Charlie, and the woman appeared to be the same one who had installed the remote control rifle.

"Well," Karen said, "at least we have faces. Maybe Indie will get lucky, and we'll have names to put to them soon."

"I certainly hope so," Sam said. "The sooner we close this case, the happier I'll be." He looked at Karen for a moment, then leaned across the desk toward her. "Karen, Beauregard says somebody close to me is likely to die on this case. He can't tell me who, but I'm asking everyone to be very, very careful. That includes you."

The detective stared at him for a moment. "Sam, if anybody but you told me an old Confederate ghost said that, I'd say they were crazy. Unfortunately, I've seen too many of Beauregard's predictions come true. Trust me when I say I'm going to be very cautious." She got out of her chair, then stopped and looked at Sam. "Sam," she said. "If anything did happen to me, you'd watch out for my kids, right?"

Sam nodded solemnly. "You know I would," he said. "And you'd keep an eye on Indie and my kids if it were reversed."

She nodded once, then walked out the door.

Steve and Walter came in about twenty minutes later, and Steve shared with Sam his conversation with Max Petrelli. When he mentioned Max's comments about the other award programs, Sam's ears perked up.

"I'm leaning toward them," he said. "Nobody hates competition like your competition."

"Well, maybe we're onto something," Steve said. "I'd like to be able to prove that it was the company they were after, and not Max. Walter thinks the poor kid is blaming himself over this, for some reason."

"Human nature," Sam said. "When something bad happens, we naturally have a tendency to believe he must've deserved it, even if we can't remember what we did to cause it."

WENDY HAD JUST FINISHED doing her stand up on the wedding they had covered, and she and Harvey were working to pack everything up. He stowed his equipment and they got into the van. The clock on the dashboard read ten fifteen. "We've got a couple hours before our next assignment," Harvey said. "Anything you want to do till then?"

Wendy smiled. "I could use some fresh coffee," she said. "How about you?"

He shrugged. They were free between assignments, so he nodded and said, "Sure. Where to?"

"Let's go over to Jefferson Boulevard," she said. "I know a little place there that's awesome!"

"Jefferson Boulevard it is," he said, and put the van in gear. "Which intersection?"

"Just hit Jefferson Boulevard and go south about a half mile, you'll see it."

Harvey drove, but part of his mind was on the pretty girl beside him. He'd known a lot of pretty girls, but this one was something special, he thought. Now, the only question was whether she would find him as interesting as he found her.

They got to Jefferson Boulevard, and he turned left to follow her directions. He'd just gotten straightened up in his lane when, just ahead, a semi truck came barreling out of an industrial complex and headed straight across the street at about forty miles an hour. Harvey saw, too fast to make a turn onto the street, and then he realized that the driver was slumped over his steering wheel. He slammed on the brakes to avoid becoming part of the wreck that was about to happen, and stared.

The truck flew past the front of the van, barely missing a small car where two kids could be seen in the back seat, and crashed into the wall of an empty warehouse on the other side of the road. Harvey threw the van into park, and reached up to his neck to shove his headset up onto his ears, then turned on the transceiver that connected him to the production room as he bolted out of the van.

"Production!" he shouted, "this is News Seven, and we've got a semi truck that just crashed into a building on Jefferson Boulevard! We're gonna roll on it, roger?"

"Roger, Seven, roll footage! Get it, guys!"

He turned to Wendy and said, "Get ready, I've gotta mic you fast, we need to get camera on this now!"

"Just a minute," she said, and was out of the van and running toward the car that had almost been crushed. Harvey jumped into the back of the van and got her mic and earpiece, then grabbed his camera and went out the side door, running after her.

The woman in the car was crying hysterically, and Wendy was trying to calm her, telling her that she was okay. Harvey shoved the mic and earpiece at Wendy. "Get these on, or we're not gonna be okay! Come on, this is news, let's get it!"

She took them and put the earpiece in, then stepped to the middle of the road. All the traffic had come to a stop, and the crashed truck and crumpled wall could be seen behind her.

"We're hot, and go!" Harvey yelled, and Wendy looked into the camera.

"This is Wendy Dawson, reporting for Channel Six News. I'm standing in front of an abandoned warehouse in the eight hundred block of Jefferson Boulevard, where a semi truck has just crashed through the wall and into the building, narrowly missing a car with children in it. We don't know the cause of the accident as of yet, but it appeared that the truck driver was slumped in his seat, and may have been unconscious. I can hear sirens now, as police and fire trucks are responding already, and there's an ambulance just coming around the corner. We'll stay here and keep you updated as we learn more!"

"Excellent, excellent, excellent," they heard through their earpieces. "Camera, keep rolling, stay on that truck!"

"I'm on it," Harvey said, "and here's the cops, now!"

Harvey kept the camera rolling as four police cars, a fire engine, and an ambulance roared up to the scene, and Wendy waited until one of the officers began directing traffic before she stepped up to him.

"My cameraman and I were here when it happened," she said. "It looked like the driver just collapsed onto his steering wheel. He was moving pretty fast, there was no way he could have stopped."

The officer looked at Harvey. "You didn't happen to get it on camera, did you?" he asked, but she shook her head.

"No, we got the camera out afterward. I just thought you'd want to know what we saw. Can I get you on camera?"

He looked over his shoulder. "Wait till we've actually got something," he said. "I'll let you know when we do."

Wendy nodded and walked back to stand by Harvey. He was keeping his camera focused on the police and fire trucks as the officers and firemen went about their duties. The paramedics in the ambulance were getting out their equipment and getting ready to start extracting the driver.

They waited about ten minutes, while the policemen watched everything that was going on. Finally, the officer who had spoken to Wendy turned and came back toward them.

He turned on the transceiver again. "Production, we're going live again, got a policeman ready to talk, I think."

"Roger, Seven, we're ready."

Wendy stopped where the action was behind her, and the officer came to stand beside her. "Okay, the driver's alive; it looks like he had a seizure or something and lost control. I can give you a basic statement, if you're ready."

"Sure," Wendy said, "that's great. Give me a second. And your name is?"

"I'm Officer Stratton," he said, "Branden Stratton."

"Okay, great, and I'm Wendy Dawson with Channel Six," she said, and turned to Harvey to give him the "ready" sign, closed fist with a thumb popping up out of it. Harvey nodded, and she looked into the camera.

"I'm here with Officer Branden Stratton of the Denver Police Department," she said, then turned to face him. "Officer Stratton, can you tell us what's happened here?"

"Yes, Wendy," he said. "Apparently the truck driver, whose name I cannot release at this time, was leaving the terminal across the street when he suffered what appears to be a seizure and lost control of his vehicle. His foot must have pushed on the accelerator pedal, and the truck sped up and shot across the road to crash into the side of an empty warehouse. The driver is alive and not seriously injured, but he's being taken to the hospital for observation and treatment for the seizure. We're just fortunate that no other vehicles were involved, and no one else was hurt."

"Yes, we are," Wendy said. "Thank you, Officer Stratton."

"My pleasure, Wendy," he said, and winked at her as he turned to walk away. Harvey cut the camera and asked, "How's that, guys?"

The production engineer came back instantly. "Excellent work, Seven, we got it! Get out of the way now, and let them do their jobs, you've done yours and done it very well!"

"Roger that," Harvey said. "We're going dark now." He cut the feed from the camera and shut off the transceiver, then started stowing his gear. He ignored Wendy until she stepped up behind him and passed him her microphone and earpiece.

"That was a good bit," he said. "We're doing real news, girl, this is awesome."

Wendy was smiling. "Yeah," she said. "And Officer Stratton asked me for my phone number! Isn't that great?"

Harvey forced himself to smile. "Yeah," he said. "Great."

11

"Jade Miller is on line 3," Jenna said. Sam picked up the phone and punched the button.

"Jade? How's it going?"

"Actually, it's going very well, sir," Jade said. "My cover is working perfectly, and everybody has been very cooperative. I understand you had a bit of an adventure here today, though."

"Yeah," Sam said. "We found out their head video producer was the one who gave information to the shooters. He's being questioned, and he's cooperating. Did you get the photo I sent you?"

"Yes, sir, I did. I had a thought on that, by the way. I've been given access to all of their video, including the raw footage from all the cameras in the arena that night. I can access it from home, so I thought I would take a good look tonight and see if I can spot either of them in the audience."

"That's an excellent idea," Sam said. "Bear in mind, the tech guys say that they would have been sitting right about the middle of the auditorium, right under the spot where camera 4C would have been at that moment. That would be the most important area to look at."

"Excellent," Jade said. "I'll let you know what I find. Now, the other thing I learned today is that this company makes an awful lot of money, especially for one that is not publicly traded. It turns out that only a few people own stock in the compa-

155

ny, and John and Annie hold the majority of it between them, like over ninety percent. The rest was given as bonuses to some of their top executives, but nobody owns more than two or three percent. What that boils down to is that John and Annie are each taking home well over a hundred million a year."

"Isn't capitalism a wonderful thing?" Sam asked with a grin. "Makes me wish I was the kind of genius who could come up with ideas like that."

"Yeah, you and me both. The thing is, I was going over the stats on the website today for a little while, and an interesting little side note on this shooting is that their traffic is up. Now, I would've expected to see a spike for a day or so after the shooting, but it's been four days. The traffic has gone up each day since the night of the shooting. What that translates to is an increase in the ad revenue the site generates. There's also been a surge in subscribers to their e-zine, WebVid. At almost 30 dollars a year, that's going to add up to some additional income, as well."

Sam was quiet for a moment as he thought. "Jade, are you getting any sense that the company may have known something like this was going to happen?"

"I'd have to say absolutely not, sir," she replied. "I wasn't meaning to imply anything like that, I just found it pretty interesting. To be honest, I don't think anybody could have predicted that something like this would actually increase their profits. I mean, that just seems completely opposite of what I would expect."

"Unless it's the car crash syndrome," Sam said. "People tend to go toward a car crash, rather than away from it. Same for a building fire, people rush toward it to get a better look. It's an unhappy part of human nature, I guess. That could be what you're seeing, that something bad happening to the company is drawing more attention to it."

"Well, my dad was in show business for years," she said, "and he used to claim that there was no such thing as bad publicity. I mean, take a look at a lot of the big companies today. Something goes wrong for them, and for weeks they're all you hear about. Somewhere in the middle of all that news, the bad stuff seems to fade away and the news starts getting better. Look at Tesla; they had problems with their autopilot and somebody was killed, but they came through that and now they're more popular than ever."

"Maybe that's what it is," Sam said. "Bad publicity drawing attention to the good parts about the company. How did things go with Stacy, by the way?"

"Hey, she's awesome," Jade said. "They told everybody she was an efficiency expert, and she jumped right into the role. She's been all over people about turning off lights when they leave the room, making sure they recycle everything, it's almost like she's actually done it before. We both laugh about it when we find ourselves completely alone for a minute."

Sam grinned. "Just remember, she's there to watch your back, not just have fun. Anything else?"

Jade hesitated, and Sam caught it. Before he could ask, she began speaking again.

"I was going over some of the feedback on the website," she said. "There was one feedback message that caught my attention, but I don't know if it really means anything or not. It was done anonymously, so it doesn't really matter a whole lot, but it said Web Wide Awards should watch its back, and that this might only be the first tragedy to strike them. It didn't go into any kind of detail, and it wasn't exactly worded like a threat, but it bothered me."

"Yeah," Sam said. "Did you show it to anyone?"

"Actually, I showed it to Annie Porter. She read it, then just shrugged her shoulders and said she didn't think it really meant anything. I don't know, Sam, it just bothered me."

"All right," Sam said. "If you run across anything else like it, let me know. Other than that, just keep watching and listening, and make sure your back is covered at all times."

"Yes, sir," Jade said, and then she was gone.

Sam left the office right after and was driving home when his phone rang. He pulled it out and glanced at it, saw Ron Thomas' number on the display, and put it to his ear.

"Ron?"

"Hey, Sam," Ron said. "Just checking in. How's everything going back there?"

"It's pretty wild," Sam said. "I posted my report just a bit ago, but I'll give you the gist. We found the insider. One of their video producers was blackmailed into giving a schedule of how the show was supposed to go to a couple, a man and a woman. We've identified the woman as the one who actually mounted the gun on the camera, and we've managed to get photos of their faces. Indie is running them through facial recognition now, but it's likely to take a while to get any results. I've got Jade inside Web Wide Awards, working undercover as we planned, and she's trying to get a feel for the people who work there. Summer checked a guy out, but he turned out not to be a problem. As it stands right now, we're just trying to identify our suspects and track them down."

"Good. Jeff and I will be stuck out here for at least the next two weeks, so you'll need to handle anything that comes up. Keep me posted, and I'll check in when I can. That may be kind of sporadic, it turns out this conference is a lot bigger than we thought. Representatives from just about every country are gathering at the Javits Center to talk about the future of the internet, including a ridiculous number of internet gurus and several world leaders. Our own Secretary of State will be there, along with leaders and diplomats from a dozen other countries. They're going to be talking about things like satellites that will make the internet free for everybody, and how internet video is going to take over what we think of as television and movies. It's pretty exciting."

"It sounds like it," Sam said. "Where are you getting the security personnel?"

"We're actually subcontracting with several other companies," Ron said. "We had to come up with almost four hundred security guards, and that was the only way to do it. Anyway, like I said, keep me posted."

"You got it," Sam said. He put the phone back in his pocket and drove home.

Mackenzie opened the door as soon as she heard the Mustang pull in, and Sam swept her up into a hug as he entered the house. Bo was in the playpen in the middle of the living room floor, standing up and clinging to the side as he said, "Da da da da," over and over. Still holding Kenzie, Sam leaned down and scooped him up as well and carried them both to the kitchen.

Indie was putting the finishing touches on a large homemade pizza, and turned around to wrap them all in a hug and steal a kiss from her husband. She held onto them for a moment, just looking into Sam's eyes.

"What?" Sam asked with a grin. "You're staring."

Indie shrugged and shook her head with a grin of her own. "I was doing a little spring cleaning today," she said, "and I opened one of the closets upstairs and found my old suitcases. Remember those, the ones I had when you found me and Kenzie living in my car?"

"Of course I remember," Sam said. "That was one of the best days of my life."

She let go and stepped back, and Sam set Kenzie on the floor.

"It was absolutely the best day of mine," Indie said. "I remember tracking you down at Taco Bell and begging for food, and you checking me out and finding out about Mackenzie. I was so scared at that moment, because I knew if you turned me in right then, I would've lost her. Instead, you offered us a place to stay."

"Yeah," Sam said, "and you thought I was trying to get you into a compromising position."

She giggled. "Yes, I did at first," she said. "And I was actually going to accept it, because I was that desperate. But then you said no strings, and you convinced me you were serious. I think that was the moment when I actually started to fall in love with you."

"Baby," Sam said, "I look back over the last few years, and I realize that I started falling for you the moment you sat down across the table from me. By the time you'd been here a week, I already knew I wanted to be with you forever."

"Wow," she replied. "We're actually quite a love story, aren't we?"

"Yes, we are," Sam said. "And homemade pizza only makes it better."

Indie smacked him lightly on his arm, then turned away to put the pizza in the oven. Sam set Bo in his high chair and got a bottle of water out of the refrigerator, then sat down at the table beside his son.

"Herman having any luck?" Sam asked.

Indie looked around, a grimace on her face. "Nothing," she said. "They're not in the FBI's facial recognition database, or the NSA's, so I'm going to check Interpol. I don't know how they managed to stay off the radar so far, but I'm not giving up."

"Daddy," Kenzie said. "Is it getting warm enough to go swimming?"

"Well, the air is plenty warm enough, but the water might be cold. Maybe we can give it a try this weekend, see how it feels. I'll go out in a bit and take the cover off the pool, then I can turn on the filtration system and start getting it ready."

"Yay!" Kenzie yelled. "I love swimming!"

"Would be nice get into the pool," Indie said. "We could invite some friends, fire up the grill, and have a pool party."

They sat around the table and talked about the possibility until the pizza was done, then sliced it up and carried it into the living room. They found a movie to watch together, and Sam decided to put work away for the evening. He was at home, with his family, and he wanted his mind to be there with him.

12

Summer had left the office a few minutes before Sam, feeling a little frustrated. The only leads she had uncovered in the case thus far had been dead ends, and she liked to feel productive. She had spent part of the day going over the list of employees again, trying once more to find someone who might be part of the problem, but with Charlie Barr's confession, she knew the odds of finding anyone else inside the company involved were pretty slim.

She had taken her phone out and looked at the photo of the suspect couple. The tall, bald man was probably the alpha of the pair, but the only one they'd actually seen involved in setting up the shooting had been the woman. It wasn't often that true hit men worked in teams, and she'd never heard of a couple working together as hired killers before. The whole concept got her adrenaline flowing, and made her want to find a way to bring them down.

Sitting at home in her apartment didn't seem appealing, so she decided to go out for a drink. Summer was a girl who liked the heavy beat of rock music, and she absolutely loved to dance, but she knew better than to drink on an empty stomach. She zapped a couple of chimichangas, took a quick shower and changed into dancing clothes, then pointed her Jaguar toward her favorite watering hole.

The Proof is one of Denver's hottest night clubs, with music videos playing for the patrons to dance to. The music is a mix of modern and retro, but it's always full of energy and fun. Summer had begun going there not long after moving to the city, and a lot of the regulars knew her well enough that she heard her name called out as she entered. She turned in the direction it came from and broke into a big smile.

"Harvey!" she yelled back. "You ready to dance, boy?"

"Oh, yeah, baby," the guy called back, forcing his way through the crowd. "Let's shake it up!"

Harvey Reilly was one of the first people she had met when she moved to Denver a year earlier, and the first man she'd dated there. They had gone out together for a couple of months, but both of them were busy with their respective jobs and had a habit of canceling dates. They'd finally decided that being friends was easier than trying to have a relationship, and still managed to have fun together whenever they both ended up at the club.

Harvey caught up to her and they went to the bar to get her a margarita, then found an empty table near the dance floor.

"So, how you been, sweetness?" Harvey asked. "Ain't seen you in a while."

"I've been busy," she answered with a smile. "Like always. How about you?"

"Same old same old," he said. "Got a new gig since we saw each other last, I'm working for Channel 6. I'm the new cameraman for Wendy Dawson."

"Wendy the reporter? Wow, you've come up in the world. Is she as big a bitch as she seems to be?"

"Who, Wendy? She's a sweetheart! As long as you're not on the wrong end of her microphone, anyway. The girl does ask some pretty hard questions, but that's just her job."

Summer stared at him. "Oh, Lord, you're sweet on her. Getting anywhere?"

Harvey made a face that told her the answer. "I am not," he said. "Besides, she's into cops and tough guys. What are you working on these days?"

"Ahaha," Summer said. "I'm not telling you, or you'll be bringing Wendy around looking for a scoop. Let's just say I'm on something big and leave it at that."

"Ouch, you hurt me! I'd never tell Wendy what you're doing, that wouldn't be cool at all. Besides, she ever gets a look at you, I'll never hear the end of it. That would guarantee I'd never have a chance—assuming I ever wanted one!"

"So? We've been over for a long time. I'm no threat to her."

"And if I'd told you back when we were dating that I knew this *other* gorgeous blonde who was sexy as hell and that I sometimes hang out with, would you have been okay with it?"

"Hmm. Okay, probably not. So, you won't tell her anything, then?"

He dragged his finger across his chest in a big X. "Cross my heart and hope to get lucky."

Summer stuck her tongue out at him. "Keep hoping," she said. "Okay, fine. You heard about the shooting at the Canterbury Arena the other night, the awards show?"

"Oh, yeah," Harvey said. "That was nasty! What are you doing on that?"

"Web Wide Awards hired us to find out who did it," Summer replied. "I'm on the Windlass investigation team, remember?"

"Well, yeah, I know that. I mean, are you getting anywhere with it?"

"Not very fast. We managed to get a lead on the people who set it up, a man and a woman. They used a remote controlled rifle mounted on one of the overhead cameras. We don't know who they are, yet, but we got a picture of them."

"Cool, lemme see! I won't tell Wendy anything, I promise, I'm just curious."

Summer looked at him for a moment, then took out her phone and called up the photo. She turned the phone so he could see it, and watched his face as he looked into the eyes of the killers.

He stared, and something about the look on his face made Summer's neck crawl. "What?" she asked.

"These are the people who shot that kid?" Harvey asked. "Are you sure?"

Summer nodded. "We've got video of the woman actually placing the gun on the camera, and they blackmailed one of the employees for the cue sheet. That's the schedule of camera angles and stuff."

Harvey grunted. "I know what a cue sheet is, sweetness. The reason I'm asking if you're sure," he said slowly, "is because I know that guy."

Summer's eyes flew wide open. "You what? Who is he?"

"Okay, let me rephrase that," Harvey said. "I don't actually know him, but I've seen him several times. He's been staying in my building for the past couple months. I think I've seen the girl with him, too, but I'm not sure."

Summer's eyes were about to bug out. "Are you freaking serious? Harvey, what apartment is he in?"

"3G, right across the hall from mine. Listen, if you're gonna call the cops to go get him, I really should let Wendy know."

"Not just yet, I'm not. I'm going to go down there and make sure it's them, first." She got to her feet. "Would they be there now?"

"Now? Well, I don't know, but I think they're usually there in the evenings."

"You still live in the same building, right?"

"Well, yeah, but..." He started getting to his feet. "Wait, I'm going with you."

"Harvey," Summer said, "do you carry a gun?"

"Well, no..."

"I do, and if it's them, they're wanted for attempted murder. Stay here." She turned and headed for the door before he could say anything else.

Harvey lived in a nice apartment building on Washington Street, near the 7th Avenue intersection. It took her about twenty minutes to get there, and she parked her car around the corner at a different building.

She walked to the front door of Harvey's building, holding out her phone and staring at the picture so that she'd have it memorized. She put the phone back into her pocket as she got inside, took the elevator up to the third floor and turned right to get to 3G. Harvey's door, as he said, was directly across the hall and she stopped and knocked on it, instead.

There was no answer, of course. She stood there for a moment as if waiting, and just listened. There was soft music coming from 3G, behind her, and she could hear a voice speaking but couldn't make out anything that was being said.

Each of the doors had a peephole, so she stood there for another moment and tried to look agitated. She took out her phone and glanced at the time, shoved it back in to her pocket and knocked again. She waited another thirty seconds, then turned around and knocked on the door to apartment 3G.

A woman's voice came through the door. "Yes? Can I help you?"

"Hey, I'm really sorry to bother you," she said. "Do you know Harvey, the guy who lives across the hall?"

The door opened a couple of inches, and the woman behind it peeked out at her. Summer looked closely, keeping her smile in place while she tried to decide if the partial face she was seeing was the same as the woman in the photo.

"I don't really know him," the woman said. "I've only seen him a couple times, is all."

Summer looked back at Harvey's door and put a knuckle into her mouth. "Have you seen him today? I've been trying to reach him, and he hasn't answered his phone for a couple days, and I just found out he hasn't been at work."

The door opened slightly more. "No, I don't think I did. Have you knocked on the door?"

"Yeah, loud and hard. I'm really getting worried, you know?" She choked a bit, as if she were about to start crying right there in the hallway.

The woman hesitated a second, then said, "Just a minute, let me get my husband." The door closed, and Summer moved a bit further away from it. If this was the couple they were looking for, the last thing they might want would be a woman having an emotional meltdown in front of their apartment door.

The door opened again, and this time it swung wide. A man stepped out, and Summer felt a rush of adrenaline as she recognized the face. It was him, all right, unless he had an identical twin.

"What's the problem?" he asked, and Summer pointed toward the door across the hall.

"Harvey Reilly," she said, "the guy who lives there? He isn't answering his phone and he hasn't been showing up for work, and I'm afraid something bad happened to him. Have you seen him lately?"

The guy scowled. "I saw him leave this morning," he said, and Summer realized he had a slight accent, something European but not specific. "He seemed fine, then."

That was what she needed. There was no way she was going to try to take down a professional killer alone, so she needed a way to get away and call for backup in a hurry. "Oh, are you sure?" she said, her eyes flicking from the man to Harvey's door and back. "Maybe he's just having one of his episodes, I mean, he's been known to just avoid everyone for a few days. I just sort of thought he was over that, at least with me." She looked him in the eye. "If you're sure you saw him, then I guess I'll wait a couple more days before I panic. Listen, I can't thank you enough, this was really awesome of you."

The bald man smiled. "It's no problem," he said as he went back into his apartment and closed the door. Summer saw the woman for a brief second, looking at her warily, just before the door closed completely.

She walked quickly toward the elevator, carefully leaving her phone in her pocket until she was inside and the doors were closed, and then she snatched it out and dialed Sam's cell phone.

"PRICHARD," SAM SAID as he answered. "Summer? What's up?"

"I found them," Summer said breathlessly. "The man and woman in the photo you sent, I found them. Apartment 3G, 715 Washington Street. I just talked with them, they're there right now."

Sam's eyes went wide. "Can you keep a watch to make sure they don't leave? I'll get police and be there right away."

"I'm on it," Summer said. "They won't get away."

Sam cut off the call, then dialed Karen Parks. It took him only seconds to relay the information, and Karen cut him off to call for backup. She would meet Sam at the building.

Sam looked at Indie. "Summer found our shooters," he said. "With any luck, we can get them tonight."

"Go," she said, "but be careful, Sam. Remember what Beauregard said—watch everyone, okay?"

"I will." He kissed her quickly and was out the door, the Mustang's big engine roaring to life.

Sam shoved his foot into the carburetor, and the big 428 uttered its famous growl as the car ate up the road. Sam was cranking almost a hundred miles per hour when he got to 6th Avenue, but his four wheel disc brakes brought the speed down drastically by the time he got to 7th. He fishtailed around the corner and slid to a stop at the curb two buildings down from his target.

Karen spotted him as she came up the street and pulled in behind him, jumping out of her car as he climbed out of the Mustang. They spotted Summer rushing toward them, and then a pair of squad cars came up the street with lights and sirens off.

"Okay, I saw them both," Summer said. "The apartment they're in is on the back of the building, so I really don't think they could've seen us. You guys ready?"

"Hold your horses, cutie pie," Karen said. "Are you wearing a bulletproof bra? Then you're staying outside. Take a position where you can see the back exit, just in case they decide to make a run for it at the last second. Sam, you go with her."

Sam's eyes went wide. "But I..."

"No argument, Sam," Karen said. "This is a police matter, and we're going to handle it. You and Summer can keep watch on the back."

As much as he wanted to argue, Sam knew she was making sense. She and the uniformed officers were wearing bulletproof vests, while Sam and Summer were not. He grabbed Summer by the arm and pointed toward the back of the building.

They had to cut between the target building and the one next door, but they got behind it quickly. Karen and the uniformed officers went in the front, with two of the uniforms going up the stairs while Karen and the other two rode up in the elevator. They waited until the officers in the stairwell caught up, just to be sure the perpetrators hadn't tried to get out that way, and then they converged on the door.

Karen knocked. "Police," she called out loudly, "open up!"

There was a loud *boom,* and a section of the wall next to the door vanished. The officer who was standing there fell to the floor, his right hip a bloody mass from where the shotgun blast had taken him. Karen and the others stepped back, aimed their guns at the doorway, and opened fire.

One of the bullets struck the door latch, and the door flew open. The woman was laying in the floor a few feet past it, and blood was pooling around her as she tried to reach for the shotgun she had dropped. Karen rushed in and stamped a foot down on top of it, pointed a gun at the woman's face, and ordered her to freeze.

The woman looked up at her, but the eye contact lasted only a few seconds. Her eyelids drooped as blood loss caught up with her, and then Karen saw the gouge on the side of her neck, where a bullet had taken out a section of her jugular.

The other officers were rushing through the apartment, shouting "Clear," as they found no one in each room. Karen cursed as she realized the man had gotten away through an open back window that led out to a fire escape. She leaned out the window, hoping to see her quarry down at ground level with Sam and Summer keeping him covered, but there was no sign of any of them.

Some instinct made her turn her head to the right, and she found herself looking down the barrel of a gun. She tried to jump back, bringing her own gun around toward the man who was grinning and squeezing his trigger, but she knew it was too late. The only thought in her mind was that she had made Sam promise to watch after her kids, and then the sound of a gunshot filled her ears.

Holy crap, she thought instantly, I'm not dead! Her eyes were wide as she stared at the bald man who was tumbling over the rail around the fire escape landing toward the ground far below. The bloody stump where his gun hand had been caught her completely by surprise, until she looked around again and saw Sam standing in the alley, his gun still raised and aimed up to where the man had been about to kill her.

When the killer hit the ground, Sam hurried over to make sure he wasn't moving, but it was clearly not going to happen. His head was bent at an impossible angle, his neck broken, and there was no sign of life.

Residents of the building were screaming and fleeing, rushing out as fast as they could. A dozen more police officers and a few ambulances had arrived, and some of the paramedics were busy with panic attacks among the residents. One elderly woman seemed to have suffered a mild heart attack, and was rushed to the hospital along with the officer who was wounded.

Sam called Indie. "Tell me something," he said. "Has anyone ever changed the outcome of one of Beauregard's predictions?"

"Not that I know of," Indie said slowly. "Why, Sam?"

"Because," Sam said, "our shooter had Karen dead in his sights, and she said he was grinning like a maniac and squeezing the trigger when I shot him. A split second later, and she would've been dead."

"Oh, Sam," Indie said. "I don't know what to say. To be honest, I've never known him to be wrong, but maybe you were in the right place at the right moment."

"Yeah," Sam said. "I don't know when I'll be home, it's gonna take a while to get all this wrapped up. I love you, babe."

"I love you, Sam," Indie said. "Come home when you can."

Sam ended the call and walked over to where Karen and the officers were waiting. Summer was with them, watching as the body of the shooter was photographed and observed by the medical examiner. He was dead, his neck broken from landing on his head when he fell, as was the woman in the apartment.

"Other than the ME taking out the woman's body," Karen said, "I'm sealing the apartment. Your tech people are a lot better equipped than our CSI, and the mayor gave you lead on this case. Just make sure I get copies, okay?"

"Yeah," Sam said.

Karen looked at him for a moment, because his eyes seemed to be seeing something miles away. "What's going on in that head of yours, Sam?"

"It doesn't make any sense," Sam said. "He goes out the window, but she makes a suicide stand? It just doesn't add up."

"What doesn't add up," Karen said, "is why he would have thought he could get out that way. This guy was some kind of pro, he should have expected there to be someone watching the back. He couldn't possibly have really thought he was going to escape, could he?"

"It's possible," Sam said. "He would've expected the biggest force to come to the apartment door, so he might have thought there was a chance he could fight his way past us outside. But still, to leave the woman behind to die, just to cover his escape? He must've had some powerful kind of control over her."

"Well, at least we have a chance now of finding out who they were. Odds on, their fingerprints or DNA will turn up in some database, somewhere."

"Hey," Summer said suddenly. "He had an accent, something European but I couldn't pin it down. I don't think she had any kind of foreign accent, she sounded more like maybe from the Midwest. Illinois, Indiana, somewhere like that."

"All right," Karen said. "Be sure to put that in your statement. And, hey, Summer? Excellent work. I don't know how you found them, but I'm awfully glad you did."

Karen turned to Sam and just looked at him for a moment, then threw both arms around his neck. "I'd be dead if it weren't for you," she said. "That was one hell of a shot, Sam."

"It wasn't all that great," Sam said. "I was aiming for center mass, a body shot."

"Summer! Hey, Summer!" Summer turned around and looked, and sure enough, there came Harvey, with Wendy Dawson running right beside him. "Summer, this is Wendy. She heard about this on the scanner and called me, so we rushed on down. You don't mind giving her a statement, do you?"

"Back off, Wendy," Karen growled. "Give me a couple of minutes, and I'll give you a statement, but you leave Ms. Raines alone."

"Come on, Detective," the reporter said. "I already know she's a Windlass investigator, and she's standing right next to Sam Prichard; do you really think I'm going to leave that alone?"

Karen went nose to nose with her. "You will if you ever expect anything more than a 'no comment' out of me in the future," she said. "I know you, and you're trying to build your career on this case. You piss me off, and you won't get anything. Do you understand me?"

Wendy scowled. "Fine, as long as I get something good. Is it true you got the people who shot that kid at the award show?"

Karen glared at her. "Fine," she said. "Let's do this." She composed herself quickly and then managed a smile.

Harvey aimed the camera at Wendy and Karen, then pointed at the reporter. "Go," he said.

"This is Wendy Dawson with Channel 6 news, and I'm standing here with Detective Karen Parks of the Denver Police Department at the scene of a police shooting." She turned to Karen and Harvey widened the shot. "Detective Parks, can you tell me exactly what's happened here this evening?"

"Earlier this evening, an investigator for Windlass Security determined that the suspects in the recent shooting at the Canterbury Arena were occupying an apartment in the building behind me. She notified police, and we responded to attempt an arrest. The suspects resisted, seriously wounding one officer in the process, and one of them was killed at that point by police. The other suspect attempted to escape out the window, and was just about to shoot another officer when he himself was shot by Private Detective Sam Prichard, who is the chief investigator for Windlass. We can confirm that these are the suspects we have been looking for, and that they are both deceased."

"Sam Prichard has become quite a hero around Denver over the last few years," Wendy said. "Will we be able to speak with him about his involvement in this shooting?"

Karen glared at her for a second, then looked around and motioned for Sam to come closer. He stepped up beside her and Wendy turned her attention to him.

"Mr. Prichard, thank you," she said. "We learned yesterday that Windlass Security is actually running this entire investigation into the shooting that took place at the Web Wide Awards presentation. I'm assuming that means you are in charge?"

"Yes," Sam said, "I'm the lead investigator on this case, but as we told you yesterday, we're working directly with Detective Parks and the Denver PD."

"Mr. Prichard, do you believe the suspects presented a danger to the public while they were here?"

"I'd have to say yes," Sam replied. "They were being sought for attempted murder, and we know now that they were armed and quite dangerous. We're probably lucky that they didn't find a need to harm anybody else, at least as far as we know."

"Were the suspects local? Are they from around here?"

"I don't believe we've identified them just yet," Sam said, "but I'm not really at liberty to discuss any other details of the case at this point. I'm sure the Denver PD will issue a statement when the time is right, and you'll have to wait for that information."

Wendy knew she was being dismissed, and turned to face the camera. "That's all we have at the moment," she said. "Stay tuned to Channel 6 news, and we'll bring you more information as it becomes available. This is Wendy Dawson, for Channel 6 news."

13

Steve Beck and Darren Beecher showed up at the police station after they heard on the news what happened. Because they weren't involved in the shooting at all, they were forced to wait in the lobby until Sam and Summer finished making their statements. Karen had gotten back by then, and completed her own report. The shooting would automatically be reviewed, and Karen would be relegated to desk duty until the review was complete.

Detective Jim Storch, newly promoted from uniform, was assigned to take over the management of the investigation for the police department, even though it was almost considered to be over. The DA's office had sent Margaret Lee, one of their newest assistant prosecutors, to oversee the reports and collect information about the shooting. She assured both Karen and Sam that the review would show it to be a good shooting, and the homicides justifiable.

It was well past midnight when Sam and Summer finally came out of the back rooms, and they went with Steve and Darren to an all night coffee shop.

"So, how did you find them?" Darren asked Summer. "We didn't have any kind of leads at all, the last I knew."

"Freaky good luck," Summer said. "I was down at Proof, talking to a friend of mine, and I happened to show him the picture Sam sent me. He took one look, then told me he'd seen the guy in the apartment across the hall from his. He thought he'd seen the woman as well, but he wasn't sure, so I went down and pretended I was worried about him to get a look at them. As soon as the guy stepped out and I saw his face, I knew it was them."

"I don't believe it," Steve said. "We all go out there and bust our asses to try to get a lead on these people, and you stumble into a case breaker at a bar. You wearing some kind of magic panties or something?"

Summer grinned at him. "Why, Steve, I think that's the nicest thing you've ever said to me. And wouldn't you like to know."

"So, where does this leave us, boss?" Darren asked. "Is the case closed, now?"

Sam shook his head. "Not even close," he said. "Denny is on his way to London right now, to follow up the lead on Starbright. He's got reason to believe that Benjamin Hickam, the owner of Starbright Awards, might have been the one who paid for this. While he's working on that, our job is to trace these two people backward, find out everything we can about them. I want to know everything they've been doing, because I can't believe this was a one shot operation. No pun intended, by the way."

"I think you're right," Steve said. "Something about this smells. That poor kid gets shot, and our clients are supposed to get the blame, right? Thing is, you don't ruin a company with just one bad day. It takes more than that, just look at how many times one of the big car makers got caught covering up a flaw in their designs. They get a little bad press, but sales don't seem to slow down that much."

"That's my point," Sam said. "Most people would've figured that the kid getting shot was going to be such a shock to the public that the company would suffer because of it, right? In reality, though, the company is the one who's getting all the sympathy. Yeah, I know, people are worried about the kid, but Jade was telling me about all the feedback on the company's website. Seems like ninety-five percent of it, maybe more, is all positive and supportive. They're actually getting more traffic and more subscribers than they had before."

"Hey, even bad publicity is publicity," Darren said.

"Yes, but people are apparently a lot more forgiving than we give them credit for. Max Petrelli got shot, and even though everybody's upset about it, the only ones blaming the company has been the news media. That makes me wonder when the other shoe is going to drop, you know?"

"Then, you think there's going to be another attack on them?" Summer asked.

"My gut says so," Sam said, and both Steve and Darren agreed. "Somebody spent a hell of a lot of money setting this up, that much I'm sure of. Just the fact that those two were still here, that they hadn't already gotten as far away as they could, tells me that this isn't over. The only question is whether they already have something set up, or if it was still in the works."

"You need to put Walter on this," Steve said. "He needs to hear all of this, and anything else we come up with on John and Jane Doe. If anybody can make a reasonable guess about what's coming next, he's the one."

Sam nodded. "I have to agree," he said. "I also have to get home. I'll see you all at the office in the morning, nine o'clock.

Everybody go home and get whatever sleep you can. I've got a feeling this is just getting started."

INDIE HAD BEEN IN BED asleep when Sam came in, and he made certain to be quiet and let her stay that way. In the morning, however, he woke to find her sitting up on the bed beside him.

"Hey, babe," he said. "Good morning."

"Hey," Indie said. "So, how did everything go last night?"

"A lot of paperwork," he replied. "Had to surrender my gun for ballistics testing, just so they can be sure it was really me that shot the guy. I wasn't alone, Karen and three other officers were involved in shooting the woman, so all of their guns are being tested, as well. Karen's going to be on a desk for a day or two, and they put a new rookie detective on the case until she's back."

"How are you doing? I know it takes something out of you when you have to shoot someone."

"It comes with the job," Sam said. "I guess I can handle it, but there's always that feeling that I might've done something differently, something that wouldn't have ended up with a body on a slab in the morgue." He shrugged. "Hindsight is always 20/20."

"No, Sam," Indie said. "If he was about to shoot Karen, you really didn't have any other options. I don't think there's any way you could have saved her without taking that shot, and I would bet you that she would agree with me."

Sam grinned. "I know," he said. "It's just the way I deal with things, I guess."

"Well, at least you know they're not going to hurt anyone else. That's something, isn't it?"

Sam let out a sigh. "That's actually what I'm working on today. Several of us, including Steve and Darren, think that they had to have been up to something more than just that first shooting. There was some reason they stayed in town, and for all we know, they may already have something set in motion. We need to find out everything we can about them, try to back trace their steps and figure out what it might be."

He threw off the covers and got out of bed, then took a quick shower and got dressed. By the time he got to the kitchen, Indie had the coffee hot and poured for him, and was flipping eggs and bacon. He sipped the coffee for a few moments, and then she set a plate in front of him.

He ate rapidly, because the day was already getting away from him. He had slept until almost 8, but he had told everyone to be in his office at nine. It wouldn't do for him to be the only one to show up late, so he shoved the last of the egg and bacon into his mouth, swallowed the rest of his coffee, and kissed his wife goodbye as he grabbed his spare pistol and tucked it into his holster.

Ballistics might have his usual gun, but Sam had learned that it was a lot better to have a weapon and not need it, than to need one and not have it. He had bought a couple extras, and made sure Indie knew how to get to all of them, just in case any of his enemies ever tried to harm his family again.

The sun was shining brightly and it was already warm when he stepped out the front door, so he reached inside the Mustang and hit the garage door opener, then rolled his big Honda Shadow out and climbed onto it. His cane went into the special holster on the front forks, and he hit the starter button. The big bike roared to life, and Sam took the helmet off the mirror and snapped it onto his head.

It was the first time he'd ridden the bike since the year before, and it felt good, rumbling under him once again. He caught himself smiling, and remembered the old joke about how to tell a happy motorcycle rider when you saw one: by counting the bugs in his teeth when he smiled. If there were more than five, he must've been ecstatic.

He parked the bike in his assigned space, then got off and walked into the building. He carried his helmet all the way to his office and set it on his desk, then turned to go and get some coffee from the break room.

He didn't get very far. Jenna was standing just outside his door, holding not one, but two large coffees out to him.

"Well, thank you," he said.

"Thank your wife," Jenna said. "She called me and said you didn't have time for a second cup at home."

Sam grinned and raised his cup in salute to Indie. He sat down at his desk, but he was only there a moment before Steve, Walter, Darren, and Summer all came in together. Sam picked up his coffee and started toward the conference table, and they all followed.

"Walter, I don't know if you've heard much about what happened last night..."

"Steve told me," Walter said. "I think you're right. I think there's something else about to happen. That's the only reason they would have stayed around here."

Sam nodded. "That's what I thought, too. What I'd like us to do..."

He was interrupted by the phone ringing on his desk, so he reached over and hit the button on the speakerphone on the table. "Yes?" He asked.

"Karen Parks is on line 1," Jenna said. "I can patch her through to the conference table."

"Yes, go ahead," Sam said. There was a beep, and Sam said, "Karen?"

"Hey, Sam," Karen said. "I thought you'd like to know, AFIS kicked back IDs on the fingerprints we ran. The man was Juergen Schroeder, born in Germany and raised in Edmonton, Alberta, but he moved to Ithaca, New York when he was only fifteen. He was not quite thirty years old, and he's been the main suspect in at least fifteen different murders since he turned twenty. In each case, police were fairly certain he was their guy, but there just wasn't enough viable evidence for charges."

"Sounds like a pro, then, just like we thought. What about the woman?"

"Her name was Bernadette Jones, and she was twenty-six. She and Schroeder have been together since she was about eigheen, and she's long been considered an accomplice to his crimes. Again, there was just never enough evidence to make any charges happen."

"Well," Sam said, "at least we know who they were. I'm going to put some of our people on digging into their backgrounds and trying to find out what they've been up to around here. We've all come to the conclusion that they were preparing another attack on the company, or they would've already left the area. The only question is whether they've already got something set up and ready to happen, or if they were still working on it when we took them down."

"I don't know, but let me know what I can do to help. I got a call from John Pemberton already this morning, and he's confident the review will be finished sometime today. I should be back on the case by morning."

"Good," Sam said with a chuckle. "I'm not too sure what I think of Mr. Storch just yet."

"Jim's okay," Karen said. "He just doesn't have any experience to speak of. The main thing I like about him is the fact that he's smart enough to realize that."

"All right," Sam said. "You're on speakerphone on the conference table. Stay with us for a few minutes, okay?"

"Sure, no problem," Karen said.

He turned back to his team at the table. "I think we need to start looking at what these two were up to the last few weeks. We know they set the shooting up long before the show began, so they had several weeks to work on the next phase of whatever plan was laid out. Anybody got any suggestions on where we start?"

"I'd like to look at the apartment," Walter said. "And their car, if they have one. I want to see if I can get any ideas about what they were going to do next."

"That's an excellent idea," Sam said. "Karen?"

"I'll clear it now," Karen replied. "You can go whenever you like this morning. Just don't forget to send your tech people out. God only knows what they'll find."

"Okay. What else?"

"We need to find out anything we can about how they were paying their bills," Darren said. "They undoubtedly had some kind of financial arrangements, even if it was just a prepaid debit card of some sort. That might give us some kind of leads on where their money was coming from."

"All right," Sam said. "Darren, can I put you on that?"

"No problem, boss," Darren said. "And while I'm at it, I'll see what I can find out about where they called home. They probably have bank accounts and cell phones and internet and everything else, wherever they come from."

"Do it. Summer, I want you to try to find out if they held cover jobs or had any friends around here. Anybody they hung out with, anybody they spent time with, we need to know as much as possible about them."

"You got it," Summer said.

"Okay, then. Let's all get to it."

"Sounds good, Sam," Karen said. "Call if you need me." There was a click as the line went dead.

Summer turned to Walter and Steve as they got out of their chairs. "I'm heading over to the apartment building now," she said. "You guys want to follow me?"

"We'll be right on your tail," Steve said. They followed her out of the office, while Darren stayed behind for a moment.

"Sam," he said. "I had a thought, and you're not going to like it. What if these two weren't working on their own?"

"What do you mean?" Sam asked, his eyes narrowed.

"Professional assassins are, by definition, serial killers. Many of them display the same personality patterns we find in serial killers who are not motivated by money. If I were to build a profile on these two, I'd start with the fact that the woman seems to have sacrificed herself to try to let the man get away, which indicates that he was the dominant one in their partnership. When we find serial killers working together, we usually find that one of them is dominant over the other, but there's always an underlying relationship of some sort. In cases where we've seen couples, that relationship is almost always at least somewhat romantic. They tend to be dependent upon one another, and the killings are usually related to some sexual component of their relationship."

"Okay," Sam said. "So, it seems odd the guy would run out and leave the girl behind him to be killed?"

Darren nodded. "Yes, if we were talking about a typical murder couple. There have been a couple of cases, though, where the couple turned out to be non-romantic. In those cases, both the male and the female were subservient to a third individual, the actual alpha. A couple like that would probably still have one member dominant over the other, but that relationship takes a back seat to the primary. If I look at this that way, the woman was the most expendable. The alpha, whoever it is, would have expected her to sacrifice herself for her partner, so he would think no more of her loss than if a pet had died."

Sam stared at him for a moment. "You're right," he said, "I don't like it. What you're telling me is that they have a boss out there somewhere, the guy who is really calling the shots on this thing. Right?"

"I'm afraid that's how it looks," Darren said. "I'll start digging, see if I can find any connections they had that might be the alpha."

"Call me the instant you find anything," Sam said. "I don't care what time it is or what I'm doing. If there's an alpha out there, that's our top priority right now."

"Yes, sir," Darren said, and then he headed for his own cubicle to get started.

SUMMER, STEVE, AND Walter arrived at the apartment building along with Q and his tech crew, and they all took the elevator directly to the third floor of the building, where a uniformed officer was sitting in a folding chair just outside the ruined door to apartment 3G. They flashed their IDs, and the officer nodded.

"Detective Parks called," he said. "Go on in."

Steve took down one end of each strip of the crime scene tape that crisscrossed the door and pushed what was left of the door open. The six of them stepped inside and stopped, looking at the large blood stain just ahead of them.

"Q," Steve said, "let's give Walter a few minutes before you start in, okay?"

The stocky man nodded. "No problem," he said. "We're just gonna stand back and watch."

Walter stood where he was for a moment, just looking all around the area he could see. They were standing just inside the living room of the apartment, and the blood stain was eight feet ahead of them, just in front of the entrance to a short hallway that led to a bedroom and the bathroom. The kitchen and dining area were through another door that was in the wall to their left.

Slowly, Walter walked around the living room. He looked closely at the sofa and chairs, the coffee table with some magazines and a laptop sitting on it, then at the entertainment center that held a cheap, flashy stereo and a large LED television set. He spotted the remote for the TV on the arm of a chair and pressed its power button. The screen lit up, and a popular talk show came on.

He turned off the TV, then sat down on the couch and looked at the laptop. It was on, so he touched the space bar to make the screen come to life. A browser was open, and they were suddenly looking at a live video feed from just inside the main entrance of the building.

"They knew we were coming," Summer said. "They saw the police coming through the door."

Steve nodded. "Looks that way."

Walter took a look at the browser history, and found that it had visited the Web Wide Awards website numerous times. There was also a number of visits to YouTube, and several to a Gmail account. He clicked on that one, but it was set to log out when closed, so there was no username or password.

Walter got up from the couch and walked to the edge of the blood stain. He stood and looked at it for a moment, then turned and went into the bedroom. Steve and Summer followed, standing in the doorway and watching him as he looked at the bed, opened some dresser drawers, and looked in the closet. From what they could see, the woman's clothes appeared to have been in the dresser, while the man's clothing was hanging and on shelves in the closet. On the shelf above the hanging clothes in the closet, Walter found a box of shotgun shells and another of thirty-eight caliber ammunition. He left both where he found them.

Two suitcases and an overnight bag were tucked neatly under the bed, and each of the two occupants seemed to have a couple pairs of shoes sitting neatly together by the wall.

Walter came out and skirted around the blood to get into the kitchen. The cabinets and refrigerator seemed to be fully stocked, and there were two six-packs of beer in the refrigerator. A glance in the trashcan revealed a few empty cans, along with the typical garbage associated with the kitchen. There were a few dirty dishes in the sink, but the kitchen itself was very clean.

Looking under the sink, Walter found a number of different cleaning products. He looked at a few of them, then put them back and closed the cabinet.

Across the hall, Walter walked into the bathroom. Like the kitchen, it was quite clean. There was nothing in the medicine cabinet over the sink, but a cup held a pair of toothbrushes and a tube of a popular toothpaste.

"They weren't ready to carry out another attack," Walter said. "They already did what they came here to do, and they were just waiting for further orders. It might have nothing to do with the award company."

Steve lowered his eyebrows and looked at Walter. "Nothing to do with them? You think shooting that kid was the only attack they were going to make on the company?"

"It might be about the company," Walter said. "The company was definitely targeted by somebody, but these people were waiting for orders about what to do next. Somebody told them to wait here until they were told what to do, or were told to leave and go somewhere else."

Summer cocked her head to one side. "What makes you think that, Walter?"

"They were watching the company's website, but they weren't posting anything on it. They were checking emails several times a day, but they weren't sending any out. Emails were their only means of communication, because there are no social media accounts on the computer, and there are no phones or cell phone chargers in the apartment. There are no tools, no supplies to make bombs or poison, and the only guns they had with them were the ones they used to try to protect themselves.

They've been keeping a low profile and trying to act like a normal couple as far as any of the neighbors could tell, but the man had been sleeping on the couch while the woman slept alone in the bedroom. All of that told me they weren't really interested in the company at all, except as part of their job. That first attack was done, but then they were told to wait here for whatever was their next job."

Steve and Summer looked at one another, then Steve nodded. "He's making sense," he said. "Anything else we need here, Walter?"

Walter shook his head. "No. We need to go back to Sam."

They went out to the living room and Steve told Q that they were done. He and Walter went to the elevator, while Summer began knocking on neighboring doors.

14

"So, what you're telling me," Sam asked, "is that our mystery couple might not have been planning any further attack on Web Wide Awards? Walter, what makes you think that?"

"Because," Walter said. "If they were already working on a new plan or had something set up, there should've been some kind of evidence of it in the apartment. They weren't trying to do anything, they were just hiding. They were waiting for some kind of orders, but they hadn't gotten any yet. If they had other weapons or equipment, it was stored somewhere else, so they may turn up eventually in storage lockers that go unpaid. We'll know more about it when Q gets into their emails. That was the only means of communication they had, so that has to be how they were supposed to get their orders."

Sam leaned back in his chair and steepled his fingers under his chin. "This is probably one of the most confusing cases I've ever seen," he said. "From what little we know so far, I would have bet just about anything they were planning another attack."

"There is going to be another attack on somebody," Walter said. "It just wasn't ordered yet."

Sam had invited Darren to sit in on the conversation, and now he turned to him. "Any thoughts?"

"I'd have to say that I agree with Walter," Darren said. "I had already come to the conclusion that these two were underlings, both under the control of some greater alpha. That alpha is still out there, and so far we've got nothing to indicate who it might be."

Sam bit the inside of his cheek and shook his head. "Denny told me something a couple days ago," he said. "There's a European assassin who had been spotted in the U.S. The last time he was seen was in St. Louis, I think, at the airport, maybe. We had come to the conclusion that he probably wasn't involved in this, but now I'm starting to wonder."

He leaned forward to his computer and opened his emails, then found the one Denny had sent him with Reynard's picture in it. He opened the photo, and then his jaw dropped.

"Son of a bitch," he said. "I am such an idiot. When Indie got the pictures of Schroeder and Jones, the couple who was killed last night, I thought they looked familiar." He turned the monitor so that the others could see it.

It was the photo he had looked at before, showing Reynard with a red circle around his face. He was apparently walking with and talking to a man and a woman, and it was obvious they were the same couple from the night before, Juergen Schroeder and Bernadette Jones.

"There's our alpha," Darren said. "Do we have any idea where he is now?"

Sam shook his head. "Denny said the FBI missed him at St. Louis, and now he's in the wind. If they were working with him and waiting for orders, then God only knows what they might've done next."

Darren was leaning close to the monitor. "Is that Pierre Reynard? It is, I recognize him. We used to call him the French Fox, and that's only partly because of his name. He was always able to sneak into and out of just about anyplace, and anyone he agreed to hit was doomed from that moment on. He was in the States a few years ago, when I was with BAU. We tried every possible way to corner him and take him down, and he always walked away."

Sam pulled the monitor around and forwarded the email to Indie. "This is a long shot, but I'm going to see if Herman might be able to find some trace of this guy." He picked up his phone and dialed his wife.

"Indie? Babe, I just sent you an email with a photograph. The guy with his face circled in red is apparently the man in charge of this whole thing, an alpha assassin who was actually running the two we got last night. That picture was taken in St. Louis, at the airport there. Do you think there's any chance Herman could track him down?"

"I can put him to work on it," she said. "I'll start with searching the archives of the St. Louis airport security videos, then move out from there to other cameras close by. I might be able to get some idea of which direction he went, but actually finding him would probably be impossible."

"I know that," Sam said. "I'm just hoping you might pick up some kind of lead on where he went after St. Louis. With any luck, he might've gotten onto a plane so we can check its destination."

"I'm feeding his photo into Herman now," she said. "I'll let you know what he finds. Sam, the time stamp on this photo is from two and half months ago, did you know that?"

"Yeah, I know," Sam said. "Again, I'm just hoping to pick up a lead."

"Okay. I'll get back to you."

"I DON'T KNOW ABOUT you," Jade said to Stacy, "but I'm about ready for some lunch."

"Yes, that sounds good," Stacy replied with a grin. "Shall we eat in the cafeteria?"

"Works for me," Jade said. "The food was pretty good yesterday. I could eat another of those taco salads."

"Oh, you should try the chicken with dumplings that I had yesterday," Stacy said. "It was incredibly good. I'm going to have it again."

The two of them got up and left the office they were sharing, which was directly adjacent to Annie Porter's office. Jade poked her head in to let Annie know where they were going, but the woman was nowhere in sight.

"It's lunchtime," Jade said. "She'll figure it out. Let's go."

They went to the elevator and rode it down to the third floor, where the cafeteria was located. They could smell the delicious variety of foods as soon as they stepped into the hallway, and Jade couldn't resist a soft moan of epicurean delight.

"Oh, I can smell the chicken from here," she said. "I think you're right, I'm going to try the chicken and dumplings today."

They made it into the cafeteria and both of them were surprised at the number of people who smiled, waved or called their names. A couple of women sitting at a table by themselves motioned for Jade and Stacy to get their trays, then come and sit down. Jade shot back a thumbs up, and they started through the line.

When they were finished and had paid, they made their way to the table and sat down. The women waiting for them had been friendly since they met the day before, and had even been helpful on a couple of occasions.

Bridget Bristow, who was short and dumpy with pink hair, reached over and patted Jade on the hand as she sat. "Hey, Jade, how are you doing? Are they driving you crazy yet?"

Paulette Berkowitz, her friend and coworker in the printing room, rolled her eyes. "Geez, Bridget," she said. "I don't think anybody's going to drive her crazy, she's Ms. Porter's assistant. Nobody wants to get on her bad side, right, Jade?"

Jade chuckled. "I really don't think it's as bad as all that," she said. "Everyone's been very nice."

"Well, that's good," Bridget said. "Believe me, it's not always that way around here."

"Oh, really? What do you mean?"

"She's just running off at the mouth," Paulette said. "This is one of the best places I've ever worked."

"Oh, it's a great place to work," Bridget continued. "But not everybody is nice all the time. I mean, you let traffic slow down a little bit, and even Mr. Morton can become quite a bear. Ms. Porter, she's usually a sweetheart, but I've even heard her do some yelling at people now and then."

"Which probably means they had it coming," Paulette said. "Ignore her, dears, she's our in-house gossip columnist. If there's anybody in the whole company you got a question about, she can tell you a whole lot more than you want to know."

Jade grinned. "Oh, is that so? What can you tell me about Jacqueline Bridges? She was trying to show me how to do the daily reports earlier, and she seemed so nervous I was afraid she was gonna have a heart attack."

Bridget smiled from ear to ear. "Jackie? Oh, my goodness, Jackie is almost always like that. If you didn't know better, you'd swear the world was fixing to cave in on her pretty much all the time. I've tried to talk to her a few times, but it's all you can do to get her to speak. It's like she's scared to death of everything and everybody, I swear."

Jade nodded. "That's pretty much the impression I got," she said. "And yet, she's in charge of doing the daily traffic and income reports. It made me wonder if she's ever made a mistake and gotten in trouble over it, you know?"

"Well, I won't say there haven't been a few discrepancies along the line," Bridget said conspiratorially, "but she always seems to live through it, somehow. About seven months ago, she got called up to Mr. Morton's office at the end of the day, something about her totals not matching up to the ones that came out of the accounting office. Usually, getting called up there at the end of the day means you're out of a job, so we all thought she was gonna get fired, but she was back at her desk the next morning. I don't think there's been any issues since then, though."

Jade narrowed her eyes. "What about the accounting department? Did anybody get in trouble over there?"

"Nope. You'd think somebody would have, if it turned out Jackie was right and they were wrong, but nobody had any problems that I heard about."

"That does seem kind of odd," Jade said. The conversation continued for a while as they ate, occasionally touching on other employees that Bridget seemed to have her eye on.

When lunch was over, Jade and Stacy went back to their office. Jade sat at her computer and started looking at the reports that Jackie submitted every day, and going back over the last year of them. She was surprised to find that some of them had been edited, the totals changed after the report had been submitted, but the computer recorded all the edits as being done by Jackie herself.

Just as glaring was the fact that, seven months earlier, Jackie had suddenly started submitting her reports an hour later than she had previously done. Prior to that time, her report preceded the report of the accounting office; since then, however, it was always submitted only a minute or two before Jackie would leave for the day.

Jade switched over to the accounting office and examined their daily totals on the sales ledgers. All of them matched up perfectly to Jackie's, but in some cases, it matched up to the edited version rather than the original.

"I think we need to have a talk with Jackie," Jade whispered to Stacy. "Do you think we're secure in here?"

"I would not trust it," Stacy replied the same way. "I can see at least two dozen places a microphone could be hidden in here. With the technology this company deals with, it would surprise me if they aren't recording most of their employees."

Jade nodded, then got up and walked out of the office. Stacy jumped up to follow as she walked straight to the elevator, then went to the income bookkeeping office where Jackie worked. That was on the fourth floor, only two doors down from the main accounting office.

She stepped inside and caught Jackie's attention, then asked the girl to step into the hallway.

"Hey, Jackie," she said. "Listen, I want to talk with you some more about what you do, because it's really interesting, but I have to run a couple of errands. Are you super busy right now?"

Still nervous, Jackie glanced at her desk, but then she turned to Jade and shook her head. "I'm not real busy," she said softly. "What do you want to know?"

"Well, I've got to run and pick up some medicine from the pharmacy, and I have to do it right now. Would you ride along with me, so we can talk without wasting a lot of time?"

"Oh, I might get in trouble if I leave..."

"No, you won't," Jade said. "I have plenty of authority over that. Come on, we'll only be gone a half hour or so. I'll buy you a Starbucks."

The mention of Starbucks actually got a tiny smile out of the girl. "Okay, then," she said. The three of them, Jade, Stacy, and Jackie, took the elevator to the first floor and walked out toward Jade's car. They climbed inside and left the parking lot, and Jade looked at Jackie.

"Why is it that you only file your reports just before you leave for the day?" Jade asked her.

Jackie turned beet red. "Well, I—I have to," she said. "Sometimes our totals don't match up with accounting, and they have to. Mr. Morton said I have to make sure at the end of each day that they match, even if I have to go in the computer and change them, so I just do mine last."

"Jackie, do you have any idea why they wouldn't match up? I mean, you get the same data that accounting does, right?"

Jackie looked down at her hands, which were fidgeting in her lap. "Maybe we make mistakes," she mumbled.

"I don't think anyone in your office is making any mistakes," Jade said. "I think your totals are perfect and accurate, and you're being forced to fudge them because somebody is hiding some money. Am I right?"

15

Jackie continued to look at her hands in her lap and said nothing. After a moment, Jade reached over and took one of the girl's hands in her own.

"Jackie, do you know where that money is going?" Jade asked softly. "You're not in any trouble, I promise you. It's just that my job is to look at everything, and when I saw the edits that change your original totals, that raised a red flag for me. The only reason for you to have to fudge your totals is to make sure they match up with what the accounting department is reporting. The differences don't look like a whole lot day by day, but over the last six months they've added up to well over a million dollars. That's not enough to make much difference when they file their corporate taxes, so I'm pretty sure that money is being spent, somewhere. If I'm going to do my job properly, then I need to find out where."

"I don't know," the girl said suddenly as tears began to roll down her cheeks. "I don't have anything to do with where money goes, I just have to watch when it comes in. Everything goes out through accounting, either through payables or disbursements."

Jade squeezed her hand. "I told you, you're not in trouble. Tell me this, why is it there is a separate department to monitor the income? Why isn't that handled in accounting, too?"

Jackie swallowed and her face made a grimace. "Mr. Morton says safety comes from redundancy," she said, "so he wanted to split all the bookkeeping into different parts. My office adds up all the money that comes in, then it goes to accounting, where they double-check it and figure up what part of it is taxable and what part isn't, then they send it to payables. That's where the bills get paid from, and after that it goes to disbursements. Disbursements takes care of things like the executive payrolls, travel allowances, bonuses, prize awards, and stuff like that."

"I hope you'll forgive me," Jade said, "but that actually sounds like a recipe for disaster. Are there ever any discrepancies between accounting and payables or disbursements?"

Jackie shrugged. "I don't know," she said. "I can't see those from my computer."

"Okay, let's back up a bit. Do you actually handle any of the money, either in cash or by having control over any specific accounts?"

Jackie hesitated for a second, then nodded. "Whenever there's a big local event, like the award show the other night, all the cash from the box office, from merchandise sales, everything, it all comes straight to our office to be counted. A couple of the girls there, they stack all the bills up neatly and put them in the counter, and the change just gets dumped into a machine that sorts it and counts it all at once. When that gets done, it's all locked into transport boxes, and then the bank sends people over to pick it up with an armored car. That's the only time we deal with any cash. Everything else, all the money that comes through the internet, goes through several different PayPal accounts, so we have to check each account and report all the totals, but then it's up to accounting to transfer the money from there to the appropriate bank accounts."

"And you do this every single day, right? The same procedures, over and over?"

Jackie nodded. "Yeah. It's boring, but it pays good."

"And yet, somehow you seem to make a mistake in the totals every day. Jackie, if that were actually true, you'd probably be fired. When was the last time you got a raise?"

Jackie's voice dropped to a whisper. "Three months ago," she said softly.

"And you got another one three months before that," Jade said. "And the month before that, that's when you started changing when you input your totals. Now, while the missing money might not save the company a lot on their taxes, I'm pretty sure the IRS would get really upset about losing any money at all. How do you think all this would look to them?"

Jackie slowly raised her face and turned to look Jade in the eye. "It'll look like I'm the one doing it, won't it?"

"Well, on the surface, that's definitely what it looks like," Jade said. "If I hadn't dug a lot deeper, I would've thought you were embezzling money. I was still thinking that until a little while ago, when I heard about Mr. Morton calling you into his office. The rumor went around that your totals were wrong and everybody expected you to get fired, but you didn't. A month later, you got a big raise, and three months later you got another one. That tells me that you were ordered to do something, and you're being rewarded for obeying orders. That sound about right?"

A lot of Jackie's nervousness seemed to be gone. "Ma'am," she said, "if you tell anybody we had this conversation, I'm probably out of a job. You know that, right? I got kids, I'm just trying to take care of them, and that's all."

"I know, I checked your personnel jacket. Tell me what's going on, Jackie."

Jackie looked over her shoulder at Stacy, who smiled at her from the back seat and gave her a thumbs up, then turned back to Jade. "Mr. Morton called me in that day because there was an error, but it wasn't in my totals. It was caused by the fact that he had moved some money around for some kind of special project, but he said it had to be a big secret until it was done. He had somebody in accounting who could actually handle moving the money without leaving a trail, but he needed to be sure that all the figures here matched up. The only way he could do that without changing the entire bookkeeping procedures was if he had somebody he could trust in income bookkeeping." She shrugged. "He said if he could trust me to help him, he'd give me a raise. He had to wait a month, so nobody would think it was funny that I got a raise right then, but I'm making more money than I ever have in my life."

"Which makes it a lot easier to take care of your kids," Jade said, "but also to overlook the fact that you could be the one to get in trouble over this. I know Mr. Morton seems like a very nice man, but I'm pretty sure he'd throw you under the bus if the IRS started asking questions."

Jackie grimaced again. "I figured that out myself," she said. "I asked him about it one day, and that's why I got another raise."

Jade nodded her head. "That makes sense. He's trying to keep you happy, so that nothing blows up in his face. Now, I've only got one more question, and I hope you can give me the answer. What is the secret project he's using the money for?"

"I honestly don't know," Jackie said. "But I can tell you this. He says it's going to make him richer than he ever dreamed he could be."

JADE AND STACY HAD just gotten back to their office, letting Jackie go back to her own, when Sam called.

"You girls doing okay out there?" Sam asked.

"It's been quite an interesting experience," Jade said. "I've actually got a few things I'd like to discuss with you, but not over the phone. I was thinking of clocking out early here, anyway, so can I drop by and see you?"

"Well, I was actually calling to tell you that we believe the threat to Web Wide Awards has been neutralized. There don't seem to be any further attacks planned, but this may not be entirely over for us just yet. Why don't you come on by, and we'll sit down and discuss it?"

"Sounds good," Jade said. "We'll be there shortly." She ended the call and looked at Stacy. "Looks like we may be done here," he said. "Sam thinks the problem is over as far as this company is concerned."

Stacy made a pouty face. "Already? I was enjoying this. Most of my friends are men, I do not have a lot of girlfriends."

Jade grinned. "Well, you do now," she said. "You can hang out with me anytime you want."

She got up and went next door, where Annie was leaning back in her chair, a big smile on her face. She had a pair of earbuds in her ears and was just about dancing in her chair to whatever music she was listening to. She must've sensed Jade's presence in the doorway, because she opened her eyes suddenly and seemed mildly startled.

"Oh! Sorry, I didn't hear you come in."

Jade smiled. "No problem. You seem to be in an awfully good mood. Something going on?"

Annie smiled again, and her face wore an expression of relief. "I just got off the phone with Canterbury Soft Drinks," she said. "After the shooting, they were talking about removing their sponsorship from the company, dumping us. They just told me they're going to stick with us, and they just committed to doubling their ad budget with us. That'll make the company another eleven million dollars a year, isn't that great?"

Jade's eyes went wide, and her smile matched Annie's own. "Wow, that's awesome," she said. "Listen, I hate to barge in to your party, but can I have a minute?"

Annie nodded and motioned for her to enter. "Sure, come on in."

Jade entered the office and closed the door behind herself, then sat in the chair in front of Annie's desk. "I'm going to be leaving early today," she said. "I need to go back to the office and talk with Mr. Prichard, but he seems to think your company is no longer in any danger. I just thought you'd like to know that before I leave."

A look of relief flashed across Annie's face. "Do you really think so? God, that would be even more good news, because this has been a nightmare the last few days. I'm just so glad Max is going to be okay." She shivered. "I don't know if I could have handled it if he had died."

"Well, the last I heard, he was doing well. He should probably be going home pretty soon, and hopefully he'll be making new episodes of Freaktown High again very soon."

"I'm sure he will," Annie said with a smile. "He really is quite a genius when it comes to video production." She looked at Jade. "So, will you be coming back tomorrow? Or is this goodbye?"

"I don't know the answer to that, right at the moment," Jade said. "I guess it depends on what Mr. Prichard has to say. If it's really over for you guys, then you might not need me anymore."

Or I might need to come back and figure out just what your boyfriend is doing with all that hidden money, Jade thought to herself. *There's got to be something fishy about that, I just can't put my finger on it yet.*

"Okay, then I guess you'll let me know?"

"I sure will," Jade said, rising from her chair. "And if I don't see you again, I want you to know that I wish you the best of luck in the future."

Annie echoed the phrase, and Jade left her office. Stacy was waiting in the hallway, and the two of them took the elevator down and walked out the door.

"So, and now that we are away from there, what do you think of the things Jackie told you?" Stacy asked.

Jade shook her head. "I'm not sure what to think," she said. "There's something fishy going on, some reason John Morton wants to have money available he can spend without anyone knowing about it. In my experience, the only time hiding money is good is if you're saving up for some kind of major surprise for someone you love. You know, like buying an engagement ring, or surprising somebody with an expensive dinner, that sort of thing."

Stacy shrugged. "Perhaps Morton is buying Ms. Porter something very expensive?"

"Could be, I guess," Jade said. "I keep going back to the fact that he gave Jackie a couple of big raises. He really wants her to keep it secret, and nothing I've seen gives any indication that Annie knows about it at all. With the kind of money we're looking at, about the only gift he could surprise her with would be a yacht. No, he told Jackie it was going to make him richer than ever. That makes me think there's some kind of secret deal going on, something under the table that might look bad if it came out."

Traffic was light, and they were back at the Windlass headquarters building in thirty-five minutes. Jade found a space in the parking lot and the two girls walked inside, then hugged each other as Stacy turned toward the section of the building reserved for the security agents. Jade walked directly to Sam's office and smiled at Jenna.

"I'm supposed to see Mr. Prichard," she said.

"Yep," Jenna said. She picked up the phone and pushed the button, then said, "Jade Miller is here." A moment later, she'd hung up the phone and motioned for Jade to go in.

16

Sam was on his feet when she entered and motioned for her to take the chair in front of his desk. He waited until she sat down, then settled into his own chair again.

"You said you had some things you want to talk about," Sam said. "Go ahead."

"Well, it might not be that big a deal," Jade began, "but my gut is telling me there's something fishy going on out at Web Wide Awards. I found out that Morton is one of those people who doesn't like to let his left hand know what his right hand is doing. He has all of the bookkeeping split up into four separate sections, and the girl running one of them has been pushed into helping him hide a fair amount of money."

Sam raised his eyebrows. "Well, the IRS might be interested in that," he said, "but that's not something we should have to report. Under our contract with the client, anything we learn in the course of our investigation that is outside its scope falls under privilege; we're actually not supposed to reveal such things, ever."

"I don't think it's a tax issue," Jade said. "To be perfectly honest, I get this really tingly feeling down deep in my gut that makes me think this money is somehow connected to what happened at the award show."

Sam leaned forward and his eyebrows came down. "Are you saying you think Morton might have been directly involved somehow?"

Jade grimaced, and shook her head. "I can't say that, necessarily," she said. "I just feel like there's some kind of connection between the fact he's hiding what amounts to over a million dollars in the last six months, and the fact that somebody tried to arrange to have the company ruined."

Sam looked at her for a moment, then asked, "Jade, did you find anything while you were there that might indicate a connection between Web Wide Awards and any of the other award organizations?"

She shook her head again. "No," she said. "If anything, I think they consider Starbright to be their biggest competition. John and Annie have both been over to London to talk with Starbright's Board of Directors about different things, mostly stuff that has to do with the indie video industry as a whole. I don't think there's any love lost between the two of them, but they both seem to have some sense of responsibility when it comes to how the industry is growing. You know there's talk of regulating it, of the government trying to impose some kind of rules on what can be independently published in video."

"I read a couple of articles on that," Sam said. "I really don't think it has much chance of getting anywhere, at least not here in the U.S. Europe, on the other hand, might actually impose some limitations sometime in the next couple of years, but even there I don't think it will last long. Indie film has always been pretty popular in Europe."

"Europe and the U.K. do things differently than we do here in the States," Jade said. "That might work to our advantage over here."

SUMMER HAD SPENT THE day speaking with neighbors of the shooters, and finding out that they were the type of people who stayed to themselves. Neighbors said they always smiled and were friendly if they happened to run into them in the hallways, but they didn't socialize and didn't seem to have any friends.

They also didn't seem to have jobs. There were several theories around the building as to what they might do for a living, but the general consensus was that they had money and seemed to be very wrapped up in one another. They were always close when they were seen, often holding hands as they walked through the halls, but those were the only obvious signs of affection.

They didn't own a car, and some neighbors claimed to have seen them using public transportation occasionally, while others said they'd spotted them getting into taxi cabs. After several hours of asking the same questions and getting the same answers, Summer was getting frustrated.

She was just leaving the building when she ran into Harvey coming in the front door. He broke into a smile, but the glare she gave him melted it away almost instantly.

"Look, it wasn't my fault," he said. "When we got to the building and you were there, I didn't have any choice but to tell her I knew you. It wasn't me that told her you were an investigator, it was one of the cops. Soon as she found that out, she was all over me to get an interview. It wasn't my idea, I promise."

Harvey stared at her pursed lips for a moment, thinking that some of his worst moments in life had begun with pursed lips on a woman. He was just about to try again to appease her when she shrugged and gave him a grin.

"I understand," she said. "Just don't let it happen again, okay? I really don't want to have to break her nose, but if she ever tries to get in my face again, I just might."

Harvey breathed a sigh of relief. "I will do my level best to keep her completely across the city from where you're at," he said. "But if you hit the scanners, she'll hear it and then I won't be able to stop her. My job is to follow her around with the camera, but she's actually the boss."

"Okay, okay," Summer said. "Sorry I took it out on you. I just don't need my face plastered all over the news, right? Sometimes I have to go undercover, and it's hard to do that when everybody knows what you look like."

"Yeah, I understand. Can I ask a couple questions, though? Just for my own curiosity?"

"Sure, as long as they don't get back to you know who. What do you want to know?"

"Well, those people that lived across from me," Harvey said. "They really were the ones who shot that kid at the arena, is that right?"

"Yes, that's true."

Harvey shook his head. "How sick is that? Any idea why they did it?"

Summer shrugged. "We figure they were trying to hurt the award company. Make them look bad, you know, some kid getting shot while receiving their award?"

"Huh," Harvey said, his eyes narrowed. "Seems to me it would have the opposite effect."

"Why would you say that? The company should have made sure the kid was safe, right?"

"Well, yeah, within reason," Harvey said. "But—well, corporate crisis management is something that I've kind of studied, because I originally majored in business administration. One of the most famous corporate crises in history was the Tylenol poisoning scandal. Twelve people died after they took Tylenol that had been laced with cyanide, back in 1982. Now, Johnson & Johnson handled it pretty well, recalling a hundred million dollars' worth of their product and working with the police and FBI to find out what happened, but the thing is that, when it was all over, Tylenol came out bigger and stronger than ever. While the people who died were victims of the killer who put cyanide in the bottles, the public saw Tylenol as the real victim."

"Well, yeah, that was before my time, but I've heard about it. Still, you can't really expect that kind of response."

"You can't? Pepsi had a case once where people were putting syringes in cans and claiming they found them there, and while it turned out to be a hoax, the public thought Pepsi was the victim. Same thing happened, Pepsi came out of it stronger. There have been a lot of cases like that, to the point that some companies have been known to orchestrate a crisis in order to build themselves up."

Summer stared at him for a moment. "Are you trying to say you think this could have been some kind of publicity stunt?"

Harvey shrugged. "I've seen cases where people stoop to some pretty low levels, in my studies. People have even been known to sacrifice their own kids to gain sympathy, because it works. If you can make your company look like a victim, your customers and clients will rally around you. It's happened over and over in recent history, and I wouldn't put it past anybody in business today. Believe me, it's something every business admin student learns about."

"Harvey," Summer said, "I take back every nasty thing I said about you last night." She grabbed his shirt and pulled him close, kissed him quickly on the lips, and then hurried away.

Harvey stood there, staring as she vanished through the door.

SAM'S PHONE RANG, AND Jenna told him Summer was calling. "Hey, Summer. Learn anything interesting?"

"Oh, boy, did I ever," Summer said. "You know, everybody expected Web Wide Awards to be seriously damaged by the shooting, but what's happened is that they seem to be more popular than ever. I ran into an old friend of mine and we got talking about that, and it turns out this is a fairly common phenomenon. He was telling me about the Tylenol poisonings back in the eighties, and something about Pepsi, but it seems like whenever a company is attacked this way, it's not uncommon for the public to rally around them as long as they at least try to handle the situation honestly and diplomatically."

"Yes, I've heard of things along that line before, myself. A few of us have discussed the possibility that someone might've anticipated this kind of result. Are you leaning that direction, now?"

"I'm leaning so hard I'm about to fall over," she said. "Sam, I can't help wondering if John Morton might be involved in this somewhere. Do you have any reason why I shouldn't explore that possibility?"

"Everything I've seen indicates he's clean," Sam said, "but you're not the first person to wonder. What have you got in mind?"

"Why, just being my normal, gracious little self. Do you think you could arrange a meeting between me and him? I mean, just me and him? If he's dirty, Sam, I'll find out."

Sam bit his bottom lip for a moment. "Summer, John Morton is going to be speaking at the big internet conference in New York next week. If he's involved in this, we need to know it before that happens. I'll call him now and see if I can set something up. He's probably going to be busy tonight, but we'll see what he has to say. Just do me a favor and don't lay it on too thick, all right? Remember, he has a girlfriend."

"Sam, if he isn't dirty, what I got in mind won't affect him. If he is, then we need to know it. Right?"

"Right," Sam said. "I'll call you back in a few minutes."

He cut off that call and dialed Morton again. The phone rang three times before the man answered, and he sounded slightly out of breath.

"John? Sam Prichard again. Are you okay?"

"Oh, yeah, Sam," Morton said. "I've been out running. I do a five-mile run every day, right after work. Keeps the brain sharp."

"Oh, sorry to interrupt, then. I was wondering if you would have some time to meet with one of my investigators this evening? We've got a few questions that we think will help us to wrap this case up."

"Sure, no problem. You want to just send him to the house?"

"Actually, I'd like you to meet my investigator alone. Have you had dinner yet?"

"No, not yet. Annie is spending some time with a friend of hers this evening, so dinner would be okay. When and where?"

"How about Vesta? Say, seven thirty?"

"Sure, it's not too far away. I was just getting home, so I'll take a quick shower and be on the way. Who am I meeting?"

"Her name is Summer Raines," Sam said. "She'll know you, so she'll be waiting just inside the front entrance."

"No problem," Morton said. "I'll see her there."

Sam called Summer back. "Okay, you're meeting him for dinner at Vesta at seven thirty. Good luck, and let me know what you find out."

"I sure will," she said.

Sam hung up the phone, then decided to call it a day. He headed out the door, pulled up at home about forty-five minutes later, and Kenzie met him at the door once again. He scooped her up into a hug, got a kiss and a second hug, then went into the kitchen to find Indie.

SUMMER HAD JUST GOTTEN home when she called Sam, and stripped while she was waiting for him to call back. As soon as he confirmed her meeting with Morton, she stepped into the shower, scrubbed thoroughly and washed her hair, then dried off with a large, fluffy towel. She stood naked in her bathroom while she blow-dried her hair and put on her make-up, then took a moment to examine the scars she had collected.

On her right thigh was a round white spot where she had once taken a bullet while on a security detail, protecting an American politician who was touring American military facilities in Afghanistan. Her left breast bore a more recent wound, where a bullet had passed all the way through. Fortunately, it had been a small bullet, and had been fired through thick glass and slowed down considerably, so it hadn't done nearly as much damage as it might have. There were simply two round, pinkish welts on each side.

On her left side, just above her hipbone, there was a thin scar that was the result of a knife-wielding maniac she had once encountered. She hadn't even been on the job at the time, but this man had decided he found her appealing and wanted to peel her. He managed one quick stab before she broke his arm, his nose, and his jaw.

All in all, things could have been worse, she figured. While scars weren't necessarily appealing, the rest of her body was still in as good a shape as it was when she was a cheerleader back in high school. She worked hard to keep it that way, and it paid off in many different kinds of dividends.

Inventory complete, she stepped out of the bath and went to her closet. She slithered into thong and pantyhose, chose a fairly simple bra, and then a midnight blue dress that clung in all the right places. She lifted it up and let it drop down over herself, quickly adjusted where it needed adjusting, and then contorted her arms to do the buttons in the back. A pair of two-inch heels gave her legs the perfect shape, and one more quick touch up with the hairbrush meant she was ready to go.

She collected her phone and purse, then headed out the door to her car, a 1982 Jaguar XJS convertible. The car had originally come with a V12 engine, but Summer liked a little power under the hood. She had thought the car was sexy when she saw it, but after owning it for a month, it just didn't have the *oomph* she wanted. She had been dating a man at the time who was notorious for building high-powered hot rods, and she wheedled him until he agreed to make a few minor modifications.

The V12 came out, and a Chevy 383 stroker crate motor went in. He backed it up with a six-speed automatic transmission, and the car could leave just about anything else at the starting line. It wasn't that she felt she really needed all that much power, but if she decided to really put her foot into the carburetor, she wanted to have something there that would respond.

Getting to Vesta didn't take long, and she got there with fifteen minutes to spare. She went inside and took a seat in the area where people wait for a table, then took out her phone to play a trivia game while she waited for Morton to appear.

John Morton arrived at almost exactly 7:30. Summer saw him come through the door and dropped her phone into her purse as she got to her feet.

"John?" she asked, and he turned to her with a smile.

"Ms. Raines? Yes, I'm John Morton."

"Summer, please," she said, returning the smile. "Ms. Raines makes me feel like a schoolteacher."

John looked her up and down, his eyes appreciating every curve. "I don't think there are any schoolteachers like you," he said. "At least, there weren't any when I was in school."

She giggled and touched his arm. "Well, thank you," she said. "Shall we find a table?"

The hostess led them to one that was off by itself, and asked each of them what they would like to drink. Summer asked for iced tea, while Morton opted for raspberry lemonade. The drinks arrived a moment later, and the waitress took their orders.

"Sam said you had a few questions," Morton said. "How can I help you?"

"Well, I'm actually kind of curious about how your company seems to be doing so well after the shooting. To be honest, it reminded me of stories I heard about the Tylenol crisis back in the eighties. Do you think there's anything particular that you did that helped your company to make it through this particular crisis?"

"Oh, I don't know," Morton said. "Of course, the first thing we did was make sure that Max Petrelli's medical bills were all covered, I think that helped us a bit in the PR department. We immediately used social media to spread the word that we accepted the responsibility for what happened, and publicized the fact that we were going to employ professional security in the future. Just mentioning Windlass Security probably did us a lot of good, considering all the good press your company has gotten lately. Other than that, I really can't think of anything special we did."

"Maybe that was enough," Summer said with a smile. "It seems that the people really like your company, and all of the commentary I'm seeing and hearing about it now is very positive. That first couple of days, there were a few bad comments out there, but they seem to have faded away quickly."

"I think that's just human nature," Morton said. "We sometimes feel that any kind of failure is an indication of failures to come, but when we see that failure in the light of an unavoidable circumstance, or in this case, deliberate malice, then the object of concern takes on the persona of a victim. To be honest, I think Windlass has helped to put that idea out there, that the company was a victim of some malicious intent."

"You know, we had somebody working undercover inside your company for a while," Summer said. "That was because we had to be fairly sure that no one inside was involved. Don't get me wrong, I know they found out that one of your video people was blackmailed into cooperating with the shooter, but I'm saying that we wanted to be certain there was no one inside the company who was willingly involved."

Morton cocked his head slightly. "Are you saying that was an actual suspicion?"

"Well, not so much a suspicion as a precaution. Windlass has a reputation that we protect very carefully, and, given that human nature is as you described it, we naturally had to consider the possibility that someone might have anticipated a positive result from this type of situation. If that someone happened to be within your company and have some kind of control over it, we needed to be in a position to ascertain that."

"Well," Morton said. "I have to say you've caught me off guard. Summer, I don't think there's anyone in our company who would consider doing something like this, no matter what might be gained from it."

"Oh, please don't get me wrong," she said. "I'm certainly not trying to imply that you're under suspicion now. I was just explaining why we went to the lengths we did, as far as putting someone in undercover. Now, let's change the subject. I understand you're going to New York?"

"Yes, I've been asked to speak at the International Internet Video Conference that's being held there all next week. I'll be talking about the future of internet video, and how television is probably on its way out. With all the content being produced for the internet, now, broadcast and cable TV is probably about to go the way of the dinosaur. You've got all the streaming services like Netflix, Amazon Prime Video, Hulu, Starbright, and more out there, so people can watch whatever they want, whenever they want. Keeping television profitable is going to be difficult in the face of that kind of competition, and I'm just one of several people who seem to be able to see that coming without panicking over it."

"That brings up another question," Summer said. "You mentioned streaming services; I'm curious why you don't have a streaming service of your own. I mean, after all, just about every indie video producer out there wants to win your awards; it would seem to me that having your own streaming service would be a natural extension of what you already do."

"We toyed with the idea for a while," Morton said. "In fact, I've even had talks with Netflix and Starbright about some sort of joint venture. Netflix was only exploring the possibility, they weren't really serious about it at all, but Starbright—well, we got down to the point of negotiating the benefits to each side, but they were a little greedier than I care to deal with. When they got stubborn and wouldn't budge, I walked away from the table."

Summer smiled at him. "I like a man who can make a decision," she said, "and isn't afraid to act on it, regardless of the consequences. Are you considering any kind of similar joint venture in the future?"

"Oh, I don't know. I suppose it could be possible, but only if I could work with someone who was more sensible than either of those were. I don't think there's any reason for me to have to give up a massive share of my company so that we can both make extra profits. The way Starbright wanted to do things, I'd have a bigger customer base, but a smaller percentage of profits. In the long run, I stood to make less money while doing more work, and that just doesn't make any sense."

"Then, I'll go back to my original question. Why don't you want your own streaming service? With the standing your company has now, I think the vast majority of internet video fans would jump at the chance to sign up. I mean, you've got the reputation already, you know what's good and what's not. If you set up your own streaming service, you could have the cream of the crop as far as internet video goes."

"Again, we toyed with the idea, but it isn't something we have in the works at the moment." He gave her a conspiratorial smile. "If I let you in on something, can you keep it from getting public? I don't care if you share with your company, just don't let it leak out."

"John, we *are* a security company," she said, giggling. "Keeping secrets is what we do."

He looked around the room for a moment to be sure no one was listening, then leaned toward her over the table. "We do have something we're working on," he said. "Our research people have been working on some code that we're pretty excited about. We've found a way to break video up into tiny little packets of data, which can then be downloaded in batches. What it will do is increase the download speed for video streaming by a ridiculous factor, so that you can get true high definition video through a data connection. No buffering, no pausing, the video is all preloaded in the background of your computer or smart TV, and will be reassembled and streamed as smoothly as if you were watching it live."

Summer gave him an admiring smile. "That sounds like something that's going to be pretty profitable," she said.

"I certainly hope so. We'll be unveiling this new technology next week, and we're certain that every video streaming application out there is going to want to make use of it. Now, what that will mean is that even the smallest video producer will be able to stream high definition video, and the big streaming services will be able to do several times as much streaming on the same bandwidth they're using now. That is going to be one of the biggest innovations this year, and I could not have hoped for a better way to announce it than at this conference. We already make a lot of money every year, but the licensing fees on this technology will multiply our earnings by a factor of at least thirty."

Summer whistled. "So, you're talking about making billions of dollars every year, right?"

"Right now, we're projecting revenue for the first three years at more than ninety-five billion dollars. It'll be the biggest innovation in video since YouTube, and it's going to cut costs for video producers and streamers, even after licensing the technology from us. This is going to be huge, and I'm extremely excited about it."

"I'll bet. I bet your girlfriend is even more excited about it than you are, isn't she?"

"Annie? Annie is not as materialistic as you might think, she doesn't care as much about the money as she does about the company. I let her make a lot of the decisions as far as employees and such, because she has such a good heart. We pay our people very well, and it makes them extremely loyal to us."

"She sounds wonderful," Summer said. "See, this is the problem I always run into. All the good guys like you are taken, so a girl like me ends up lonely all the time."

Morton's eyebrows went up. "You're lonely? Forgive me, but you got to be kidding, right? Summer, you are probably one of the most beautiful women I've ever seen. I can't imagine you being lonely."

Summer was smiling, but suddenly her chin was quivering. A single tear started to make its way down her cheek from her right eye. "Hey, you know what looks like these will get you? A lot of attention, but most of it from men who only want that famous one thing. All the really decent guys seem to be intimidated by my looks, so they either won't pay any attention to me at all, or they try to pretend to be something they're not because they think it's the only way to get my attention. The truth is, all I really want is someone who will care about me for who I am, rather than what I look like."

Morton was quiet for a few seconds, then reached across and laid his hand on hers. "I'm sorry you feel that way," he said. "You seem like an incredible woman."

Summer looked at his hand and then raised her eyes to meet his. "You have a gentle touch," she said. "I hope you'll forgive me for being so bold, but I would bet you are an incredible lover."

Morton yanked his hand back. "Oh, my goodness," he said, "please forgive me if I gave you the wrong impression just now. I wasn't trying to..."

"Relax, John," Summer said with a grin. "I wasn't, either. To be perfectly honest, that was just my way of kinda checking you out. See, I can learn an awful lot about a man by leaving him an opening to flirt with me, and then watching how he makes his moves. I left you an opening, and you jumped away from it. That tells me you're a pretty good guy, and Annie is lucky to have you."

Morton swallowed, his eyes wide. "Listen, I understand what you're saying and I appreciate your honesty. I was really just trying to be comforting, because you looked upset. It didn't even occur to me that it might be taken as flirting. I really do apologize..."

"Seriously, chill out," Summer said. "Like I said, John, it was a test and you passed. Sometimes I do this type of interview when we're trying to clear someone, or prove that they have good character qualities. It's all about perception, and you'd be surprised how many men fail miserably."

"Actually, I don't think I would be," Morton said. "My Annie is a beautiful woman herself, and she's always dealing with men hitting on her. I can't tell you how grateful I am that she's devoted to me, so I'm certainly not going to be anything less than devoted to her."

The waitress arrived with their dinner, and they put aside any serious conversation while they ate. They talked about simple things, such as what they each liked about their work, and went their separate ways when dinner was over.

Summer called Sam from her car, catching him relaxing on the sofa with his children in his lap as they watched a movie on TV.

"I think we can eliminate John Morton as any kind of suspect," she said. "There aren't a lot of guys in the world who are still genuine, but he's definitely one of them."

"I'm glad to hear it," Sam said. "My own gut tells me he's clean, but there are enough little discrepancies that we have to consider the possibility someone inside his company is still involved. Any other possibilities come to mind?"

"Sam, I don't know anybody else in the company. You find a suspect, I'll be happy to vet him, but I don't know of any at the moment."

"Okay. See you at the office tomorrow."

"I'll be there." She hung up the phone and dropped it into her purse, then took it back out. She found a name in her contacts and hit the dial button.

"Hello?"

"Harvey," she said slowly and seductively. "Would you like some company?"

THOUGH IT WAS ONLY a little after three, Sam decided to take off early. He told Jenna that he was going home and that he had forwarded his office phone in case something came up, then walked out the door and got into the Mustang. He was just backing out when his phone rang, and he picked it up to see Karen's number on the display.

"Karen? What's up?"

"Well, you're not going to believe this," she said. "Somebody just took a shot at Max Petrelli, right through his hospital room window."

"No way! Was he hurt?"

"No, the bullet missed completely, and your security guard spotted where the shot came from and returned fire, striking and killing one person. Unfortunately, another person with him got away. We need you down there, Sam. I'm on the way myself. And by the way, we are not releasing the information about the shooter being killed."

"I'm rolling. I can be at the hospital in less than ten." He ended the call and dropped the phone into his pocket, then took off toward the hospital.

Despite a couple of lights that might have turned red just before Sam blew through them, he made it to the hospital in less than nine minutes. He parked his car right outside the front entrance and grabbed his cane out of the back seat as he climbed out, then hurried inside and into the elevator. There were police officers all over the place when he emerged onto Max's floor, but they all knew who he was. He paused when he got to Max's door, letting his face show through the small window before he opened it and stepped inside.

Heath Blevins, the security guard on duty, recognized Sam. "Mr. Prichard," he said. "I got one of them, but one got away. I called in, and Roscoe Jordan is on the way back to relieve me. I have to go down to the police station to make a report."

Sam nodded. "That's normal procedure," he said. "Good job on getting the shooter, but the police want that kept away from the press, so don't speak to the reporters on your way out. Did you get a good look at the one that ran?"

"I did, sir," Blevins said. "That's one of the advantages of a high-powered scope. I've already given a description of her to the police."

Sam's eyebrows rose. "Her? It was a woman?"

"Yes, sir, a man and a woman. The man was holding the rifle, and the woman was spotting for him with binoculars. I just happened to be looking toward the window at that moment and I saw the flash, so I immediately aimed to return fire. I had the shooter in my cross hairs, so I squeezed the trigger and then tried to adjust my aim for the woman, but she was running already. I fired, and I think I hit her, but she didn't stop."

Sam walked to the window and looked out. There were several police officers on top of a building a short distance away, and Sam pointed. "Is that where they were?"

"Yes, sir," Blevins replied. "I don't know who it was, sir, but he's definitely a pro. Max was walking back to his bed from the bathroom when the shot was fired, and I believe the bullet was slightly deflected as it came through the glass, or he could be dead right now."

Sam turned to Max, who was sitting in a chair out of sight of the window. "You okay, kid?"

Max gave him a nervous grin. "I'm okay," he said. "I just wish people would stop shooting at me."

Sam nodded. "Yeah," he said. "You and me both."

There were two police officers in the room, and Sam told them he'd be back. He went out of the room and back down the elevator, then started out the door. He was planning to go to the building where the shooter had been, but he suddenly had microphones in his face. Several reporters had gathered, but Wendy Dawson and her cameraman actually got to him first.

"Mr. Prichard, can you tell us what's going on? We heard that Max Petrelli was shot again, is that true?"

For a split second, Sam regretted his earlier comment to Karen about how he had learned to like the press.

"There was a shot fired into Mr. Petrelli's room, but he has not been injured. Windlass Security has been maintaining a security guard with him all week, and our security officer was able to keep Mr. Petrelli safe. The police are currently investigating, and they will have more information for you before long."

"Mr. Prichard," Wendy said, "do you believe this is related to the last time Max was shot? Is someone trying to kill him because he won the award last week?"

"At this moment, I can't speak about the motive of the shooter, or about any connection this might have to our ongoing investigation. Again, you'll have to wait for the police to release whatever information they have."

Sam pushed his way around them, and the reporters finally backed off. He walked down the sidewalk in front of the hospital, leaning on his cane lightly as his hip began to protest the distance.

Several policemen and Detective Dolby were standing in front of the building the shot had come from, and Dolby was delighted to escort Sam inside and up the elevator. When they got to the top floor, they got out of the elevator and went to the emergency stairs that led to the roof. Sam held onto the rail as he climbed the stairs, and then they were out under the sun. Dolby walked with him across the roof to where the shooter lay on his back.

For a moment, Sam thought he was seeing a ghost. The man laying on the tarred roof was almost a twin for Juergen Schroeder, but there were some differences. This man wasn't quite as tall, and he had a slight mustache under his nose.

"I don't suppose he had any ID on him?" Sam asked.

The police officer standing next to the body shook his head. "No, sir," he said. "No ID, no wallet, nothing in his pockets at all."

"Did anybody see where the woman went? Were there any witnesses who might have gotten a good look at her?"

"Again, no, sir. We know she made it down the elevator, but no one reported seeing her come out of the front door. It's almost like she vanished out of the elevator."

Sam took out his phone and dialed a number. "Steve? You heard already? Okay, get Walter up to where the shooters were. I want his take on this as soon as possible, but the police are not releasing the information that the shooter is dead."

"We'll get there as soon as possible," Steve said. "And don't worry, I don't deal with reporters, and I don't let them anywhere near Walter."

Sam put the phone in his pocket and looked at the shooter again. Blevins had definitely done a good job, because there was a hole in the center of the man's forehead.

"I've got my crime scene specialist on the way," Sam said to Dolby. "Make sure he gets up here, and that nobody touches anything until he does."

"Yes, sir," Dolby said. Sam went down the stairs to the elevator, and limped his way back to the hospital.

Most of the reporters were talking to some police officers, but Wendy Dawson and her cameraman were standing off by themselves, both of them staring at Sam as he approached. He started to enter the hospital and ignore them, then stopped. He looked around quickly, then motioned for them to follow him inside.

He didn't have to tell them twice. A few seconds later, he had taken them aside in the hospital lobby.

"I give you a quick, brief statement," he said, "but I want you to promise me you'll run it exactly the way I give it. Can you do that?"

"Of course," Wendy said. "All I have to do is tell the boss that was a condition of getting it. Our producers would do just about anything to get an exclusive statement out of you, Mr. Prichard."

"Okay, then tell me when you're ready."

It took Harvey a couple of seconds to get the camera onto his shoulder and turned on, and then he nodded. Wendy stepped up to Sam, showing the camera her profile.

"Mr. Prichard, what can you tell us about what's going on right now?"

"Wendy, Windlass has been working on investigating this case all week, and we've come across some disturbing information. I can't go into any detail, but it appears at the moment that the shooting last week, and this attempt on Mr. Petrelli today, may actually be connected to an attempt by an unknown entity to damage or destroy the Web Wide Awards company. Now, that's not conclusive, but we've come across evidence to back it up. The only question we got now is whether anyone inside Web Wide Awards might be aware of what's happening."

"Inside the company? Do you suspect there might be some kind of collusion between Web Wide Awards and the unknown entity you mentioned?"

Sam frowned. "It might be premature to say we suspect collusion," he said. "Let's just say we're exploring all possibilities."

Sam dragged a finger across his throat, and Harvey turned off the camera and lowered it. "We're off," he said.

"Wow," Wendy said. "You just launched a whole string of conspiracy theories, you know that, right?"

"I don't care about conspiracy theories," Sam said. "I'm actually trying to throw a scare into somebody, and hopefully it might help me figure out exactly what's going on, here."

"You put one into me," Wendy said. "I worked for Web Wide Awards for a short time, and I hate to think anybody there would be involved in a plot like this. I mean, to shoot a kid?"

"I agree with you, it's despicable. Hopefully, we'll know something more concrete pretty soon." He turned and walked into the elevator, leaving them where they stood.

Karen was in Max's room when he got back up there, and he asked her to step out before he told her what he'd seen on the other roof. "The guy was almost a ringer for Schroeder," he said, keeping his voice low. "Blevins said there was a man and a woman working together, so I'm about convinced that Reynard had more than one team here, working this assignment."

"But why would they try to kill Max now?" Karen asked. "Trying it before only made Web Wide Awards stronger, it didn't hurt them."

"And that's what they're trying to do," Sam said. "If Morton really is involved in this, then he was expecting the kind of result he got. Another attempt on Max's life right now, when it's obvious that it's the company who's the actual victim, is only going to strengthen that. Somebody, and it could possibly be Morton, is out to build Web Wide Awards up."

"But why? Just to make more money?"

"I don't think so," Sam said. "Do you know what you do with the turkey before Thanksgiving?"

Karen looked at him like he was crazy. "Keep it frozen?"

"Nope," Sam said. "You fatten it up before the slaughter. Somebody is getting Web Wide Awards ready to be plucked and stuffed."

THE NEWS ABOUT A SECOND attempt on Max Petrelli's life spread like wildfire, and Wendy's prediction came true. The network grabbed Sam's statement and ran it nationwide, while CNN happily paid the ridiculous amounts of money the station demanded so they could run it globally.

On social media, there was a tremendous outpouring of love and support for Max, but almost as much for Web Wide Awards. Even people who noticed Sam's statement were unwilling to believe the company could possibly be involved in wrongdoing, and a few even posted some disparaging comments about Sam, himself.

Back in Denver, however, John Morton was stunned when he saw the news. Hearing Sam say that they were still investigating whether someone inside the company might be involved was a shock, and one that rocked him to his very core.

"Annie, do you think he's trying to say it's us?" Morton asked.

"Oh, John, why would he think that? You're not doing anything to be worried about, are you?"

"No, no, of course not. No, you're probably right, it wouldn't make sense for him to suspect us. That wouldn't make any sense at all."

"Of course not," Annie said. "After all, what was the first thing we did? We hired Windlass Security, and we're the ones who are paying them to investigate this thing. I'm sure we wouldn't have done that if we were somehow involved in making it happen."

"Yeah, you're right," Morton said. "I'm sure you're right."

RON THOMAS CALLED AS soon as he heard the news, and Sam brought him up to speed on what was going on. Ron suggested they double the guard on Max, and Sam was happy to agree that it was a good idea.

"You realize," Ron said, "this actually doesn't make any sense at all. They had already achieved what they were after, if you're correct about this being a plot to build the company up. Why take another shot at Max?"

"I think it's about fattening them up for the kill," Sam said. "If I'm reading this right, somebody wants the company to be as solid as possible when they make their move. At least, that's the only scenario I can envision that's going to make any sense."

"I can't fault your logic," Ron said. "I trust your judgment, Sam, so you handle this however you feel the need to. I'm quite sure you're doing the best job anybody could on it."

"Well, thanks for the vote of confidence," Sam said. "Listen, Steve is calling. I had him take Walter up to where the shooters were, I'm hoping Walter can figure out how the woman disappeared."

"Go ahead, I'll talk to you later."

Sam flashed over to Steve's call. "Go ahead, Steve," he said. "What have you got?"

"Well, Walter figured it out," Steve said. "The woman took off and went down the elevator, but she never came out on the ground floor. Apparently she really was hit, because there are drops of blood on the stairs down from the roof, and a few inside the elevator. We're checking floor by floor to see where she got off the elevator, but right now we're pretty sure she never got out of the building."

"I'll be right there," Sam said. He turned to Karen. "The female subject with the shooter may still be in the building over there. She's been wounded, and leaving a trail of blood drops."

"What are we waiting for?" Karen asked, heading out the door with him. They fought their way past the reporters, then made their way to the other building and inside. Steve and Walter were standing in the lobby, and Steve had a grin on his face.

"Damn, Sam," he said, "you should have seen it! We checked every floor, us and the cops, and there was no sign she got off the elevator. Walter, here, he went back in the elevator and looked around for a second, then jumped up on the little rail that goes around the thing and punched the emergency hatch in the ceiling, then pulled himself up. I heard a scream, so I climbed up there, too, and find him standing over the suspect, holding the gun she tried to point at him."

"I wasn't gonna shoot her," Walter said. "I just didn't want her to shoot me."

"Where is she?" Sam asked.

"I've got two uniforms up on the elevator, keeping their eyes on her. She's hit just under the collarbone, and she's in a lot of pain. The officers got the bleeding under control, but she needs a hospital. I've got paramedics on the way, now."

Sam looked at Walter. "Way to go, Walter," he said. "Did you know she would be up there?"

"Yeah. I should have figured it out sooner. I just went up there to make sure, but she tried to shoot me so I took her gun away."

"He did that," he said. "And I think he broke two of her fingers while he did it."

Sam shrugged. "That'll teach her not to point guns at Walter."

The paramedics arrived a few minutes later and they ended up having to open the doors on the second floor in order to get the woman out. She was unconscious by that time, and they rushed her out to the ambulance even though it was less than a block to the emergency room. Sam followed and found Karen standing just outside the exam room where doctors were stabilizing her, but then they hurried her off to surgery. One of the nurses said it would be at least the following day before anyone could speak to her.

Police officers were assigned to keep watch on her when she came out of surgery, but there was nothing more Sam could do at that point. He turned to Karen.

"Not much more I can do around here," he said. "I think I'm going to head back to the office for a bit before I go home. Give me a call if anything happens or you need me, okay?"

"Yeah, I got this," Karen said. "I don't think she's going to be talking, anyway. Watch out for the reporters as you leave."

Sam grinned. "Don't worry, I will."

He walked out through the ER entrance and was immediately mobbed by the press. He glanced at the crowd of reporters and was surprised that he didn't see Wendy Dawson shoving a microphone at him, but then he spotted her and her cameraman standing off to the side.

"Mr. Prichard, can you tell us who was just taken into the emergency room? Was that the person who tried to shoot Max Petrelli?" Those and a dozen other questions were shouted at him, and he held up a hand to get everyone to stop.

"All I can tell you at this moment," he said, "was that it is someone who was wounded in this most recent shooting. I don't have any other information to give you at this time. The police will make a statement once they know more." He pushed his way past them and headed toward his car, climbed in, and started back toward his office.

When he got there, Sam turned to his computer and began looking through all the reports on the case since it had begun. Something was bothering him, but he couldn't put his finger on it. The only thing he could do in a case like that, he figured, was go back over all the notes, all the references, all the information they had collected since the case started.

The first thing he read through was the original description of the case, provided by John and Annie when they had first contacted Windlass Security. The initial contact usually came through the internet, on the company's website. There was a form to be filled out with all relevant information, including the names and pertinent details of individuals involved, the service requested, a general description of the situation that needed to be investigated or protected against, and any comments the applicant might like to make.

John Morton and Annie Porter had done a good job of filling out the form. They had provided all of their own information, and then gone into a lengthy description of the shooting, and the circumstances surrounding it. They had specified that they wanted to hire the company for security for all future events, as well as for the Star Tour that was to begin shortly, and then requested assistance with investigating how the shooting had come about.

They had also gone beyond what was required, providing video clips that were taken from the production of the award program. While it was streamed live, it was also recorded and archived on their website. Sam remembered watching as it actually happened, because he and Indie watched a lot of the web-based programs, and recalled his shock at seeing the boy collapse. The hair on the back of Sam's neck had stood right up, and he wasn't even slightly surprised when they turned him over to see the blood on his chest.

There were four different camera angles included with the application, and Sam hadn't seen them before. He clicked the play button on the first one and watched the drama unfold.

Aaron Zachary and Jennifer Larkindale were there on the screen, and Sam watched as Jennifer read off Max's name from the card. In the original production, the scene had cut to Max behind the curtain, being congratulated by the other nominees, but this was the full shot from a single camera. The camera stayed on Aaron and Jennifer as they turned and looked toward the curtain where Max should be stepping out. Slightly to their left, Sam could just see the curtain opening up, and then Max appeared in the gap. He seemed to stumble once, stood straight, and then just fell on his face.

Everyone froze for a couple of seconds, and then a stagehand appeared from the left. Aaron and Jennifer jogged across the stage, and got to them just as the stagehand rolled Max over. Jennifer let out a small scream, something Sam hadn't noticed at the time, and then the clip ended.

Sam went to the next one and clicked the play button. This was a different angle, from the other end of the stage. On the left, Sam could see Aaron and Jennifer facing out to the crowd, which was also to the left. The same scenario played again, and Sam watched the stagehand, Aaron, and Jennifer as they played out their parts in the drama.

The third camera was apparently mounted up in the fly loft, over the stage. It was looking down at a slight angle, and slightly behind where Aaron and Jennifer stood at the podium. From this angle, Sam could see all of the stage and the curtain, which was curved more than he had suspected previously. When Max's name was announced once again, the curtains opened toward the top of the screen, and Max started to step out.

From this angle, Sam could see that what appeared to be a stumble was actually Max reacting to the impact of the bullet.

It had struck hard enough to knock him backward for a second, but he had caught himself and managed to get his balance just before shock set in and he lost consciousness. That would be the moment when he fell flat on his face onto the stage.

The high view also allowed Sam a clear look at the blood on Max's chest. The spreading stain looked bigger than it had looked from the other angles, and Sam realized that it was growing as the blood spurted. Seeing that, Sam knew that Max was even luckier than he'd originally thought. Spurting meant that the bullet had, at the very least, nicked an artery.

The fourth video was actually from the camera on which the rifle had been mounted. Sam had expected it to be a distant shot, but the camera was apparently zoomed in pretty tightly. Once again, he watched as Jennifer announced the winner, then the curtain opened and the camera adjusted itself and zoomed in a little tighter. Max stepped into view, and suddenly Sam heard a *thump*.

If he hadn't been halfway expecting it, he never would have caught it. He actually heard the shot that fired the bullet that struck Max. The muffled sound wasn't loud, but it was distinctive, and the picture wobbled for a split second. That would've been due to the recoil of the rifle, Sam figured.

A thought struck him, and he refreshed that video and played it again. Sure enough, he thought, this was the actual view he had seen on the live webcast. The producer had been streaming that particular camera at the time, and Sam suddenly remembered the cue sheet. That had told the shooters which camera would be used for that particular shot, which explained why they had chosen it to mount the rifle on.

He went back to reading the description of the shooting, and was frankly amazed that John and Annie, or whichever of them had actually filled out the application, had done such a precise job of describing it. They had gone into great detail, almost split second by split second, from the moment Jennifer read off Max's name to the moment when the paramedics rushed onto the stage. After he'd been thinking about it for a few moments, Sam concluded that they had gone over the video footage more than once themselves, trying to make sure they described everything properly.

Next, Sam began looking at the first reports from the investigators. Walter's was at the top of the list, and Sam was always surprised at the clear and grammatical manner in which he wrote his reports. Perhaps he should not have been; shortly after his first case with Windlass, Sam had the opportunity to review a file on Walter, and learned that Walter was an extremely rare individual. While he had been diagnosed with a form of autism known as Asperger Syndrome, he was also classed as a multiple Savant.

Savant syndrome refers to certain abilities that seemed to be inherent in an individual. In the general population, less than one percent have any type of savant ability, but within the population of people diagnosed with any type of autism, that percentage raises to around ten percent. Not every autistic person will develop a savant ability, despite the misconception that the public gained from the movie *Rain Man*. Not every autistic person can do incredible mathematics or count instantly, and while these are not uncommon abilities, there are many others.

Walter's doctors had determined that he had four specific savant abilities. He could perform even the most complex mathematics in his head; he had a grasp of mechanical and visual spatial relationships that allowed him to imagine and visualize complex relationships between objects; he had unusually acute sensory discrimination, which meant that he could see, hear, smell, taste, and feel things that most people would never notice at all; and he had what amounted to an eidetic memory, because any detail that he read, heard, or saw remained in his memory to the point that he could call it back at any time and examine it as if he were experiencing it all over again.

Unlike many autistics, he did not have extreme difficulty with communication skills. While he often spoke in very short, almost broken sentences, he could speak and write with perfect clarity whenever he chose. He could also, although this is not considered a savant skill, type accurately at close to two hundred words a minute.

Walter's report on his first examination of the crime scene was extremely detailed. He not only described the arena building in great detail, but he listed his impressions of every step from the point he entered the building until he climbed on the rail of the catwalk to photograph the rifle.

"As I stepped onto the catwalk," his narrative read, "I observed that the floor of the catwalk was made of steel grating with rectangular holes that were one half inch wide and one and one quarter inches long. The steel strips that divided the holes from one another were nine-sixteenths of an inch tall and three thirty-seconds of an inch thick. They were attached to one another by interlocking grooves and were spot welded by the application of electricity and pressure. They were more than sufficient to withstand the weight of myself and the others with me. I further observed that there were small amounts of dirt and other substances on their top edges and sometimes running down the vertical sides of the strips. Some of the other substances included road tar, mud, coffee stains, spilled soft drink residue, chocolate, small pieces of gravel, pieces of cigarettes and cigarette filters, bits of grass, small seeds, flower petals and other items I did not take time to identify."

All of that, Sam thought, *after only a few seconds of looking at the catwalk. The only thing I noticed was that it was made of metal, and I wouldn't even have been sure that it was steel. As far as all that other stuff, I never would've seen it all, and probably still wouldn't see if I went back and looked again.*

"When the camera was manipulated to just over our heads, I stepped up onto the railing of the catwalk, spreading my legs to maintain my balance and looked closely at the top of the camera. There I saw an articulated platform that appeared to be movable by means of remotely controlled electric motors, cables and solenoids. The proper combination of signals would result in movement of the top mounting platform of approximately ninety degrees on the z axis (horizontal rotation), approximately seventy degrees on the X axis (vertical rotation), and zero degrees on the y axis (longitudinal rotation). Mounted atop this platform was a modified AR-15 rifle that had been stripped down and had the addition of a large sound suppressor, video camera sighting mechanism and a solenoid controlled lever that could depress the trigger. I also observed a considerable amount of dust that had accumulated on the camera, with only a much smaller layer on the rifle, indicating that the rifle had been in place for a relatively short period of time."

Unbelievable detail seemed to be the hallmark of every report Walter wrote, and Sam often wished that he had an entire team of Walters.

Steve Beck had also written a report, and his was good. It showed the attention to detail common among police officers and detectives, who know that their jobs depend on their ability to see clues that others might miss. Still, he couldn't hold a candle to what Walter had written.

One by one, he went through all of the reports that had been written over the last four days. From Summer to Jade to Denny to Darren and back to Walter and Steve, including their reports on the scene of the most recent shooting, until he was certain he had read every possible word that could be used to describe any of what was happening in this case.

Still, something was bothering him. He had the feeling that there was one little detail that he had been presented with that wasn't fitting, like having one jigsaw puzzle piece that was cut slightly wrong and wouldn't fit where it needed to go.

The latest development, apparently a second attempt to kill Max Petrelli, simply didn't fit. The original shooting had been designed to generate a wave of sympathy and support for the company, as well as for Max, but was it really likely that they would gain even more support if Max were to be killed? Sam just couldn't see the logic behind it. About the only thing he could do was hold out hope that the woman in the hospital might be able to shed some light on the subject.

Sam shut down his computer and headed for home. What he needed, he figured, was an evening of relaxation with his family. That should clear his mind, and he would think about all of this in the morning.

17

*T*hank God it's Friday, Sam thought. He and Bo were at the table, having their early morning moments before Indie and Kenzie got up. Sam knew they weren't going to last a lot longer this way, because Bo was getting tired of having to sit in the bouncy seat on the table, and he'd pretty well outgrown it, anyway.

"Maybe next time," Sam said, "we'll do this in the living room. That way, you can be in your playpen and not stuck in one spot. Is that a good idea? Yeah? You think that's a good idea?"

"What's a good idea?" Kenzie asked as she entered the kitchen.

"Bo thinks it would be a good idea if he and I start having our coffee time in the living room. He's about had it with the bouncy chair on the table."

"Yeah, that's a good idea," Kenzie said.

"What's a good idea?" Indie asked.

"Daddy and Bo having coffee in the living room," Kenzie said.

Indie looked at Sam. "Having coffee?" she asked. "Sam..."

Sam held up a hand in self-defense. "Don't worry," he said, "it's like I always say, his coffee comes in a bottle and tastes a lot like milk. He's not quite ready for my kind of coffee yet."

"And he won't be, not for another fifteen years or so." She gave him "the look" that meant he'd better not try to argue, so Sam only smiled and nodded.

"Yes, dear," he said. "Anyway, he's outgrown his little bouncy chair, so I told him we'll start doing this in the living room in the mornings, so he can be in his playpen."

Indie grinned sleepily. "Yeah, that probably is a good idea. I'm going to give the bouncy seat and a lot of his baby clothes to Nadia, anyway. She's only known she's pregnant for a week, but she's convinced it's going to be a boy."

Sam looked up at her. "Nadia? From my office?"

"Yep. Eileen called me on Monday, she's putting together a baby shower. I'm surprised you hadn't heard about it, I think everybody else up there knows."

"Well, most of the women hang out together up there," Sam said, "especially in the break room. They put a couple of tables together so they have a big one over in the corner, and they make it pretty clear that men are not allowed."

"I think that's because most of the men up there are a bit intimidating," Indie said. "I don't think you should take it personally."

Sam rolled his eyes. "Oh, trust me, I don't."

Indie walked up behind him and put her arms around his neck, then kissed him on the cheek. "That's my good boy," she said. She let go and went to the refrigerator, and it wasn't long before Sam could smell bacon starting to sizzle.

His phone rang, and he picked it up to see that it was Karen Parks calling. "Hey," he said as he answered. "Anything new?"

"Actually, I have something good to report, for once. We ran the fingerprints of the dead shooter and the woman we captured yesterday through AFIS and got a hit."

Sam's eyebrows rose. "You did? Who are they?"

"Well, he was David Green, ex-Marine who's been mixed up with a lot of different anti-government groups since his discharge three years ago. FBI has been looking for him for a while, now, but he always seemed to slip away before they could grab him. They lost track of him a year ago when he somehow made it to Paris, and this is the firt time he's been seen since then. As for the woman, her name is Suzanne Kushner, and she's ex-army. She got out with an honorable discharge two years ago, and hasn't been seen or heard from since until now. No family, she grew up in the foster system in Ohio. I'm headed for the hospital to talk to her now, and thought you might like to go along."

"You bet," Sam said. "I'll meet you there."

Sam got up and kissed his wife and kids, then headed out the door. The Mustang roared to life, and he actually got to the hospital two minutes before Karen did.

"Do we know if she's said anything?" Sam asked.

Karen shook her head. "She hasn't even really been awake yet," she said. "I spoke to the doctor a little bit ago and he said they've kept her out, but they're ready to wake her up, now. I asked him to wait until we got here, and he agreed."

"Sounds great," Sam said. "Are we ready?"

They stepped inside the hospital and Karen asked the information desk where to find Doctor Whitaker. The woman there gave them directions to his office on the second floor, and they took the elevator up. A moment later, they stepped into the doctor's office.

"Doctor Whitaker?" Karen asked. "I'm Detective Parks, and this is Sam Prichard, Windlass Security. We are here to speak with our suspect."

"Yes," Doctor Whitaker said. "Give me just a moment." He finished typing something into his computer and then shut it down, removing an access card from a slot in the front of the computer. He tucked the card into a pocket and rose to his feet. "All right, sorry about the delay."

The doctor led the way down the hall, and they saw two police officers sitting just outside the room. Both of them nodded as Sam and Karen followed the doctor inside, where Suzanne Kushner was lying in the bed. Her eyes were closed, and the doctor inserted a hypodermic needle into her IV line and depressed the plunger.

"Give her a minute," he said. "That should wake her up within a few seconds."

As he spoke, the woman's eyes began to flutter, and she opened them after a few seconds. She looked around the room wildly for a moment, then her gaze settled on Sam.

Karen stepped up to the bed. "Ms. Kushner," she said. "You're in the hospital, and you're in custody. I'm Detective Karen Parks from the Denver Police Department, and this is Sam Prichard, from Windlass Security. You remember how you got here?"

She nodded. "Yes," she said, her voice raspy. "David?"

"He was killed, I'm afraid," Karen said, "which means you are completely on your own. Who hired you to try to kill Max Petrelli?"

Kushner closed her eyes for a moment, and a couple of tears leaked out of them. "I told him this was a stupid job," she said. "He wouldn't listen." She was quiet for a moment, then she opened her eyes and looked at Karen. "I have no idea who hired us. David was the one who took the orders, and he never shared that information with me. All I know is that we were told to come here and fire a shot at that kid. It wasn't even a real hit, we were supposed to miss. We didn't expect anyone to be able to shoot back."

"Our security guards," Sam said, "are almost all former special forces. The man who returned fire did it instinctively. Now, why in the world would someone want you to take a shot like that and not hit your target?"

"I don't know," she said. "Probably some sort of distraction from something else. Like I said, David never shared any information with me."

"When did you get these orders?" Karen asked.

"Couple days ago. We were in New York, and David went out to get some food, and when he came back he said we had to come here. He always got orders when he was out, away from me. He never wanted me to know who hired us, anything like that." She gave a wry chuckle. "He always said I'd talk too much if we ever got caught. Guess he was right."

"Good," Sam said. "Because right now, you're looking at charges that include murder, accessory to murder, and attempted murder, so the only hope you've got is to talk your head off and help us figure out what's been going on in this case."

"Murder?" Kushner asked. "But, I haven't killed anyone!"

"Maybe not," Karen said, "but being involved in a crime where someone dies is an automatic murder charge. Just the fact that you were with David Green while committing a crime, during which he died, makes you guilty of murder, and your association with him implicates you as an accessory to both his death and the attempted murder of Max Petrelli a week ago. You're probably looking at spending the rest of your life in prison. If you cooperate, tell us everything you possibly can, the judge might be willing to be a little more lenient when it comes to sentencing."

"But I don't know anything," the woman said. "I told you, David never told me anything about who we were working for. I was just supposed to be his helper, I've never even actually fired a gun on one of our jobs."

"You didn't hesitate to aim one at my investigator," Sam said. He glanced down at her right hand, with two fingers in splints. "I'm just glad he was quick enough to take it away from you."

"It wouldn't have mattered," she said. "I wasn't going to shoot anybody. I was scared and hurt, but I just thought he might run away if I pointed the gun in his face." She held up her hand and grinned. "Boy, was I wrong."

"You are lucky," Karen said. "Anyone else would've shot you and finished you off. How did David receive his orders?"

"His cell phone," Kushner said. "Everything was by email, but David wouldn't use a computer. He did everything on his cell phone, and never let me near it."

"How long have you been with David?" Sam asked.

"About six months, I think," she said. "I was with another guy before that, but he got killed. I got away, so they put me with David, instead."

"They?" Sam asked. "Who is 'they?' Who are you talking about?"

Kushner grimaced. "You're not going to believe me," she said, "but I don't know. Couple years ago, when I got out of the Army, I got offered a job to come to work for this security outfit in France. They took me over there for training and said we were special contract operatives for different governments. Our job was to eliminate people that the governments who hired them said were threats to their security, but it didn't take long before I knew that was BS. The only problem is, once you're in, you're in. If you try to quit, they kill you."

"You must know the name of the security company," Sam said. "What was it?"

"Well, the name they gave me at first was Fawkes Security, but they never used that name after I got there. From that point, we were just called the organization. There were a lot of us there for training, about a dozen teams. One man, one woman, always. The idea was that we could always pose as a couple."

"Who was your first partner?" Sam asked her.

"His name was Julio, but he was pretty crazy. I was with him for about a year, but he spent more time beating me up than going out on his assignments. He wouldn't let me go out with him like I was supposed to, he'd leave me tied up wherever we were staying. When he got killed, I was tied up for two days, trying to get loose. I was gonna just run away, but they found me before I could get free. They took me back to their headquarters and put me with David."

"Where is the headquarters at?" Sam asked.

"Here we go again," Kushner said. "I don't know. They put you inside a van with no windows, so you can't see where you're going. I can tell you it's about a six-hour ride after you leave Paris, but I couldn't even guess what direction."

"Wait a minute," Karen said. "What you're telling us is that you were recruited by some sort of international murder organization?"

Kushner gave her a sheepish smile. "I guess that's what I'm saying, yeah," she said. "I can tell you they recruit people by promising them jobs as security personnel, but when you get there you find out the truth. If you don't agree to do what they want, and if you're not convincing about it when you do, they literally just shoot you in the head and toss your body in a ditch. They've got a tractor there with a front bucket on it, and they just throw dirt in over you."

Karen looked at Sam. "This is way over my pay grade," she said.

"Suzanne," Sam said, "do you know any of the people in charge?"

"We aren't told any names," Kushner said. "Everyone there goes by an animal name, like Bear or Rhino. None of us are allowed to use our own names until after we're teamed up and sent out on assignment. After that, the guy is in charge and the woman is supposed to be his helper and camouflage. He's always the important one, so us girls are usually expendable."

Sam looked at Karen and nodded. "That explains a couple things," he said. He looked back at Kushner. "You and David Green are actually the second pair we've had to deal with. Did you know Juergen Schroeder and Bernadette Jones?"

She shook her head, then winced. "Not by those names, I don't. If I ever met them at all, it would have been with some other names." She blinked several times. "Look, you're probably going to think I'm crazy, but this is probably the best possible thing that could've happened to me. I couldn't get out, but even spending the rest of my life in prison will be better than being stuck in that outfit. I'll tell you anything you want to know, but they went to a lot of effort to make sure we didn't know much."

Sam nodded, then motioned for Karen to follow him into the hall. When they were outside the room, he turned to her.

"This is a lot bigger than just a local case," he said. "I think we should turn her over to DHS. I doubt she knows anything that is really going to help us on this case, anyway, but she might be able to help figure out where that training camp is and who the organization behind it really could be."

Karen shrugged and rolled her eyes. "That's fine with me," she said. "I wouldn't have a clue where to start with all this information."

Sam grinned and took out his phone, and walked further down the hall. He dialed a number and put the phone to his ear, and grinned when it was answered.

"Sam, boy? Why are you calling an old man and interrupting his vacation?"

"Oh, give it up, Harry," Sam said. "You love it when I call, and you know it."

"There could be some truth in that, but don't tell my wife. Ow. Never mind, she heard me. What can I do for you, Sam?"

"Hey, I've stumbled across something and I'm not sure what to do with it. I'm working on a case here in Denver, but some of the players involved are apparently connected to an international hitman ring. Have you ever heard of Fawkes Security?"

"I can't say that I have. What else can you tell me about them?"

"Apparently, they put out teams to handle hits, always a man and a woman. The man is the killer, the woman is his helper and is considered expendable. One of the pairs that we dealt with put that to the ultimate test, because the man went out a window and left the woman to try to fight off the police. She died, and luckily we got him, as well, but I had to shoot him. The second pair wasn't quite as easy; they took a shot at someone we were protecting, and our security guard managed to hit them both. The man died instantly, and we found the woman hiding on top of an elevator. She is in custody, in the hospital. She's the one who's been telling us about this organization. They seem to be based in France, or at least that's where she believes the training camp was."

"Do you have any principals? Any names?"

"One possible. Have you ever heard of Pierre Reynard?"

Harry was silent for several seconds. "Now you're making a little bit of sense. Pierre Reynard is known as the French Fox. You said this outfit was called Fawkes, right? That's just an alternative spelling of the word Fox, so that would make sense if he's involved. But, whatever you do, don't underestimate Reynard if you end up dealing with him. He was originally a French-Canadian named Armand Tredeau, who immigrated to the United States. Sam, there was a time when he was one of the best wet work men the CIA ever had. He turned his back on America about fifteen years ago, and he's been independent ever since."

"Well, that's just wonderful," Sam said. "Harry, I think I'm going to turn this woman over to DHS. She doesn't seem to have any information is going to help me on my case, so maybe she can do something for them."

"Sam, do me a favor," Harry said. "Can you just sit on her for a little while? Let me make a couple of calls, and I'll have somebody get in touch with you."

"Sure, Harry," Sam said. "I'll talk to you later."

Sam hung up the phone, then stood and looked at it for a long minute. Karen stayed quiet, waiting for him to be ready to say whatever was on his mind. She knew him, and knew that he would; he always shared his thoughts with her when he was ready.

"That was Harry Winslow," Sam said. "He's retired, but he still has more contacts than anyone else I know. He's going to make a few calls and get back to me, or have somebody else call me. I think he just wants to make sure she goes to the right department."

"That's fine with me, like I said. I wouldn't know what to do with her, that's for sure."

"Harry seems to think Pierre Reynard may be more of a problem than we anticipated. Apparently, he was some sort of CIA assassin back in the day."

Karen's eyebrows went up. "So, he thinks you should be careful?"

"Yeah. He says not to underestimate Reynard if I end up having to deal with him."

"In that case, the sooner you get her turned over to somebody bigger than us, the better I'm going to like it. I know you dealt with international assassins before, but that's definitely not in the job description at the Denver PD."

Sam nodded. "Believe me," he said, "I understand that completely. Keep your people watching over her, because I wouldn't put it past this Reynard to try to silence her."

Five minutes later, Sam's phone rang.

"Sam Prichard," he said.

"Mr. Prichard? This is Hunter Grayson, with the CIA. I understand you have a package for me."

"I believe I do," Sam said.

18

Sam headed toward his office, leaving Karen to see to security over Kushner. Thinking about the things Harry had told him about Reynard was only getting Sam riled up, and he needed to get himself focused back on the case.

He was fairly certain they were on the right track, and that someone had anticipated the beneficial effect the shooting would have on Web Wide Awards. The company had experienced significant growth in the last week, and that would only translate to greater value to the independent video industry players who received the award. The greater the company's following, the more the awards would promote the individual shows and artists who won them.

The big problem was that he hadn't figured out the motive behind it. The only people who really stood to gain from a greater financial value of the company would be the two people who owned the vast majority of the stock, which was John Morton and Annie Porter. From what Jade had told him, no one else owned enough stock to ever see any true benefit, because the stock was not publicly traded. While it was possible to sell the stock privately, it would probably be difficult to sell to anyone outside the company itself.

A sudden thought struck him, and he picked up his phone. He dialed John Morton, who answered on the second ring.

"John, this is Sam Prichard," he said. "I'm still trying to get to the bottom of this thing, and there are couple of things that are confusing."

"Yeah, I'm pretty confused, myself," Morton said. "I got the news yesterday afternoon, when you were talking about someone inside the company possibly being involved. I thought we had already settled that."

"Well, to be honest, I'm not sure of that anymore. John, I understand that you and Annie own ninety percent of the stock in your company. Who owns the rest?"

"The rest of the stock? We gave some to some of our executives, like bonuses. They get dividends on it every year, so it's basically just a way of rewarding them for all the extra stuff they do beyond their jobs."

"Okay, I can understand that," Sam said. "Have any of them ever tried to sell the stock?"

"Well, no," Morton said. "There's a clause in their contracts that says they can only sell the stock back to the company, and they have to sell it back if they decide to leave the company. Why? What brought all this up?"

"John, somebody anticipated the beneficial effect your company received after Max Petrelli was shot. I'm trying to figure out what could motivate anybody to want to see your company grow and suddenly be worth more money, and the only thing that would make any sense was if they had some way to benefit financially from it. Have you made any plans to go public?"

"We talked about it from time to time," said, "but that's as far as it's ever gone, just talk. An IPO would probably quadruple the value of the company, but it would also limit my control over it. It's something I probably will do within a few years, but there are no plans in place to do so anytime soon."

"So, nobody who owns stock in your company right now could benefit from the value of the stock going up, am I right?"

"Absolutely not. In fact, unless we go to IPO, the stock itself doesn't really have any value. All it does is entitle the owner of the stock to receive the dividend when we declare one, which we usually do about every quarter. In fact, we haven't missed a quarter in five years."

"Okay. Then let's talk about the company's revenue. Is there anyone who would benefit directly from the company making more money?"

"Well, Sam, we are actually considered a pretty innovative company. One of those innovations is the fact that all of our employees receive a percentage of the company's profits, rather than a conventional salary or hourly wage. What that does, of course, is turns every employee into a salesperson or ambassador for the company, because they all want to see the business grow."

Sam took the phone away from his ear and stared at it for a moment. When he put it back, he was shaking his head. "John, you just handed me more than two hundred possible suspects. If everyone gets a percentage, then everybody there stands to benefit if the company makes more money."

"Well, yes," Morton said, "but bear in mind that the percentages are very small. We use what we call a points system, where each point is worth one one-thousandth of a percent. Our lowest level employees, which is about a hundred of them, get two point five points, which equals .0025 percent of the revenue. The revenue is calculated weekly, so that they get a pretty decent paycheck each week. Some of our top executives get as much as one hundred points. Everybody makes good money, but the amount of increase we've seen in revenue over this past week wouldn't add more than a dollar or two to any of the smaller paychecks, and may be as much as fifty bucks to the bigger ones. I really don't see that being worth whatever it would've cost to pull this off."

Sam sighed. "No, I guess not. This is just—I don't know what to say. Unless we can figure out the motive behind this, John, we may never find the person who is actually responsible."

Morton was quiet for a few seconds. "The only ones who stand to benefit financially from the increase in revenue," he said slowly, "are myself and Annie. The problem with that is that we didn't do it."

"All right, then let's look at competitors. We had originally thought someone was trying to run you out of business; is there anybody else who might benefit if you suddenly grew bigger?"

"No, nobody I can think of. And realistically, Sam, I can't even see how it makes any sense that somebody was trying to build us up, and here's why. I'm going to be announcing something very soon, a whole new way to encode video that will make it so much faster that it's going to be possible to stream high definition video online, even over the slowest connections. Now, this is proprietary new technology, and it's probably worth five times what my company is worth today. The increase in revenues we've seen over this mess, even stretched out over a year, will probably be less than half of one percent of what we'll make once I release that technology. Every video company out there will need to license it from us, just to stay competitive, but it'll mean that even the smallest producer can stream high def video. Max Petrelli? He'll be able to upload high definition video and know that everyone in the world can see it just the way he wants them to."

"Is there anyone else who will earn money off that technology? Any of your development people, maybe?"

"Only in the sense that an increase in revenue will increase their paychecks. The company owns the technology outright, and I actually did some of the development work myself. I had to call in some programmers to work out the kinks, but we got it done. This thing is going to be huge, and every video streaming network in the world is going to need it. If I wanted to make extra money, I could've announced this six months ago."

"John, we've already concluded that you and Annie are not suspects," Sam said. "I'm not calling to sound accusatory, I'm just trying to figure out who else could possibly have a motive for making this happen."

"And I wish I knew what to say, Sam. Yes, we are making a bit more money, but not so much that it's that big a deal. I mean, just to generate an extra million dollars a year, we have to increase our regular traffic by almost five hundred thousand people. That's an awful lot of traffic hitting the website, which means we have to increase the number of backup servers we have online. It's not all profit, not by a long shot."

"So, even though you're making more money, it's costing you more to be able to take care of all the new traffic?"

"Oh, gosh, yes," Martin said. "If things hold steady, our traffic should be up by about seventeen million people this year. Now, that sounds like an awful lot of money when you think about the ad revenue, but it's going to cost me half of that just to maintain the site and the servers and everything else involved."

"Seventeen million people? That's more than the populations of a lot of small countries."

Morton laughed. "Yes, that's true. Our total traffic is actually much bigger than that, almost sixty million. That's a pretty big accomplishment, and there's not a lot of companies who can boast that they get that much traffic."

"That is a lot," Sam said. "Sixty million people a year? I have trouble even imagining…"

"Oh, Sam, no," Morton said. "I'm talking about sixty million people a day."

Sam's eyes got wide. "You got sixty million people a day looking at your website?"

"Yeah," Morton said. "Scary, isn't it?"

"John, that gives me a whole new list of suspects. How many of your advertisers are going to see serious increases in their own revenue over that?"

"Our advertisers? Oh, wow, I don't know. Probably quite a few of them, to be honest. An extra seventeen million pairs of eyeballs every day, we're talking about the potential for another few hundred thousand sales."

"I need a complete list of all of your advertisers, John," Sam said. "How soon can you get that to me?"

"Um, let me get hold of Annie," Martin said. "She handles all that, and I can have her email the list right over to you. Give me fifteen minutes, okay?"

THE LIST OF ADVERTISERS came through on schedule, and Sam called Jade into the office. He had printed out the list and passed it over to her.

"Something new," he said. "It turns out that several of the advertisers are going to benefit heavily from the sudden increase in traffic that Web Wide Awards is getting. We need to figure out which ones are most likely to see a significant upswing in revenues. Do you think you can handle that?"

"Well, yes, but I'd like to ask Darren to help me out, if that's okay. And I might need to ask Indie for help, as well."

"Call her if you need her," Sam said. "That's the reason we keep her on retainer."

"Then I'll get on this," she said. She took the stack of papers and left the office, headed for her own cubicle, or possibly Darren's.

Sam turned back to his computer and started looking through the list, himself. Canterbury Soft Drinks was the biggest advertiser, but they were also the one who had nearly pulled out on them. That didn't necessarily mean they couldn't be involved, but it did lend them a bit of credibility.

The next biggest advertiser was actually one of their competitors. Starbright Awards, the European competition to Web Wide Awards, also owned the Starbright Streaming Service. They boasted over twenty million subscribers worldwide, and streamed hundreds of Internet-based television programs and other videos directly into homes all over the world. They even carried a number of the independent programs that had won the Web Wide Award, and it was a safe bet that their ads on the award company website were responsible for a lot of those subscribers. A sudden upswing in traffic for Web Wide Awards was likely to mean an upswing in subscribership for Starbright.

Sam made a note to himself to check them out more thoroughly, and then was surprised when Jenna announced that Jade and Darren wanted to speak with him.

"Send them in," he said.

The two of them came in and sat in front of Sam's desk, and Darren said, "Sam, there's one advertiser that we think looks suspicious."

"Starbright?" Sam asked.

Both Jade and Darren grinned. "That's the one," Darren said. "I noticed in Summer's report that Morton said he had considered merging with them at one point. The purpose of that merger, I would suspect, was so that Starbright could take better advantage of the traffic that Web Wide Awards already has. If we're looking at advertisers who would benefit from a sudden boost in traffic, they would come out on top of the list."

"I agree," Sam said. "I was just thinking along the same lines, myself."

"Well, anyway, I asked Denny to see if he could find out anything. He's supposed to get back to us pretty shortly, but I got a hunch we might be onto something, here."

"Then, let's dig into it and find out. I really want to know who was behind this, as soon as we possibly can."

"You got it," Darren said. Jade only smiled as the two of them left the room again.

DENNY CORTLANDT WAS getting frustrated. If he was told he had to jump out of an airplane behind enemy lines, crawl on his belly through mud for twenty miles, find a single left-handed blind shoemaker and drag him back to the U.S.A., his only reaction would be one of excitement. Adrenaline would kick in, and no matter how bad things got, he'd only be having fun.

Sitting at a computer, on the other hand, was one of the few things that he honestly dreaded. He was exceptionally good with them, and could generally find whatever it was he was looking for, but he hated the thought of sitting in one spot for hours at a time, pounding on the keyboard and doing nothing more exciting than reading what somebody else thought about his topic of research.

Checking out advertisers was even more boring than usual. Starbright Awards, the one he was currently looking at, was situated in London. Like Web Wide Awards, they were known for providing a lot of information to the public on the shows they followed, but most of theirs were based in Europe. They did follow some American shows, and had even given awards to a few of them, but most of their award business seemed to be concentrated on the east side of the Atlantic.

Their revenues, however, were more substantial than Web Wide Awards', because, while they also learned a large part of their money through advertising, they had also expanded into a streaming service of their own, and part of the award they offered included a contract for the winning shows to be included in their lineup. The streaming service was subscription-based, and they had more than fourteen million subscribers throughout the U.K. and the European Union. They had recently began expanding the service into the U.S. and Canada, which explained why they wanted to advertise on a competitor's website.

To Denny, that made them stand out as probable suspects in this particular case. While the vast majority of the people who worked for the company probably knew nothing about it, Denny would've bet one of his secret identities that someone at Starbright was somehow involved in the shooting of Max Petrelli. The sudden boost in popularity of Web Wide Awards and their partner companies, like the magazine as such, meant a lot more people on this side of the pond were finding out about the Starbright Streaming Service. They were already boasting almost 6,000,000 subscribers from the west, but Denny suspected that number was growing rapidly since the traffic had increased so drastically over the last week.

The question was how to make sure. He sat and stared at the company's website for several minutes, then reached over and picked up a phone. He dialed a number from memory, and then waited for the call to connect.

"Lord Chamberlain's residence," said a male voice.

"Put the bugger on," Denny said. "Tell him it's his favorite nephew."

There was a loud laugh from the other end of the line. "Denny, is it really you? What in the world are you up to these days? I haven't bloody heard from you in a year."

"I'm a spy, uncle Devon," Denny said. "Do you really want to hear from me that often?"

"Well, a postcard would be nice once in a while. Surely you can take a moment to send one from whatever exotic locale you might be snooping around. What can I do for you, lad?"

"Listen, I'm working as an investigator in the States," Denny said. "We're trying to find out some information about a company in London, and if I remember correctly, you should be pretty familiar with the bloke who owns it. Think you could dig up a bit of dirt for me?"

"Well, only it depends on who we're talking about. What sort of company is it?"

"It's called Starbright Awards," Denny said. "They give awards to..."

"Oh, yes," Devon Chamberlain replied. "That's Ben Hickam's company. I get them on my telly, some wonderful programs. What is it you think they're up to?"

"Did you hear about the boy who was shot on the awards program a few nights ago? Happened over here, in Denver."

"Oh, yes, very sad. Although, I understand the lad is going to live, is that right?"

"Yes, he's doing well at the moment, though someone does seem to have tried again. We've come to the conclusion, however, that the shooting wasn't actually about him. It seems to be an attempt to actually build up the company behind the awards, and Mr. Hickam 's company is one of the biggest advertisers. What that means is that he is likely to benefit from the fact that the company is getting a lot of new traffic to their website, ever since the shooting happened. Right now, it appears that somebody hired a professional assassin to make the attempt on the boy's life, and since Starbright stands to make a lot of money off advertising to all the new traffic, that puts them high on my suspect list."

"Well, what is it you'd like me to find out? I can't exactly call Ben up and accuse him of attempted murder, now, can I?"

"And why not? Surely it'd get someone's attention, right?"

"Why, yes, and if you're correct about them, it might get me the kind of attention I don't want. If you're trying to get me killed, you can give it up. You're not in my will, lad."

"What? After all I've done for you? Look, I don't want to be in your will, and I don't want you dead, I just want to know if someone in the company might be conspiring to boost our client in order to improve their own sales rates over here."

"And how the bloody hell, pray tell, am I supposed to find that out? Have you a plan laid out for me?"

"Uncle Devon, when did you ever need anyone to lay out a plan? As I recall, you were one of the most successful bloody investigative reporters the *Times* ever had. Surely you can think of some way to probe the mud for me, can't you?"

There was sputtering on the line for a few seconds. "Well, fine, then," Chamberlain said at last. "But you'll bloody well owe me a favor."

Denny grinned. "That works for me," he said. "Let me know what you find out, right?"

"Shouldn't think it would be too difficult," Chamberlain said. "I'm due to meet Ben at our club for whist in half an hour, anyway. I'll call you when I get back home tonight. It'll probably be after eleven, will you be up?"

"Uncle, I'm in Denver. That will only be four o'clock this afternoon, for me."

"Well, good. Hate to think I might wake you." There was a click, and the line was dead.

Denny replaced the handset and grinned. "Sly old bugger," he muttered.

He got up from his desk and walked down the hall to Sam's office. Jenna looked up and smiled, then announced him. Sam told her to send him in.

"I've been checking out Starbright, as Darren asked," he said as he sat in the chair in front of the desk. "They've been doing some expanding lately, got their own TV service going, and they've been working hard to get subscribers over here to get even bigger. Since they advertise with our clients, and those ads are likely getting an awful lot of attention lately, I rang up my uncle Devon in London. He knows just about everybody over there, and as I thought, he knows the owner of that company well. They're playing cards tonight, and he's going to see what he can find out. I should hear back from him at some time in this afternoon. He's going to dig around a bit, see if he can find out just how likely they might be to be involved in this thing."

"Denny, are you sure that's a good idea? These people, whoever they are, don't seem to be shy when it comes to murder or attempted murder. You could be putting your uncle in danger."

Denny scoffed. "More likely, I've put his friend Ben Hickam in danger. Hickam owns the company, and uncle Devon is no man to mess with. He spent nigh twenty years untangling the politics of Parliament to uncover all sorts of governmental corruption for the *Times* of London, and more than one tried to shut up and died for their efforts. He's a master at getting people to admit to things they'd rather keep quiet; in fact, they often don't even remember that they said anything at all."

Darren Beecher had walked in as they were talking, and he suddenly grinned. "Uncle Devon?" he asked. "And he was a reporter for the *Times*? Are you telling me Devon Chamberlain is your uncle?"

Denny look surprised. "You bloody know him?"

"Only by reputation," Darren said. "Anytime we were working with Scotland Yard, it seemed like one of his articles would be in the file. Sam, this guy not only covered a lot of the major corruption stories in England, he actually caught quite a few of the culprits involved, handed them over himself to Scotland Yard. Quite an amazing fellow."

"He sounds like it," Sam said. "Remind me to see that he gets something for doing this."

"Aw, bloody no!" Denny said. "The old fart'll be calling us every day looking for work if we do that. This way, he'll only want a favor in return one day, and I can live with that."

Sam smiled. "Okay, I'll let you manage him, then. Let me know what he finds out, okay?"

"Will do," Denny said. "It'll be in my report by the end of the day."

19

Lord Devon Chamberlain, who was afforded the title for no better reason than the fact that his father had been a Duke of some small area that nobody bothered to remember anymore, walked into the Travellers Club a few minutes after eight in the evening, fashionably late as was his habit. Benjamin Hickam, David Darwin, and David Cross were waiting for him around the whist table, and one of them had already seen to it that his whiskey sour was waiting.

He sat down, picked up the drink and took a sip, then greeted his friends. "Ben, David, David," he said. "Do you know, I always feel just a bit ridiculous saying that. You should put Benjamin between the two of you, so that I won't feel quite so stupid the next time."

"Not much chance of that," David Cross said. "You manage to make yourself feel stupid for the silliest reasons, Devon. Who are we to take away a good one?"

"Oh, and that's why you are such good friends. It's also why, if truth be told, I so enjoy taking your money at these little games."

"Oh, shut up and deal," Ben Hickam said. "You're last in, so you deal first."

Devon grinned as he picked up the cards and began shuffling. He enjoyed playing whist with his friends, and the penny ante bets they made only helped to make it more fun. He finished shuffling and let the cards fly, demonstrating that he was still the fastest dealer among them, just as he had been when they were all recruits in the Royal Navy.

"Hearts is trumps," he said. "It's to you, David."

David Darwin arranged his cards carefully, taking far more time than was necessary. The two Davids were a team, while Devon always partnered himself with Ben.

"Good heavens, Darwin," his partner said, "Will you toss out a card already?"

"Well, it's got to be the right one, dunnit?" Darwin asked. "We don't want to be feeding these blighters our tricks, now, do we?" He huffed a couple of times, then tossed out the ace of clubs.

Hickam was next and laid the deuce, followed by Cross with the trey. Devon tossed out the five, making Darwin groan.

"Chamberlain, you broke that run," he said. "Every time we start with ace through four, David and I end up winning."

"Well, it's glad I am I didn't have the four, then," Devon said. "You took the trick, so you lead again."

"Bastard," Darwin muttered. He laid out the five of diamonds. Ben dropped the queen of diamonds on it, Cross laid the seven, and Devon followed up with the nine.

"Ours," Ben said, pushing the cards toward Devon, who stacked them neatly and laid them beside his glass.

"Your go," Darwin said. Ben laid out the king of diamonds, Cross added the four, Devon dropped the deuce, and Darwin chuckled as he took the trick with the five of hearts.

"I saw that coming," Cross said. "Far too many diamonds in my hand, I knew somebody was short."

The play continued, and the two Davids took the hand with eight tricks, for a score of two. It was Darwin's turn to deal, then, and he shuffled the cards with as much noise and fanfare as he could manage. Somewhere, he had learned the trick of slapping a card down so that it made a loud noise, and Devon noticed several of the other members glaring their direction.

"Darwin, can you be a bit more gentle? I think you're beginning to annoy some of our fellows, what with making such a racket as you deal."

Cross nodded. "He's right," he said. "It's bad enough when you slam the cards during play, but when you do it as you deal, it sounds like a small war in here. Had more than enough of that, long ago."

"Which it might be," said Lord Fancher from a couple of tables over, "if he keeps that up. Down the racket, Darwin, you're making an ass of yourself again."

Darwin grumbled under his breath, but laid the rest of the cards out quietly. Devon took the opportunity to look at his partner across the table.

"So, Ben," he said conversationally. "Did this horrid shooting in the States cause your company any grief?"

Hickam seemed completely unfazed by the question. "And why should it?" he asked. "D'ye think I care much what the Yanks do?"

"Daresay not," Devon said, "but they seem to be sort of a cousin to your firm. Awards, all that rot. Just wondered if it's going to affect your move into the States." They picked up the cards and began sorting them.

"Can't see why it would," Hickam said. "We don't depend on the Yank market, but we're bound to pick up a lot of them as subscribers. I could bloody care less who gives awards for the vids, that only costs me money. Putting them on the telly, that's what stuffs my bank accounts."

"Good point, that," Devon said. "I had been thinking that that poor lad getting shot in the middle of their broadcast might cast some dirt on then, your competitors, but now I've been hearing a lot of stories that say it's actually gone the other way. On you to go first, by the way. Diamonds is trumps."

Hickam laid out the king of hearts, and Cross followed it with the four. Devon laid the six, and Darwin the five. Devon picked up the cards and laid them by his glass.

"What do you mean, gone the other way?" Hickam asked.

"Well, that bloody American company has been cast as some sort of victim, so that there has been an outpouring of support for them. I read today where they've gone up half again in their revenues and traffic. Don't know about you, but to me that seems a bit odd, dunnit?"

"S'pose it would," Hickam said. "Be a shame to have some poor lad die to build them up, though."

"Oh, the boy's alive," Devon said. "Heard it on the news, they say he's going to be fine. Probably make him a bloody superstar, what with the sympathy and all. And I understand that the company's advertisers are the ones reaping the greatest benefit of all. You advertise on them, don't you?"

"A bit," Hickam said. "I do hope the boy will be all right, I already sent word to him that I want to run his show. Bigger it gets, more subscribers I can sign up, especially out of the Yanks."

Devon laughed. "Now, hadn't thought of that," he said. "Was that the plan, then? Have the boy shot, then use his program and all those new eyes on your advertising to boost your sales?"

Nobody else would've noticed it, but nobody else had spent so many years ferreting out the corruption in the royal court and parliament. It was Devon Chamberlain who had done that, for more than two decades as the star reporter of the *Times*' government section. He learned early on to spot the flash of anger, the split second of shame, the tiny minute expressions that cross our faces when what we say is at direct odds with what's in our minds.

Hickam flashed guilt for a split second, then anger, and then one more split second of fear. All of them passed so quickly that the card he dropped hadn't even hit the table by the time they were all gone. His face was perfectly normal again, and the laugh that came from him sounded absolutely natural.

"Terrible thought," he said. "Wish I'd thought it myself, and I might have to think of variations on that theme to use in the future, but this time it was nothing but dumb luck. Come now, Chamberpot," he said, using the old nickname they'd given Devon when they were recruits. "D'ye truly think me capable of something so evil? I mean, I confess to a love of the filthy lucre, but you can't truly believe I would stoop that low. Can you?"

Devon flashed him a middle finger. "Capable? Absolutely. Guilty of it? Now, that's another whole matter. I am quite certain, however, that you will take advantage of any possible opportunity to make more of that 'filthy lucre' that you confess to being so fond of. Besides which, this would be beyond your intelligence." He grinned at David Darwin. "Darwin might be smart enough, however. Perhaps he did it, just to help you out. After all, he does take a lot of your money in these little games."

All four of them chuckled, as the cards continued to drop onto the table. They played until well after ten, and Devon finally ended up being the winner of the evening. He raked up his winnings, a total of four pounds fifty pence, and walked out to the lobby where Charles, his faithful companion, butler, and driver, was waiting.

IT WAS NEARLY FIVE by the time Denny's phone rang, and he snatched it up instantly. "Cortlandt," he said.

"Do you remember," his uncle said, with just enough slurring in his voice to tell Denny that he'd been drinking, "just a few hours ago when you referred to yourself as my favorite nephew?"

"I do," Denny replied.

"Well, consider yourself disowned," Devon said. "I went to the Travellers Club with the full intent of coming back to tell you that there is absolutely no way my friend Ben Hickam could be involved in the crime of which you spoke. Unfortunately, I am forced to report to you that he is almost certainly guilty. I don't mean that he actually fired the shot, but there is no doubt in my mind that he paid someone to do it. This is completely devastating to me, dear boy, because Ben and I have been friends since we were barely out of school. We joined the Navy on the same day, finished training together, served on the same bloody ship for three solid years, and each of us saved the other's arse numerous times. Have you any idea what it does to

me, tonight, to think that he could truly stoop so low as to con-
done the murder of a young man for no better reason than to
try to make his business more money?"

"Uncle Devon," Denny said, "I'm sorry. Can you tell me
what makes you believe he did this?"

"Well, I've no evidence to give you," Devon said. "All I've
got is the certain knowledge. I jokingly accused him, and the
guilt was written all over his face, though only for a brief second. Right after, he got angry, but then he got a little scared.
I laughed it off, and assured him I didn't actually believe any
such thing. I even went so far as to accuse one of our other
friends of doing it to try to help him out, just to make myself
sound completely absurd, and I believe it worked. If I'm dead
by morning, we shall both know that it didn't."

"Uncle, do you honestly think you might be in danger? I
could..."

"Oh, of course not," Devon said. "Even if he thinks I believe him guilty, he knows bloody well I couldn't prove it. Ben
Hickam is so much smarter than me that it would be like Al-
bert Einstein being afraid of Forrest Gump. I've no intention
of pursuing this matter, not in any way, but I promised you a
report and so I've given it. Now, I'm going to stumble up to
my bedroom and drink the rest of the bottle of bourbon that's
sitting there waiting for me. With any luck, I shall sleep until
well after noon tomorrow, and won't have to think about anything more complex than taking a piss until then. Good night,
nephew. I hope you bloody sleep well, for I won't."

The line went dead and Denny replaced the handset. He sat
there for a few seconds, then got up and walked toward Sam's
office.

Jenna was just picking her purse up off the desk as she prepared to leave.

"Is he in?" Denny asked.

"Yes, but he's about to go home. Is it important?"

"Well, we'll let him be the judge of that, shall we?" He walked past her and tapped on Sam's office door.

"Come on in," Sam called out.

Denny stepped through the door and shut it behind him, then sank into the chair in front of Sam's desk once again.

Sam looked at him for a moment, then nodded. "I take it you heard from your uncle?"

"Too bloody right," Denny said. "He says there's no doubt in his mind that Ben Hickam, who owns Starbright, was some way or other behind this whole thing."

"And you believe he's correct?" Sam asked.

"Devon Chamberlain never once failed to spot when people were lying to him," Denny said. "All the way up to the royal family, he could always tell when they were being untruthful. He knows the secrets that could literally destroy the royalty of Britain, and they bloody well know that he knows, but they also know that he'll keep his mouth shut about them. If he says Hickam is guilty, then he's guilty."

Sam leaned back in his chair and looked at Denny for a moment. "How do we use this information, then?"

"We need to find a connection between Starbright and Reynard. There's no doubt in my mind they work for him, but it's going to be bloody hard to prove any link between the two." He rubbed his hands over his face. "I need to go to London, boss. I need to get into Starbright and find that connection."

"And how do you plan to do that?" Sam asked. "I mean, where would you even look?"

"Starbright is a bloody video company," Denny said. "I've never been to their headquarters, but I'm certain it's everything you'd imagine. They're bound to have security cameras and such all around the place, and if they do, then there will be some trace of Reynard. He'll show up on it, somewhere."

Sam stared at him for a moment. "How would you get in?"

"That's my specialty, Sam," Denny said with a grin. "All I need to do is get into that building and find where they store their security treasures. If I'm wrong about that, there will still be something. I'll get all of their phone records, steal Hickam's cell phone, whatever I've got to do. That bloody bastard has to pay for this, Sam."

"Denny, you seem a lot more upset now than you did when we talked earlier. What changed?"

"You want the truth? What changed was hearing the grief in my uncle's voice. He and Ben Hickam have been friends for many years, since they first enlisted in the Royal Navy. You should have heard him, Sam. It's like—it's like his spirit was broken. Hickam needs to pay for having that boy shot, but he also needs to pay for betraying not only my uncle, but everyone who knows him. He's considered one of the great philanthropists of the U.K., gives millions of dollars to charity and good works, but if he could stoop so low as to do this..."

"Okay," Sam said. "Okay, I get it." He turned to his computer and started tapping on the keyboard. "I'm authorizing you to go to London. There will be a jet waiting for you at nine o'clock tonight, to take you to Heathrow. Denny, I want you to check in with me every day. If you get stuck on the security video or anything like that, I want you to call Indie. If you can figure out how she can get into their system, she can find anything they've got."

Denny nodded. "Thank you, Sam," he said. "I'll get what we need, and get back here as soon as I can."

"Wait a minute," Sam said. "What happens if you get busted over there? How do we get you back out?"

Denny grinned, but there was no humor. "I've got friends over there," he said. "And I've also got enemies. The nice thing about having enemies, in my old line of work, is that I know where an awful lot of bodies are buried. I won't have any trouble getting free, if I run into a snag."

"All right," Sam said. "Just remember to talk to me every day. I want regular updates."

"You'll get them. I'll find what you need to nail these bastards."

He got up and walked out of Sam's office, and Sam began shutting down his computer. He walked out the door a few moments later, got into the Mustang and headed for home, his mind racing around everything he had learned that day.

He parked the car beside the Honda Ridgeline that was their family vehicle and leaned on his cane as he walked up the steps. Some days, his hip made sure he remembered that it was bad, and this was one of those days. He walked in the door, and was surprised to find no one there to greet him.

"Indie?" He called out. "Where is everybody at?"

She stuck her head through the door from the kitchen, so that he could see her through the dining room. "Where you think I am? I'm making dinner. How was your day, babe?"

"It's been interesting," he said. "I just sent Denny off to London, to check out a new theory we've got on the motive behind the shooting. Turns out that the company has gained so much new traffic that the advertisers could end up making millions more dollars over it. Well, one of those advertisers is Starbright Streaming Service, out of London. Denny spoke to his uncle over there, who used to be an investigative reporter, and I guess the old man looked into it and is convinced that they are behind it. Denny is going over to infiltrate their headquarters, to see if he can find evidence. He's probably going to be calling you, by the way."

"No problems," she said. "That's what you guys pay me for, remember?"

Sam walked up behind her where she stood at the range and slipped his arms around her waist. She leaned back into him as he kissed her cheek, moaning happily.

"So, what's for dinner?" Sam asked.

"I decided on something simple, tonight," she said. "Spaghetti and meatballs. Your son and daughter have driven me crazy today, and I just need to take it easy for the evening."

"I can certainly understand that," Sam said. "Tell you what. I'll even do the dishes tonight."

She turned around in his arms and put her own around his neck. "That, Mister, will get you an even bigger surprise later tonight."

20

The Gulfstream touched down at Heathrow at just before one PM, which was six AM back in Denver, and Denny picked up his bag and walked straight through the terminal. He found his way to the car rental kiosk and quickly selected a Jaguar F type, filled out the paperwork and swiped his company card, and took off into the city. He followed the M4 to North Circular Road, then turned north up to Wembley.

He took out his phone after he made the turn and called his uncle. Lord Chamberlain answered on the fourth ring.

"Lord Chamberlain's residence," he said. It was the way he always answered his phone at home.

"Uncle Devon," Denny said. "I'm in the city, can we talk?"

"Well, that didn't take you very bleeding long. I thought you'd be coming, but I didn't expect you for another day or so. Do you realize, lad, that you have left an old man quite depressed?"

"I'm sorry about that, Uncle," Denny said. "Right now, though, I'm a bit more concerned about your physical health than your mental. Where is a safe place we can meet up?"

"Is it absolutely necessary, Dennis? I'm actually somewhat inebriated at the moment. Seems to be the result of getting some terribly bad news last night."

"Fine," Denny said, "I'll come by your house. Open the garage for me, I don't want anyone to know I'm here just yet."

"No. No, do not come here, I forbid it. I'll have Charles drive me down to the Green Man. We can speak privately out in the smoking area outside, and you can get yourself a bloody room. How long till you can be there?"

Denny thought for a moment. "Probably twenty minutes. I'll see you there." He hung up the phone and put it back in his pocket.

He understood why his uncle was being hostile, but it didn't help his mood any. The old man could well be in danger, although his assessment from the night before was probably fairly accurate. Hickam might guess that Devon suspected him of being involved in the shooting, but it had been eight years since Devon Chamberlain was active in any investigations. Hickam wouldn't be worried that Devon could prove anything, and he could undoubtedly cast plenty of doubt on any accusations that might be made. If there's one thing Devon Chamberlain would never stand for, it was being made to look like a fool; he'd keep his mouth shut about his suspicions, and since they were old friends, he'd probably never bother to look for any kind of proof.

Hickam had nothing to worry about. The only thing Denny worried about was whether Hickam understood that.

The Green Man Hotel is less than a mile from Wembley Stadium, and well known to many seasoned world travelers. Its pub is one of the finest in the area, providing the kind of food and atmosphere that both tourists and locals yearn for in a pub. The hotel is decent, though the rooms have rather plain furnishings and décor.

Devon was correct, however. With nothing exciting happening at the stadium, the hotel was only sparsely booked.

Since smoking was not allowed inside, there was an outdoor smoking area set up that was even heated with fire pits maintained by the staff in the wintertime. Denny stopped at the bar for a glass of ale, then took it outside to wait for his uncle.

It wasn't a long wait. Devon came walking up onto the covered porch a few minutes later, and sat beside him.

"Well?" The old man glared at him from the corner of his eye. "You've flown all the way across the bloody pond, I suppose to further ruin my life?"

"Uncle Devon," Denny said, "would you rather have gone through life not knowing the truth?"

Devon spun his head to look straight at Denny's face. "As opposed to learning that one of my dearest friends might be a murderer? Why, yes, I would've preferred to remain in ignorance. I realize you are only half a Chamberlain, since my sister married that bloody American wastrel who pretended to be your father, but I think you are fully aware of what the Chamberlain blood does to you. Do you know how we came by the name?"

Denny sighed. He had heard this particular discourse on numerous occasions when he was a child. "Yes, Uncle," he said. "Your great-great-great-great-great-grandfather served as Chamberlain to Queen Victoria, and was knighted by her because of his unwavering dedication to seeking out the truth about her political enemies. Until she knighted him as Sir Reginald Chamberlain, his name was Reginald Higginbotham. All Chamberlains since then have devoted themselves to becoming investigators of one sort or another."

"Exactly," Devon said. "As much as I might like to pretend I don't know what Ben has done, I simply cannot. Now that you

have forced me to look at this awful truth in the eye, I must
see that it is brought to light, and that my oldest and dearest
friend is properly punished. In this case, since a murder on foreign soil orchestrated by a citizen of the Commonwealth for
the purpose of corporate gain would be certainly prosecuted as
industrial espionage, Ben will face a high probability that he
shall spend the rest of his life in prison."

"And you don't think he deserves such a penalty?"

"Of course he does. And when I find evidence of his guilt,
it will undoubtedly be the fate that awaits him. My anger with
you is due to the fact that I was happily ignorant of his guilt until less than twenty-four hours past. Now that you have thrust
it in my face, I have no choice but to do whatever is necessary
to see him charged and convicted."

"Well, perhaps I can relieve you of that burden," Denny
said. "That's the reason I'm here, Uncle. I've come to find that
very evidence, so you'll have no need of seeking it."

The old man's hand was lightning fast, and Denny barely
managed to brace himself before it slapped him across the face.

"How dare you? How dare you come to me the way you
did, make me confront an old friend with an accusation I had
no reason to believe in, and then think you can simply waltz in
here and put me at ease? Ben Hickam is my friend, and I am a
Chamberlain. It is my duty to get to the truth."

"I'm not disputing that, Uncle Devon. I'm only trying to
tell you that you don't have to do this alone. I was sent here to
find the very evidence that you are looking for; I shall be more
than happy to provide you with a complete copy of everything
I find. I fully agree that it should be you who brings it to the

government. My job is to produce the evidence to the prosecutor in Denver, which is where the crime itself took place."

"What makes you think you can find such evidence? Ben is absolutely no fool, as evidenced by the fact that he has made billions of pounds. Do you think he would not have taken great pains to cover his involvement?"

"I'm quite certain he did," Denny said. "I am also certain that evidence still exists. There are very few people who can truly do anything without leaving some trace of it to be found. This is especially true whenever money is involved, and there is no doubt in my mind that money changed hands. Somewhere, there exists a record of the transactions involved, and I intend to find it."

Devon stared at him for a moment. "You would do better to look for transactions that do not exist. Variations in bank ledgers that do not seem to have a transaction connected to them. There are certain men in London who see to such things, so that men like Ben Hickam do not have to get their hands dirty. Payments to such facilitators are often disguised as ledger errors, or the distribution of funds for investment purposes."

Denny nodded slowly. "Then perhaps, Uncle, we should do better to work on this together. You wish to uphold the Chamberlain name and bring evil before the light; I seek to prove that the events that took place were deliberate and calculated, rather than the result of negligence on the part of my client."

Devon reached into his pocket and took out a pack of Dunhill cigarettes, shook one out, and then produced the gold lighter that Denny had given him years earlier, for his birthday. He held it out and looked at it for a moment, then lit the cigarette and put the lighter back into his pocket.

"Together, then," he said. "How do you propose to do this?"

"I'm going to get into his building," Denny said. "I need to get access to his computers, and then an associate of ours can find just about anything we need inside it."

"That should be a start, at least. I think that we might also consider a direct confrontation. He knows me, so he knows it's likely I figured out what he's done. Together, you and I can probably wring a confession from the bastard."

"And it may come to that," Denny said. "First, I want to try my way. It won't take me long, I can assure you."

"How long?" Devon asked.

"I slept some on the flight over," Denny said, "and I'll get a bit more this afternoon. I'm going into the building tonight, and I expect to have the answers we seek by this time tomorrow."

Devon sat quietly for a couple of minutes, occasionally puffing on his cigarette and looking up at the canopy overhead. At last, he put the cigarette out in the ashtray beside him.

"Then we shall meet here again, at this time tomorrow. If you have not succeeded, then we should do things my way. Agreed?"

Denny grinned. "Agreed, Uncle."

The old man got up and walked away without another word, and Denny went into the hotel. He went to the front desk and got himself a room, then went back out to his car and got his bag. He carried it up to his room and set it on one of the beds, then laid down on the other and set an alarm on his phone for six.

WHEN HE AWOKE, DENNY took a quick shower and then turned to his bag, sitting on the bed. He opened it and took out his clothing, then began removing items from the hidden compartment in the bottom.

The night before, even before leaving Denver, he had made a few calls to other old friends in London. From them, he had learned that the Starbright building used highly sophisticated, state of the art security. Digital combination locks secured every door from the outside, and many of the interior doors required biometric identification—fingerprints—before they would open.

One of those old friends, who happened to be in charge of a large database of military records, found a copy of Benjamin Hickam's fingerprint card from when he was in the Royal Navy and emailed it to Denny. With that, a CAD program, and a fairly simple 3D printer, Denny was able to create thin, flexible copies of Hickam's thumbs and fingers that could be slipped over his own. Those would, with the application of a bit of moisture from his own palms, handle all the biometric locks. The digital combinations were even easier, since Denny had an app on his phone that would allow him to plug a cable into the digital lock and read its combination. All such locks had a place for the cable, because that was how they were programmed when the combinations were changed.

Also in the hidden compartment was a gun. He had chosen a Walther PP Q4, set up to receive a suppressor, which he added. Even with the silencer in place, the pistol was light and small, easily concealed under his shirt.

With all of these things tucked into pockets and under his clothing, Denny headed out. He had every intention of getting the information he was after that very night, so that he would have plenty of time to consult with Indie if necessary.

The drive to the Starbright building took him almost an hour, mostly because of the evening traffic. There were an awful lot of vehicles on the road in London, and many of its streets were still narrow from the days when automobiles were a novelty, rather than the norm. Even some of the main thoroughfares were narrow enough to cause some traffic congestion when so many people were trying to get out and enjoy the nightlife, or begin the nightly hunting rituals that most singles engage in.

Of course, a company like Starbright had people working at all hours. Denny knew that he would have to be careful, but he had learned years earlier that people had a tendency to ignore someone who looked like he knew what he was doing and had a reason for being wherever he was. The building was large enough that he doubted there were too many people who could be certain they knew everyone who worked there, so all he really had to do was make himself fit in.

He parked the Jaguar in the company's car park, then approached one of the side doors of the building. With a practiced ease that came from a lot of experience, he slipped the cord into the digital lock and tapped the icon on his phone. It took less than six seconds to display the combination, and he was able to punch it into the lock, open the door, and slip his phone into his pocket in one smooth movement. If a security guard happened to be watching the monitor showing that door, it would have looked perfectly natural.

Fortunately, there was no one in the hall that he entered. He kept his face downward, avoiding the overhead security cameras, then made his way through the halls in search of the computer rooms. It took him less than five minutes to find them, and he was pleased to see that they had large windows set into their interior walls, allowing him to see inside without having to open a door and surprise someone. One of the rooms was completely empty, and he pressed his right thumb against the security scanner.

The scanner flashed red, indicating that it did not recognize the thumbprint. He hadn't been sure whether Hickam was right handed or left, so he quickly tried his left thumb instead, and the scanner turned green. The lock clicked, and he opened the door and walked into the computer room.

He plugged the USB adapter for his phone into the computer, and another app began running. This one looked for security passwords in the operating system on the computer, and once again it was able to get him the answer within a matter of seconds. He tapped the keyboard and entered the password, then took hold of the mouse and began scrolling through the files.

A moment later, he realized he had hit the jackpot. The main computer system for the building not only held all of the communications for every employee, but also kept all of the internal security video. He worked quickly, creating a Split Multi Link Trunking protocol connection, assigning a port to it and then creating a password protected entry point. The whole process took only eleven minutes, and meant that he could give Indie easy access to the back end of Starbright's entire computer system, but the system was far too large to try to copy. Remote access was the only way it could be safely searched.

That was all he needed to do, so it was time to leave. He got up and walked out of the computer room, letting the door secure itself behind him as he strolled nonchalantly through the hallways again. He passed a few people, smiled and nodded at each one, and made it all the way back to the door through which he had entered with no problem.

And then he ran into a snag. While the door could be opened from the outside through the use of a digital combination, on the inside it was nothing but a fire door. Pressing the bar to open the door would sound an alarm, and that was not something he wanted to do.

He turned around and walked back into the building, wandering through the halls for several minutes and checking every exit door he could find. Except for the ones at the front of the building, right in front of the security guards at the front desk, every single one of them was rigged to sound an alarm if opened from the inside.

As long as he was deep inside the building, the security guards had no reason to pay any attention to him. If he was inside, naturally, he must belong there.

Trying to leave by the front doors, on the other hand, might prompt one of the guards to ask for his ID. Denny really didn't want to have to use a weapon, simply because it might create problems he'd actually prefer to avoid. Still, it seemed that it might be the only way he was getting out of the building, so he prepared himself to take the risk.

He started toward the front lobby, and almost bumped into a young woman who was stepping out of her own workstation.

"Oh, your pardon," she said. "I'm sorry, I didn't see you."

"No trouble, luv," Denny said. "I'm just on my way out. A bit knackered, too many of these late nights lately."

"Oh, I know," the girl said. "This is my third in a row this week. You'd think his Lordship would bring on some new help, it would surely make him look good, creating dozens of new jobs. He certainly doesn't seem to like paying the overages on our wages, does he, now?"

"That's so true," Denny said. "Are you going off, as well, then?"

She looked up at him shyly, and smiled. "Yes," she said. "I finally finished the user ratings I've been working on the last three days, and I truly cannot wait to get home and just relax."

Denny smiled back. "In a rush, then? I'm more than a bit famished, and I'd love some company over dinner. Would you care to join me?"

She giggled. "Well, now, that depends on where you plan to eat. I'm a bit picky, I'm afraid."

"Then, that's perfect," Denny said. "You can pick the place, and I'll pick up the check. Where should we go?"

She pretended to be deep in thought as they walked along, and didn't object when Denny slipped an arm around her shoulders. When they reached the front lobby, the security guard at the desk looked up briefly, grinned when he saw Denny obviously trying to charm the pants off the girl, and looked back at the magazine laying in front of him.

Denny and the young lady, whose name was Alice, walked out the front door and turned right to get to the car park. Alice had chosen a chip shop nearby, and Denny promised to follow her straight there.

Five minutes later, Alice was genuinely surprised when her date failed to show up. Denny was already three miles away in the opposite direction, headed back to Wembley and the Green Man Hotel.

He checked his phone for the time, and saw that it was not yet nine. That made it just a bit before two in the afternoon back in Denver, so he dialed Indie.

21

Saturday, at the Prichard household, was not always a day of rest the way they liked it to be. Sometimes, it seemed to be just a continuation of the rest of the week, with plenty of work to do around the house. Sam, for instance, was using his riding mower to take care of the yard, the first time he had a chance to mow it himself since the previous fall. Kenzie was upstairs, cleaning her own room, and Indie was folding clothes when her phone rang.

"Hello?"

"Miss Indie, this is Denny Cortlandt. I'm across the pond in London, and Sam told me to give you a call when I had certain arrangements made."

Indie smiled. "Yes, Denny," she said. "Sam told me you might be calling. Let me get to my computer, give me just a moment."

"No rush," Denny said. "I've set up an SMLT protocol connection to the target computer, and I'm hoping you'll be able to get in to it."

"Oh, I can," Indie replied. "Okay, just a few more seconds. I'm letting Herman wake up. Okay, he's ready. Got the IP address for me?"

Denny gave her the IP address, the port number, and login information, and she fed them into Herman. When she turned

293

him loose, she watched the monitor closely to see if there was any sign her intrusion was being detected.

"Hey, you did good work," she said after a moment. "Herman is in, and has full access to everything."

"Well, there were a lot of protected files in there," Denny said. "Not too sure what you'll do about those, but..."

"Herman can get in," Indie said. "This is a Windows system, so he can find the Credentials Manager, which will give him access to the passwords necessary to open any locked files. The only one he'll have to really work for is the Windows administrator password, but those usually aren't that hard to crack. Do you have any specific ideas what we're looking for in there?"

"Well, certainly, anything connecting Starbright to the shooting at the arena," Denny said. "Also, you might need to look through the security videos pretty hard. My gut says that Reynard may have been to the building, and probably met with Benjamin Hickam, the owner. If you can find his face..."

"Well, if he's there, I'll find him."

"Good. I've got a pretty solid reason to believe that Hickam was the one who arranged that shooting, and he would certainly have the money Reynard would charge. If there's a connection, and I'm dead certain there is, you'll find it in that computer system."

"I'm feeding in the various data and photographs now," she replied. "That's an awfully big system, so it's not going to happen in a few minutes. Is this a good number to call you back on?"

"Yes, my cell number," Denny said. "Let me know as soon as you can, please, if you find anything definite. Or even something indefinite, if it seems to be a lead I can work with."

"I sure will. And you ought to call Sam. I think he may have something to tell you."

"My very next call, luv, I assure you," Denny said.

"Give it a minute, though, because he is out on the lawnmower. I'll tell him to shut it down and wait for your call."

"Will do," Denny said. The line went dead and Indie put down her phone as she went to the back door. She slid it open and leaned out, waving until she got Sam's attention.

He rode the motor close to the deck and shut down the engine. "Hey, babe," he said.

"Thought you'd like to know that Denny is going to call you," she said. "Probably about any second now."

Sam grinned and pulled his phone out of his pocket, and it rang at that very moment.

"Denny? It's Sam," he said. "How are things going over there?"

"It all went well," Denny said. "I got in with no problem and set up the connection. Mrs. Prichard is working on it now, looking for anything to connect Hickam and Starbright to Reynard."

"Awesome. You didn't run into any problems, then?"

"None," Denny said. "I asked Miss Indie to look for any sign Reynard made contact with Hickam, or vice versa. My gut says she's going to find it, Sam."

"Good," Sam said. "We're fairly certain, now, that Morton was not actually involved, but there's still a chance that someone inside his company could be. Indie might find something along that line, but I'm more interested in connecting Hickam and Reynard, at this point. Any evidence that ties them together will help us bring this thing to a close. I don't know about you, but I'm ready to wrap this case up."

Denny sighed. "So am I," he said, "and uncle Devon is right there with us. Sam, this whole bloody thing was probably just about Hickam building up his company as it moves into the American market. By giving Web Wide Awards a boost, he put his bloody advertising in front of millions more Americans who might sign up for his streaming service. I can't think of a worse motive for what that poor young man endured."

"I agree," Sam said. "Unfortunately, it's the only scenario that actually makes any sense. By building up Morton's following, he increased his own presence inside the American video market. I'm going to ask Indie to see if she can find any evidence that their own sales have been increasing since the shooting. Hey, maybe we'll be lucky and get a lead on Reynard, himself. I'd love to be involved in bringing him down."

"Sam, that's harder than you think. Reynard has never failed to take out his target, and he always seems to be a step ahead of whoever's after him. If we get close to him, he's going to know it."

"Then maybe we can find something we can turn over to NSA and they can take him down. Every criminal makes a mistake sooner or later, and maybe this one will be his time."

"Listen, I'll do some digging over here, see if I can pick up any kind of intel on what he's up to. I asked Miss Indie to let me know what she finds, but she said it's going to be a while. I'll work on learning all I can about Reynard until then."

"Good job," Sam said. "Keep me posted if you learn anything."

Sam hung up the phone and sat back in the seat of the mower. He was finally starting to feel like the jigsaw puzzle was coming together. Maybe soon, he would be able to see what the final picture was going to be.

He fired up the mower again and went back to giving the yard its trim.

HERMAN CHIMED, AND Indie went to the computer to see what he had found. The monitor displayed several links, and she clicked the first one. It opened to reveal an email that had been sent more than three months earlier from Ben Hickam's account on the server.

From: Hickam, Benjamin
To: elim@otromail.com
I've gotten the word that we should proceed. Ideal target would be winner of Top Discovery Award from WWA. Can you make that happen during the webcast?

There was a reply attached to it from the recipient.

Consider it done.

Indie stared at the screen. There before her was very solid evidence that Benjamin Hickam, owner of Starbright Awards, had specifically ordered the shooting of Max Petrelli, though it was unlikely he knew that Max would be the winner at that time.

The wording seemed very strange, though. Hickam seemed to be saying that he had received authorization, apparently from someone else. Was it possible that his entire Board of Directors was involved in this plot? That would make it a massive conspiracy, since a simple internet search turned up the fact that there were more than twenty people on the board. Some of them were even diplomats and officials in the U.K.

She went back and clicked the next link, and an audio file began to play. There were two voices, and while she didn't recognize either of them, the context led her to believe that one of them was Hickam, himself, while the other was an electronically distorted voice with an American accent. The date stamp on the file indicated that it had been created the day after the email she had just looked at.

American: "Hey, just checking in. Is everything all set over there?"

Hickam (?): "Everything looks good on our end. I've managed to put together the entire package, and everyone over here is on board for the venture."

American: (chuckling) "That's excellent. This is gonna be the biggest thing since eBay, and I can't wait. We'll be in the driver's seat from now on."

Hickam (?): "I agree. We should be cautious, though, because if any of this comes out, we'll all be ruined. Let's not speak again until after the Web Wide Awards webcast."

The American didn't even bother to say goodbye.

She went back and clicked the next link, and found herself reading a copy of a letter that was sent to Max Petrelli, offering a substantial amount of money in return for the right to stream Freaktown High on the Starbright system. It wasn't exactly a fortune, but considering that the show was made with essentially no budget whatsoever, it was definitely going to make it even more lucrative for the boy than it already was.

She clicked the next link and found herself looking at a soundless video. It appeared to have been taken by a camera in the company's parking lot, because there were several cars on the screen. One of them was facing toward the camera, and the driver's face was just visible. Herman had applied facial recognition to it, and concluded that it was Pierre Reynard, superimposing that name so that it floated just over the driver's head.

Another car was parked beside him, facing the opposite direction. It appeared that Reynard was talking with whoever was driving the second vehicle. Indie zoomed in on the license plate, then spent fifteen minutes tracking down the U.K. auto license database and hacking into it.

The tag came back to Starbright, but it was one of several vehicles owned by the company. It would take finding the vehicle's records in the computer system to determine who might have been driving it, but her gut feeling was that it was almost certainly Benjamin Hickam.

Sam came in at that moment, and she showed him the page of links.

"Okay," he said. "What is all this?"

"Well, to me it looks like evidence that Denny was right. Take a look for yourself and tell me what you think." She clicked the link to open the email she had read a few moments earlier.

"This is absolutely incriminating," Sam said. "Can you get anything on that email address?"

"That mail server doesn't even come up," she said. "It's probably something the guy can turn on and off when he wants to use it. I can't even find a DNS record for it, so it's probably an anonymized redirect of some sort."

"Okay," Sam said, and she clicked the next link.

"This one is an audio file," she said. "Take a listen to it."

She waited quietly while Sam let it play through. When he finished, he looked at her and said, "I don't suppose there's any way to identify the voices?"

"My gut says the first one is Hickam, but I'd have to find a way to undistort the other one, and then I'd need a voice sample to compare it to. If I can find the right frequency, I might be able to clear that voice up somewhat, but there's no guarantee. The simplest way, I can have Herman try to find the call records; we might be able to back trace the number the call came from and figure out who it is that way."

"It's worth a try," Sam said, "but it probably won't get us anywhere. Whoever these people are, they know the tech world inside out. I'm pretty sure they're not going to leave any bread crumbs for us to follow." Sam had clicked the next link himself. "Now, this video is interesting. Herman says that is Pierre Reynard in the car?"

"Facial recognition," Indie said. "That face matches the photo I fed him on at least eighteen points, or he wouldn't have declared it a positive match. He's absolutely dead certain that's Reynard, and I'm pretty confident that he knows what he's doing. The other car belongs to Starbright, but I haven't been able to identify the driver yet."

"Is there a way to do that?" Sam asked.

"Yeah, I've got Herman searching the computer system for their vehicle records. It should say who the car was assigned to, or who might have signed it out on that particular day. When he finds it, I'll let you know."

"This is excellent work, babe," Sam said. "Go ahead and send this to Denny. I'm pretty sure he'll know what to do with it over there. In the meantime, I'm going to forward it to John Pemberton at the DA's office, and give him a call. Knowing him, I'll probably have to spend the next hour explaining how we got it. Luckily, John can't prosecute for burglaries in England, so Denny is safe."

"Just as long as he doesn't want to prosecute me," Indie said. "My record is clean, and I want to keep it that way."

"He won't," Sam said. "You haven't done anything wrong, anyway. With an international involvement, we can now lean on DHS and claim this is a form of economic terrorism. That'll cover you."

"Okay, I'll just let you handle it, then. Will I need to testify?"

"Possibly, and maybe to a grand jury. A lot will be dependent on whether he wants to try to prosecute it locally, or turn it over to the feds. I'll let you know what he has to say."

Sam walked onto the back deck, took out his phone, and called John Pemberton's cell number. It took him nearly half an hour to explain the email he'd forwarded, and everything that it seemed to imply, but John finally got his head wrapped around it.

"Sam, we can extradite Hickam, old buddy," he said. "I don't know how long it will take, but I'll start the paperwork right away."

"Thanks, John," Sam said. "I had a hunch you'd feel that way, once you saw the evidence. Let me know if you need anything further from me, okay?"

"Oh, trust me," Pemberton said. "If I'm going to be involved in this at all, you're going to be sitting right beside me."

Sam's next call was to John Morton at Web Wide Awards. "John, it's Sam Prichard," he said. "Just wanted to give you a heads up. We have uncovered some fairly damning circumstantial evidence that seems to indicate the shooting really was orchestrated by one of your advertisers. You're familiar with Starbright, out of London?"

"Oh, of course," Morton said. "Are you serious? I know Ben Hickam pretty well, and while we certainly are in competition in some ways, we've always gotten along. There was even a time when we considered teaming up on a global streaming service."

"Why did you not go ahead with that plan?" Sam asked.

"Oh, just business. His Board of Directors wanted a bigger stake in our company than I was willing to give up. Since we make a higher annual revenue than they do, I didn't see any reason to give them a bigger share of our company than we were getting in theirs."

"I guess that makes sense," Sam said. "Tell me something, if the shooting had actually done your company a lot of damage, would you have been willing to reconsider? Go ahead with that deal?"

"No, not at all," Morton said. "In fact, I would have probably cut all of our strategic alliances with competitor companies. I built this company from the ground up, and if I had to bring it out of a major crisis, I'd do it the same way I did before. We would have concentrated on our own services and what we can do to rebuild public image, with as little connection to other companies as possible."

"That sounds like a solid strategy," Sam said, "especially since it's already proven. Anyway, we're working on getting actual proof, but I thought you'd like to know that we're making progress. The DA's office is going to be filing charges against Hickam, and working to extradite him over here to face the music."

"I appreciate it, Sam," Morton said. "I know Annie will appreciate it, as well."

Denny had called again while Sam was on the phone with Pemberton, so he called him back immediately when he got off.

"Sam," Denny said as soon as he answered, "I'm going to have to take this information to CPS."

Sam's eyebrows narrowed. "CPS? Child protection services?"

"No," Denny said with a chuckle. "Crown Prosecution Service. They handle any type of criminal prosecutions in the U.K., and your Indie has provided enough evidence for them to take an interest. If we fail to report what we've learned, we could conceivably be guilty of concealing a crime from the crown, which is a pretty serious offense in its own right. Not one I'd bloody well like to be charged with, for certain."

"Do what you gotta do," Sam said. "The local DA is filing charges against Hickam, and will be seeking to extradite him to Denver for prosecution. I'm also calling in DHS over here, since we have an international component, and apparently Reynard, involved now. How is your uncle taking this?"

"Haven't told him yet," Denny said. "Bear in mind it's past nine thirty, over here. I might wait until—oh, bloody hell, that's him ringing in now. I'll call you tomorrow, Sam."

"Okay," Sam said. "Good luck."

Sam hung up and put the phone into his pocket, then went back inside the house.

"So?" Indie asked. "How did it go?"

"Pemberton says he's going to file charges against Hickam Monday morning," Sam replied, "and start the extradition proceedings. With any luck, this case will be coming to an end pretty soon, and a lot of that is thanks to you and Herman."

She grinned at him. "We're just doing our jobs, sir," she said. "By the way, Herman wants to know when he gets a paycheck."

"As soon as he gets a Social Security number and walks into the office to fill out all the paperwork," Sam said with a grin of his own.

22

"Dennis?" Devon Chamberlain said. "Forgive an old man's impertinence, or blame it on the liquor if you prefer, but I wonder if you've come across any further information?"

"Actually, I was planning to come 'round in the morning," Denny said, "but as you are already up and besotted, perhaps now is as good a time as any. Shall I come to the house, or would you prefer to meet somewhere else?"

"Charles is already in bed," Chamberlain said. "I suppose you can come up, but do try to be quiet about it. The neighbors complain when I have too much noise at night."

"Uncle, you don't have any bloody neighbors," Denny said, but he realized he was talking into a dead phone. He shook his head and put it away, then went down and out to his rented Jaguar. It started up instantly, and he drove toward Chamberlain Manor.

When he was a boy, Denny used to love going to visit the Manor. It was one of the big old mansions that England is so famous for, with more than forty rooms and tons of history. There were suits of armor standing in the great room that had been actually worn in battle several hundred years past, and the family had amassed various other historical treasures. Over the mantelpiece hung the very large and sharp continental sword that beheaded Anne Boleyn, which Devon's father Ansell had painstakingly tracked down after more than thirty years of research, and Devon himself had somehow acquired the pistol that seventeen-year-old Marcus Sarjeant had used to fire six blanks at Queen Elizabeth in 1981. It hung over the mantle, as well, just below the sword.

History had always been of interest to Denny, and he still loved it. One of the reasons he had joined the SAS was because it would give him an opportunity to participate in things that would eventually be considered historical, and he had been very proud of his association.

He pulled up to the house and parked just outside the garage, then walked up the ramp that had been built for Devon's father, when old age had put him in a wheelchair. It took him onto the grand porch of the house, and he rang the doorbell.

He stood there for more than a minute, and finally Devon opened the door. He had a whiskey glass in his hand, and motioned with it for Denny to come inside.

"We'll talk in the garden," the old man said. He led the way through the house and out through a back door into the luscious garden. There were several benches and tables scattered about, and he walked to the furthest one from the house and sat down. Denny noted that the whiskey bottle was already on the table.

"So?" the old man groused. "Did you find any evidence?"

Denny sighed as he sat across the table from his uncle. "I'm afraid I did," he said. "I slipped inside and created a way for one of our people to get into Starbright's computer system, and she was able to find several items that are rather incriminating.

Would you like to see them?" He had his large smartphone in his hand.

"I don't need to see a bloody thing," Devon said. "I saw the guilt in his eyes, I don't need you to confirm it for me. I only want to know what you found so that I won't look like a bloody sod in front of the Crown Prosecutor. Tell me what it is, that's all."

Denny nodded. "Very well," he said. "There was an email sent by Hickam that said he had received authorization from someone to target the winner of the big award on the show. That turned out to be the boy who was shot, of course, so we can tie him directly to the shooting. There is a recording of a telephone conversation between Hickam and an American whose voice is digitally distorted, where they talk about how, after the award program, they will gain some sort of power. And then there is a bit of security video footage that shows a known assassin, Pierre Reynard, sitting in a car and speaking with someone driving a Starbright vehicle. The footage was taken in the Starbright car park, and our people back in the States have linked Reynard to the people who actually arranged for the boy to be shot. Taken altogether, there is sufficient evidence to launch an investigation, and I shall be taking it to CPS in the morning."

"They shall be glad to get it," Devon said. "The Chief Executive, Arthur Lansdowne, called me a bloody nincompoop when we had dinner tonight. Couldn't believe it, he said, without evidence. I told him you were here, and would be getting the evidence. And don't you take it in without me. That bloody sod is going to apologize, mark my words."

Denny's eyes were wide. "You told the Chief Executive of CPS that Benjamin Hickam ordered a shooting in the States, and that I was bloody burglarizing Starbright to get evidence? Have you gone bloody daft?"

"I told him about the shooting, and that I'm absolutely certain of Ben's guilt. All I said about you was that you work for some bleeding company that's investigating, and that you would be bringing me proof. He told me I was mad, that Hickam would never do such a thing, and then he called me a nincompoop."

Denny was on his feet and looking around carefully. "Uncle," he said, "I think it might be best if we take a drive."

"At this bloody time of night? Now who's daft?"

"Uncle Devon, Arthur Lansdowne is on the board of directors of Starbright. If you told him what's going on, then Hickam knows about it by now. If he'd order an American teenager shot, just what do you think he'll do to you?"

"He'll not do a damn thing to me," Chamberlain said. "D'ye know how many times I saved his life?"

"Yes, well, and now you're about to put his neck in the noose! I don't think he's going to be thinking a lot about favors he might owe you, he's going to be thinking about how to shut you up." He reached out and took hold of the old man's arm and tried to lift him to his feet, but Chamberlain slapped him away.

"Get your hands off," the old man shouted. "I'm not going anywhere, except possibly to bed when I've drunk enough of this rot."

"Uncle Devon, please," Denny said. "You're drunk, so listen to someone who's sober. I need to get you out of here, to somewhere safe. Ben Hickam won't hesitate to order your death, probably less than he hesitated to order that boy shot. Remember when I was a teenager, running with my mates? What did you tell me then? 'Friends, my boy, will always stab you in the back sooner or later.' That's what you said, and I need you to listen to your own advice for once. Now, come on, we need to find somewhere to keep you safe until..."

The sound seemed to come from behind him, but Denny knew full well that was a trick of echo. It was a loud cough, and he recognized it instantly as the sound of a silenced rifle. His uncle sat up straight suddenly, and his eyes went wide open, and then he let out a long sigh and slowly toppled over onto the ground.

Denny had dived under the table, his pistol in his hand even before he moved. A second shot struck the flagstones beside him, throwing sparks and chips of rock that peppered his face. He couldn't tell where it had come from, because the sound suppressor was also hiding the muzzle flash. He fired a couple of shots in the general direction he thought might be close to the shooter, then scrambled over to his uncle and checked for a pulse.

There was none. He looked quickly at the old man's back and knew that the bullet had undoubtedly pierced his heart.

He heard a rustling in the brush and jumped to his feet. The shooter was running, and Denny had no intention of letting him get away. He started to run in the direction of the sound, but then spun and ran through the house, out the front door, and toward his car.

A vehicle started somewhere on the road as Denny leaped behind the wheel and hit the button to start the engine. He slammed the car into reverse and backed out just as a Land Rover shot past the end of the driveway.

"Oh, no, you bloody don't," Denny said as he slammed the car into drive and floored the accelerator. It fishtailed out of the driveway onto the road, and he held the throttle wide open as he raced after the shooter. The Land Rover's taillights were visible a quarter mile ahead, but the distance seemed to be growing smaller.

A Land Rover is a marvel of British engineering, but it cannot corner like a Jaguar F type. Every time it came to one of the sharp curves in the road, the brake lights flashed on and the distance grew smaller. The Jaguar hugged the curves as if it were on rails, and Denny was steadily gaining on the bastard who had killed his uncle.

He hit the button to roll down the window and thrust his pistol out into the night air. As soon as the Jaguar came out of the next curve, the Land Rover was straight ahead. Denny had once been trained in the art of shooting from a moving vehicle, and aimed the gun at where he thought the driver's head would be, then squeezed the trigger twice.

The Land Rover lurched to the left, then straightened up and kept going. Denny followed it for another quarter mile, and then it suddenly began to slow. The driver seemed to have lost interest in fleeing, or even in controlling the vehicle, for it veered to the right and came to an abrupt stop in the midst of a stand of trees.

Denny screeched to a halt behind it and got out with his pistol held ready. He made his way to the car and looked inside, where the driver was leaning back against the headrest. His shots had missed his intended target, but both of them had punctured the back of the seat. The driver was gasping, and the loud, bubbling noise told Denny that he had hit a lung.

He yanked the door open and grabbed the driver's face. "Who sent you?"

The driver only stared at him, and then he coughed. Blood sprayed out and struck Denny in the face, and then the light in the man's eyes faded away. Denny slapped him twice, trying to get him to revive enough to answer, but he was already gone.

He stood there for a moment, grief and rage boiling through him, then used every trick he had ever learned to get his emotions under control. He took out his phone and called 999, the emergency services code in the U.K.

"What's your emergency?"

"Lord Devon Chamberlain has been murdered," Denny said. "I've pursued and shot his killer. Track my GPS and send police, now."

"What is your name, sir?"

"This is Leftenant Dennis Cortlandt, retired, SAS. Lord Chamberlain was my uncle."

"Are you certain he was dead, sir? I can send an emergency care team."

"Yes, do so," Denny said. "He's in the garden behind the house, and the front door is open."

He hung up the phone and stood there, staring down at the man who had shot his uncle. He resisted the temptation to search the fellow, but he was fairly certain he would've found no identification in any case. He took the silencer off his pistol while he waited for the police and threw it as far as he could into the woods.

It took almost ten minutes for the local police to arrive, and two cars stopped where he was while two more and an ambulance sped on to the house. The policeman approached him cautiously, and he held out his identification as they drew near. He used his retired military ID, first, then followed it up with his Windlass Security ID.

"You're the one who called in, are you?" asked one of the officers.

"I am," he said. "I was visiting with my uncle in his garden when he was shot by this man. I gave pursuit, and fired two shots to try to stop him. My aim was apparently better than I had thought."

Two of the policeman were looking at the dead shooter. The one who had initially spoken turned back to Danny. "Have you disturbed the body at all, sir?"

"No. I'm a professional investigator, so I knew not to touch anything. He was alive and gasping when I got to him, but he didn't even speak before expiring."

"And why were you carrying a weapon, sir?"

"As I said, I'm a professional investigator. I'm also a contract Special Agent with the American Department of Homeland Security. I'm authorized to carry a weapon at all times, and we have reciprocity with the U.K."

"I need to verify that, of course, sir," the officer said. "And I shall need your weapon."

"Yes, I know," Denny said. He took the pistol out of his waistband and removed the magazine, then cleared it and caught the ejected bullet in the air. He offered all of it to the officer, and then had to wait while the officer procured a plastic bag to put it in. The bag was sealed and Denny was given a receipt for the pistol. Another ambulance arrived, and the paramedics carefully checked the driver of the car before taking him out and strapping his body to a gurney. They loaded him into the ambulance and drove away, while a tow truck appeared to take away the driver's vehicle.

The officer looked at Denny again after putting the bag into his car. "Are you staying at the Manor?"

"No," Denny said. "I have a room at the Green Man. Incidentally, my uncle's butler, Charles, is probably asleep up at the house. You might want to let the police there know, so they don't accidentally shoot him if he wakes and comes down."

The officer took out a phone and made a call, and Denny overheard him warning the other policemen about Charles. A moment later, he put the phone away and turned back to Denny.

"The butler was awake when they arrived," he said. "They found him in the garden, weeping over Lord Chamberlain. I take it they were very close?"

"Charles has been with him for more than forty years," Denny said. "Do not read any further implications into it than that."

The policeman blinked. "Of course not, sir," he said. "I'm afraid you're going to have to come with us for tonight. Is there anyone you need to call?"

Denny shook his head. "Not before morning," he said. "Then I shall need to speak with Arthur Lansdowne of the CPS."

"Yes, sir. Under the circumstances, I must ask you to ride in my car. If you like, I can have my partner bring yours along."

"Well, I certainly don't want to leave it on the side of the road. Yes, yes, have him bring it along, please."

They left the side of the road a few moments later, and arrived at the police station after about twenty minutes more. Denny followed the officers inside and took a seat at the desk, where he was told to wait for a few minutes.

The process didn't take nearly as long as he had expected. An hour later, after giving his statement and having his connection to DHS confirmed by the U.S. Embassy, a CPS clerk arrived. He also took Denny's statement, although a shorter version, and shook his head.

"Shame," he said. "Lord Devon was a wonderful man."

Denny stared at him. "Is that all you've bloody got to say? I just sat here and told you that your own chief executive must certainly be the one who tipped off Hickam, who is the only bloody person in the world who could have a motive to kill my uncle, and all you can say is it's a bloody shame?"

"Now, see here," the man said. "I admit it looks rather strange, that he should be killed just after making a statement to the chief executive, but you have no evidence whatsoever to connect the two together. Now, this evidence you provided regarding Mr. Hickam, that will have to be reviewed back at CPS. If we find that you are correct, that he was indeed involved in this American shooting, then you can rest assured that we will take action. If that leads us to believe that Mr. Hickam might have been involved in your uncle's murder, then you can expect us to prosecute him for that, as well."

"I stand so relieved," Denny said. "Of course, all of that depends on your abilities to find your own arses, abilities of which I have grave doubts at this moment."

Denny was told he was free to go. He collected his car keys from the officers and walked out, slid behind the wheel, and then took out his phone to call Sam.

"Denny? How did it go with your uncle?"

"They killed him, Sam," Denny said. "The silly old scunner had dinner with the CPS Chief executive last night, and told him about Hickam. Needless to say, the bloody fool chief made a phone call, and an unknown assailant murdered my uncle right in front of me. I got the bastard, but there's nothing to connect him to Hickam, and even though CPS admits it's a bloody strange coincidence, and even after I showed them the evidence you sent me, they won't so much as pull the bastard in for questions. They say they've got to review it to see if there's enough for a conviction, and whether trying to prosecute Hickam would be in the public interest."

Denny could hear the sorrow in Sam's voice. "Denny, I'm so sorry," he said. "What can we do?"

"We can hang that son of a bitch, that's what," Denny said. "I don't care what we've got to do, Sam, I want Hickam to spend the rest of his life in the worst prison the U.S. or the U.K. can find."

"They won't even question him?" Sam asked. "Don't you have any favors you can call in over there?"

"Too right, if I wanted him dead. One bloody phone call, 's all it would take. Unfortunately, that's not the way we bloody do things, so we've got to keep it all legal. I've got to get more evidence, Sam, but it's nigh certain they know I've been in there already. I might bloody well not get another shot."

"Indie is still going through their computers," Sam said. "She might come up with something else we can use, something more concrete. For now, what I need you to do is watch your back. If they know you've been in the building, they might be out to get rid of you, as well. Get some sleep, and we'll talk tomorrow."

"I don't know if I can sleep," Denny said, "but I'm dead on my feet. I'm going to find someplace to lay low and rest, and I'll give you a call tomorrow."

"You do that," Sam said. "I'll talk to you then."

23

Denny had gone back to the Green Man, and immediately dug his spare pistol out of the bottom of his bag. This one was a Bersa Thunder .380, a compact pistol designed for concealed carry. He loaded the magazine and worked the slide to chamber a round, then ejected the magazine and inserted another round. They gave him the pistol's maximum capacity of nine shots: eight in the magazine and one in the chamber.

Since there was no doubt in his mind that the assassin who killed his uncle had been sent by Ben Hickam, then he had to consider it likely that an attempt would be made on his own life. Unlike his uncle, though, Denny was a well trained commando who had been in life-threatening situations before. He didn't actually have any proof that he was in danger, but he had every intention of minimizing the possibility anyway. Since Hickam had his own private source of information smack in the upper offices of the CPS, Denny was sure it wouldn't be difficult for Hickam to find out where he was staying. Therefore, it behooved Denny to make sure any assassin would be aiming in the wrong direction.

In the Green Man, each room held three beds. There were two full size beds and a twin, and Denny set to work creating a dummy of himself in each of them. He would not sleep in one of the beds, but stuffing blankets and pillows under the covers on each of them should at least cause an assassin to waste a few rounds trying to hit whichever might hold the real sleeper, while alerting himself to the presence of an intruder.

There was also a closet in the room, and it was reached through a pair of sliding doors. The closet itself was six feet wide by two feet deep, and Denny found that he could lay comfortably in its floor. Even the closet was carpeted, and the Green Man was the kind of hotel that believed in thick padding under the carpet. It cut down on noise complaints from people in rooms below, and was one of those little touches that many visitors considered somewhat luxurious. Getting up in the middle of the night to go to the bathroom didn't require one to put slippers on, because the carpeted floor was so comfortable to walk on.

It was nearly three AM by the time Denny got to lay down, but despite what he had said to Sam, he never had trouble going to sleep. He was quite certain he would mourn his uncle for quite some time to come, but he was able to force it out of his mind for the moment. He needed to get what rest he could, because he was confident the next few days were going to be lively.

He left one of the closet doors open an inch, so that he could see into the room without having to make any noise. He had slept for slightly more than an hour when a barely discernible sound woke him, and he lay perfectly still and watched the gap for any sign of motion.

It came a moment later, as a shadow passed the gap. Part of that shadow, he could tell, was the leg of a man passing by the closet. This man was focused on the lumps on the beds, and Denny waited for the sound of the muffled shots that he was sure were about to come.

He had gone to sleep with his pistol in his hand, the safety on. Denny had personally filed part of the safety switch and smeared it with white lithium grease, so that it could be removed without making a click. He wrapped his left hand around the gun as his right thumb removed the safety, and then carefully aimed between the doors.

Phwtt, phwtt! Phwtt, phwtt! Phwtt, phwtt!

Three double taps. This was a killer who wanted to get the job done, and the sound suppressor was so efficient that Denny barely heard the shots at all. He heard the floors under the carpet creak slightly, as the killer moved to check his handiwork, and then Denny swept one of the doors open and rolled his upper body into the room in a single motion.

The door made just enough noise to catch the killer's attention, and he spun around to find himself facing the business end of the Bersa. Denny had the drop on him, and he knew that he couldn't even aim his gun without causing Denny to squeeze the trigger.

"Put the gun behind your head," Denny said, "then transfer it to the other hand, barrel first. Bring it around in front of you and let it drop to the carpet between us. Do anything else, and I'll put a bullet through your eye."

The killer removed his finger from the trigger as he did as he was instructed, grasping the gun by the sound suppressor threaded onto the barrel. He brought it out in front of himself with his left hand, held the tip of the suppressor with two fingers and let it drop.

"Now, hands on your head and back away. Sit down on the furthest bed. You and I, mate, are about to have a little chat."

The killer backed away slowly, his hands on his head, until the backs of his legs struck the bed. He sat down on it and stared at Denny, who stared back.

Denny kept his eyes on the man as he got to his feet, then kept them there still while he bent down to pick up the silenced pistol. A split second glance told him that it was a Ruger LCP, with an extended barrel that was threaded to receive the sound suppressor. The little Ruger had a magazine capacity of only six rounds, so unless there was a seventh in the chamber, it was empty.

Denny pointed it at the killer, a typical blue-collar type fellow, who suddenly looked frightened. He kept his hands on his head, but his eyes closed and he almost seemed like he was trying to duck away.

"Bloody hell, mate," Denny said. "You think I'm a pillock? You already emptied the bloody magazine, but did you have one in the chamber before you started?" He pointed the gun at the killer again, and the man flinched once more. "Aye, maybe you did. 's alright, but I think I'll keep my own piece in hand, anyway. I mean, I don't mind waking up the whole bloody hotel. Now, who the bloody blazes are you?"

"Name is Murphy," the man said. "Giles Murphy."

"You're no fool, Murphy," Denny said. "Took you only a second to figure out that I've no need for you if you don't talk, right? So let's get on to the real question. Who sent you to kill me?"

"I don't know," Murphy said, a touch of a Scottish brogue entering his voice. "I got a call, told me where to find the money, and it was there. I got paid, so I came to do the job."

"Sounds like a gobshite way to do business. Suppose it was a copper who called; he'd have a fair cop on you just for going to pick up the money. You been in this game long?"

Murphy shrugged. "Couple years," he said. "Done some work for some of the gangs, so people know how to find me. And the coppers around here, they're all on the dole. Not a lot to fear."

"Had another bloke a bit earlier, shot and killed my old uncle. Thought he was going to get away, but he couldn't outrun my bullets. He's probably on the slab next to my uncle right now. Can you tell me why I'm not putting you on the next one?"

Murphy shrugged again and grinned. "You're not quite ready to wake the hotel yet?"

"Bit more than that," Denny said. "If I kill you, I'm going to be downtown answering more bloody questions tonight, and I'm in need of my beauty sleep. The question is, what the hell can I do with you while I'm sleeping?"

Murphy just stared at him.

"Ah, you're right," Denny said. "If I tie you up, there's always a chance you might get loose and we have to dance like this again. Or you might even get away, in which case I have to give up hours of my time to track you down. It'll just be better if I go ahead and kill you now."

"I might have a suggestion," Murphy said, his eyes bouncing back and forth between the barrels of the two pistols pointed at him. "If I don't go back home, whoever hired me will probably suspect I failed. Would it be better for you if he thought I succeeded?"

"It might, but do you think I'm stupid enough to let you go and trust you?"

"I don't know about that," Murphy said. "All I know is this: in my line of work, you never, ever go back on your word. If I tell you I won't come after you, or I won't let anyone know I didn't kill you, then you can believe me. If you're not comfortable with trusting me, though, then you could just come with me. I live alone, my garage is built right into my house, and nobody can see inside, so no one will know you're there. You come with me, you can rest as much as you want. I'll watch your back."

It was all Denny could do not to burst out laughing. "You're actually very funny," Denny said. "No, seriously, you should go on one of those talent shows, be a comedian. Has it not occurred to you that the fact my body doesn't end up on another slab might tell whoever hired you that you didn't keep your word?"

Murphy shrugged once more. "It was only a thought," he said. "And if you think I won't trade my word and a few hours of being your protector for my life, you should think once more. That's all I'm saying, is we can make a deal. I go home, either with you or without you, and you're safe for at least a few hours. At my place, you can sleep as long as you want, then get up and leave when you choose. As for my reputation, I think I'm ready to retire from this line of work. I've got a new name all set up, and the old family place waiting back in Scotland."

"And all you want out of the deal is your life?" Denny asked.

"That's right," Murphy replied. "That's all I want. I'm just not quite ready to give up living just yet."

"Well, you should have thought of that sooner." Denny raised the silenced pistol and pointed it at Murphy's forehead, then squeezed the trigger.

There was a round in the chamber after all. Luckily, Denny jerked the barrel up at the last second, and the bullet passed over Murphy's head and struck the wall. Murphy ducked and flinched, then stared at Denny with his eyes wide.

Someone in the room on the other side of that wall pounded on it. "Har! People trying to sleep over here!"

"Well, damn," Denny said. "You did have one in the chamber. Silly bugger me, I almost killed you. Now if I decide to kill you, I have to go ahead and wake up the whole bloody hotel."

Murphy swallowed hard. "I meant what I said," he said. "I give you my word, I won't betray you."

"Well, I think we're going to find out. Have you any idea who I am?"

Murphy shrugged. "Didn't get a name," he said. "Just told me what room you were in and to kill you before morning. That's all."

"Are you from around here?"

"Twickenham," Murphy said. "Been there nigh ten years."

Denny nodded. "Then you'll know who Lord Chamberlain was?"

"Oh, aye," Murphy said. "Fine old fellow. Did you say was?"

"Yes, was. He was my uncle, who was murdered earlier. I'm Dennis Cortlandt, his heir. Now, Giles Murphy, can you think of any reason why I might want you alive?"

"I can think of two," Murphy said. "First, you want me alive so somebody else thinks you're dead. Second, you want me alive because you want to know who killed your uncle."

"Doesn't really matter who he is, he's already dead. What I do want to know is who paid him to do it. A man in your line of work might be able to find out. And that, Mr. Murphy, might be worth your life."

Denny left his car at the Green Man and rode with Murphy, hunkered down in the passenger floorboard with his gun still aimed at the killer. "Anyone come 'round your place in the mornings?" he asked.

Murphy shook his head. "Never," he said. "I've got no one. My daughter, but she lives back in Scotland, and I haven't spoken to her in years. Neighbors all think I'm eccentric, because of my hobby; I build things, inventions, I calls 'em. Machines to do stuff I'm a bit too lazy for, that sort of thing."

"Really? What sort of machines?"

"Odd ones," Murphy said with a shrug. "Built a big hoover to clean up the yard, and a ride on mower with an overhead blade, to trim all the low branches on the trees, that sort of thing."

"Overhead blade? Sounds a bit risky, that. Bounce off the seat and get a haircut down to your neck."

"Oh, it has a guard. Got fingers in it, to guide the branches to the blade, and a chute so they don't land on top of me, but fall out the back. The Hoover picks 'em up, then, it tows behind."

Denny grinned. "You're an interesting fellow, Giles Murphy. How did you become a killer?"

Murphy shrugged again. "Was an accident," he said. "I had a niece, she got raped and left for dead by five local lads. She knew who did it, but the police said they couldn't convict just on her word alone, and there was no other evidence. I found one of them walking in the rain one night, nobody about anywhere, so I stopped and chatted him up, got him to boasting about what he and his mates had done. I only wanted to make him say it, but I got so angry that I beat him to death, right then and there. Stood in the rain till the blood was all off, then drove away and waited for the coppers. They never came, and a few days later I came across the second one, he'd had a flat and didn't have a jack. He didn't know me, so I offered to help, then cracked his skull open with the jack handle."

"And the other three?"

Murphy smiled. "Took me a few months, but I got them all. By then, I was enjoying it. Some of the gangs, the old ones, not the punks we get today, they let it be known they might have some work for whoever did it, and I've been up to it ever since."

"What kind of jobs?" Denny asked.

"Mostly gang rivalries. Take out the competition, that sort of thing. That's what the caller said about you, you were cutting into his business."

Denny grunted. "You might be a bit more selective in the future, Giles. I'm an old MI6 lad; had you gotten the job done, they'd have come looking, and they would have found you."

"Aye, 'twas obvious you're not the typical gangster," Murphy said. "I'm wishing I hadn't taken the job, right enough."

They rode in silence for a few minutes, then Murphy put on the turn signal. "Almost there," he said. "Stay down till I get us inside the garage. The shades are all drawn, so once the overhead comes down, no one can see inside."

"And how is it," Denny asked, "that I can be sure you're not going to cut my throat as I sleep?"

Murphy sighed. "Well, I suppose you're going to tie me up. Since it's going to keep me alive, I suppose I shouldn't complain."

"You really are an interesting fellow, Murphy. You're not the most intelligent killer I've ever met, and you've obviously never run up against anyone like me before. How is that you managed not to get yourself killed?"

"Guess I've been lucky, eh? To be frank, you're making me think seriously about that retirement I mentioned."

"Really? That may be the most intelligent thing you could do. Tying you up sounds like a good idea."

Murphy nodded. "There's plenty of rope in my garage," he said. "Or I've got handcuffs, if you prefer."

He made another turn and Denny heard gravel crunching under the tires. A moment later, they stopped and Murphy pushed a button on the remote clipped to the sun visor. He waited until the garage door had opened, and then the car eased inside. Denny sat where he was until the door had closed behind them.

"All right, let's step out gently," Denny said. "No sudden moves."

"Wouldn't dream of it," Murphy said. He climbed out the driver's door and stood there, his hands on the car, as Denny got out to the passenger side. "Rope is hanging on the wall," he said, pointing.

"Get it, then, and let's go inside. Might as well make you comfortable."

Ten minutes later, with Murphy securely tied to a kitchen chair that had been brought into the living room, Denny sat in an easy chair facing him. "I'm going to nap for a bit," he said.

"Getting out of that would make some noise, so I don't think there's much chance you can escape and get the jump on me. Give me a couple hours, and then we shall see what to do next."

Murphy nodded, but said nothing. He watched in amazement as Denny leaned his head back and seemed to go to sleep only a moment later.

DENNY WOKE TO FIND the sun shining in, and looked immediately at Murphy. The hired killer was still tied to the chair, his head drooped against his chest as he snored.

"Oy! Murphy!" Denny called out, and Murphy yanked his head up. "What bloody time is it?"

"Looks to be around nine," Murphy said. "Clock's on the wall in the kitchen, only one I've got."

"Around nine is close enough," Denny said. He got up from the chair where he'd been napping and walked over to Murphy, then reached down behind him and pulled an end of the rope. A moment later, it came free and Murphy began moving his arms and legs to get the circulation working again.

"I've been thinking," Murphy said after a moment, "about how to find out what you wanted to know, about who paid for your uncle's murder. I can call some of the gang boys, one of them might know something."

"And how do you think they'll take you asking about it?" Denny asked. "Might make them wonder a bit about you, wouldn't you think?"

"Nah, not so much. All I've got to do is say I'm pissed there's someone else working 'round here, and I want to know who's tossing work out there without calling me."

Denny shrugged. "I suppose it's worth a try," he said. "See what you can learn."

Murphy went into the kitchen and made a pot of tea, then sat at the table and used the wall-mounted phone, while Denny sat across from him and watched. An hour later, he finally hung up for the last time and shrugged.

"All I can tell you," he said, "is that none of the locals heard anything about it. Most of them are pissed, and I mean very pissed, that the old Lord Chamberlain is dead. Most of them knew him, and he was always good for chipping in when somebody was in need. I'm supposed to let them know if I find out who hired it done." He shrugged again. "Couple of them even talked about having me go deliver a little justice."

"Then I'm almost tempted to tell you who it was," Denny said. "Unfortunately, I want the bloody sod to pay for his crime, and getting killed is the easy way out." He sat back in his chair and stared at Murphy for a moment. "Which leaves me with a dilemma. Should I let you live, even though you didn't find out what I want to know? Or should I just kill you now and get it over with?"

Murphy licked his lips. "Well, I suppose that's going to be up to you. I'm quite sure you know what I would prefer, but you are the one holding the gun."

Denny chuckled. "That was a nice little nap," he said. "Now, come on, take me back to my car. I've got to make arrangements for uncle Devon."

Murphy seemed surprised when Denny simply got out of his car and let him drive away. Denny had contemplated calling the local police and turning him over, but he knew that Murphy was right about the policemen in the area. The "gangs" that he kept referring to were not the types of gangs that are prevalent in the United States, but something closer to the organized crime that used to dominate American cities. They were involved in loansharking, prostitution, some drug distribution, and other crimes that were highly profitable, and the vast majority of police in the area accepted the occasional gift to look the other way. Turning him in would probably only result in a few wasted hours, because Murphy would undoubtedly be back on the street before the day was over.

Denny quickly went up to his room and gathered his things, then checked out and drove off in the Jaguar. He headed into London proper, but chose a hotel that was off the beaten path and accepted cash. The last thing he needed was for anyone to figure out where he was staying now, because he had several things to accomplish before he headed back to the States.

His first move after getting a new room was to call his uncle's barrister, an actual friend of the royal family named Sir William Winningham. The old lawyer knew Denny from his younger days, and had handled the estate when Denny's mother had passed away a couple years earlier.

"Dennis, old boy," Winningham said. "So sorry to hear about Devon. I understand you were there when it happened?"

"Yes, and I shot the bloody bastard who did it. Listen, Willie, I don't even live in the U.K. anymore, but I have dual citizenship, between Britain and the States, because of my father. What's going to be involved in handling uncle Devon's estate?"

"Why, almost nothing," Winningham said. "Your uncle put all of his assets into a living trust, which passes to you. One of our younger associates is the current trustee, and she has done a marvelous job thus far. I would highly recommend that you keep her in that position."

"That's all? What about taking possession of the estate?"

"Under the terms of the living trust, it became yours at the moment of your uncle's passing. I believe his friend Charles has the keys and paperwork for you."

"Well, that part was bloody painless," Denny said. "Are there accounts I need to settle? Debts, anything like that?"

"No, no," Winningham said. "You should speak with your trustee, her name is Margaret Milligan. She'll need to establish you on the banking accounts, of course, but I know that she keeps all of the debts paid. Hold a moment, and I shall transfer you to her."

Denny waited only a few seconds, and a pleasant voice picked up the other end of the line. "Mr. Cortlandt? This is Margaret Milligan. I need to set an appointment with you to arrange a few minor matters, when would be convenient for you to come in?"

"I'm about ten minutes away," Denny said. "If we can do it now, that will be best. I'll be returning to the States about any time."

"Well, I actually have an appointment this afternoon, but your uncle was a valued client. Do come down as soon as you can, and I shall simply take the time."

"All right," Denny said. "I'll come down now."

Thirty minutes later, Denny had signed all the necessary paperwork to put his name on the estate accounts, he had signed an authorization for Charles to continue living at the Manor for the rest of his life, and he had confirmed Margaret as the trustee. He left her office feeling accomplished, and finally decided to call Sam.

"Denny?" Sam asked. "How's it going over there?"

"Bloody buggers, Sam," Denny said. "I'll tell you most of it when I see you. I'm about done over here, though, since Charles will arrange the burial, though the actual funeral won't be for a few weeks. Where are we on your end?"

"There won't be anything new until Monday. That's when the DA is going to file charges and start the extradition proceedings. I don't know how long all that will take, but I think we can start to consider this case solved."

"It won't be bloody solved until Benjamin Hickam is sitting inside a jail cell," Denny said. "Extraditing someone from the U.K. to the States, especially a British national, is probably going to take months. I doubt these bloody bastards over here will ever even take him into custody, so he's going to get plenty of chances to skip out. That simply isn't going to work for me, Sam."

"Denny, I understand," Sam said. "Unfortunately, there's not much else I can do. I suppose I could ask DHS to look into it, but I can't even do that before Monday."

"Bloody hell," Denny said. "I guess I need to come home, then. Can you arrange me a flight?"

"Sure," Sam said. "No problem at all. Too bad you can't invite Hickam to come along. If he happened to set foot on American soil, the warrant our DA gets Monday would be all we need to pick him up."

Denny was quiet for a moment. "Now, suppose that could be arranged, Sam. Would the bloody bugger be able to get out on bail?"

"Him? I seriously doubt it," Sam said. "He's a billionaire from another country, so that makes him an absolute flight risk. I don't think there's a judge in the world who would allow him bail. Just exactly what are you thinking, Denny?"

"Me? Why, I'm only thinking about inviting the bloke for a holiday."

"Yeah, well," Sam said, "I don't think that would necessarily be a good idea. The last thing we need is for the U.K. to be trying to extradite you back up there to face kidnapping charges."

"True. Oh, well, it was a nice idea while it lasted. Give me a flight, Sam, I need to come home and take some rest. This has all been a bit much, I'm afraid."

"I'll get on it right now," Sam said.

24

"But who in the bloody world would want to kill the old blighter," asked David Darwin. He, David Cross, and Benjamin Hickam were at the Traveller's Club, where they often met for breakfast. "That's what I want to know. Old Chamberlain never hurt a soul in his life, unless you count those rotting bastards he caught in their own corruption. It certainly seems to me that only a true bastard would want to cause him any harm."

"Why, 'twas Ben what did it," said David Cross. "After all, Chamberpot called him out the other night, remember, it was all over the plot to kill that lad in the States in order to make more money. Old Ben had to hush him up, don't you know, save himself from ruin."

"Oh, aye," Hickam said. "Can't have him running around spilling out my secrets. Bloody bastards, the both of you. All four of us been friends nearly fifty years, and you can sit here and make light of Devon being murdered. Should have bloody well been one of you, instead of him."

"Only I'm not making light," Darwin said. "That was Cross, not me. All I said was nobody would want to hurt the old boy, unless they were a true bastard."

"Calm your knickers, Hickam," Cross said. "No one believed you would hurt Devon. Old boy was getting a bit dotty, I might say, what with all that rot he was saying. According to

Arthur Lansdowne, he actually believed you might have been involved in that thing, poor old bugger." He shook his head. "Sad, that, when a man's mind starts to go."

Hickam nodded. "Very sad. I'm putting up a reward, you know, to help the police find whoever paid the killer. He was some sort of professional, they're saying. It was Devon's nephew that shot him, you know. Dennis, he was SAS a while back. I understand he also told the police that he believes I arranged it." He snorted. "Bunch of rot. I used to bounce that lad on my knee."

"It'll pass, Ben," Darwin said. "Far too many people know what a generous sort you truly are, they'll not believe stories like this. Flash in the pan, you will see."

Hickam's phone rang. He glanced at it, then excused himself and went outside to take the call.

Cross looked at Darwin. "He's bloody guilty as hell, if you ask me," he said softly, once Hickam was out of earshot. "Lansdowne thinks so, but he says there's not enough proof to try to make a case."

"Not a doubt in my mind," Darwin replied. "Just make bloody sure he thinks we don't believe it, or we'll end up just like Devon." He knocked back his glass and signaled one of the attendants for another gimlet.

Cross stared at him. "I've no idea how you can stand to drink gin with breakfast."

"It's easy," Darwin said. "All I have to do is imagine what the day would be like if I was sober. All the motivation I need, right there."

Hickam had answered the call as he was walking out, telling the caller to wait a moment. Outside, he made sure there was no one who could possibly overhear before he put the phone back to his ear again.

"Is it you?"

The distorted voice came through the earpiece. "Yes. We have some problems over here. The investigators think someone inside our organization is involved."

"Bloody hell," Hickam said. "Do they actually know anything? Or is it just speculation?"

"As far as I can tell, they're only guessing. We've taken great pains to make sure there is no evidence linking us to the events, but someone made another attempt to kill the boy a few hours ago. Do you know anything about that?"

"Me? Why should I know anything about it? You're the one who set up the whole damn thing, not me. All I did was hold the money, and I wouldn't have done that if I'd known what you were doing. This thing has gotten so far out of hand I'm wishing I never agreed to any of it. I was forced to order the death of my own best friend just two nights ago, all because he told the wrong person he suspected I might be involved."

"Then we both have problems. Have you made sure to clean up the mess on your end?"

"I said he's dead, didn't I? I don't know that it did any good, though, because his bloody nephew is going 'round pointing fingers at me, now. Fortunately, the top man at the Crown Prosecutors is one of my big investors. That's probably all that's keeping me from being held on remand at the local prison, right now. I hope you've got someone equivalent watching over you."

"No one suspects me. Even if they believe someone in our company was involved, no one is going to point the finger at me. Now, are you prepared for the next phase?"

"Yes, yes, I'm ready. Just make certain everything goes as planned. I don't think we could recover if anything goes wrong, and we'll certainly never get another chance."

"We only need one," said the voice. The line went dead, and Hickam took a moment to compose himself before going back inside.

DENNY SLEPT ON THE flight. He'd certainly been in need of sleep, and since the flight would last slightly under nine hours, he figured it was the perfect opportunity to catch some rest. The only problem he had run into was the flight attendant, who suggested that he might like to watch a movie and have a bite to eat.

"I've had about five hours sleep out of the last forty-eight," he said. "I ate fish and chips before I got on the plane, and the only movie I want to watch is playing on the backs of my eyelids. Now, if you can find a way to sit quietly for the duration of this flight, I shall be more than grateful, which you will know because it will mean that I will not hogtie you to one of the seats. Do I make myself clear?"

"Perfectly," said the man. "I'll—I'll just go put the earphones in and watch the movie myself."

"You do that," Denny said, "right after you fetch me a blanket and pillow, there's a good lad."

Unfortunately, Denny's mind took that particular opportunity to start reminiscing about his uncle, and sleep did not want to come. Between the grief and the turbulence they experienced numerous times on the journey, he actually didn't get much sleep at all.

The plane had left Heathrow at five thirty in the morning. It arrived at Denver International at nine AM, all thanks to the fact that the plane was fleeing the sun the whole way. Denny stepped off refreshed and ready for whatever they might throw at him, until he got to the customs desk. There, an overpaid, undereducated miscreant, in his opinion, tried to tell him that his DHS identification was not sufficient to allow him to bypass the customs inspection. Denny decided that he was either going to have to put up with the inspection, or spend some ridiculous amount of time in jail before somebody at DHS would make the right phone calls to get him out.

If he hadn't had a gun stuffed in the hidden compartment of the bag, he might have decided that sitting in jail a few hours would only mean getting some more sleep. As it was, though, he didn't think he wanted this jackass to feel like he'd actually caught someone doing something wrong. There was basically no possibility that the jackass would find the gun, so Denny handed over his bag and passport.

It was close. The idiot actually found the false screw that would release the hidden compartment, but he didn't turn it the full one hundred eighty degrees. If he had, somebody in D.C. would've had to make that call after all.

Finally, Denny was allowed to escape the airport. He took his bags, which were bound together so that they could all roll on one pair of wheels that he dragged behind him, and headed for long-term parking. He got into his car and stopped at the gate to pay its ransom, then headed for home.

Denny Cortlandt lived in a nice area of Denver, a gated community known as Lockwood. His house was modest compared to many of the others, with only three bedrooms and four baths, but it suited him well. He parked his car inside the garage and walked in through his kitchen, dropping his bags in the utility room as he headed straight toward his bedroom. He stripped out of his clothes and entered the bath, took a fast shower, and then climbed under the covers.

A moment later, he sat up and picked up his phone. He hit the button to dial Sam, and held the phone up to his ear.

"Denny?" Sam asked as he answered.

"It's me, mate," he said. "Just got in a bit ago, but I've not had any sleep to speak of. If it's all right with you, I'm going to catch a few hours now."

"That's fine," Sam said. "Nothing's going to happen before tomorrow, anyway. See you at the office in the morning?"

"Yeah," Denny said. "Assuming I wake up, that is."

Sam chuckled. "Get some sleep. We'll talk tomorrow."

SAM HUNG UP THE PHONE and turned to Indie, who was just cleaning up after their late breakfast.

"Denny is back," he said. "I'm about half dreading tomorrow, but at least we'll have a shot at bringing this case to a close."

Indie turned away from the sink and walked over to put her arms around her husband from behind.

"It'll be okay, Sam," she said. "You'll handle it the way you always do."

JADE MILLER WAS SITTING in her kitchen, tapping at the keyboard on her computer. She would type consistently for several seconds, then stop and read whatever was appearing on her monitor, only to begin typing once more. Darren Beecher, who had spent the night at her place and was sitting across the table, finally got up and walked around behind her to try to see what she was doing.

"Jade? The look on your face makes it seem like you're onto something big over here."

"I wish," she said. "Got something stuck in my teeth, and I'm trying to get it out. When I was working undercover at Web Wide Awards, I came across something that seemed to be unrelated. According to one of the employees, John Morton has been diverting some cash for the last several months, and it's driving me nuts not knowing what he wanted it for."

"Did you ask him?"

Jade shook her head. "I mentioned it to Sam, and he felt like it was unrelated. He said our contract requires us to ignore anything not related to the case, so there really wasn't much point. The more I think about it, though, the more it drives me nuts."

Darren pulled his chair closer to her so he could see what she was looking at. "I can understand it driving you crazy," he said. "Do you think it actually is related, somehow?"

"I don't know," she said. "I honestly can't say that it is, but it's still driving me mad. I was just curious and checked to see if they had cut off my access to their computers yet, and it turns out they hadn't, so I'm digging around to see if I can find any kind of indication on what it was for. I mean, we're talking more than a million dollars that he's funneled off into some secret hiding place. I don't know that you can have a legitimate reason to hide a million dollars, do you?"

"It's possible," Darren said. "Maybe it's an emergency retirement fund, just in case the company goes belly up on them. Or it could be that he's investing the money in something new; Summer mentioned that he's about to announce a new video algorithm or something, right? Maybe it's related to that."

"He's got one of the bookkeepers covering up for it, Darren," Jade said, "and he's given her a couple of very generous raises since she agreed to help him hide the money. She swears up and down she doesn't know what it's for, but it's just bugging me." She pointed at the screen. "Look here, at this part. Her original report for the day said that they brought in one million, nine hundred and twenty-three thousand and change. What that means is that she and the girls in her office actually counted that much, either in the cash that came in from various sources or in the accounts they use, like PayPal. Later, though, she edited the report to say one million, eight hundred, ninety-six thousand. That's twenty-seven thousand dollars that just disappeared. The only way that could be possible is if somebody transferred it to a secret account, somewhere. Morton makes this bookkeeper change her daily reports every day if it doesn't fit what's left over by the time it all gets done at the accounting office."

"Well, I'll admit it does sound strange," Darren said. "On the other hand, unless you can come up with something to justify your interest in it, there really isn't a lot you can do. I mean, you can report it to the IRS, I guess, but he'll undoubtedly have some way to justify it as a deductible expense, so that probably wouldn't get you anywhere, and might get you in a little bit of hot water with Sam."

"Well, I can't help it," Jade said. "I'm like a dog with a bone, sometimes. I just can't stop gnawing on it, no matter how worn out it may be."

"But are you getting anywhere? Are you finding anything to make all your effort worthwhile?"

"Not just..." She suddenly froze and stared at the screen. "Holy granola," she said. "Darren, take a look at this is, tell me what you think it is." She pointed at a line on the screen.

"Well, that looks like a record of transfers from one account to another," Darren said. "That spreadsheet is showing almost 200 lines, and the amounts I can see range from about twenty-five thousand up to around thirty thousand. Look, they're all going to one particular account number. Any idea what bank it's in?"

"Not yet," Jade said. "But let me run those numbers through the FINCEN database and see what comes up." Her fingers flew across the keyboard again, and a moment later she let out a low whistle.

"Darren," she said. "John Morton is transferring money to an account in the Royal Bank of London. Now, what makes that so interesting is that it's the same bank where Starbright keeps their accounts. Same branch, everything."

"Is there any way to actually tie it to Starbright?" Darren asked.

"Not without hacking into the bank," Jade said. "Unfortunately, that's not among my talents." She turned and looked at Darren. "But I know who can do it."

She picked up the phone and called Indie, and it was answered on the second ring.

"Indie? It's Jade. How would you feel about hacking into a bank in London?"

"Is this part of the investigation you guys are working on?" Indie asked. "Sam seems to think it's just about over."

"Well, let's just say it's connected, okay?" She gave Indie a quick rundown of the reason she was trying to track the money, explaining that she had found a spreadsheet in the Web Wide Awards computers indicating that all of that money had been transferred to the account at the Royal Bank.

"Just a minute," Indie said. "Let me get Sam in on this conversation. I'm putting you on speaker, okay?"

"Yeah, that's fine."

"Okay, Sam's here. Tell him what you just told me."

"Hi, Jade," Sam said.

"Hey, Sam," Jade said. "Um, I should probably mention that Darren is here with me, too. Anyway, I've been going a little bit crazy over that money I told you about Morton hiding, remember that? Well, I've just been poking around in the Web Wide Awards computer system this morning, and I finally found an accounting sheet that shows that money being transferred to another bank, the Royal Bank of London. Now, what got me all excited about that was that is the same bank that Starbright uses."

"Okay," Sam said. "That does seem pretty strange."

"That's why she called," Indie said. "She was asking about having Herman take a look inside the Royal Bank and see if there's a connection."

Sam was quiet for a couple of seconds, then spoke again. "I think we should check it out," he said. "Is it going to be difficult?"

"For Herman? Not really. Okay, Jade, first, give me the information to get into your account on the Web Wide Awards system. Let me see the spreadsheet you're talking about."

Jade gave her the login and password, and then directed her to where she had found the spreadsheet, in a folder marked "Special Project S3." Indie looked it over, and found the information she was looking for.

"Okay, I've got the account and routing numbers, and the Swift code," Indie said. "Herman's actually been into that bank before, so this shouldn't take more than a few minutes. Hang on, let him work his way into that section."

A minute passed, and then Herman chimed. "Bingo!" Indie said, and then she gasped. "Oh, my. Sam, look at this. Jade? Are you sitting down?"

Jade had the phone on speaker, so that Darren would be able to hear as well. "Yeah, we're sitting down. Did you find something?"

"Well, I found that the account number you gave me goes to an account owned by Starbright Research Technologies, which is a wholly owned subsidiary of Starbright Enterprises, LTD. Starbright Awards is also a subsidiary of Starbright Enterprises, as is Starbright Streaming Service. Now, that's interesting enough by itself, considering we're talking about money coming out of Web Wide Awards, but then there's the fact that the account has made several transfers to a bank in the Cayman Islands. There's a total of only about fifty dollars left in the account."

Jade and Darren stared each other. "Oh my God," Jade said. "The Caymans? Rather notorious for money laundering, they are, aren't they?"

"Yes," Sam said. "Very much so. Honey, is there any way to find out whose account that was in the Caymans?"

"Highly unlikely," Indie said. "The reason people use banks in the Caymans is to keep anyone from knowing anything about their money. However, most of the time, any money sent to the Cayman Islands is transferred right back out pretty fast. They use it for a pass-through account, basically, and sometimes the bank is set to send it right back out as soon as it comes in."

Sam grunted. "So, it's probably going to someone who doesn't want to be traced, right?"

"Yes, and those banks hide the actual accounts they send the money to, so even if I hack in, I won't be able to track where it actually went. It'll say it went to an account that won't exist by the time I get to it."

"Jade," Sam said, "it sounds like you've actually found something important."

"You think?" Jade said. "Does this look the same way to you guys as it does to me?"

"I hate to admit it," Darren said, "but I think it does. It looks to me like Web Wide Awards provided the money that was used to hire Reynard to arrange the shooting."

Jade nodded. "That's how I see it. Sam?"

"I would have to agree," Sam said. "Unfortunately, unless we can prove conclusively that Morton was aware that's where the money was going, or that Reynard actually received it, making such an accusation stick would be very difficult. Have we got anything else on this we can work with?"

"I'm afraid not," Jade said. "It's just too big a coincidence, Sam. He's been diverting money and hiding it, then sending it to Starbright in London, and then it gets transferred to the Caymans? There can't be any legitimate explanation for that."

"I agree," Sam said. "Again, the problem is how we prove it. At this point, I don't even want Morton to know we've discovered this. We're going to have to find some way to connect him to the money, and the money to Reynard."

"Connecting him to the money isn't going to be that difficult," Jade said. "The lady who runs the income bookkeeping office is unlikely to take the fall for him, and I've already talked with her about this once. I'm pretty sure I can get her to come forward, if I let her know just how serious the problem might be."

"The only problem I have with that is that she might go running straight to Morton," Sam said. "I want to keep this under our hats for the moment, something we can bring out when we need it. If we can find anything else to indicate his involvement, then as circumstantial as this is, it could help cinch the case."

"Then we'll get back on it," Jade said. "If he did this, Sam, we cannot let him get away with it."

"Trust me," Sam said. "We won't. My office, eight thirty in the morning."

"Sam," Indie said, "hold up a minute. Remember that phone recording, the one with the distorted voice that we think was talking to Hickam? Well, I never managed to find the call record, so I haven't been able to track the call itself. On the other hand, if I could get a sample recording of John Morton's voice, Herman could do a comparison on speech patterns and cadences, stuff like that. That could tie him directly to Starbright."

"That won't be a problem," Sam said. "It could be a recording over a phone, right?"

"Oh, yes, of course."

"I'll have it for you in a few minutes."

25

Sam called Morton and talked with him about simple things for a few minutes, with Indie recording the call on the computer. Ten minutes after he finished, Herman gave them his opinion.

"Sorry, Sam," Indie said. "Herman says that is definitely not John Morton. Less than a seventeen percent similarity in speech patterns or cadences. Even with the distortion, there's no way to hide things like that. It's not him."

Sam nodded. "I'm actually glad to hear it," he said. "Summer spent some time with John the other night, and she came away convinced he's clean. We're looking for somebody else inside his company, but who else would benefit? I went over this with John yesterday, and there's nobody who owns enough stock in the company for it to really make them any money."

Indie looked at him. "There is one other possibility," she said. "We've just been going on the guess that this is a male voice. What if it's Annie Porter?"

Sam stared at her for a moment, then took out his phone and called Jade again. "Jade? Sam. Listen, we just checked the recording against Morton's voice, and it is definitely not him. However, Indie just made a good point. We've been going on the assumption that whoever that voice belongs to is male, but there's no reason it couldn't be a woman. Could you give Annie a call and get a recording?"

"Um, yeah, sure. I'll give it a try now."

Fifteen minutes later, Sam's phone rang again. "Hello?" He put the phone on speaker so Indie could hear.

"It's Jade. I just emailed you a recording of a phone conversation between me and Annie Porter. Did you get it yet?"

"Oh, let me go to my computer," Indie said. "Yep, there it is. Let me get it set up. Okay, I've fed it into Herman and told him to compare it to the distorted voice on the recording from the Starbright computer system." She set a number of parameters for the comparison, then turned him loose.

A box popped up on the screen that said it would take an estimated eleven minutes to complete the comparison. This was because Herman was taking each audio file apart in tiny little fragments, and looking for identical fragments in the other audio file. Finding a sufficient percentage of identical fragments would make it possible for him to generate a statistical probability of a match.

"Okay, Herman says it's going to take him eleven minutes," Sam said. "I'll give you a call back and let you know what he decides."

"Okay, Sam," Jade said. "If I'm being honest, I'm really hoping it's not Annie. I actually kind of like her."

"Well, we'll know pretty soon."

A little more than ten minutes later, Herman had finished the comparison, and had concluded that there was slightly less than an eighty-nine percent probability that it was the same speaker.

"Herman," Indie said, "eighty-nine percent?" She looked at the screen for moment longer, then turned to Sam.

"Okay," she said. "He says it's about an eighty-nine percent chance that is the same voice, but I need to qualify that for you a bit. At eighty-nine percent, about all he's really saying is that the two voices are extremely similar, but probably not the same. They speak in much the same way, they probably even sound very similar, but anything less than a ninety-seven or ninety-eight percent similarity means that it's highly unlikely that it's the same person on both recordings. I'm not saying it absolutely isn't, I'm saying this is simply not conclusive. It's possible that similar speech patterns could be learned in school, or if they spent time in a similar environment, that sort of thing."

"Then, you're saying this probably wouldn't hold up in court?"

"Oh, I'm sure it wouldn't," Indie said. "Any halfway decent lawyer would be able to cast doubt on it, I'm sure of that. It just couldn't be considered a definite match, Sam."

"Okay, sweetheart," Sam said. "So it didn't rule Annie out, but it doesn't confirm that it is her, either."

"Right," Indie said. "I wish I could give you something more definite, but I can't. And my gut says it's not her. Eighty-nine percent just isn't close enough to believe it could be the same person speaking."

"Okay." He called Jade back and told her that Herman didn't believe it was Annie's voice on the distorted recording.

"I'm really kind of glad to hear that," Jade said. "I just wish we could come up with someone else to compare it to."

"We'll just add that to the things we're going to talk about in the morning," Sam said. "I'll see you both then."

Sam hung up, then turned to his wife. "I really thought we were about to close this case out," he said. "I wanted it over with. Now I'm not sure what's really going on."

"Let's talk it out," Indie said. "There's no longer any doubt that someone at Web Wide Awards is involved, right?"

"No doubt at all," Sam said. "The only problem is figuring out who it could be. The plot seems to have been intended to build up the company, make it more valuable. The only people who really benefit from that are the owners, John and Annie, or the advertisers, and Starbright in particular. We know that Starbright is involved, but even if we proved that, we don't have anything on a motive for whoever is the inside man."

"Or woman," Indie said. "So, what other ways could somebody benefit from this? Is there anybody who might end up with a better job out of it?"

Sam shook his head. "Not likely," he said. "And the way they do their compensation system, everybody ends up making more money when the company does, but not so much that it will make that big a difference. From what John told me, there's nobody who would see their income go up enough that it would conceivably be a motive for this type of thing."

"Okay. And yet, we know that somebody inside the company is working with Starbright to make this happen. Maybe Starbright is paying them."

Sam looked at her for a moment. "That's definitely conceivable," he said. "Starbright is trying to expand their streaming service into the U.S.A., and the increase of traffic on Morton's website means a lot more Americans are seeing Starbright advertising. Is there any way to find out whether they had a big increase in American subscribers?"

Indie bit her bottom lip. "Well, I can try going into the connection that Denny set up in their computers, see if I can find their subscriber database. The only problem is that they may have figured out that I have a backdoor, and either put a stop to it or set a trap on it."

"What would that mean, if they set a trap on it?"

"Well, they could conceivably backtrace to my computer, or even hit me with a virus. I don't think it would really do me any harm, because Herman would automatically block any data packet that was pushed toward us. The only real risk is that they might figure out exactly who hacked into them. The last thing I want is Interpol showing up here to haul me off."

"No, that won't happen," Sam said. "Like I said, when we're dealing with economic espionage, DHS has a lot of latitude in how we acquire information. Unless you think they could actually do some damage to Herman, I think it might be worth a try."

"Okay," Indie said. "Wake up, Herman, you got work to do."

Herman got into the connection easily, and Indie was surprised to find that no one seemed to have even noticed it.

"Okay, here we go," she said. "I'm looking at their accounting section, and there has been—well, I have to say a moderate increase in American subscribers. Of course, all that new traffic has only been there for a few days, and most people see an ad many times before they actually click on it. While it doesn't look like a huge increase right now, they'll probably keep growing at a pretty steady rate for some time, now."

"Then that establishes a motive for Starbright," Sam said. "Increase their American subscribership, and they increase their entire global revenue stream. The only question is what they would've paid somebody inside Web Wide Awards to do this, but then we have the additional question of the money that was sent out of Morton's accounts to Starbright. This just isn't adding up. You know, conventional wisdom for police is to follow the money, but in this case it's going from victim to perpetrator."

Indie was staring at her monitor, clicking the keys so rapidly that it sounded like a rhythm of some sort. "Sam?" she said slowly. "What if the inside person stood to gain something a whole lot bigger than just money?"

Sam's eyebrows lowered as he looked at his wife. "Such as?"

Indie turned to look at him. "Stock. Starbright has been privately held among a small group of investors until now, but it's going public next month. Everything's all set up for their IPO, and they even have arrangements made with Chase Manhattan so that they can trade on the American Stock Exchanges. They just split their stock so that there are five billion shares total, and it's being predicted that they'll open at almost 10 dollars a share. Benjamin Hickam owns ninety-two percent of all the stock, so what if he agreed to give a few million shares to whoever is helping him out?"

The eyebrows suddenly shot upward. "Then somebody becomes a multimillionaire overnight, and they even stole money from Morton himself to do it. Indie, I think you may have just broken the case."

"But there's nothing that says who," Indie said. "All I see is that the stock was split, and there are a few blocks that appear to be earmarked for certain people, but it doesn't say who."

"Then all we need to do is find out who inside Web Wide Awards is suddenly very interested in the stock market."

There was the sound of feet on the front porch, and Sam got up and went toward the door. A glance through the glass made him smile, as he saw his mother's face, but then an aroma found him as he opened the door.

"Samuel," his mother said, "we brought something." She held up a large serving dish, then waited for Kim to step inside and pushed the door shut with her butt as she went past him toward the kitchen. "Indie invited us over for dinner, so I wanted to surprise you."

Sam broke out into a smile of his own. "Mom," he said, "you can't surprise me when it smells that good. You made your beef stroganoff?"

"Yes, just the way you like it, with rum and broccoli. Kim thought I was crazy when she saw me cooking the beef in rum, but when she tasted it, she understood."

"Oh, my goodness, that was good," Kim said. "Come on, let's get it into the oven before it gets cold."

Sam grinned and let the ladies precede him into the kitchen. His mother's beef stroganoff was one of the things he loved to remember about growing up. It had been his father's favorite dish, and became Sam's during his teens. They set the oven on low and put it inside, to keep it warm while the rest of dinner was prepared.

Twenty minutes later, with hastily made side dishes of instant mashed potatoes and cream style corn, they all sat down to the table. Indie had taken the stroganoff out of the oven last, and it was absolutely perfect as they began dishing it out.

They chatted as they ate, and when it was finished, Indie broke out ice cream for dessert. She had just set a dish in front of everyone when Kim suddenly shook her head and turned to look at Sam.

A chill went down Sam's spine. He had seen that look too many times, and hated it. It meant that Beauregard had taken over his mother-in-law for a moment, and that always meant that he had a message for Sam.

"You're looking good, Sam," he said. "I was sorry to hear about your friend's uncle. I hope he did not suffer."

Sam swallowed, but looked directly into Kim's eyes. "As far as I know," he said, "the old man died instantly. I wish I had been able to interpret your warning, so that we might have saved him."

"I'm afraid he was not the one I was speaking of, Sam," Beauregard said. "I regret that I must give you even more bad news, but Death has not struck yet. I know very little more than I did before, but that it will happen suddenly, without warning. Death is stalking someone close to you, and you will not be able to prevent what is to happen."

Sam bit back the anger that tried to swell up within him, and stared into his mother-in-law's eyes. "Is there anything at all you can tell me that may let me avoid this? Any way in the world that I can stop it, prevent someone from dying?"

"I am afraid not, Sam. However, I am somewhat confused about this, myself. I know that death will strike someone you care for, and yet I see a point beyond that moment with all of your friends and family gathered around you. I wish that I could tell you what this vision means, but I cannot."

"But if you see them all with me, doesn't that mean they all survive?" Sam asked. "What else could it mean, Beauregard?"

"I have not got an answer for you, Sam. Would that I did, but all I see are the visions. In my vision of death, I see the dark Angel hovering over everyone close to you, and reaching out a hand, but I am not able to see whom he touches. In my vision beyond that moment, I see only that all of your friends and family are gathered, and I cannot see anyone missing. Unfortunately, I have never had a vision of death that did not come true, so I do not understand the meaning of these conflicting visions."

"Then I'm going to cling to the second one," Sam said. "I'm going to cling to the hope that everyone survives."

Kim nodded her head. "That is what you have to do, Sam," she said, in Beauregard's voice. "I have one more thing to tell you, and then I shall leave poor Kimberly alone for this evening. I told you before that you may arrest the wrong person for these crimes; I no longer see that problem, so I am quite certain that you will determine who is guilty and bring them to justice. I would urge you only to be certain that everyone involved be brought to justice, for there are more than one."

"How many?" Sam asked, but Kim was blinking. She looked at the way Sam was staring at her, and frowned.

"Beauregard?"

Sam nodded, but forced himself to grin. "Yes, but at least this time he gave me a bit of good news."

MONDAY MORNING. AS Sam walked into his office, he suddenly remembered how he used to dread Monday mornings on the police force. Monday always seemed to be the day that something would go wrong, but on this particular Monday he was feeling pretty confident.

At eight thirty, Sam and the entire team were gathered around the conference table. He waited until everyone had coffee and settled in, then began speaking.

"Jade has discovered that John Morton has been diverting money from his company, and keeping it hidden. She and Indie were able to track that money yesterday to an account in London that happens to belong to Starbright. The money had been transferred into that account, and then transferred out to a bank in the Cayman Islands. Needless to say, we are now working on the possibility that this money was involved in the arrangements to hire Reynard, which means that there is someone inside Web Wide Awards who was working with Hickam. What we've got so far is pretty solid evidence of collusion, but we are still looking for anything that can lead us to the person responsible. If any of you run across any information that might give us a lead, I want to know as soon as possible."

He paused to take a sip of coffee, then looked at them all again. "I've secured the backing of the DA's office, who is filing charges against Benjamin Hickam today, charges that include attempted murder, murder, and economic espionage. Pemberton, the DA, will immediately start extradition proceedings, and we're lucky enough that the U.K. is generally pretty cooperative about such things. When he gets here, I plan to question him pretty heavily about his involvement with Reynard."

"Speaking of Reynard," Steve said, "what happens if one of us actually runs up against him? I mean, if he's honestly involved in this thing, and we've already taken out four of his people, there's a pretty good chance he's going to show up here. I want to know what to do if that happens."

"That's a very good point," Sam said. He reached over and pushed the button on the speakerphone in the middle of the table. "Jeremy? Could you come in here for a moment?"

"Yes, sir," replied Jeremy Levins. Jeremy was Sam's legal consultant. He came through the door just a few seconds later and took a seat at the table. "How can I help?"

"We have reason to believe," Sam said, "that Pierre Reynard, a known killer who has been active in political assassinations and has been classed as a terrorist in other countries, could show up in Denver and take some kind of action that may affect our client. If any of our investigators are able to come face to face with Reynard, what limitations would they be under regarding the use of deadly force?"

Jeremy thought for a moment, then nodded to himself.

"As private investigators, they would be limited to the use of deadly force only in the case of self defense, or to prevent immediate harm to others. However, as agents of the Department of Homeland Security, they would be fully justified in taking whatever action was necessary to kill Mr. Reynard. He is classed as a terrorist, and a presidential finding, equivalent to an executive order, made by President George W. Bush after the events of 9/11, authorizes the use of targeted killing against any terrorist suspect. That finding is still in effect today, and allows any agent of the United States government to use deadly force against any terrorist or terror suspect. It is not necessary to arrest or attempt to arrest the person first. It's basically a shoot to kill order, and if you happen to get the opportunity to kill Mr.

Reynard and do so, you would automatically be considered to be operating as DHS agents at the time."

Summer was staring at Jeremy. "Being a DHS agent is a license to kill? I thought the United States didn't actually have those."

"Any federal agent or member of the military can choose to use deadly force against any known terrorist or suspected terrorists. That's the way the presidential finding was worded, and it still stands. As for a license to kill, there's no such actual document, but with that presidential finding in effect, any federal badge is essentially a hunting license for anyone labeled as a terrorist."

"No shit?" Steve asked. "Man, that sucks."

Summer looked at him. "Why, Steve?"

"Because, honey, under certain current laws, just about any group that opposes something the government does can be classed as a domestic terrorist organization. Remind me to quit griping about paying taxes."

Everyone looked to Jeremy. "Jeremy?" Summer asked. "Is he right?"

"Unfortunately, he is. Under the U.S.A. PATRIOT Act, any action which seeks to influence any policy of the government, such as taxation or gun control, through the use of intimidation or coercion, which can be defined as something as simple as a protest, can be considered an act of terrorism. Therefore, any person or group that condones the attempt to influence that policy is automatically considered to be a terrorist or terrorist organization. And yes, that does mean that they could theoretically be subject to targeted killing. Fortunately, so far, that hasn't happened."

"Well, let's hope it stays that way," Steve said.

"Okay, you heard the man," Sam said. "Unless you honestly believe you can take him alive, then I'm going to agree. If you are absolutely certain you're face to face with Reynard, do not take any chances. He is considered a terrorist, so you can take the first shot."

26

"Let's get back to the inside person," Steve said. "Are we sure it isn't Morton, himself? This whole plot has always been about sympathy, right? Making the public feel sorry for the poor company that got attacked. Well, I've been kicking some ideas around with Walter, and he says I might have come up with something that makes sense."

"Maybe," Walter said. "I said maybe."

"Okay," Sam said. "And what would that be?"

"What if something were to happen to Annie Porter? We know that there are professional killers involved, right? That kid got shot and the company got this massive outpouring of sympathy and support. What do you think would happen if Annie Porter, who everybody knows and loves, were to suddenly get killed?"

Everyone but Walter was staring at Steve. It took a moment, but finally they began to regain their voices.

"I guess it's always possible this is his way of getting rid of her," Summer said. "If she dies, her stock would probably revert back to him. That would leave him in total control of the company, all by himself."

"I don't think it's about control," Sam said. "From what I was told, Morton runs everything. Annie owns stock, but he makes all of the major decisions. I'm not sure what the split is, but either he owns fifty-one percent or her stock is nonvoting.

I don't think he would have to eliminate her, even if he wanted to make some major change in the company."

"That doesn't mean he doesn't want to get rid of her," Summer said. "With billions of dollars involved, could you imagine the palimony if he kicked her out? Let's face it, this would be the perfect opportunity."

"Feeling a little cynical, today, Summer?" Jade asked.

"Not really," Summer said. "I'm really just thinking out loud. I spent some time with Morton and saw nothing that indicates any kind of unhappiness in his personal life, but I always try to look at every possible angle."

"We all do," Sam said. "I can tell you that he sounded genuine whenever he talked about his feelings for Annie. I never got any impression that there was any problem between them."

"I agree with Sam," Darren said. "Nothing I know about Morton would fit the profile of the person behind this. There's no doubt in my mind that we are correct and Hickam is involved, and I have to say he is likely the originator of the plan. Thanks to Google, I've been able to learn a lot about him, and he's actually quite a piece of work. Starbright is his latest business, but it's not the only thing he's ever done. He's run several different businesses right into the ground, starting with a motorcycle dealership shortly after he got out of the Navy. He followed that up with a financial services company, ended up in trouble with HMRC, the British tax authority, and then went into the scrap metal business. He did well in that for about ten years, but then it turned out that he was spending money faster than it was coming in and the company went belly up. Starbright was actually started by his nephew, as more of a hobby than a business, but Hickam saw the potential and talked the boy into selling it to him. Somehow, he managed to round up investors and raised almost half a million dollars, and built it into not just a video awards system, but the U.K.'s biggest video streaming service. He's done extremely well with this one, but there are rumors that the company might not be quite as solid as it appears. If his company keeps growing at the rate that it is, his new publicly traded stock values will probably triple within a year."

"Okay," Sam said. "So he fits the profile you're building, then?"

"Perfectly," Darren said. "On top of all of that about his business ventures, I also found out that he's been suspected more than once of paying to have someone killed, especially a competitor. One of the reasons he did so well in scrap is because two of his competitors in the London area met with suspicious accidental deaths. Hickam was a suspect, but no evidence was ever found to prove he was connected. A few years before that, an HMRC investigator who was digging into his financial company also met with a suspicious and untimely end. It was set up to look like a robbery, but when the thief was caught, he said somebody he couldn't identify paid him to kill the investigator and make it look that way. Again, Hickam was suspected, but no evidence was ever produced."

"He definitely sounds like our boy," Sam said. "Now, if we can figure out where Reynard fits into this, we might have a chance of killing two birds with one stone. Any thoughts on that, anybody?"

"Pierre Reynard is a professional killer," Darren said. "I contacted an old friend at Interpol and got a dossier on him, and this guy is one hundred percent pro. He's credited with more than eighty successful assassinations, more than half of them of prominent figures in business or politics. He's absolutely without scruples of any kind, because he's known to have taken contracts to kill children, eliminating competitive heirs to an estate. In more than one case, when getting to the target alone proved to be impossible, he resorted to mass destruction that meant lots of collateral damage. The Swedish ambassador to France was a target, and Reynard planted a bomb on a carousel where the ambassador often took his nine-year-old daughter. Six children were killed, and eighteen more were critically injured."

Denny nodded his head. "When I was with SAS, he was high on our list. Shoot to kill, those were the orders."

"And if any of us," Sam said, "were to come face to face with him, those are the orders now. He is listed as an enemy combatant of the United States, because he has ties to terrorism. Under the law, Jeremy says, we are authorized to use deadly force. Don't warn him, don't try to arrest him, just shoot the bastard."

"You honestly think we might run into him?" Jade asked.

"I'm sure it's probably a long shot," Sam said, "but it's like Steve says, he's definitely involved in this case somehow, so it's possible. All I'm saying is that you cannot hesitate if the opportunity for the shot comes along. I understand that goes against the grain for most of us, to shoot first without warning, but this guy is dangerous. If you don't take him out first, he's probably going to kill you."

"That's a fair assessment," Denny said. "We lost eight men in SAS because they thought they could take him alive. The single survivor claims Reynard was on the floor and handcuffed when he suddenly got his hands on one of the weapons and managed to shoot the entire team. He is rumored to have escaped from several different jails over the years, and restraints don't seem to hold him."

"I read about him," Walter said suddenly. "He knows how people think. He can make people do what he wants. If you look at some of the people he killed, it wasn't because someone wanted them dead, it was because their deaths would make other people do certain things. Hickam hired him, but Reynard is probably the one who is running this whole operation. He was hired to make sure Web Wide Awards grew quickly, but he's the one who decides how to accomplish it."

All eight of the others stared at him, and Sam slowly began to nod his head. "It makes sense," he said. "The mind behind this whole thing has been ruthless, and that fits perfectly with what Darren just told us about Reynard. If he's running the show, then he is almost certainly going to turn up here before this is over." He looked around the table. "All right, we have two missions. First, we need to identify the inside person at Web Wide Awards. Second, we need to find some way to put a stop to Reynard. Anybody got any suggestions?"

THERE ARE SOME PARTS of Denver where the tourists do not go, unless they happen to be looking for a glimpse into the seedier side of life. There are not many such sections, but Denver has its share of bars, dives and diners. Some of them are particularly well suited to the criminal element, but there are a few that are occasionally frequented by some of the most dangerous people in the world.

Crandon's Diner just off Wewatta Street, near Union Station, was one such place. Though it has never been depicted in movies or television shows, locals knew very well that the diner had seen a number of criminal plots hatched. It was a place where everybody watched everybody else's back, because an attempt to kill the person at the next table could easily get you killed, as well.

The man sitting at the back table close to the lonely old video game machine knew how to fit in perfectly. His clothes were decent but not expensive, and he gave the impression that he was seeing everything around him, even though his eyes never seemed to leave the coffee cup he held. Most of the people in the place figured he was waiting for someone, and they were close to the truth.

The cell phone in his pocket vibrated, and he took it out and put it to his ear. "Yes?"

"It's me," came the voice he recognized as Benjamin Hickam. "We—we have a problem."

"And that is?"

"I was nearly exposed over here," Hickam said. "An old friend of mine figured out that I was involved, and went to the CPS. Luckily, their top man has been in my pocket for years, so he warned me about it. I took care of the situation, but I'm afraid it only got worse. My old friend, it seems, has a nephew who is busily trying to dig up proof. I tried to take care of that, as well, but the fool I sent to do it managed to make a botch of it. The man got away, and now it turns out he's an investigator, working for the people out of Denver."

"Then find him, deal with it."

"Well, and that's the problem," Hickam said. "I just learned he's left the country, and is back in Denver. From what I've heard, they may have figured out what's actually going on, and that you are involved."

"Who is this 'they' of which you speak?" The man in the diner suddenly seemed menacing to those around him.

"It's that bloody security company Morton hired. Windlass, they call it. Seems their top man is famous for a number of things, I guess he was some kind of secret agent for the American government. Samuel Prichard, that's his name."

There was silence on the line for a few seconds, and then the man in the diner cleared his throat. "I know of him," he said. "I have not yet had the pleasure of meeting him, but he is not a threat. The plan will continue, and I shall do what is necessary. It will cost a bit more, however. We were not supposed to run into these problems."

Hickam sighed. "Of course," he said. "How much more?"

"We will determine that when the objective is reached. It will depend on the difficulty, but nothing shall change. Call me again if you learn more that you believe I need to know."

He hung up the phone and put it back into his pocket, then went back to nursing his coffee. He sat there for several minutes, just thinking about the situation.

Sam Prichard. Sometime back, the man in the diner had considered accepting a contract that would have brought the two of them together. He had been promised a powerful position in an entirely new order, by a man named Chandler. The job was simple and straightforward, to eliminate an associate of the Pope, but Reynard had always trusted his own instincts. He'd already heard about Prichard at that point, because of his contacts in the American intelligence community. The fact that Prichard had prevented a terrorist from setting off a nuclear device in Lake Mead was public knowledge; the fact that he had been instrumental in stopping some even bigger terrorist threats was not, but such things found their way to the ears of those who live in that shadowy world.

Pierre Reynard did not fear Sam Prichard, but he detested the idea of being on the losing side of anything. He could care less about the morality of any situation, but his reputation had been built on successes. There was no way he was going to be part of any plan that was doomed to failure, and Prichard had been working with a rogue agent named Long. Long was probably the equal of Reynard, so for the two of them to be working together could conceivably present an obstacle Chandler was unlikely to overcome. For that reason, Reynard had declined the job.

And now, Prichard was running the investigation into the current situation. Reynard had been following the news, keeping an eye on the developments as they happened. He hadn't actually expected Prichard to be a problem in this particular case, but perhaps he had underestimated the man slightly.

"So," he mused to himself. "Fate brings us together after all."

The nice thing about knowing your enemy was that you then knew his weakness. Reynard took out the phone and called up his email app.

Possible mission forthcoming. Acknowledge.

He sent the email and put the phone back in his pocket. It would be several hours before a response could come in, and he had things to do in the meantime. He signaled the waitress for a coffee refill, and then continued to sit where he was.

"I HAVE ONE," WALTER said. "I was thinking about the original shooting. We know that woman put the rifle on the camera. We saw that on the security video. It occurred to me that I missed something. The rifle was where I knew it had to be, but how did it get there?"

Sam looked at him, confused. "Like you said, Walter," he said. "The woman, Bernadette Jones, put it there. We know that from the video, there's no possibility it was someone else."

"I mean, how did the camera get there? The camera moved to come down to where she could reach it. I looked in the control room, and it's a very confusing place. Most people would never be able to figure out how to move the camera. I don't think the man with her would have known how to do it."

"Holy smokes, he's right," Steve said. "We never looked at who was in the control room that night. How in the world did we miss that?"

"Actually, we didn't," Jade said. "I checked it on the arena security cameras, but the camera in the control room wasn't working that night. I asked somebody about it, and they said it had blown a fuse. They didn't fix it until a couple of days later, when they noticed it."

"The gun was mounted in the early morning hours," Sam said. "There wouldn't have been anyone in the control room who actually works there, unless..."

"Charlie Barr," Darren said. "Sam, how did we miss this? He told us he gave them the cue sheet and the code to get into the building, but if he had given them instructions on how to move the camera, he would've said so. I'll bet fifty bucks right now he went in there and moved it for them."

Sam reached over and hit the speakerphone. Jenna's voice came through a second later. "Yes, sir?"

"Jenna, get Karen Parks on the line for me."

"Yes, sir," Jenna said. It was less than a minute later when Karen's voice came through the speakerphone.

"Sam? You there?"

"We are all here, Karen," Sam said. "Listen, we've got a lot to bring you up to speed on, but right now I have a question. What happened with Charlie Barr the other day?"

"Well, he's being charged as an accessory, but Pemberton decided to go easy on him. They're already talking about a plea deal for probation. Why?"

"I need to talk to him again," Sam said. "When Bernadette Jones mounted the rifle onto the camera, somebody in the control room moved the camera down to where she could get to it. It's highly doubtful her partner could have done that, but Charlie could have. Any chance you could pick him up, so I can come down to the station and question him?"

"I'll go you one better," Karen said. "Since your company is still in the lead on this, I can pick him up and bring him right down to your office. You got a room to use for interrogation?"

"We'll create one in a hurry," Sam said. "I'll get somebody started on that, and you can go find him. He may have been more deeply involved in this than we thought."

"I'll be there as soon as I can track his ass down," Karen said. There was a click, and she was gone.

"Sam?" Jade said. "You think Charlie could be the inside man?"

Sam looked at her. "I guess it's possible," he said. "Frankly, though, I didn't think he was that smart."

Darren shook his head. "I have to agree, Sam," he said. "Charlie Barr doesn't fit the profile I'm working up on this."

"Speaking of your profile," Sam said, "have you got far enough you could share with the rest of us yet?"

"Well," Darren said, "I think we're looking for someone who is extremely intelligent, but probably feels neglected and underrated. This person is motivated strictly by a desire for wealth, but there is a revenge component involved, as well. I would expect this person to be friendly and personable, but with some deeply hidden anger against the company, or against Martin. Using him and his company to make himself rich is part of what fills the need this person has for revenge. It's probably somebody under thirty-five, and could be either male or female."

"Charlie's in his late forties," Sam said, "and I don't think he's all that intelligent. It's possible he was fooling us, but I certainly didn't get that impression."

"No, neither did I," Darren said. "Quite the opposite, in fact. He's not entirely stupid, you can't be and do good video work, but he's not the kind of person who can manipulate others very well. The person we're looking for knows how to do that, and how to do it very well."

"Okay, anybody else got any ideas?"

All five of the investigators looked at one another, but it was Walter who finally raised a hand.

"Walter?" Sam asked. "Go ahead, what are you thinking?"

"Jade said John Morton is the one hiding money," Walter said. "Did we find any proof of that? Is it possible it could be somebody else? The reason I'm asking is because I looked up a few things about Morton's background. Besides the fact that he's a programmer, he's also a licensed CPA. If he wanted to hide money, he could probably find a lot of ways to do it that we never would discover."

All of the others stared at him, and Jade began to shake her head.

"No," she said. "I never saw any proof that it's him doing it. I actually was told that by one of the employees who says he forces her to fudge the paperwork, but I only have her word for it, now that I think about it." She turned to Sam. "Maybe I should go pay her another visit."

"Go ahead," Sam said. "But take Summer with you."

27

It took Karen almost an hour to find Charlie, but Sam was ready by the time she got him to the offices. There was a room near the front door that was used for small meetings, and had just a table and four chairs. They took him in there, with Sam, Karen, and Darren.

"What's this all about?" Charlie asked. "I already told you everything I know."

"That's what we want to find out, Charlie," Sam said. "See, there's one little detail we haven't been able to figure out, and we think maybe you can shed some light on it for us."

Charlie shrugged. "Okay, if I can. What is it?"

Sam had brought a tablet into the room, and he turned it around so Charlie could see it. He tapped the screen, and the security video showing Bernadette Jones mounting the rifle onto the camera began to play.

"Take a look at this," Sam said. "That's the woman who set up the rifle. Notice anything funny about this video?"

Charlie looked at the screen. "Looks like she's trying to dress like a man," he said. "Is that what you mean?"

"No," Sam said. "No, what I'm talking about is the fact that the camera moves down to where she's standing. Now, we know enough about the control room to know that it's very complicated. It's very doubtful that her partner would have been able to figure out which controls moved the camera well enough to have brought it down to her that perfectly. That would take somebody who was familiar with those controls, somebody who really knew how to use them. Any idea who might have been in the control room at three o'clock in the morning?"

Charlie suddenly looked nervous. "I—how would I know? I already told you, I gave them the cue sheet, but that was it."

"No, you also admitted to giving them the access code for the door," Darren said. "Charlie, it's time to come clean, buddy. That was you in the control room, wasn't it?"

Charlie stared at him, swallowing repeatedly. "I—no, I wouldn't..."

"See what I mean, Sam?" Darren asked.

Sam grinned. Charlie was tapping his pinky against his palm. "Charlie, give it up. Your body language is giving you away, right now. We know it was you in the control booth, but I want to know what else you know about this. Now, you can either talk to us here, or you can talk to the prosecutor when he adds accessory to attempted murder to the charges against you. I think you can kiss any hope of probation goodbye, if that happens."

Tears started to run down the man's face, and Charlie gave in. "It was the same thing," he said. "They threatened to rat me out if I didn't help. They just told me what time to be there and which camera they wanted, that's all I did, I swear. As soon as they were done, they went their way and I went mine, and I never saw them again."

"What this means is you spent more time with them than you told us before," Darren said. "I want to know what they talked about while you were with them. Did you know they were planting a gun?"

"No, no, I swear I didn't know that," Charlie said. "I told you, they said they were reporters and they were trying to get the scoop on everybody else. I thought they were hiding their own cameras up there, I swear I did."

The questioning went on for nearly an hour, but Charlie never gave up any more information. When they were done, Sam and Darren agreed that he probably didn't know anything else of value. With Karen's cooperation, they decided not to take this additional information to Pemberton.

Karen drove Charlie home, and Sam and Darren began once more trying to figure out who the inside person was.

JADE AND SUMMER WALKED into the Web Wide Awards building and told the security guard at the front desk that they needed to speak with Jackie Bridges. He consulted his computer and then looked up.

"I'm sorry, but Ms. Bridges didn't come in today. According to the computer, she didn't even bother to call in, and personnel hasn't been able to get hold of her."

Jade looked at Summer, then both of them took out their IDs and shoved them in the security guard's face. "My name is Summer Raines, and I'm an investigator with Windlass Security," Summer said. "Give me her address, right now."

He looked at the ID for a moment, his eyebrows trying to crawl over his forehead, and then slowly shook his head. "Ma'am, I'm sorry," he said, "but I'm not allowed to give out that kind of information about employees here."

Summer leaned across the desk until she was almost nose to nose with him, and gave him her sweetest smile. "Daniel? It says Daniel on your name tag, that's you, right? Listen, Daniel, I'm not the type of girl to really push a guy, but if you don't cough up that address in the next five seconds, I'm going to make you wish you were born female, because then it wouldn't be so embarrassing when you have to sit down to pee. Now, you don't have to believe me, because it won't take me ten seconds more to prove it. Five—four—three..."

"Hang on, hang on," he said. "They don't pay me enough for this stuff. Okay, look, I can't give you the address, even though it's right here on the screen on my computer, I can't give it to you, do you see it? I'm not allowed to read that off to you."

"Got it," Summer said, and the two women bolted out the door. They had come to the building in Summer's Jaguar, and the big engine roared as she dropped it into gear.

Behind them, a man stood and stared after them through the glass of the front doors. Neither of them had noticed.

Jackie's house, according to Jade's GPS, was nearly 20 minutes away. It was less than fourteen minutes later when Summer slid to a stop in her driveway. The two girls jumped out and headed for the front door of the house, each of them with a hand on a weapon.

Jade knocked, but they waited more than a minute with no response. Summer signaled that she was going around the back, and Jade nodded as she knocked again.

The backyard was fenced in, and Summer found the gate and made her way into it. She slipped around the back of the house, keeping a close eye out in case anyone was watching, and walked up to the back door. It was on a small concrete porch, and she looked through the window on the door before she tried the knob. There was no one in sight, but the knob was unlocked so she opened the door and stepped inside. She had her gun in her hand, keeping it low until she managed to get the door closed quietly behind her.

The kitchen opened directly onto the living room, and she cleared it quickly. She went to the front door and opened it, putting a finger to her lips to tell Jade to be quiet. The two of them, both with guns in their hands, started moving through the house.

A hallway led off from the living room, and they found Jackie laying on the bed in what must've been her own room. There was a needle hanging out of her left arm, and Jade made a face as she reached down to feel for a pulse.

Her eyes flew open. "She's alive," she said to Summer, who immediately dialed 911.

Jade yanked out the needle and started slapping Jackie in the face. "Jackie? Jackie, can you hear me? Jackie, it's Jade, come on, respond to me."

She got a simple moan, but Jackie wasn't truly responding. She kept trying until paramedics arrived almost 10 minutes later, and they got out of the way as they started doing what they could for her.

"Any idea what she took?"

"No, we found her this way. I removed the needle, it's right there on the bed beside her."

The paramedic took a look at the needle, then rolled his eyes. "Meth," he said. "Any idea how long she's been using it?"

"I'm pretty sure she hasn't been, before now," Jade said. "She works for a company that requires regular testing, and not just urine. They get very serious about it, so there's no way she was using meth regularly." She showed him her ID. "She was a potential witness in a major crime investigation. I personally suspect foul play. Any idea whether she'll make it?"

"That depends on a lot of things," the paramedic said. "How much she took, how strong her heart is, and a lot of other things. I started an IV drip to get fluids into her, and we're taking her to the hospital now."

As the paramedics were leaving with Jackie, two police officers arrived. Jade gave them Jackie's basic information, and the officers began taking the steps necessary to locate and arrange care for her children.

Jade called Sam and told him what was happening, and he gave her the okay to go to the hospital. She and Summer headed there immediately.

Surprisingly, Jackie was awake in the ER when they arrived. Showing their ID got them past the hospital's security, and they were able to walk into the room where she was still connected to IV lines.

Jackie saw Jade and began to cry. "They said you found me," she said. "They said I might've died if you hadn't found me."

"Don't worry about that, right now," Jade said. "What we want to know right now is how this happened. Do you use meth regularly?"

"Oh, God, no," Jackie said. "I don't do any drugs at all. I've got kids, you know?"

"That how did this happen? How did you end up with a needle hanging out of your arm, overdosing on methamphetamine?"

Jackie looked at her as if she was confused for a moment, then her eyes went wide. "Somebody broke into my house," she said. "It was right after the kids left for day care, they ride a van in the mornings. I was getting dressed, getting my make-up done and all that, and somebody broke in the back door. I heard a noise, and then somebody grabbed me and held me down on the bed, and somebody else stuck a needle in my arm." She shook her head, tears flying. "That's all I remember. Who would do that?"

"Jackie, did you recognize them?" Summer asked.

"No, they—they had some kind of cloth over their faces, all I could see were their eyes." She looked around for a moment, then her eyes came back to Jade. "This is because I talked to you, isn't it? Somebody's afraid I told you too much, they're trying to shut me up."

"I have to say that's possible," Jade agreed. "But don't worry, my boss is putting security on you. No one is going to get close to you again, and we'll make arrangements to protect your children, as well."

"My kids? You think they might try to hurt my kids? Oh, God, I have to get out of here, I have to..."

"You're not going anywhere," Jade said. "Right now, this is where you need to be. The police are going to pick up your kids, and they'll bring them here, I already arranged that. I've got security guards on the way right now, they should be here any minute. You just lay back and relax, and do what the doctors tell you."

Jackie was still crying, but she nodded. "My kids," she said. "If they think you're doing drugs, they can take your kids."

"I already explained to the police that I know for a fact you don't do drugs regularly, so they're cooperating with us. I'm sure they're gonna want to talk to you, but you just tell them the same thing you told us. They can't hold it against you if someone injects you with drugs against your will."

"No, we can't," said a voice behind her, and Jade and Summer turned to see Karen Parks walk in. "Sam called me, and I'd already heard on the radio anyway. What's going on?"

"Summer and I were going out to talk to Jackie again, about some things she told me when I was working undercover. I'm sure Sam told you we have evidence that money has been transferred from Web Wide Awards to Starbright, and might be the money that was used to pay for the shootings. Well, Jackie was the first one to notice discrepancies in the accounting, and she told me that John Morton was requiring her to keep her mouth shut about it. He even gave her a couple of big pay raises, to keep her quiet, but it's actually scaring her pretty badly. I think she knows that, if it ever comes out, the fact that she was covering it up isn't going to look good on her."

Karen nodded. "And now, it looks like somebody wanted to shut her up permanently. Any idea who?"

"Well, Morton is my number one suspect," Jade said, "but Sam doesn't agree with me. He doesn't want any of us to confront Morton right now, unless it turns out there's nobody else in the company who could be involved."

"Yeah, Sam gave me a quick briefing. At the moment, I'm agreeing with him." Karen turned around as two Windlass security guards suddenly came through the door. "Looks like your reinforcements are here. I heard a couple minutes ago that they found her kids, and they're on the way here right now. Let me talk with your witness for a bit, so I can make my report."

Jade and Summer stood back while Karen took Jackie's statement, and then the two of them sat down on the sides of her bed.

"Jackie, I found out where all that money was going," she said. "Do you know?"

Jackie shook her head. "No, it's completely out of my hands once it leaves our office. All I know is that I get an email at the end of the day telling me what our total should have been, and then I go in and fix it if I have to. Can you tell me where it was going?"

"I don't think you need to worry about that right at the moment," Jade said. "Jackie, do you know anything about the bank account? Who has access to them, that sort of thing?"

"Not a whole lot," she said. "Like I said, all we did was tally up the money that came in, and then it was up to the different sections in accounting to transfer it to where it needed to go. We didn't even have access to any of the bank accounts."

"Okay, then, can you tell me anybody inside the company who would have access to that information, and who you think I could trust?"

Jackie wiped away a tear and gave her a half grin. "There's only one person involved in all of the accounting that I trust at all, and that's Andy Wilson. He's the senior accountant, and that means he's the guy who actually has to okay transferring the money, but he's about as nice as they come."

Summer looked at her. "Jackie, if he's trustworthy, why would he be involved in a plan to hide money?"

"I don't actually think he is," she said. "See, the way it's all set up, there are different people in the accounting office to handle individual accounts. Only one of them would need to know what money was supposed to be transferred out, and that amount would be missing from her daily report. Andy would never see my totals until he went to reconcile everything the following day, and he couldn't see that it had been edited."

"So, who is it that tells you every day how much you have to take off your totals to make it match up to accounting? Wouldn't that be Mr. Wilson?"

"Oh, no," Jackie said. "That actually comes in an email, in a special email account they set up for me. I'm not really sure who sends it out every day, it could be one of the accountants for all I know."

"Or it could be John Morton," Jade said. "He's the one who told you to make the totals match, right?"

"Yes," Jackie said. "He was very nice about it, but there was something about that meeting—almost like it was in some kind of spy movie or something, it was weird."

Summer's eyes narrowed. "Tell us about the meeting," she said. "Tell us everything about it, from the moment you got called to it, to the moment it was over."

Jackie blinked, but she nodded. "Okay. Well, it was toward the end of the day, and I remember it was on a Thursday. Somebody came by the office and told me that Mr. Morton wanted to see me about some kind of mistake I had made, and I thought that was pretty odd, since I'd never made a mistake in all the time I worked there. Anyway, I got up and went up the elevator and went to his office, but his secretary was already gone for the day. I knocked on the door and he told me to come on in, but when I stepped inside it was kind of dark. He was sitting behind his desk, in the dark, and he said he had a headache and that's why the lights were out."

"Have you heard of him having headaches like that before?" Summer asked.

"Well, pretty much everybody knows he gets migraines sometimes," Jackie said. "Sometimes he just goes home, and we don't see him for a day or two."

"Okay. Go on."

"Well, anyway, he said he wanted to talk to me about the difference between the totals from my office and the totals that were being reported from accounting. I said they should match, and that's when he told me that he was setting up something special, and needed to move a little bit of money every day into a secret account. In order to do that, he said that my totals had to match what accounting said at the end of the day. Well, at first I told him there was no way I could do that, because our reports are finished before the money is released to the accounting department. That's when he told me he knew that I could edit my reports, and that he wanted me to start doing it. He told me about setting up the new email account for me, and said that I had to check it every day at quitting time, and then edit my reports to match what it said in the email."

"And what did you say then?" Jade asked.

"Well, at first I tried to say I couldn't do it anyway, but he promised me it wasn't anything bad and that it would be something that was going to make him and Annie richer than ever. He said it was something really good that everybody was going to want when he finally told the world about it, but that he had to keep it a big secret until then, so nobody else would steal it and beat him to it."

"So you agreed?"

"Well, yeah," Jackie said. "Like I said, he promised me it wasn't anything bad and that nobody would get in trouble, and then he told me he'd give me a raise if I would go along with it." She shrugged. "I got kids, and it's expensive to raise them. I said okay."

"Jackie," Jade said, "you said it was dark in the office. Are you sure it was John Morton you were talking to?"

"Well, yeah," Jackie said. "You can't work there more than a week without getting to know his voice perfectly. He walks around through the building all day, every day, just talking to everybody. He's the best boss I've ever worked for, and I'm not just saying that because I got the big raises. He's just a great guy, he really is."

"Jackie," Summer said, "I'm just curious, but did he happen to tell you never to mention this outside of that meeting? Even to him?"

Jackie narrowed her eyes. "Yeah," she said. "He said he didn't want to take a chance on anybody else overhearing it, so if I had any questions or anything, I was supposed to send them to him with the email, from the email address he gave me. He said that was a super secure email, so nobody could get into it."

Jade patted her hand. "Jackie, you've been a great help. Now, you need to do what the doctors tell you and stay put, and when they let you go, our security guards are going to take you to stay somewhere safe."

"But, my job," Jackie said. "I have to go to work tomorrow."

"No, what you have to do is be safe. Right now, I don't believe going to work is the way to stay that way. As you pointed out, this attack probably happened because somebody wanted to shut you up. Apparently they just didn't realize how hard it is to fatally overdose on meth. I'm pretty sure they meant for you to die, Jackie, and I don't plan to let that happen."

Jackie nodded, but they could see that she was still somewhat confused. Of course, she was still suffering some of the effects of the methamphetamine she'd been injected with, and that was probably having some effect on her thinking processes.

Jade and Summer promised to check in on her again, and left. When they got outside the exam room, they found that Karen had been holding back the officers with Jackie's children, and the doctor was fuming as he stormed past them.

"I told him it was important that you girls interview her alone," Karen said. "He said it was important that he get in there to treat his patient. I asked him if she was about to die, and he said no, so I told him that forcing his way into that room would constitute interfering in a police matter." She grinned. "Be sure to tell Sam I did that for you. I'm sucking up for the next time you guys have an opening in the investigations department."

Both the girls chuckled, and promised they'd relay the message to Sam. "We'll tell him as soon as we get back to the office," Jade said. "That's where we're headed right now."

"Cool," Karen said. "I think I'll follow along."

28

Jade, Summer, and Karen walked into Sam's office. When he saw the three of them, he motioned for them to follow him to the conference table and they all sat down.

"Okay, here's the situation," Jade said. "Jackie can't be certain that it was truly John Morton who told her to fudge the numbers. She was told one night to go up to his office, but his secretary was gone and when she went inside, the lights were out. I guess Morton gets migraines, so that didn't surprise her all that much, and she said she was confident that it was his voice she was hearing. Personally, I think it was somebody who could either impersonate his voice very well, or who was using a voice changer that was programmed to sound like Morton."

Sam nodded. "That would make sense. That's probably the only way somebody else could enlist her cooperation. On the other hand, you said she got raises for going along with this. Wouldn't Morton have to approve those?"

"Maybe not," Jade said. "From what I was given to understand, Annie Porter actually handles a lot of the personnel matters. She could probably authorize a raise, but it could also be that the payroll department simply got a call from somebody who sounded like John. If they thought they knew his voice, they probably would do whatever he asked without questioning it."

"True. Alright, so how is Jackie?"

"She's apparently going to be okay," Karen said. "Somebody tried to OD her on meth, but unless you got a weak heart or other health problems, that's not all that easy to do. She'll probably spend the rest of the day in the hospital, and I'm glad you put security on her. It's entirely possible whoever tried to kill her will try again."

"That's why I did it," Sam said. "At some point, we are undoubtedly going to need her testimony. Now we just need to figure out who was playing John Morton in that meeting. Any suggestions?"

"Actually," Summer said, "I might have one."

Sam looked at her and cocked his head to the side. "Go ahead," he said. "Who?"

"Somebody I already declared beyond suspicion," she said. "Annie's brother, Tom Linden. Jade was telling me what Indie said about the voice comparison thing. Tom grew up in the same house as Annie, so there would be similarities in the way they talk, right?"

"Yes, I'm sure there would. Think you can get us a recording of his voice, so Indie can check it out?"

Summer smiled. "Give me fifteen minutes," she said. She got up and walked out of the office, and Karen looked at Sam.

"What did she mean, somebody she already declared beyond suspicion?"

"She had a meeting with Linden last week, and came away convinced that he was innocent. I think there's just been too many little things going crazy, lately, so she's willing to revisit the possibility that he's not."

"HI, TOM?" SUMMER ASKED. "Hi, it's Candy, remember me?"

"Oh, yeah," Tom said. "How have you been?"

"Oh, I've been doing okay," she said. "Listen, I wanted to let you know that I got a call from my doctor, and it turns out I don't have herpes after all. Apparently, it was just a nasty attack of hives, but it's all cleared up now."

"Oh, really? Well, I guess that's good. I've been meaning to call you, but I've been really, really busy lately. Maybe, maybe we can get together again sometime soon. I mean, if you want to."

Summer chuckled. "Look, boy," she said, "I just told you it's safe to get in my pants. Kind of sounds to me like I want to get together again, don't you think?"

Tom burst out laughing. "You are about the most unusual girl I have ever known," he said. "Listen, I'm going to be tied up for the next week or so. How about I give you a call next weekend, if I can get free?"

"You'd better," she said. "You wouldn't want me to think you didn't like me, now, would you?"

"No, no way," Tom said. "I'll call you as soon as I can, I promise."

Summer hung up the phone, then emailed the recording she had just made to Indie. As soon as it went through, she called Indie to let her know that it was there. Then she went back to Sam's office and sat at the conference table once again.

It was fifteen minutes later when Jenna announced that Indie was calling. Sam reached over and hit the button on the speakerphone.

"Hey, babe," he said. "You get the results?"

"Sam," Indie said, "Herman says there is a ninety-nine point seven percent probability that the distorted voice on the recording from Starbright's computer is Tom Linden. I don't think there's any way he could get closer than that, especially with that voice distorted the way it is."

"That's the break we've been looking for," Sam said. "Thank you, sweetheart, until I can give you better thanks when I get home."

"Oh, I'm gonna be looking forward to that all day," Indie said with a giggle. "Bye-bye, Sam."

"Karen, I think we need to pick Linden up for questioning. Do you mind?"

"Hell, no, I don't mind. You got an address for him?"

Summer rattled it off from memory, and Karen punched it into her phone. When the app began to speak, she got up and headed out the door.

"I really wish it hadn't been him," Summer said. "He actually seemed like a very nice guy, and I'm sure this is going to devastate his sister."

"I think it may be worse than that," Jade said. "Annie seems to really adore her kid brother. This might be one of the worst things she ever goes through."

TOM LINDEN PUT DOWN the phone and leaned back in his desk chair. He hadn't expected a call from "Candy," because he'd been sure he had handled the situation properly the first time he dealt with her. Of course, he hadn't realized then that she was actually an investigator with Windlass; it wasn't until just a few hours earlier, when he'd seen her dealing with the front desk security guard, that he had figured that out. If he was being honest with himself, he felt rather stupid about that.

Why would she call me now? Tom asked himself. *Unless they've suddenly become suspicious of my involvement. Gotta handle this quickly.*

He picked up his phone again and dialed the number that was marked "Vancouver Rehab" in his contacts. He was careful to turn on the voice changing app, to distort his voice once again.

"Yes?"

"I have a problem," Tom said. "These investigators, Windlass Security, I think they may be on to me. One of them just called me, posing as a girl who wants to go out with me."

"What a pity," Reynard said. "These people seem to be interfering in everything I'm trying to do."

"Yeah, well, I need some help. We need to shut them down, like right away."

"Yes, I suppose we do. Of course, this will further increase my fees. We won't know how much until everything is done, but I will do what is necessary. Just make sure you are prepared to pay when the time comes."

"No problem," Tom said. "Just make it happen." He cut off the call and got up from behind his desk. There was no way he was going to sit around and wait for someone to come and get him. He walked down the hall and told his sister that he needed to run an errand, then headed for his car in the parking lot.

LOCATE AND OBSERVE the home of Sam Prichard, the investigator. Take no further action until ordered to do so. Keep your phone on. That was the order that had come through an hour earlier.

Locating Prichard's home had not been difficult, because he was still listed in the Yellow Pages as a private investigator. Nolan pointed his house out to Laura as they drove past it.

"Now we have to watch," Laura said. "How boring is that?"

Nolan grinned at her. "It's all part of the job, remember? This is what we do."

"No, this is what we end up doing," Laura said. "Our job is actually killing people, not sitting around watching them have dinner." She was squinting through a pair of binoculars that were trained on the big picture window at the front of the house. "I see the wife, just sitting there with a little girl. Boring, that's what I said, boring."

"He only said to observe for now," Nolan said. "Sounds like you'll get your chance to kill them. Just be patient, I mean, what choice do you have?"

She put the binoculars down and looked at him as they went past the house. "We could go in and kill them now," she said. "That would definitely not be boring."

"Yeah, good luck with that," Nolan said. "Remember what happened the last time somebody hit a target before they were told to? I have never seen somebody disemboweled alive before, and I don't ever want to see it again. And I especially don't want it to happen to me, so get yourself under control."

"I'm not going anywhere," Laura grumbled. "I just hate when he says to observe." She made a face. "Observe this, observe that," she said, dripping with sarcasm. "It's been months since I got to kill anybody. He knows it builds up in me, why won't he let me put it to work more often?"

"Because you get sloppy," Nolan said. "You go off half cocked, and things end up nasty. Why do you think he makes us work in pairs? He's teaching us to be the best at what we do, so the least we can do is show him some respect."

"Yeah," Laura said, "because it's the best way to stay alive."

Nolan chuckled as he pulled the car over to the curb. "There's a lot of truth to that," he said. "So, we just observe. Until he says otherwise."

Laura let out a sigh. "Yeah, fine," she said. "I just hope he doesn't wait too long. I'm starting to get antsy."

"You can get as antsy as you want," Nolan said. "Just keep your pants on until we get orders."

"God," Laura said, "you sound like a good little soldier. Wait for orders, wait for orders, that's all I ever hear out of you."

"That's because you're always ready to go off on a wild tangent of your own. At some point, you need to decide what you want. Continue to flaunt the orders you're given, and your name may end up on one of our lists."

Laura shook her head. "God, you're such a pain in the ass. Maybe you should tell him that it's just the wife and kids there. Maybe he'll give us the go-ahead."

Nolan looked at her for a moment, then took out his phone. He called up the email app and sent the message, then put it back into his pocket.

IN THE DINER, REYNARD sat sipping his coffee. His phone was laying on the table in front of him, and he took another look at the message that came in when it vibrated.

Prichard is gone to his office. Only wife and children there.

"What are you up to, Sam Prichard?" Reynard mused to himself. He had been thinking about the call from that boy, the one who had started all of this. Of course, it was necessary to now get Prichard under control quickly, before he could ruin everything.

He already knew that Prichard and his team were closing in on Hickam, but it might be best if he never got a chance to question the man. Hickam was soft, and while Reynard was confident that he, himself, could avoid arrest or capture, it would be a shame to have put in all this effort and see it fail.

Eliminating Hickam, on the other hand, was not feasible. He was the one who had brought in Reynard to bring the boys' plans to fruition. The final success of the operation depended on both of them being in place, and Reynard wasn't going to remove either of them.

Therefore, it was time to get some leverage in place to use on Prichard. He had thought this through carefully before coming to a decision, but that was one of the reasons he had been so successful. He never rushed a decision if there was time to think it through. He looked at his phone and sent a reply.

Acquire Prichard's wife and children and hold them. Do not harm them without further orders.

His remaining team in Denver was not his best, but they would do. Or he would kill them.

ACCORDING TO GRACE Prichard, who was a real estate broker, the thing to do when you had no appointments for the day always included sleeping in, tuning out the world, and enjoying the pure luxury of not caring what was happening anywhere other than the bed in which she was luxuriating.

Occasionally, however, those hours of self-indulgent luxury were interrupted by a frantic knocking on her bedroom door. This turned out to be one of those days.

"Go away, Kim," Grace shouted. "It's my day off! I like to sleep on my day off!"

"Grace, you have to get up," Kim yelled back. "Grace, it's—it's Beauregard! He says we have to go to Indiana, and we have to go now."

"We'll go after I get up! Now, leave me alone for an hour or two!"

"Grace, Indiana and the children are in danger! Beauregard says we've only got a few minutes to spare! Now, get your ass out of that bed!"

Grace raised her head and pushed the sleep mask off her eyes. Kim hardly ever used language like that. "What? What's going on?"

"Just get up and get dressed, I'm calling Indiana."

The covers flew off and Grace was up and on her feet. Her fluffy nightgown hit the floor as she yanked open her closet.

Outside her bedroom, Kim had her phone in her hand and was frantically searching for the speed dial icon for Indie. She actually passed it up once, then found it and went back to smack it with her thumb.

"Hey, Mom," Indie said.

"Indiana, it's Beauregard," Kim said instantly. "Grace is getting up now, we'll be on the way in a few minutes, but he says you and the kids are in danger right now!"

Indie had been walking from her kitchen to her bedroom, and she didn't even slow down. "What kind of danger?" She went into the bedroom and directly to her closet, punched in the four digit code on the safe on its top shelf, and withdrew the little thirty-two caliber pistol Harry Winslow had once given to Sam.

"All he knows is that there are three people coming after you," Kim said, "and they're killers. He thinks they're not supposed to hurt you, but to take you somewhere."

"Over my dead body," Indie said. "I gotta go, Mom, I'm calling Karen Parks." She cut off the call without another word, then hit the button for Karen's cell phone.

"Detective Parks," Karen said. She had just stopped for a quick lunch after leaving the Web Wide Awards building, where she had failed to find Tom Linden.

"Karen, it's Indie. Mom just called and told me Beauregard says three killers are coming after me and my kids."

Karen dropped the paper plate she was holding into the trashcan beside her. "I'm on the way," she said. "I'm calling in backup, lock up and stay in the house."

Indie had gone back to the living room, picked up Bo out of his playpen and told Kenzie to follow her, and they'd gone into the kitchen. "Okay," she said. "I've got my gun, and the kids and I are in the kitchen so I can see in every direction."

"Good, stay there," Karen said. She had already made it to her car and fired it up. "I'll call you back."

She hit another button on her phone as she roared out of the driveway.

"Detective Dolby."

"Dolby, this is Parks. I just got an anonymous tip, and I need backup at 13551 Triton Avenue, possible abduction attempt in progress. How fast can you get there?"

"Triton Avenue? I'm probably fifteen minutes away."

"Get there! Dolby, that's Sam Prichard's house. His wife and children are the intended victims, if my tip is correct."

"I'm on the way." Karen heard a siren start through the phone, as she kicked on her own.

Indie had Bo in his high chair, tucked behind the refrigerator, and Kenzie was in a chair right beside him. The little girl was nervous, because she could tell her mom was upset, but she knew to obey instantly whenever things seemed frantic. She sat in the chair and talked to her baby brother, trying to keep him from sensing just how frightened their mother was.

Indie was carefully looking out windows and doors, trying to see anyone approaching the house. The only thing she had noticed so far was a brown sedan she'd not seen before, but it was parked several doors down and might be nothing. She went back toward the kitchen to check on the kids and look out the back windows.

"Come on, Karen," she muttered. "Don't make me do this all by myself."

A minute later, there was a knock on the front door.

TWENTY-FIVE MINUTES earlier, Nolan had nudged Laura. "Wake up," he said. "We've got orders."

He and Laura had decided on a nap after getting back to the apartment. "I'm awake," she said. "What's going on?"

"I just got an email a few minutes ago. We're supposed to grab Prichard's family. Not hurt them, just grab and hold them until further orders."

Laura groaned. "Whatever," she said. "At least it's doing something, rather than just sitting around and watching."

"Yeah, but where do we take them? I'm thinking we get a room in one of the scuzzy motels. Shouldn't be too hard to keep them quiet, and those places don't pay a lot of attention."

"Fine. Let Angela go get a room, and you and I can do the job." Angela was their new trainee; there hadn't been a male to pair her with, so she had been sent out with them as a spare.

"That's what I had in mind," Nolan said. "Hurry up and get dressed, so we can get moving."

He left the bedroom and Laura got to her feet.

When she came out a couple of minutes later, Angela was already gone. "I'm ready," she said.

"So am I. Angela's going to get a room in Aurora, some dump called the Pickwick Motel. It's got individual cabins instead of rooms, so that ought to be easier to handle."

He led the way out the door and they walked down the stairs of the old building. They were only ten minutes from Prichard's house, but Nolan decided to push the car a little bit anyway.

"Slow down, idiot," Laura said. "Last thing you need is to get pulled over right now."

"We won't," Nolan replied. "Cops don't bother with brown sedans unless they're going way over the speed limit. Statistical fact, look it up sometime."

"Statistics only say what usually happens," Laura shot back. "Our luck hasn't exactly been the best lately. Slow it down."

Nolan let off the gas and dropped back to the speed limit. A few minutes later, he pulled up in front of a house that was five doors from Prichard's. The two of them sat and watched for a moment, then got out of the car and started walking down the sidewalk as if they belonged there.

"How do you want to do this?" Laura asked. "Just knock on the door?"

"Probably the best way. Prichard is gone, and she's not going to be expecting any problem. We just knock on the door and grab her when she opens." He looked around the neighborhood. "Nobody around watching, shouldn't be any problem at all. After we have them contained, you can bring the car up."

"Whatever."

They stepped onto the porch and Nolan knocked on the door. He waited about twenty seconds, then knocked again.

"Who's there?" Indie asked from inside.

"Ma'am," Nolan said, "we're from the Department of Human Services. We had a complaint that your children are being abused, and we need to speak with you."

"Yeah? Well, at the moment I'm waiting for the police to arrive. I've just been warned that someone is on the way here to snatch me and my kids, so you're gonna have to wait till they get here. If you're still here then, we can talk about it."

Laura looked up at Nolan, glaring. "Screw this," she said. She reached under her shirt and pulled out a forty caliber Glock with a sound suppressor that barely did any good, then stood back and blasted the deadbolt and the doorknob. The door flew open, and she stepped inside.

And then she fell. Nolan's eyes followed her body to the floor, and when he looked up he found himself staring down the barrel of a silenced pistol.

"Get down on the floor," Indie said, as she kicked Laura's pistol across the room. "Do it now, or I pull this trigger."

"Look," Nolan said, "she was just worried about the kids and..."

Indie lowered her aim to his crotch. "I said get down on the floor."

Nolan's eyes had followed the gun barrel, but his mind was racing. He had a Glock of his own tucked in the back of his pants, just under the polo shirt he was wearing, but he knew he could never get it out before she could pull that trigger.

"Okay, okay," he said. "I'm doing it, just chill."

Very carefully, he dropped to his knees with his hands stretched out in front of him, then fell onto all fours and lay down.

"Hands behind your head, lock the fingers." Indie waited until he had done what he was told, then reached down and pulled the Glock from his waistband. His shirt had ridden up as he got down, and she had seen it. With both guns pointed straight at him, she said, "Where is number three?"

"It's just the two of us," Nolan said. "That's all, just the two of us."

"Keep your hands where they are and roll over onto your back," Indie said. "Now!"

Nolan rolled over and looked up at her. "I'm serious, it's just the two of..."

Indie pointed his own Glock at his crotch. "If I pull this trigger, you're going to be extremely popular in prison. If you don't tell me where the third person is, I'm going to pull it."

Nolan swallowed. "She went to get a hotel room," he said. "I don't know where, she was supposed to call me later."

"Wrong answer," Indie said. She steadied her aim with the Glock and shifted her eyes to his crotch.

"Pickwick! Pickwick Motel in Aurora, that's where she went. I swear, that's where she went."

"I ought to shoot you anyway," Indie said. "Who sent you after us?"

"We don't know who it is," Nolan said. "We just get paid to follow orders."

A siren could be heard in the distance, but another car suddenly stopped in front of the house at that moment. Indie kept her eyes on Nolan, but moved further back into the living room so that she could watch the door, as well.

"Kim, wait!" Grace shouted, and Indie relaxed slightly. Her mother came through the door and stared down at the two lying there, and she gasped when she saw the blood pooling around the woman on the floor.

"Indiana? Are you all right? Where are the kids?"

"Stay outside, Mom," Indie said. "The police will be here any moment, you need to stay outside until they get here."

The sirens had gotten louder, and it was Detective Dolby who arrived first. He slid to a stop just behind Grace's car, jumped out, and leveled his weapon at the two women standing on the front porch. "Freeze, hands in the air," he shouted.

"We're the grandmothers," Grace shouted, raising her hands high. "You have to go inside, she needs help."

Dolby moved cautiously toward the house, keeping both women covered as he did so. Kim had also raised her hands, but she was nodding frantically toward the front door.

Dolby looked through the open door and saw Indie holding two pistols pointed at the man on the floor, and instinctively turned his gun toward her. "Ma'am, this is the police. Drop your weapons, now."

"Watch me, Detective," Indie said. "I'm going to move very slowly and set them on my coffee table. You keep that bastard covered, please. They came here to try to kidnap me and my kids." She set the guns on the coffee table, then raised her own hands and stepped away from it. "I'm Indiana Prichard, Sam Prichard's wife."

Dolby looked down at Nolan, who was laying on his back with his hands linked behind his head. "Roll over, onto your belly," he ordered. Nolan, his face showing resignation, rolled over one more time.

Dolby took a second to look at Laura, saw the emptiness in her eyes, and put his weapon back into its holster. He put a knee in the middle of Nolan's back, then yanked his prisoner's right hand down and back and clicked a cuff onto it. He repeated that with the Nolan's left hand and then patted him down, looking for weapons. He found a hunting knife down one leg and a five-shot thirty-eight revolver strapped to Nolan's ankle. He removed both weapons and then checked Laura again.

"This one is dead," Dolby said, just as another car screeched to a halt in front of the house. Karen Parks jumped out and came running up the walk. Dolby turned as she approached the door, gun in hand.

"What's the situation?" Karen asked.

"Mrs. Prichard already had them down when I got here," Dolby said. "The woman is dead, but this guy is unhurt."

He grabbed Nolan by the arm and pulled him to his feet, then pushed him into Sam's recliner. Karen turned to Indie.

"What happened, Indie?"

"They knocked on the door and said they were from Human Services," Indie said, "and they had a complaint about my kids. I told them that the police were on the way and they would have to wait, and that bitch shot up my door. She came through with a gun in her hand, so I shot her, then I made him get down on the floor. He had a gun in the back of his pants and I took that, and I asked him where the third person was. He said she's at the Pickwick Motel in Aurora, getting a room where they were going to keep us, I guess. Bastard!"

Other police cars were arriving, and an ambulance followed. Dolby had called in for the Medical Examiner, but it was standard procedure for the paramedics to check the body first.

Karen escorted Grace and Kim into the house, and hustled them and Indie into the kitchen. Kenzie was standing on her chair, her arms wrapped protectively around Bo. Her face was pale, but she was doing her best to remain calm.

Indie picked up both of the children and held them in her lap as the police went about their business. The paramedics rolled Laura over and attempted to revive her, but gave it up after only a few minutes.

29

Karen had sent two other detectives to the Pickwick to look for the third person. All they had gotten out of Nolan was that it was a woman, but the desk clerk said only one woman had rented a room that morning. She was in cabin nineteen, the one furthest to the back of the property.

Angela had been waiting for Nolan and Laura to arrive with their captives, and she had been looking out the window when the unmarked car pulled in up by the office. When the two men came walking toward the cabin she was in, she knew they were police. She thought about trying to bolt and run, but the stupid cabin didn't have a back door. The only way out was the front, where they would see her.

She resigned herself to making a stand. If she survived, she decided she would get into her car and take off, forget about Reynard and Nolan and Laura, and just try to disappear.

Nolan had told her to bring all the extra gear with her, so she had plenty of weapons and ammunition. She picked up the rifle and carefully aimed at one of the two detectives walking toward her, squeezed the trigger and watched him fall, instantly transferring her aim to the second one. The man's reflexes were good, but not good enough. She fired again, all of the training she had received paying off when he fell beside his partner.

This was her chance, and she had to take it now. She dropped the rifle and ran out the door, got into the car and started it, then spun it around in the gravel lot. Her only hope was to vanish as quickly as possible, ditch this car and find another...

Bulletproof vests, she thought to herself as the two detectives rose onto their knees. Each of them had a pistol in his hand, and it was the last thought she ever had. The very first bullet went through her left eye and ended any possibility of thought, while the rest of them simply turned her face and head into a bloody mass.

Angela's foot fell off the gas pedal and the car coasted across the lot, causing both detectives to dive out of the way. It came to a stop when it struck cabin fifteen, and the detectives rushed toward it. A single glimpse of what was left of the woman inside was all it took to tell them that she was dead, but they checked the cabin she had come from carefully. There was no one else inside, but they were amazed at the number of weapons they found.

Karen got the call a few moments later, and turned toward Indie. "She's dead," Karen said. "They got her."

Indie only nodded. The impact of what she had done, taking a life, had finally struck home. Tears were slowly tracing their way down her cheeks as she held her children tightly to her.

Nolan had been searched thoroughly, and one of the things Detective Dolby had found had been a smartphone. It was laying on the coffee table beside his Glock, the thirty-eight, and the knife, and Dolby picked it up and hit a button.

"Parks? You might want to take a look at this," he said.

He brought the phone to her in the kitchen, and waited while she put on rubber gloves of her own before she took it. She looked at the screen for a moment, then touched the email icon.

"Well, would you look at that?" she said. She got up from the chair beside Indie and walked into the living room, where Nolan was still sitting in the recliner. "Who gives you your orders?"

"I don't know," Nolan said. "We were independents, just got hired to do this job."

"Bullshit," Karen said. "Shaved head, small blonde woman, we've seen this before. You work for Reynard, right?"

"Who?" Nolan asked innocently. "Sorry, don't recognize the name."

Karen was scrolling through the emails as she spoke to him, and noticed that all of them were short and concise. She called Dolby over to her.

"I need to keep a lid on this," she said. "No press, no statements. Anybody outside the department wants to know what happened, Mrs. Prichard had an accident. She was moving one of Sam's guns when it went off, nobody injured. No news story here, got that?"

Dolby nodded and took out his phone. It took him only a couple of minutes to make sure the police chief understood, and then the dispatcher began talking over the radio.

"All units, stand down. The incident is under control, it was an accident with no injuries. Lady was moving a gun, and it went off. No injuries, no need to respond."

A couple of news vehicles had already arrived but had been held back by police. Karen walked out to them a moment later, told them that it was all a mixup over a rifle that accidentally fired while it was being moved, and the reporters groaned as they climbed into their cars and vans and drove away.

Karen looked down at the smartphone in her hand and hit the reply button.

Done, she typed. *Awaiting orders.*

As she walked back to the house, she took out her own phone and called Sam.

"Sam? Are you sitting down?"

"Yes," Sam said cautiously. "Why?"

"Listen and don't interrupt. Indie called me just a little bit ago. I guess her mom called, and Beauregard said some people were coming after her and the kids. She called me, but two of them showed up at your house before I got there, and Indie was forced to shoot one of them. It was another team of Reynard's, Sam. Man with a shaved head and a small blonde woman. They had another woman working with them and she had been sent to a motel to secure a room where they were going to hold them. I sent detectives out, and she is also dead. The man is alive, Indie captured him, and we have him in custody. Now, the man had a cell phone on him, and there was an email in it telling him to pick up your family and hold them, but not to harm them without further orders. My guess is that Reynard planned to use them as leverage against you, to make you back off, so I've put a press blackout on this thing, and then I sent a reply email from that phone saying that the job was done and they are waiting for further orders."

That was as far as she got before Sam exploded. "That son of a bitch! He dared try to touch my family?"

"He dared, but he failed. Sam, listen to what I'm telling you. He thinks he has them. He thinks that his people have them under control, but you and I know that isn't true. They are safe, and I'm going to take them to my place for a while, to keep them that way. What you have to do is keep your cool, because this gives you something to use against Reynard. If he sends another message, I'll get it on this phone, and I'll handle whatever comes up. Are you with me, Sam?"

"I'm with you, Karen," Sam said. "Tell Indie—nevermind, I'll tell her myself." He cut off the call and dialed his wife's number immediately, and she answered on the first ring.

"Sam? Oh, God, Sam," she said. "I—I killed somebody, Sam."

"I know," Sam said softly. "Karen just called and told me what happened. Indie, you did exactly the right thing. Don't second guess yourself, don't think about what you might've done instead, just understand that you did exactly the right thing. When somebody threatens you or the kids, you do whatever it takes to keep all of you safe."

"I know," Indie said, and Sam could hear the tears in her voice. "I know I had no choice, but it still feels awful."

"It will, for a while," Sam said. "I wish I was there with you right now, but for right now, I want you to get out of there. Go stay with the grandmas, because Karen has Reynard thinking that they have you. I need to keep him thinking that way just a little longer. If I come rushing home right now, it's possible he's got someone watching me and will know they failed. Can you handle that, babe?"

"I can handle it, Sam," Indie said. "Sam? Promise me you're going to get that son of a bitch."

"You're damned right I am. Kiss the kids for me, and I'm going to bring this to an end."

They said goodbye and Sam put the phone into his pocket. The team was all gathered at the conference table, and they had all been staring at Sam after his outburst.

"Reynard sent people after Indie and the kids," Sam said coldly. "Indie killed one of them and captured the other, and the police have him in custody. Karen found the emails in his cell phone and sent one to let Reynard think they were successful. It's time that bastard goes down."

Steve nodded. "All the way down," he said. "She actually caught one of them alive?"

Sam gave him an evil-looking grin. "Never mess with the mother protecting her children," he said. "It's never going to end well for you."

"But Reynard thinks they managed to pull it off," Darren said. "This is good, Sam. If he wanted them taken, he was probably going to use them as hostages to make you back off. He's going to be contacting you with a warning, and you've got to convince him that you're stepping back from the case, that we all are. That will make him overconfident, and that's exactly how we need him."

"I agree," Sam said, "but we've got to be careful. With any luck, we're about to strip him of having any power at all."

He took out his phone again and called Harry Winslow.

"Sam? My gut tells me this is not a social call. Please tell me I am not correct on that assumption."

"I wish I could, Harry," Sam said. "Reynard sent a team after my wife and kids. Indie is freaking out because she killed one of them, but she captured the other for the police. Karen found a cell phone on one of them, and found the email where Reynard ordered them to take my family. She called for a press blackout and sent a message back to Reynard claiming that the job was done."

"Well, well," Harry said. "You must be making him nervous, Sam. This tells me that things are about to get exciting. What's your next move?"

"I'm waiting for him to contact me, warn me to back off. When he does, I'm hoping we can find some way to figure out where he is. We've identified both of the principals in the crime, but Reynard is the one they hired to accomplish everything. I'm hoping to put an end to his career today."

"Well, then I have good news, and I have bad news. Which one would you like first?"

"Oh, hell, give me the bad news first," Sam said. "That way I still got something to look forward to."

"Well, the bad news is that I just walked through the front door of your office building."

Sam blinked. "You did what?"

"Of course, Sam, boy, that is also the good news. I should be in your office in about thirty seconds." The line went dead.

Sam turned his head and looked at his office door, and simply stared when it opened and Harry Winslow walked in.

"What in the world are you doing here?" Sam asked. "Your wife is going to kill me, do you realize that?"

"Relax, Sam," Harry said. "Kathy told me to get my ass up here. When I explained to her just who Reynard is, she insisted that I come to help."

"But you're supposed to be retired," Sam said, "or have you forgotten that?"

Harry reached into a pocket and pulled out a slim wallet, flipping it open to show Sam his Windlass Security ID. "I made a deal with Ron to keep me on the payroll as a consultant, so that I can come out of retirement when I need to. My security clearance is still intact, so I am putting myself on temporary reassignment to DHS. Now, let's start planning to eliminate the French Fox."

Of the team members, only Darren had ever actually met Harry before. The two of them had occasionally worked together before Harry was exiled to Denver, and they shared a mutual respect for one another. Sam introduced him to the rest of the team, and was surprised when even Walter shook his hand.

"All right, let's figure out what we're doing," Harry said. "Sam, you're still in charge. I'm only here as a consultant."

"Well, all I can do at the moment is..."

Sam's phone rang, and the display said "RESTRICTED." He held it up for everyone to see, then answered it as they sat in silence.

"Sam Prichard," he said.

"Mr. Prichard," said a voice that sent a chill down Sam's spine. "I believe you are trying to interfere with some of my plans."

"Then you must be Pierre Reynard," Sam said. "Let me tell you that I plan to do a lot more than interfere. I'm going to stop your ass."

"Oh, I sincerely doubt it," Reynard said. "You see, Mr. Prichard, I have something to offer you, a reward for getting out of my way and staying there."

"Sorry, asshole," Sam said. "I don't take bribes."

"You should hear the offer before you discount it," Reynard said. "Mr. Prichard, I have your wife and children. I'm certain you won't believe me, so I suggest you try to reach them. I shall call you back shortly, after you have come to understand that I am quite sincere."

The line went dead. Sam sat there quietly, his heart racing as he waited. Two minutes passed, and then five. At eight minutes, the phone rang again.

"You son of a bitch!" Sam said coldly. "Where are they?"

"They are not harmed," Reynard said, "and they will remain safe as long as you do as I tell you. You will stand down, Mr. Prichard. This matter is not of your concern. I do not care if you watch it unfold, but you and your associates will cease all activity to try to stop me. If you fail to do as I tell you, your family will be killed. Oh, and just so you know, they will not all die together. Your wife will get to watch your children die, first, before she joins them. Do we understand one another?"

Sam forced himself to sit there in silence for several seconds, then spat out, "Yes. We understand one another."

"That's very good," Reynard said. "Once my business is concluded, your family will be released unharmed. Your wife will be able to call you at that point, so that you can pick them up and take them home."

The line went dead, and Sam put the phone back into his pocket.

"And the game is afoot," Harry said. "Now is the time to move, Sam. Where do we go?"

"Karen was supposed to be bringing Tom Linden, who is Annie Porter's brother, but I think what happened with Indie got in the way of that. I've got a sneaky hunch he knows we're onto him, anyway, and that's probably what prompted Reynard to try this. We need to find him, Harry. I'm just not sure how to go about it, if he's hiding."

"I'll bet I can," Summer said. "Well, not me, but I've got his personal cell number. Good chance he won't be smart enough to turn it off."

"Then I can find it," Jade said. She grabbed Summer by the arm and the two of them hurried to Sam's desk. Jade sat down and started tapping keys on the computer keyboard. "Give me the number," she said, and Summer read it off to her.

"It's a Verizon phone," Jade said. "Bingo, I got a GPS signal on it. It's on Seventeenth Street, in LoDo. He's at a restaurant, little place called Ruby's."

"Or at least, his phone is," Sam said. "He might have ditched it."

"Hang on just a minute," Jade said, "and I can probably tell you. Nope, I'm looking at the activity on the phone, and he used it three minutes ago when he got a call from the headquarters building. He answered the call and talked for over ninety seconds."

"Let's go," Sam said. "I'll call Karen on the way."

Back in part of the building where the old automotive shop had done detail work, Windlass had three special vehicles. One of them was a beat-up old Ford van, the kind that looks like it should have been in the junkyard five years ago. Sam put Darren in the driver seat, while he, Denny, and Steve hunkered down in the back. Harry, claiming the privilege of age, took the passenger seat up front.

Despite its appearance, the old van was in excellent mechanical condition. It had been built for the express purpose of clandestine work, with a five hundred horsepower crate engine that was muffled to the point of silence, except for one small hole drilled in the exhaust pipe to make it sound rough. With Darren driving, it made it into Denver in very short order and pulled up in front of Ruby's less than thirty minutes after leaving the office.

Jade and Summer had remained at Sam's office, still on the computer and watching to make sure Tom's phone didn't leave. "He still there," Jade said to Sam over his phone. "He's made half a dozen calls in the last half-hour."

"Good. Everybody ready?"

Summer had sent each of them a photo of Tom, so they knew who they were looking for. When everyone was ready to move, Sam threw open the side doors and they all boiled out at once. They rushed into the building and spotted Tom sitting in a booth by himself.

He looked up, but it was far too late and he knew it. As they moved to surround him, Sam held up his ID for everyone else to see. "Federal agents," he said. "We're taking this man into custody."

Denny grabbed Tom and yanked him out of the booth, took away his phone, and then slapped a pair of handcuffs on him behind his back. Darren took him after that and marched him out to the van. Tom climbed in without resisting and the rest of them followed. Darren got behind the wheel and they headed back toward the office building.

Tom looked at Sam. "You must be Prichard," he said. "I heard you limped, so I know it's you. You do realize you just got your family killed, right?"

"Oh, thank you," Sam said. "You just confessed to being an accessory to kidnapping. And since two of the people who were involved in that attempted kidnapping died, you will also be charged with murder. But as for my family? Don't you worry a bit, they're perfectly safe. You see, my wife is a lot tougher than any of the pieces of crap that your boy Reynard could send after her. She killed one of them herself, and captured another one."

Tom's face went white. "You're lying," he said. "He already told me he got them, and if anything happens to me, he'll kill them."

"Sorry, pal," Sam said. "I'm afraid it's all over for you. You're looking at a minimum of life in prison, and you might even be charged with acts of terrorism. In that case, you could conceivably face the firing squad, or you could spend the rest of your life inside a single room."

Tom stared at him. "Look, there's been some kind of..."

"Shut up," Sam said brusquely. "Don't even try to talk your way out of this. We've got you every way you can imagine, we even have a recording of you talking to Benjamin Hickam about making sure the winner of the Top Video Award gets shot. You're hung, kid, and the only hope you've got right now is to start talking your head off. I want to know everything about what you were getting out of this deal, I want to know where to find Reynard, I want everything, and I want it now."

Tom Linden started to cry. "I-I-I just wanted to..."

"I don't want any excuses. Don't try to tell me what you wanted to do, just tell me what you were getting out of this. Was it money? Was this all about getting rich?"

Tom sniffled a couple of times, then forced himself to stop. "A billion dollars," he said finally. "I was supposed to get a billion dollars' worth of stock in his company."

"And all you had to do was arrange for some poor kid to get killed, right? Put your sister's company smack in the middle of all the sympathy and support he could get, so that it would suddenly grow and become more valuable?"

"That was part of it," Tom said miserably. "Once he went public, then he was going to offer to buy Annie out. My stock would have doubled, and I'd be richer than John ever dreamed of."

There it was. That was the anger Darren's profile had suggested they would find, clear as day.

"And that was part of it too, right? Make yourself richer than John, show him you're not as big a waste of space as he thought you were?"

Tom looked down at the floor of the van and said nothing.

"Okay, that helps a little bit," Sam said. "That explains why you were doing it, at least. Now, if you want to help yourself and maybe even have a chance to see freedom again someday, you tell me where to find Pierre Reynard."

Tom shook his head from side to side. "I don't know," he said. "All I've got is a phone number, but it bounces around the world before it ever gets to him. He says that's so it can't be traced. I know he's here in Denver, somewhere, but I don't know where."

Sam looked at him. "He's here in Denver? Then there is something else here that he needs to do, isn't there? What is it, Tom? Why is he still here?"

Tom stared at the floor of the van for a moment, then suddenly looked up at Sam with pure rage in his eyes. "You're too late," he said. "He's going to kill John, and he's already on the way."

30

Sam's eyes flew wide open. He snatched out his phone and called John Morton, and John answered the call only a second later.

"Sam?" Morton said as he answered.

Sam cut him off. "John, Pierre Reynard is on the way to kill you, right now. Where are you?"

"To kill me? I'm in my office, what are you talking about?"

"Annie's brother Tom was the inside man," Sam said. "I'll explain it all later, but he's been stealing money from you to hire Reynard, to build up your company, and then kill you. He made a deal with Benjamin Hickam to get a billion dollars' worth of stock in Hickam's company, and I guess they figured that once you were dead, they could force Annie to sell out to him, as well. You need to get out of there, right now. We are on the way, but you need to grab Annie and find somewhere to hide."

"Oh, my God," Morton said. "Annie just went down to the lobby, somebody came in and said they needed her to sign for a package."

"Don't go down there," Sam said. "If that's Reynard, he's out to kill you, not her. You go and hide somewhere, right now. We'll be there in just a few minutes, we'll handle it."

Darren had shoved his foot to the floor, and the van was flying through the city. Sam turned and looked at Tom. "Well, at the moment it sounds like Reynard has your sister," he said. "We'll do everything we can to keep her alive, but you may have gotten her killed."

Tom stared at him. "No, he knows not to hurt Annie," he said. "He knows that."

"Young man," Harry said, looking back at Tom. "If he feels trapped, he will kill everyone near him. It won't matter what he promised not to do, it won't matter what he was paid to do, he will kill everyone as he makes his escape." Harry looked at Sam. "We should throw this piece of crap right out in front of Reynard. Then he'd find out firsthand just how loyal an assassin can be."

"Oh, no," Sam said. "I want this boy to live a long time, and remember what he's done."

It took them four more minutes to get to the Web Wide Awards building, and Darren slowed the van as he drove up to it. Its nondescript appearance might give them an extra moment of advantage, and he was planning to squeeze everything out of it that he could.

He pulled up as close to the front door as he could get and tried to see through the glass on the front of the building. "No sign of anybody in the front lobby," he said. "Sam, I don't even see the security guard."

Sam reached for the side door handle, then looked up at Harry. "Harry, do me a favor. Keep your gun pointed at this piece of shit, and blow his brains out if he tries to run." He snatched open the door and he, Denny, and Steve leapt out. Darren jumped out of the driver's door and the four of them rushed for the front of the building.

As Darren had said, there was no one visible in the lobby. Sam didn't even slow down, but ignored the pain in his hip as he ran. He opened the door and rushed inside, pistol held out in front of him as he looked around for potential threats.

Denny ran to the front desk, glanced over, and then turned to Sam. "Security guard is down," he said. "Dead, bullet through the brain." He moved behind the desk and started looking at the security monitors. "There! Top floor, headed for Morton's office, it looks like. Him and the woman, and he's holding a gun pointed at her head."

"Let's go," Sam said, and he started toward the elevator just as it opened. A dozen people came spilling out, several of them screaming when they saw the men with their guns. The second elevator opened a few seconds later, and more people came rushing out. "Stairs," Sam shouted, and they all headed for the fire stairs. Darren yanked it open and the four of them started up.

Morton's office was on the fourth floor of the building, and it only took them a few minutes to make it to the top. Sam's hip was screaming by then, but he didn't take time to worry about it. The four of them crashed through the door onto the fourth floor hallway, guns aimed straight ahead of them.

The hall was empty, so they started moving through it, checking each room as they passed. They made it to just outside of Morton's office, and then all four of them pressed themselves against the wall.

"Reynard!" Sam shouted. "Reynard, there's no way out. Let the woman go and come out of there, now."

"Prichard? Is that really you?"

"Damn right it is," Sam called back. "You dared to try to hurt my family, you son of a bitch. You're not getting away from me. Now throw down your weapons and come out, because if we come in, we shoot to kill."

"Of course you will," Reynard said calmly. "However, bear in mind that I have hostages. There are three women in this room, and I shall kill each and every one of them if you attempt to come in."

"We know your reputation, remember? You kill everyone you possibly can when you're trying to escape. We're not going to fall for that, not this time. You come out, or you die. It is that simple."

Phwt! The sound of a silenced gunshot was heard, and then they heard women screaming. Sam felt like a sledgehammer in his gut, but he knew there was nothing else he could have done. Reynard could not be allowed to escape.

"That was the first one," Reynard said. "There are two to go. Now, I'm sure you're not alone; you can try to rush me, but I will probably manage to kill at least some of you. If you wish to minimize the loss of life today, Prichard, then I suggest you put down your weapons and let me walk out of here."

"Not gonna happen," Sam said. "If I hear another shot, your chance to survive this ends."

The screaming suddenly began again, and Sam rushed through the door. He was aiming his gun wildly, looking for a shot at Reynard, while the others followed behind him, but he was gone. A door to the right stood open, and Sam suddenly realized that Morton's office adjoined Annie's.

He looked at the women in the room, and saw that all three of them seemed unhurt. Annie Porter was in the middle, hugging two other women who were weeping against her chest.

"He was bluffing," Sam said. "Denny, Darren, take the hallway. Steve, you're with me." He rushed into the adjoining office, but it was empty. The door to the hallway stood wide open, and Sam rushed out through it, only to find himself facing Denny and Darren.

The stair door was just closing, and all four of them rushed toward it. Denny and Darren hurried ahead while Sam and Steve tried to keep up, but Reynard beat them to the ground floor. The stairway door was just closing as Denny and Darren reached it, and they pulled it carefully open only to have to duck back inside because of gunfire coming at them.

Sam and Steve caught up then, and Sam yanked the door open and ran out without stopping. Reynard had already fled the building and was halfway across the wide concrete apron in front of it when Sam threw open the front door.

"Reynard!" Sam screamed, and the killer spun and snapped off a shot in his direction. Sam ducked aside, feeling the wind as the bullet flew past his ear, then raised his gun and fired twice in rapid succession. Reynard hit the ground and rolled, coming up on his knees and firing towards Sam again just as the other three came rushing out. They all fired in Reynard's direction, but he had managed to roll behind a planter, and their bullets merely bounced off.

Limping hard, Sam started toward the planter, his gun held steadily out in front of him.

"There is no escape, Reynard," Sam shouted. "Throw out your gun and give it up. This is your last warning!"

The van, sitting over to the side, suddenly opened. Harry Winslow stepped out and aimed his gun, his own view not blocked by the planter with its miniature tree. He squeezed off one shot, but missed, and Reynard turned and fired.

"*NOOOO!*" Sam screamed as Harry fell. Reynard's head was just above the planter, and he was staring toward Harry.

"Winslow?" Reynard asked, incredulously. He raised his gun again, and Sam fired once more.

Reynard's head snapped to the side, and he turned toward Sam. The bullet had only grazed the back of his head, and he raised his gun once more, aiming directly at Sam, but then Sam, Denny, Steve, and Darren all began firing together.

Reynard ducked behind the planter, but then he jumped and tried to run, heading straight towards the van. All four of the men fired, but he kept running. He had almost made it, he was just about to vanish behind the old van, when Sam fired his last round.

Reynard suddenly stopped, his back arching and his hand reaching behind him. His knees collapsed and he went down, but he turned toward Sam and raised his gun one more time. Sam tried to squeeze his trigger, but his magazine was empty and the others leveled their weapons and fired.

Reynard went down again, riddled with bullets. Sam hurried past him to where Harry lay while Denny and Darren approached Reynard. Denny kicked his weapon away from his hand, then holstered his own and rolled the man over. His sightless eyes stared upward, but they saw nothing.

Sam collapsed next to Harry and put his hand over the bleeding hole in Harry's chest. "Harry, dammit," he said. "What the hell did you think you were doing?"

"My job, Sam," Harry gasped out. "I was doing my job."

Steve was standing over them, his phone in his hand as he called 911. Sam heard him tell them to hurry, but he was concentrating on Harry.

"Your job was to watch Tom Linden," Sam yelled. "Reynard was my job!"

"Sam," Harry said weakly, "you couldn't hit him, and I thought I could. Guess my old eyes aren't what they used to be. I missed, Sam. I never used to miss." He tried to look down at his chest, but he couldn't even raise his head. "Pretty bad, isn't it? Don't let it tear you up, Sam. I've had a good run, son, and I've got nothing to complain about."

"Oh, no you don't," Sam said. "You're not going to die on me, I absolutely will not permit it! You just suck it up, you old bastard, you still got a lot of years ahead of you."

"Sam," Harry said, his voice growing faint. "Sam, it's okay. This is why I was here, Sam. Kathy told me to come and make sure you were safe, and I did. You tell her that, Sam, you tell her I did."

Harry's eyes closed, and he took one more breath before his chest stopped moving. Sam felt his throat for a pulse, and didn't find it, so he bent down and clamped his mouth over the old man's and blew into his lungs. He popped up and started chest compressions, while Darren dropped down to take over breathing for him. Darren blew air into the old man's lungs over and over, while Sam kept up a steady rhythm on his chest.

The ambulance arrived three minutes later, and the paramedics took over. They loaded Harry onto a gurney and shoved him into the ambulance, with one of the paramedics continuing CPR as they raced away. The police were arriving by then, and Karen Parks showed up. Sam told Steve to handle the police report, turned Tom Linden over to Karen, and climbed into the driver's seat of the van.

Sam pushed the old truck for all it was worth and skidded to a stop just out of the way of the ER drive. He climbed out, wishing he had his cane, and hobbled his way up to the door. As he stepped inside, he could see a lot of activity in one of the exam rooms and knew that was where he would find Harry. He hurried as fast as he could, but the people in the room suddenly started filing slowly out as he got there.

Sam shoved the curtain aside and stepped in, as he saw a doctor lifting a sheet up over Harry's face.

"Oh, no," Sam said. "Don't you dare give up on him. He's not ready to go yet, that man is an American hero. You don't stop, you keep going, do you hear me?"

The doctor turned and looked at him. "I'm sorry, sir," he said. "I'm afraid he's gone."

"No, he's not," Sam shouted. "I know, I know for a fact he's not gone. You get back over there and you keep trying, you bring him back again. This world isn't ready to be without Harry Winslow, you bring him back."

The doctor sighed, but he turned and pulled the sheet back down off of Harry. "He's lost a lot of blood," he said. "We were giving him blood, but his heart just won't cooperate."

Sam pushed past the doctor to the head of the bed Harry was laying on, and leaned down beside his ear. "Harry? Harry, damn you, you listen to me. I am not going to explain to Kathy that you got yourself killed trying to play hero one last time. That is not going to happen, so you might as well just get your ass back inside this body and kickstart that heart of yours. And don't you dare try to tell me you can't do it, I know you better than that, remember?"

He turned and looked at the doctor. "Well? What are you waiting for? Bring him back, now!"

The doctor glared at him and shook his head, but he picked up the paddles. "Charging," he said, and a moment later he said, "Clear!" He pressed the paddles down to Harry's bare chest, there was a loud thump and Harry almost jumped off the bed.

Beside Harry, the monitor continued its steady flat tone. Sam looked at the doctor. "Again."

The doctor adjusted the machine, then shouted, "Clear!" He slammed the paddles down on Harry's chest once more, and Harry jumped again. The doctor stepped back and looked at the monitor, shaking his head, but then he stared as it began a weak rhythm.

Sam was shoved aside as the doctors and nurses were suddenly frantically busy once again. He stood back, leaning against the wall, tears streaming down his face as he nodded his head over and over. "I knew it," he said. "I knew you weren't done yet, you old son of a bitch. You don't get to check out, not yet, you don't."

It took them an hour to get Harry stabilized, and by that time Sam had been pushed out of the exam room and was surrounded by his entire team, his wife and children, his mother and mother-in-law, and several local police officers. A number of the Windlass office staff and security guards were there, as well, so that the waiting room for the ER was overflowing.

Sam kept looking back toward the exam room, and finally the doctor came out and walked toward him. Sam got to his feet and met the man in the middle of the floor.

"He must be one hell of a man," the doctor said. "The bullet had struck him in the heart, to one side of the left ventricle, and that should have been the end of it. If anyone else had ever told me a man could come back from that, I would've said they were crazy, but now I've seen it. We ended up taking the bullet out right there, and the damage to his heart will be repaired. I know who you are, Mr. Prichard, and to be honest that's the only reason I kept trying, because you were demanding it. If you hadn't, he would definitely be dead. As it is, he was dead for almost four full minutes."

"Will he..." Sam began, then he licked his lips and started again. "Is he going to be okay?"

"Well, there is a risk of some brain damage, but I think it'll be minimal. He wasn't really without oxygen very long, so there's a good chance he'll come back and be his old self again. The biggest worry right now is his heart, but it's in surprisingly good shape for a man of his age." He reached out and put a hand on Sam's shoulder. "Thank you, Mr. Prichard. Because of you, I've seen a miracle here today."

Sam nodded and wiped the tears away from his face. He turned and made his way back to his chair as the doctor went back to his duties, and suddenly he found his mother-in-law standing directly in front of him. There was something about her face, and Sam stopped and stared.

"Beauregard?" Sam asked.

Kim nodded. "Yes, Sam," she said, in Beauregard's voice. "You see? My visions were right after all."

"But Harry's not dead," Sam said. "He's alive."

"Yes, he is," Kim said. "And he has you to thank for that, Sam. You see, he was dead for a little while, there. His heart had stopped, and the doctors wrote him off as being without hope. But you didn't. You refused to give up, or to let them give up, and that's the only reason old Harry Winslow was able to find his way back. And now, the second vision will be true. One day soon, all of your friends and family will gather around you again. Alive."

Kim staggered and almost fell, and Sam caught her. She looked up into his face, and realization dawned. "Beauregard again?"

"Yes," Sam said. Indie stood beside him, and he reached out to put his arm around her. "Yes, it was Beauregard. He just wanted to tell me something I needed to hear."

What'd You Think?

Thank you for reading this novel. I had a blast writing it, and I hope you had fun reading it.

If you enjoyed the book, please consider telling your friends, or posting a short review. Word of mouth is an author's best friend and is much appreciated.

All the best,

David Archer

Full List Of My Books Can Be Found At

www.davidarcherbooks.com[1]

---

1. http://www.davidarcherbooks.com/

77346770R00255